BY WAND OR BLADE

are battles fought and won in the far-distant fantasy realms of:

"Sleeping Dogs" by Jennifer Roberson—Summoned by the king when his favorite hound was about to bear a litter, the witch woman used all her arts in vain. To save the only surviving pup, she revealed an ancient knowledge that would forever change the king's own life. . . .

"The Making of a Legend" by Mercedes Lackey—In the town of Viden, Tarma and Kethry, warrior woman and sorceress, would face a rendezvous with fate—and with a minstrel only too ready to spread the tale of their adventures. . . .

"Shadowlands" by Elisabeth Waters—Her husband killed in an accident, Oriana would do anything—even spell travel to the Shadowlands—to bring him back to life. . . .

These are just a few of the spellbinding tales of spell casters and warriors you'll find in—

SWORD AND SORCERESS VI

SWORD AND SORCERESS VI

AN ANTHOLOGY
OF HEROIC FANTASY

Edited by
Marion Zimmer Bradley

DAW BOOKS, INC.
DONALD A. WOLLHEIM, PUBLISHER

375 Hudson Street, New York, NY 10014

DAW Book Collectors No. 819.

First Printing, June 1990

1 2 3 4 5 6 7 8 9

PRINTED IN THE U.S.A.

TABLE OF CONTENTS

INTRODUCTION

Wanted hen I first began this project—several years ago now—my main motive was to liberate sword and sorcery, the last macho domain of science fiction and fantasy, where rape and exploitation were the most commonplace events, and women were acted upon more than acting, not uncommonly distributed as bad conduct prizes for the heroes.

The authors who have contributed to *S&S* have since had a lot of success: Diana Paxson has published several novels, as have Jennifer Roberson and Mercedes Lackey. We imagine Dorothy Heydt and Millea Kenin won't be far behind when they get around to submitting completed novels.

The general enthusiasm for women's Sword and Sorcery has made me think seriously about the branch of women's fiction which is commonest in this country and can be found, ever proliferating on the shelves of any popular bookstore, and is recommended as surefire income for any would-be writer who can turn out the stuff. I mean the kind of soft-core pornography written for women and called Romance. Even at fourteen I couldn't stand it.

I am often asked why I personally think romances, even when combined with a few fantasy elements, are a bad thing which no self-respecting woman should read. I feel strongly that romances, even the ones which make six figure incomes for their very well-meaning and hard-working authors, perpetrate the most harmful of old stereotypes; the one which encourages women to think their primary—maybe their only value—is the finding of the right man; that all their troubles will be ended upon the procurement of love and marriage.

Now, even my worst enemies couldn't call me a man-hater; in fact, the more extreme feminists won't have anything to do with me because I have been quite forthright in saying that most of what is called women's fiction is so bad it has to be printed by women's presses because it simply isn't good enough for the mainstream. I am widely regarded by these women as having sold out to what they call the male establishment. To make matters worse in their eyes, I have been twice married, was on excellent terms with my first husband until his death, and am still on excellent terms with my two grown sons, my second husband, and my (male) agent and editors. Partly for that reason I refuse to call myself a feminist. The feminists won't have me, and I have stopped lamenting the fact. (It hurt a lot at first.)

But even so, I, who am the kind of omnivorous reader who reads the back of toothpaste cartons, can't stomach the average romance. They are more thoroughly tied to formula than the worst hack fiction in the outfield; some woman who is lonely meets a man. For no reason, except maybe hormones, she begins to feel inner stirrings for this person, and eventually, with or without any other reason, she calls this feeling love, and settles down with him to live happily ever after.

I've prodded and prodded my secretary, who devours these things by the dozen, to try and articulate what she gets out of them. I've read any number, and can't even begin to imagine; yet she must get *something*, or she wouldn't read them. It can't be pure empty-headedness, for she has more education than I do; I have a BA from a third-rate Bible college in the south, while she has an MA from a prestigous university. For years she held down an excellent job with a large corporation before going to work for me, and it took three full-time employees to replace her. (We still get pitiful, trouble-shooting calls when the equipment goes out of order, begging her to fix it.) So what's the attraction of this stuff?

Much thought and introspection has led to thinking only that they must get from them what the late J.R.R. Tolkien, in his essay *On Fairy Tales*, called, "the consolation of the happy ending." They almost always end with what their authors think of as a happy ending; which other genre fiction seldom does, namely, the man and woman end with a commitment to live happily ever after. You know, and I know, and I imagine that even the writers of these things know that wedding bells indicate, not the end of troubles, but the beginning. But for the moment, all's well, and as Sam'l Pepys says, "and so to bed." Dishes, dirty diapers, dentists, divorce and death may loom ahead, but for the moment the balance is restored, and things are going well. You can leave the characters and feel they'll be all right. And if you never go back to them, they'll be all right, too. And people—even me—want that in their books.

However, I feel that a steady diet of this kind of reading encourages young women to feel that they don't have to do or be anything in themselves, but that they need only seek out "love," meanwhile (as the message of Barbara Cartland insists) maintaining their virginity, and all will (someday, if they stay young and pretty) be well. I need not say what this theory has done to women who marry fresh out of school, never fitting themselves for any useful work, even caring for their own children. Most of these women, when confronted with the reality of motherhood are still in such an infantile state that no self-respecting SPCA would give them a kitten to raise (we prepare less for motherhood than for a driving license in this country). When, having lost her youth and beauty, she is abandoned by a husband encouraged by the prevailing climate to seek ever new "love," she frequently finds herself unprepared for anything but the most menial of jobs, and sinks into instant poverty. She is the innocent victim of our culture's idea of romance; perpetrated by a thousand books and a thousand writers.

It goes along with the idea that being the queen of the senior prom is more important than anything else in life. The fact is that the kids who are highly successful in high school, the prom queen, the star of the football team, are not really prepared for life in the real world. Today, when I go into any high school, the first thing I tell the kids is that it's okay to be a nerd. Your parents may act as if popularity in school is the key to instant success, but life just doesn't work that way; having more dates and boyfriends (or girlfriends) than anybody doesn't mean a thing. There may come a time when you'll wish you'd paid less attention to those "cute" boys across the aisle and more to your grades in English.

The way education is nowadays, the writer of a literate English sentence may soon be more in demand than ninety words a minute in typing.

So put down your romances, whose writers insist you be pretty in a conventional way—white, middle-class, virginal, and popular with boys—and start reading something where women can have adventures and be something on their own; like the stories in this book. That's why I print them.

EQUONA'S MARE
by Diana L. Paxson

Diana and I have divided the world up between us informally; specifically, I got Arthur (THE MISTS OF AVALON) and she got Tristan and Isolde (THE WHITE RAVEN). I got the *Iliad*, (THE FIREBRAND) and whatever she makes of it, she gets the Oddyssey. I get El Cid, and she gets Roland. And so forth.

Diana, who happens to be my sister-in-law, is also my dear friend; but it was the worth of her work, not nepotism, which has prompted me to give her a place in most of these anthologies. (She missed last year's because she was in the middle of writing THE WHITE RAVEN. She has also written several books about a fantasy country, Westria, (including her first book, The EARTHSTONE, for which I had the unwelcome task of suggesting to her that it had enough plot for four books, and would not sell in its present form: well, she finally made seven books out of it, and they *have* sold; which just goes to show I'm not infallible.) She has also written just about the best contempory fantasy I've ever read, BRISINGAMEN (Freya's necklace). And now there are about enough Shanna short stories to make a novel . . . is any editor out there listening? But I hope it won't stop her from writing short ones. Anyhow, I happily kick off this volume with the return of sorceress-swordswoman Shanna.

"**I** am hag-ridden by goddesses . . ." said Shanna of Sharteyn, downing another beaker of Karna ale. "And I wish they'd damn well leave me alone!"

"Don't trouble the gods, and they won't bother you, that's my theology—" Rufo Beltorix grinned and refilled her cup, then began to rattle the dice once more.

Shanna sighed. The gods didn't give you much choice, sometimes. Still, Rufo was a good lad—she surveyed the men in the tavern through an ale-gold haze—they were all good lads. The Second Equestrian Wing of the Fifth Legion, the "Emperor's Own" were a fine outfit, with the dents of the last Dorian campaign still in their armor. They filled the taproom at the White Horse tavern in Karna, breastplates of polished bronze gleaming beneath their green plumes.

Shanna fingered a loose rivet in the quilted red leather shirt she wore over her gilded under-mail, and thought that she had taken a few dents in her own journey southward, and would likely acquire a few more before she reached Bindir.

When I find my brother—if I ever do find my brother—she thought morosely, *he won't recognize me!* She had left Sharteyn as the daughter of a princely house, but though she might look a little young for a mercenary, only the black braids coiled around her head marked her as a woman now.

"How long were you in Bindir?" she asked, as Rufo spilled the dice across the scarred table. He sat back, clasping his hands behind his head. He was a big, raw-boned man with red hair—*northern blood there*, thought Shanna—*maybe a father from the Misty Isles*.

"Three moons. We were hoping for a longer duty, but there's some trouble in Mesith . . ." He watched the dice spin to stillness and grinned. "You buy the next round, and tell me what *you're* doing here."

"I'm a Caravan guard—" she signaled the bargirl, then considered him carefully. No need to tell him the whole story of how she had joined Bercy's caravan after the plague at Otey, or how the older woman had developed from an employer into a friend.

"Working my way down to Bindir. I'm looking for a man called Janos ban Artinor, or he might have called himself Janos of Sharteyn. He left on a mission to the Emperor four years ago, never came home again."

Rufo whistled. "The Imperial Court! High doings indeed!"

"Don't know why I'm asking *you*," muttered Shanna. "You likely never got beyond the guardhouse." She watched him from the corner of her eye. This was the opportunity she had hoped for when she heard that the Wing had come from Bindir. But she had not expected to have to drink quite so much ale.

"The Second took its turn at Palace guard! I've been this close to Baratir," he held apart his palms, "and there's always gossip . . ."

"Well, *did* you hear anything?" She blinked up at him.

"Might have." Rufo rattled the dice-cup suggestively. "Was he a big man, dark like you, laughs when he's fighting?"

"Tell me!"

He shook his head, grinning. "Now, now, Shanna, love—I don't give anything away! Throw you for it, though. . . ."

Shanna shook her head, too hazed to even resent what he had called her. She pulled her pouch inside out, then realized that the rest of her money had gone to pay for the last round.

"No more coin?" Rufo asked. "Well, if you lose, you could spend the night with me . . ."

That got through. Shanna pulled herself upright, glaring.

"I don't give it away, and I don't sell it, either, horse-boy! Choose again!"

"Meant no insult—" he said mildly. "If I can't ride you, then how about your pretty mare? Saw her when you came in. My own nag's gone lame, and we're off somewhere in the morning. Suppose I borrow your little lady for this campaign?"

Shanna stared. Let someone else ride Calur?

"Roll for it—Fortune is with you. . . ." She could

hear the Voice distinctly, and shook her head again, wondering just how drunk she was. *"Go on, all will be well!"*

"For a battle?"

"I don't think so—just a little clean-up job. But she's battle-trained, isn't she?"

"Yes, of course, but—" Shanna began, then shut her mouth, remembering some of the fights they had come through. "I trained her myself. She's never been apart from me."

"How much do you want my information?" Rufo asked.

To find Janos! That had been her goal for three years, and this was the first real clue she had had!

"I need more proof." She took another drink of ale.

"Does the man you're looking for wear a medallion with a phoenix on it—ruby eyes set in gold?"

"All right," Shanna capitulated suddenly. "High number takes it—now roll!"

"You hear that?" Rufo waved one of his companions over. "It's a wager! You witness it, Alusius—my information against the use of her mare!"

The big, dark man he had summoned blinked when he realized that Shanna was a woman, then grinned, and took a swig of Rufo's ale.

"Holy Equona," Shanna prayed silently as Rufo shook the dice cup. *"Make this come out right—take care of my mare!"*

Rufo slapped down the cup, uncovered a six, and grimacing, handed dice and cup to her.

"Goddess, remember!" The dice rattled in the wooden cup like dead bones. Shanna dashed the cup down on the table, shivered, and tipped it upright again.

"Huh! Equona must love me!" said Rufo.

Blinking, Shanna tried to focus on the dice. A two and a two? It couldn't be!

"You've won the horse, then? Good!" said Alusius. "I was wondering if you were going to go off tomorrow hanging on to somebody's tail!"

"I'll take her with me when I leave here," said Rufo. "We'll be off at first light. Come to think of it,

I'd better be getting back to barracks now!" He stood up and tucked his plumed helmet under his arm.

But you can't— Shanna tried to protest, but no words would come. All the ale she had drunk rose in a dark tide to drown her. The last thing she heard was Rufo's laugh.

When Shanna floundered back into consciousness, aching, shaking, hurting in every limb, the sun was shining through the open doorway of Bercy's tent. She closed her eyes again as pain lanced through her skull.

"Back in the land of the living, are you? About time!" the voice of the caravan-mistress came, far too loudly, from near at hand.

"I don't even *like* ale," muttered Shanna. "I will never, ever, drink it again!"

"Drink this, then. It'll taste nasty, but it should take the edge off the pain."

With a heroic effort, Shanna got herself upright. She slitted her eyes a little, saw Bercy holding out a mug. She reached out blindly, gulped the stuff down and coughed. Bercy had been right. But once she got her stomach under control Shanna realized that her condition had marginally improved.

"Think you'll live?" came Chai's voice in her head. Shanna turned, carefully, and saw the falcon perched on the cross-pole. *"Watching you makes me glad I'm doing this journey as a bird!"*

"Shut up, feather-brain—" Chai was condemned to bird shape for the duration of the journey, and Shanna had been delighted when she learned to communicate with her. But just she now she was not so sure.

"Quite a night you had of it—" said Bercy. "We had to carry you back to camp."

Shanna frowned. *Carry*— Then a memory surfaced through the pain. "Calur!"

An hour later she was waiting to speak to the Garrison Commandant of Karna. The day was hot and still. She could feel a new trickle of sweat gluing her undertunic more closely to breast and back, and wished she could strip off the leather shirt that covered it. But not here, where she flinched at the glance of every soldier who passed.

"Sorry, to take so long, mistress—" the aide she had spoken to came back out onto the porch of the guardhouse. "Especially when I can't give you any news. Rufo Beltorix rode out this morning with his troop, but the mission's secret. They wouldn't even tell me where they've gone!"

"But he's got my horse!"

"It was a fair wager, witnessed it myself—" a big, brown man leaned against one of the weathered sandstone columns, grinning.

It was a mistake. I was drunk! Shanna could not say that aloud. Instead, she glared at him.

"They should be back in a day or two," said the aide. "I'll tell Rider Beltorix you're looking for him!" This time, everyone within earshot laughed.

Shanna turned on her heel, a flush of fury increasing the pounding in her head. They didn't understand. Rufo didn't want a battle-trained mount for a pleasure ride. She had been insane, or deluded, to even con- sider risking Calur! As she turned toward the gate, she saw that the big man was following her.

"You're—Alusius—the friend who was with him, aren't you? Didn't he say where they were going to you?"

" 'S close-mouthed, when he wants to be, is our Rufo. *You* should know!" White teeth flashed. "You and he was getting mighty close, but Rufo's gone now. Won't I do?" He reached out to her.

Without premeditation, Shanna's knife was in her hand. She was dimly pleased that trained responses still served her even as she settled into a defensive crouch, holding his gaze.

"I'm looking for a horse, not a jackass!" she spat. "If you can't tell me anything, go piss into the wind."

"Just wanted to be friendly!" he said plaintively. "You want information, go ask old Keri Na down in the spice-sellers' quarter—she reads hands, bones, spi- derwebs. Maybe she can tell you. For sure, you won't find out anything here!"

* * *

"I was once a high priestess!" The crabbed figure that picked its way among the tumble of gear in the shadows of the hut cackled at Shanna's expression. Skeins of drying herbs hung on the walls, stoneware crocks held other things, and on the shelves were polished stone spheres, animal bones, bits of metalwork.

"Never think it, would you, to see me now! I served Kera and Koré in the great temple at Essa, but that's all gone now, burned when the Emperor put down the uprising. They never rebuilt it. The Spear-Priests'd be just as pleased if all the other cults went under, leave nobody but Toyur!"

"Can you find my horse?" Shanna asked.

"Patience, patience! When you've lived as long as I have, you'll learn. Bones don't answer, we find another way." She lifted a small jar down from a shelf sat down again in her carved chair.

Shanna took a deep breath to calm herself, smelled dust, old incense, a whiff of garbage when the wind changed. She'd had a run in with the Spear-Brothers herself, but this was no time to discuss it. She turned back to the old woman.

The crone pinched powder from the jar and cast it into the brazier, and gray smoke curled into the air. Shanna breathed in acrid fumes and felt her head begin to pound once more.

"You just sit there, that's right—and you've got some hair from the mare's mane, yes, and one of your own? Good, good, we'll lay them together, black as black—can't tell one from the other, can you? Yes, now hold out your hand!"

Shanna jumped as the bodkin pricked her finger. crone pressed her bleeding thumb against the ˌsted black hair. Scrawny throat muscles quivered as Keri Na let out a shriek that made Shanna's hair stand on end.

"*Heko, heko, hekas!* Austri, Vestri, Nodri, Sudri, world wardens hear me, spirits be near me. . . ." Her eyes had rolled back in her head. For a moment there was babble, then a new spate. "Let that which was separate come together! Red mare and red rider, no more divided—Equona, Lady of Horses, show me Thy will!" She opened her eyes, but they were unfocused. She picked up the twist of hair.

"Let what was bound, now be found—"

Someone knocked on the door.

The crone jerked, the hair slipped from her fingers and fell into the brazier, where it began to stink and sizzle on the coals.

"No, no, not yet!" the crone was making ineffectual jabs as she tried to fish the hair out of the fire. Shanna started to get up to help her, but the pain in her head pounded her back into the chair. A wave of dizziness smote her, the chair went over and she fell into the dark.

"Keri Na, old spider, you in there?"

Shanna recognized Bercy's rough warmth, tried to call out to her, but a great wind wrenched spirit from body and whirled her away.

"Remember your oaths, remember your love!" came a Voice. *"Rider and ridden you shall be!"*

For a moment Shanna seemed to glimpse a long white face with large, dark-lashed eyes. Then even that was gone.

When Shanna came to herself again, she was standing in a dusty road; standing, with all four limbs firmly planted on the ground. . . . She jerked upright, striking out hysterically, and screamed.

"Rufo!" Her ears flicked at the call. "Quiet that mare or cut her throat! We're getting near!"

A sharp pain in her jaw brought her head down; she tried to stand, but her balance was wrong. She came down on her front limbs with a shock that jarred from head to tail, while trained responses warred with stark, unreasoning fear.

"Calur! Be quiet, sweetheart—don't want them to hear us now." That terrible pressure still constrained her head, but the hand on her neck was firm and friendly. She stood, shuddering, while the voice above her murmured something soothing. "That's right, girl—

you don't want to find out if the Dark Mother's priestesses sacrifice horses as well as men!''

To either side she saw men on horses—saw them on
both sides at the same time—the realization made her
moan, but the sound came out as a despairing whicker.
She was vaguely aware of massed trees beside the
road, but from somewhere ahead she could scent running water and grass.

"What'sa matter, Rufo—your mare get a hornet up
her tail?''

"Not *my* mare," the voice above her muttered. "Beginning to think that wager wasn't so lucky after all!''

Shanna stilled, remembering, an appalled understanding of what had happened to her dawning at last.
I'll kill that old woman! came her first coherent thought,
and then—*and that fool who thinks he's riding me!*

The horse beside her reached over and whuffed
gently in her nostrils, then laid back his ears as she
jerked her head away. An order from up ahead set the
column in motion. She felt a firm pressure against her
sides and started forward, tried to figure out how she
was doing it, and stumbled. She could feel sweat on
her neck and flanks.

"Get on with it, girl," Rufo whispered. "Please!''

*I'll run away with him as soon as there's room to
turn!* she thought, *I'll scrape him off on a tree!* When
she took her mind off it, she could walk freely, but
when she thought, she tripped once more. *If I can run
. . .* she thought despairingly, head drooping until Rufo
pulled it up again. *If I don't trip over my own feet—all
four of them, and get shot down before I can get out of
range!*

"Come on, girl," whispered her rider. "We just
gotta clean out a nest of these fanatics, and then I'll
take you home to your mistress again. Fine looking
woman, looks like my ma. Sorry I ever took you away
from her. But you're never going to see her again if
you get me killed out here, eh?''

Fanatics? Were they attacking a stronghold of the
Dark Mother, then? Preoccupied by memories of the
cultists who had nearly killed her twice before, Shanna

moved out more easily. Her old enemies were hardly likely to recognize her in this guise! Not that it mattered, a greater curse than Saibel's was upon her now.

A murmur came down the line—the enemy hold was in sight—when they reached the meadow, they were to charge. The pace quickened. And then, suddenly they were galloping over sparse grass, Rufo hauling her head up when she stumbled, digging heels into her sides so that she instinctively broke into a canter with the rest. The wooden palisade loomed up with appalling speed.

"*Equona!*" she screamed silently. "*Why me? Why did you do this to me?*"

"*Sometimes the gods have to do some housecleaning, too,*" came the Voice in her head. "*The Dark Mother was served by great priestesses once, but they've gone bad since they were forced underground. As you know. Aren't you happy to be helpful?*"

Even at full gallop, Shanna found it possible to snort her opinion of *that*.

Men were struggling to close the great gate as they crashed through it. Shanna plunged as Rufo's balance shifted. The reins were loose on her neck now. A sword flickered at the edge of vision and she shied. The scent of blood filled the air.

"She said you were battle-trained!" Rufo cried. "Prove it!"

A rider's trained responses warred with the instincts of the horse in Shanna's awareness as they pushed across the open ground inside the palisade. But was it so different from unarmed combat? She struck out, felt satisfaction as a sharp hoof crushed a man's skull. And in this form she could kick with astonishing power. The lurching weight on her back told her that Rufo Beltorix was fighting his own battle as well.

Slowly they were gaining ground. A ring of stones surrounded the hall, a man's height apart and half that high. She could leap that, Shanna thought scornfully; she got her hindquarters well under her, tensed—and saw the lead horse rebound from an invisible wall. Still collected, she wheeled on her hindlegs as man and horse went down in a tangled mass. Missiles were coming through the barrier in a steady hail; she squealed as an arrow grazed her shoulder, and felt the shock as something heavier struck Rufo. The others were turning away. She started to follow, felt her rider's weight sag backward, and then the lightness as he fell.

She could see him as the panic of the other horses carried her away with them. He was half sitting, pulling a javelin from his shoulder. He got it out, tried to stand, and a dark-robed warrior darted out between the stones and pulled him inside.

"Damn! Rufo's taken!" cried one of the men.

"We've got to go after him—you know what those perverts do to captives!"

"He's dead meat for sure, and the worst is, they'll use his soul to fuel their sorceries," the captain said.

"After him, then—"

"How? Neither gods nor men can get through that barrier!"

They pulled up in a plunging mass, Shanna keeping close to the other horses while she tried to think what to do.

"Well, are you going to let them kill him?" came the Voice inside. *"I thought you were saving that pleasure for yourself—"*

"You heard the man," Shanna eyed the ring of stones. *"Nothing can get in."*

"Neither man nor god," the Voice echoed, *"but an animal's body could go through, with a woman, or a goddess, inside! Let me ride you, Shanna. Then you'll see what I can do!"*

At least, thought Shanna, this goddess was *asking.* Her nostrils flared at the heavy reek of incense from inside. She had smelled it before, though never with the sharpness of equine senses, and it made her skin crawl.

"Do I have a choice?"

"You always have a choice—but you have to keep making it," came the answer. That had implications that would take some thinking over, but Shanna had no time for it now.

"Very well . . ."

It was not, this time, like a red tide that separated her from her own awareness. The consciousness that was Shanna still existed, but she felt the weight of the goddess descending upon her as she had felt Rufo upon her back, controlling her body far more effectively than any rider could with heel and rein. She turned, and with perfect coordination began to canter toward the barrier.

"What's that fool horse doing now?" came the cry.

Shanna would not have answered if she could. Suddenly she was experiencing the full power and grace of the equine body; she tossed her head with delight, extended herself, and thundered down upon the foe. In moments the barrier was before her. With perfect timing she paused, collected herself and loosed all the strength of her body in a leap like the lift of the wild swan, up, up and over as if she were flying; then down again, forefeet taking the impact and transferring the shock immediately to the powerful hindquarters, springing into the shocked crowd of defenders and striking until they shrieked and ran.

At some point in that battle the goddess left her. Shanna, drunk on delight in the strength of this wonderful body she was inhabiting, took her own vengeance. But presently there was no one left to oppose her. Those who still lived were on their hands and knees, making the strangest assortment of noises. From the corrals behind the hall came terrified whinnying. Shanna threw up her head, listening, and it came to her suddenly what the punishment of Equona had been.

In horror, she looked at the crawling things that had once been men, and wheeled away. The Imperial Riders were moving among them, blades glittering balefully as they put the survivors out of their misery. What had happened to her own body, back in Karna?

"Calur! Please, over here . . . Calur!"

Pricked ears identified the direction of the call; she cocked her head to see. Rufo had his back against one of the stones. Blood was seeping through the fingers he pressed against his shoulder, but he was conscious. *Just 'a clean-up action' indeed! Serves you right,* she thought then. But if he died, they might give her to a Rider who would not honor the terms of the wager, and what would happen to her chances of getting back to her own body then?

She blew gustily and plodded over to the wounded man, then, much to his astonishment, knelt on one foreleg so that he could climb on.

"Oh, you beauty!" Rufo whispered as she heaved herself up again. "Oh, you wonder— Equona Herself sent you to me!"

Shanna snorted disgustedly and moved carefully through the stone circle into the yard. The other Riders were forming up again. They watched, open-mouthed, as she carried Rufo toward them.

"Did you see what she did for me? Did you see?" her rider exclaimed. Shanna sighed. If he kept on like this, the journey back to Karna was going to seem long indeed.

Shanna's saddle was beginning to gall her. She could not decide whether it had gotten knocked loose during the battle or it was something in the way Rufo was sitting. She twitched, trying to resettle it, and heard Rufo's muffled grunt of pain as she jarred his wound.

You deserve it, she thought sourly. *You've been so busy praising your wonder-horse you never thought to ask one of your sword brothers to see to her gear!* The smoke of the burning cult-hall had disappeared behind them, and just now she wished she had left Rufo inside it, but the hearth fires of Karna were dimming the skies ahead. Her nostrils flared at the scent of woodsmoke and the effluvia of crowded humanity.

Soon I can fix this damned saddle! She stepped out more smartly, hoping that was true. She could sense the terror of the loose horses the troop was driving along with them, and she did not look forward to a lifetime in their company.

"Equona? I did what you asked. Are you going to get me out of this?" Her thought probed outward. But

she heard only the creak of leather and the jingle of brass fittings and the irregular rhythms of hooves on the hard-packed road.

They were coming down the hill toward the golden sandstone walls of the city when a shadow slipped across the road. The horse ahead shied as the falcon circled, but Shanna threw up her head to see, heart lifting with the first hope she had known today.

"Where have you been?" she cried silently.

"Is that you?" Chai hung in the air above her, holding her place with an occasional beat of powerful wings.

"More or less—" Shanna replied. *"Where's the rest of me?"* For the past few hours she had tried not to remember headless bodies sprawled in the dust—bodies which neither hedge-magic nor divine intervention could reunite with their spirits now.

"Bercy took you—her—to the Moonmothers. You seem to be coping with your metamorphosis better than Calur. Interesting, isn't it?"

Shanna snorted. Until they reached the Emperor, Chai was condemned to remain in falcon form. She supposed the werewoman had a right to her opinion. Chai found a thermal to lift her and soared ahead of them as they cantered toward the gate.

"Where is the hospice?"

"Follow me—"

As they passed between the pillars of the gatehouse, the falcon veered away to the left. In a moment Shanna was trotting down the street after her, ignoring Rufo's startled oath and the pain as he yanked on the reins.

"Ho, Rufo—has your wonder-horse gone mad again?" It sounded as if some of the Rider's companions were as tired of his boasting as she was. Shanna swung into a canter, hoping to get out of sight before they stopped laughing and followed her.

The Moonmother's Temple was in the poorest quarter, like enough to the one in Otey so that Shanna would have recognized it even without the blue crescent over the door. As she slowed, Rufo jerked cruelly at the bit; she put down her head, heaved, and gently tumbled him to the ground.

The gate was closed, but it was only breast-high. Shanna shook her head, trotted in a circle to get some distance, then launched herself toward the barrier and sailed over it. She landed in a garden where the patients, lying on pallets or sitting on benches, had been brought to take the sun.

Chai swooped down to perch at the edge of one of them, and it was only then that Shanna recognized the raw-boned, sallow-skinned figure lying there. Several of the patients screamed, and a blue-robed form came hurrying through the trees. From the gate came a hollow banging. But a swift step had brought Shanna to the pallet. She nosed at the canvas restraints that held the hands.

Ah, lass, I'm sorry for the mix-up. It's a poor weak, body you're stuck in, isn't it? She could not mind-speak the mare as she did with Chai, but a low whicker seemed to soothe her. *If we get this straightened out, I will never risk you again.*

Shanna lifted her head and trumpeted challenge.

"*Equona! For the mare's sake, help us, if you won't do it for mine!*"

"*If we need you, will you consent to help again?*"

Shanna stilled. One way or another, she had had enough of being ridden to last her quite awhile. Still, with practice it seemed to grow easier, and she had seen enough of what men did in the name of their religions to understand the exasperation of the gods. She began to nod—

—but she could scarcely lift her head. Shanna blinked, trying to focus, saw something large moving away, a blur of blue bending over her. She tried to step out, but she was bound.

"Get these damned things off of me!"

"You've returned to yourself again! May the Lady be praised!" A soft voice murmured soothingly, soft hands fumbled with her bonds.

Returned . . . yes, and she had been back in her body before she finished nodding. Would Equona have done that if she hadn't agreed? She had the uncomfortable feeling that she had been tricked again, but it didn't matter. She had her own shape back. She was free!

"There she is!" It was a man's voice, hoarse with pain and laughter, and Shanna knew it only too well. The priestess helped her to sit up as Rufo staggered toward Calur, who stood trembling by the wall.

"That's my wonder-horse—she saved me, did you know that? Equona Herself gave her to me!"

"Horse-apples! That mare is mine and you know it, Rufo Beltorix!" Shanna found strength to call. He came to a wavering halt and turned.

"What are *you* doing here?"

"It would take too long to explain—" Shanna began.

"See, now, you can't come barging in here this way—" the Moonmother found her voice at last. "If that's your animal, you can take her away!"

"She's mine," said Shanna, "and he's wounded. Why don't you give him my bed. I won't need it anymore."

"Oh, you poor lad! That does look bad. Let me see!"

"Shanna, you've got to let me keep that mare!" Rufo babbled as the priestess started to peel the rough field-dressing that covered his wounded shoulder away. He was already flushed with fever. It was probably just as well he had come. "She saved my life!"

"Somebody certainly did," answered Shanna. "I wonder why? But why don't we let the mare decide? Try calling her—"

She waited, pulse pounding, as Rufo put his soul into summoning Calur, who shook her head and retreated among the orange trees. For a moment Shanna almost pitied him, then she remembered the saddle gall.

"All right," she said when he ran out of breath at last. "It's my turn." She took a deep breath, cursing this body's weakness. "Calur . . ."

The mare's head lifted, ears pricking forward, nostrils widening at the scent of human pain. Shanna began to realize what the past twenty-four hours must have been like for Calur. *Equona! What if she's too frightened even to remember me? What if she doesn't want anything more to do with men?*

"*Haven't you learned anything?*" came that Voice from within.

Shanna levered herself to her feet, sucked in air and let it out in a low whickering not really meant for a human throat. "Calur!" she called softly, and whickered again. "Come now, come to me!"

The fine head tossed. A hoof that was still blood-stained pawed the ground. Then, trembling and with rolling eyes, Calur came to her rider at last.

Rider and ridden . . . thought Shanna, stroking the sweating neck, murmuring in a language that only a horse would understand. She could feel her strength coming back to her. *But now it's my turn to be in control again.*

"*For awhile—*" came the Voice, fainter now. Shanna thought she heard a distant whinny of laughter.

"You win," Rufo gasped as the priestess began to wash his wound. "But I wish I knew—"

"You're alive. Don't complain!" Shanna looked down at him and grinned. "Lie still and let the nice lady do her job. If I see any of your sword-brothers I'll tell them where you are!"

She adjusted Calur's saddle to take pressure off the gall, and Chai came swooping down to perch at her saddlebow.

"Remember, Equona loves you!" she told Rufo as she pulled herself onto the mare's back and reined her away.

THE HAND OF FATIMA
by Shariann Lewitt

Since this was one of the few stories in this anthology to come in through an agent, all I know about Shariann Lewitt is that her story is thoroughly professional, embodying an old fantasy theme; stories laid in a psuedo-Arabian Nights world are always popular in fantasy —although that end of the world is not, in reality, very hospitable to woman writers.

But, I guess, in fantasy, anything goes. And we can use our imagination to decide whether Shariann Lewitt is a fifteen-year-old college girl (unlikely, considering that she has sold several novels), or a harried mother of five. (Don't laugh; Harriet Beecher Stowe had ten.)

The Hand of Fatima is the single, sure protection against the mischief of the unseen world. It is carved over the Gate of Justice at the Alhambra Palace just as it is painted over the doors of the meanest dwellings throughout the whole of Dar al Islam. Over the inner portal of the Gate, there is a carved stone Key. Those who know say that Granada will never fall until the Hand over the Gate takes the Key and opens the fortress.

She didn't recognize the fear at first. The faint, uneasy feeling could be caused by the brilliance of the

28

late afternoon sunlight glaring off the peaks of the Sierra Nevadas, spoiling her aim. She squinted, judged the angle again, and then let the arrow fly toward the onrushing enemy. The arrow caught the breast of the huge destrier he rode, and the man in glittering mail fell to the ground.

She urged her red Arabian forward quickly to the fallen knight. As he lifted his sword above his head, she thrust her spear into the unarmored gap under his left arm. Dead or dying, he crumbled onto the red soil.

She felt the fear again and this time she knew it. She also knew that she was not afraid of the knights of Aragon or Castile, Leone or Navarre. She was not afraid to die on the plain of Granada with the promise of Paradise before her. It was Paradise she sought.

She notched another arrow, but it flew wild because of the fear that shook her hands.

"Fatima bint Muley, you are not thinking!" the furious voice of Farid the Berber came at her back. "Look at the sun. It is near dark."

It was true. The shadows had become very long, and already there was darkness under the peaks of the great mountains. Above, the red tower wall was a black silhouette on the barren hill. She didn't move. The towers that guarded the Palace, like the Palace itself, offered less safety than battle. Less safety, even, than the invaders' camp now twinkling with myriad welcoming watchfires for the withdrawing knights.

The old man who had spoken before put his hand on her reins. "We must go, Fatima. But how many times must I tell you to think before the action, and not afterward?"

Fatima nodded, acknowledging the rebuke, and rode back at his side. They passed through the Gate of Arms into the camp of the common soldiers. As she dismounted and let the stable boy take her Arabian, the fear did not lessen. She could identify a warmth between her breasts, a warmth that had nothing to do with the sun or armor or exertion.

"Farid?" Fatima called to the Berber general. "May I join you for supper?"

He looked at her carefully with the cold judgment he had used when she was small. "The Sultana will miss you," he said slowly. "That could be dangerous. Go and wash. I will wait for you at the Tower of Spikes after evening prayers."

When she left the old man under the darkening tower, the fear closed around her, breathing over her gently like the warm sigh of evening. She walked slowly, not wanting to enter the great Palace where the Sultana Zoraya waited.

The garden between the tower wall and the royal dwelling was scented with cypress and myrtle, bitter oranges and roses. Tiny fountains drizzled reflected twilight into their ceramic basins with a sound as innocent as rain. She sat on the stone ledge by the lower fountain and her fingers went to the chain around her neck.

It was the amulet on the chain that was warm, she knew. She pulled off the necklace and held the silver filigree charm cupped in her hands. It was the same charm every child wore, and she was not alone in wearing it after childhood. The openwork depicted a hand full of whorls in the palm, a Hand of Fatima, the daughter of the Prophet for whom she had been named. Farid the Berber had given it to her when she was born, and he said it had come from a great fakir in Baghdad.

The small talisman filled her hands with faint light, a subtle glow different from the colors in the fountain or the sky. Fatima bint Muley knew why she was afraid. The brightness of battle never touched her with this darkness. But the strange things, the nights when Farid read the stars and told stories of djinn, these had always awakened the cold trembling. The fear had only made those stories more delicious, but this was no story. The talisman glowed. There must be something moving under the scented breath of the night breeze.

Fatima picked one of the heavy pomegranates hanging full and ripe on a low branch. Pomegranates had given the city its name. Yet as things walked in the twilight, the garden seemed closed and quiet and at rest. There was no hint of the watchfires under the Sierra Nevadas, no whisper that those who had taken Seville and captured the glories of Cordoba now surrounded this last fortress of the Faithful in Al Andaluz.

They were the last. They had always been the last. For the first time, Fatima was overwhelmed. The great fortress with its tower wall had seemed invincible. She had never questioned Granada's strength. Didn't they have the protection of the Hand over the Gate of Justice?

For the first time, she saw how isolated the city was, surrounded by mountains and ringed by enemies. The Berbers had twice sent help. They would send no more. The heavy fruit slipped between her fingers and shattered on the stones below, its sweet and sanguine juice running between the crevices and down into the earth.

Startled, Fatima blinked and came to herself. She stood and walked quickly to the Palace, fastening her necklace as she went. Her arrival at the royal baths surprised the attendant, who ran for soap and perfume and towels.

When she was clean of the sweat of the day, she dressed as the daughter of Muley Abdul Hasan. Her dress was silk, the color of young pears with a pattern of pomegranates and stars. The gauze veil she draped over her heavy braids was bordered to match, and her slippers were fine tooled goatskin. She slipped two heavy gold bracelets over her hand, and was satisfied that she looked like the Emirah she was.

Soft voices drifted up to her from the courtyard. "Fatima, come down."

It was her stepmother's voice, rich as the night air. The Sultana Zoraya must have seen the light. Without quite knowing why, Fatima grasped her childhood charm as she descended into the cypress shaded enclosure.

Around the Sultana's private garden, the upper rooms were brightly lit, and the lacy pierced stucco bled eerie luminosity into the lush courtyard. It was just enough light that Fatima could see the criticism in Zoraya's gaze as the Sultana inspected her. "Let me see your hands," Zoraya ordered.

Fatima held them out obediently, trying not to flinch at the Sultana's touch.

"You should not ride out as you do," Zoraya said with the trace of accent that she had never lost. "Your hands have calluses and your skin is dark."

"No one else will go," Fatima replied.

Zoraya laughed richly. "That, my dear, is why we have Berbers."

Fatima shivered. She despised Zoraya, hated the woman to touch her, hated her ice-colored eyes. "Will that be all, Doña Isabel?" Fatima asked, the words out before she realized she had said them.

The Sultana struck her across the face. "Never use that name to me," her stepmother hissed. "I wish your father had beheaded you, too, along with your brothers."

Fatima turned and fled. There was a gate from the courtyard and she raced through it into the garden beyond, and up the Tower of the Ladies to the wall. Resting one hand against the rough stone of the walkway, she panted until she began to sob. She knew better than to defy Zoraya, but her anger was beyond bearing.

The next tower was the Tower of Spikes, the place where she was supposed to meet Farid. It was long after evening prayers, and he might have gone. She sat on the wall and cried, afraid of the strange glow of her amulet and angry at Zoraya and angry at herself.

"Go on, weep like a child," came Farid's voice in the dark. "You can return to the harem and let Zoraya's son Boabdil rout Leone."

Fatima rubbed her eyes and looked up. "I hate them both," she spat.

Farid only shook his head slowly, his grizzled beard catching the moonlight. "You called her by her old name, didn't you?"

Fatima nodded. "How did you know?"

The old Berber sat down next to her. "I know you, Fatima. Zoraya, Doña Isabel, whatever name you use for her, is dangerous. You know that. You know how she bewitched your father into killing your brothers. One day," he sighed, "and probably very soon, you will be in a situation that will kill you if you don't think carefully first. Calling names will not defeat Zoraya, or anybody."

His voice sounded strange, and the light glinting off his white hair seemed too bright. Fatima blinked several times. "Farid, I have known you all my life. You were my father's general before I was born, and his father's before him. And if anyone should hate Zoraya, it's you."

The old man merely chuckled. "I read the stars the night you were born, Fatima."

His mention of the stars reminded her. "And look at this," she said, pulling the amulet from her neck. "You gave me this. And it's bright, and warm to touch, and that's what I really wanted to ask you about. You never said that it would get warm, or why. It's like in those stories you used to tell."

The old man's face changed strangely. He no longer seemed old, but he did not look young, either. Only very strange and solid like marble and clear like crystal, and his feet seemed to drift over the stone walkway softer than a butterfly.

"I didn't know it would be so soon," he said, and his voice sounded deeper than before, and as if it came from very far away. "It is a sign, but I cannot use it. It is a test, Fatima! Think! Remember, before you act. Think."

Fatima started to edge away from him, feeling the way behind her with her toes. It was not Zoraya, then, but Farid who frightened her. He, who had taught her to ride and fight, to read and chant poetry, he was the something from the unseen that made her afraid. Slowly, carefully, she stepped back on the stones, wondering how to escape. She didn't know how to escape from something of the other world.

"Wait, Fatima," Farid called.

His voice chilled her and she began to run again. She ran through the towers along the wall, ran west almost half the length of the fortress until she reached the Tower of Arms. She flew down the stairs into the narrow paths of the common soldiers' camp.

Several men stared at her, and she slowed to a dignified walk. She went to one of the fires and took some sharp goat cheese to nibble. "Supper," she said with a forced smile although it was true. She wasn't hungry, but she chewed a bit of the cheese anyway.

Twice this night she had run, she who had never run from anything, who was truly the daughter of Muley Abdul Hasan. It was Boabdil, that whining son of Zoraya, who ran away. And she had run from Farid, Farid whom she had called "Uncle" as a child. She always did act before she thought.

Farid said that she must think. She pulled the talisman from her neck and held it. It was warmer now, and brighter. She walked up the street toward the Tower, and down toward the Gate of Justice. When she approached the Gate, the filigree amulet glowed brighter, but the heat was pleasant, not painful. Farid said it was a sign he could not use, and he had read her stars. Maybe it was for her to use, if she could understand it, a tool like the astrolabes of the sailors. Astrolabes! They guided sailors on the sea, and this charm became brighter as she came closer to the Gate of Justice. Perhaps it was some sort of guide, then.

Fatima breathed deeply to quiet the throbbing in her veins. There was nothing to fear from the Gate, she reminded herself sternly. It was only stone and wood and tile, and protected by the Hand of Fatima like her own small charm. She had often seen it in the dark.

Yet the Gate loomed above her. The blue pattern on the white tiles glimmered and danced, swirling into new patterns. For a moment the colors took on the look of writing, but melted so quickly that Fatima could not read what it said. She blinked and the decorative pattern changed. The stones of the Gate were cold to the touch when they should have been warm from the heat of the day. They seemed to vibrate, tremble. The small silver charm was blazing with light.

Fatima wanted to run, but she would not run for the

third time. Like the changing tile patterns above her, she felt the pieces of the day shift and merge. The fear and the amulet, Zoraya and Farid, and above all things, Granada itself. Above the inner portal of the Gate, the large carved Key took on a terrible solidity, gathering the darkness into itself.

It was the Hand that protected the fortress, and the city. It was the Hand that would open the gates of the Alhambra to the enemy, or none at all.

Fatima felt her talisman pulling her into the heavy inner portal of the Gate. The thick walls were high and the passage was winding and narrow. Her filigree amulet was radiant light, a torch in the darkness. She found herself at the bottom of the stair that wound to the chamber above the keystone. She had climbed this stair on other days to watch the road from behind the carved sandlewood screens. But this time it was different. Here the stone quavered and drank in the light, and she could hear chanting in a strange language from the watchroom above. The stones seemed to carry the chanting, moving in rhythm to it.

Suddenly Fatima realized that she had no spear, no sword to defend herself. It was never necessary for her to carry weapons in the Fortress. She was the Emirah, daughter of Muley Abdul Hasan. No one in the citadel would harm her, no one except Zoraya, and the sword was not Zoraya's way.

Think, Farid had told her. The only true weapon is the mind. Hardly daring to breathe, Fatima dropped the talisman back around her neck under her dress. The light could not be seen through the gold encrusted fabric. She slipped out of her tooled leather slippers and set them aside. Then she pulled the gossamer silk veil from her head. Sinking down against the frigid, shallow steps, she pulled the gold bracelets off her arm. The heaviest one she tied to one end of the veil. The other she slipped into the toe of one shoe. The cold passageway numbed her feet, but she took comfort from that very ordinary thing. Nothing else was ordinary.

Carrying her slippers and veil, she began to creep

silently up the winding staircase. She could feel the pulse of the chant through the wall as she pressed her back against it. The dark congealed around her and the small bite of cheese lay like lead in her stomach. The sound of her heart was like a Berber battle drum in her ears. All the stories of djinn came back to her. She willed herself to climb. One step, and then one step more she ascended into the palpable umbra.

Back pressed hard to the wall, she negotiated the last curve of the staircase as slowly as she could. She moved like one more shadow among the many in the deep passageway. Moving only her eyes, she looked up to the doorway at the top of the stairs.

Silhouetted dark against the shimmering void beyond the open door stood a figure. He was armed, facing out toward her but not seeing her edged against the stones. A random ray of starlight filtered through the tracery of the high window, and Fatima recognized the guard. It was Muneer ibn Ahmed, one of Boabdil's men. Loyal to Boabdil meant loyal to the Sultana Zoraya.

Not daring to breathe, Fatima stood motionless. Her fear had lessened facing a danger she could understand. This was something she knew, had planned for. She threw one of her shoes down the stairs.

Muneer was alert, but he was staring well past her, into the place where the noise had originated. He glanced behind him, almost as if wondering if he should leave his post to investigate.

Fatima threw the other shoe. The guard moved down a single step, listening intently. He waited. Fatima threw the bracelet, which made a clear sound as it hit the stone and tumbled from step to step.

Muneer rushed down. Fatima waited, crouched, until he was almost past her, and then she threw the weighted veil at his legs. She had always been very good with a sling, a weapon no less deadly for being humble. The veil wound around his right leg and Fatima pulled with all her strength. His own forward motion and the depth of the staircase aided her. Muneer dived headfirst down the stairs.

Fatima waited breathless for a second that stretched into an eternity. She could not hear anything from the fallen guard. The chanting in the high chamber did not stop, nor did she hear any movement from the top of the stairs.

She descended to Muneer and found that he was unconscious, his head twisted around horribly. His neck was broken. She had seen things like this before. His body was heavy and inert, and it was hard to move him. She rocked him gently, building momentum, until she could snatch the knife at his belt. Then she cut his throat expertly and without feeling, a better death than his wound would have given him.

His sword had fallen even farther, and she fetched it before beginning her ascent a second time. As she approached the now unguarded chamber, a sudden, sharp sound echoed through the entire Gate. The massive masonry seemed to heave and toss in its foundation, and there was a low keening as if the stone itself had cried in pain. She grasped the hilt of the scimitar close to her, but it gave her little comfort.

Think. These were the things she had not wanted to know, had never wanted to face. She shut her eyes and tried to pray, but the words gave her no comfort. The vast walls shuddered and settled again. She knew she had no choice but to enter the upper chamber. Farid had told her, but she hadn't understood, that he had read her stars, and that he didn't know it was so soon. It was this that he had meant. Her destiny lay in the shadows above her.

Moving softly, she peered into the open doorway. Moonlight filtered in through the carved sandalwood and stone in the windows, casting arcane silver patterns on the floor. Small oil lamps illuminated a circle in the center where a woman stood facing a thing that only walked in nightmares. Between them lay the great stone Key from the inner portal.

It was the monster *ifrit* that held her eyes, and she almost gagged. It was nearly as tall as the roof with the features of a man crudely molded, as if a child had made it of clay. Its skin was green, glistening with moisture, and the eyes were yellow like those of a rabid dog. She did not need to look further to know the *ifrit* was one of the evil djinn who followed Satan into the bowels of the earth.

The woman turned and smiled at Fatima. It was Zoraya. "You are too late," the Sultana said, pointing to the key.

Fatima understood only too well. Dona Isabel, who had once been her father's prisoner and then the Sultana, had planned from the first to deliver Granada to their enemies.

Around Fatima's neck, the charm burned. She was no magician like Suliman to bind the *ifrit*. She was no astrologer like Farid to read the meaning of this in the stars.

Think, Farid had told her. She needed time. "You still need the Hand," she said, feeling the throbbing of the charm over her heart. "You need the Hand of Fatima." She said the words before she heard them. "You need the Hand of Fatima," she repeated, to listen again and taste the words. A plan was forming in her mind. No, she was not a sorceress like Dona Isabel the Sultana, but she was Fatima the daughter of Muley Abdul Hasan.

Carefully, Fatima laid down the sword. It would be no use against the *ifrit,* and she had the knife for Zoraya. In any case, she needed her hands free. She moved slowly, letting her mind race. *Think,* Farid had said. This was a test. There had to be an answer somewhere.

The stories she had heard as a child came back to her. The *ifrit* were evil and canny, could not be fought with sword or spear, or controlled by any save a great magician. But they were proud and loved riddles and honored their bargains. They could be tricked.

"Ifrit," Fatima said, trying to keep her voice as bold as if this were a mortal enemy, "you have brought the Key to Granada, but not the Hand. I challenge you, Ifrit, to bring the Hand of Fatima here now. Because if you cannot, I can!"

The *ifrit* laughed, a sound of hollow, ringing brass.

"I would like to see *you* bring that hand, daughter of Adam."

"If I can," Fatima replied, "then will you take this sorceress with you and return to the place you were called from immediately?"

The *ifrit* laughed again. "Yes, daughter of Adam, I will take her and return."

Fatima smiled grimly. There was little reason to believe that it would work, but it was the only thing she could think of. She unclasped the silver necklace and held it to her palm. It blazed to life, burning, the silver whorls spreading across her own hand. It painted her like quicksilver henna, not at all painful but somehow *fitting,* as if she had drawn on a glove. The power entered with the color, seeping deep into her tissues, into her blood, and all fear was extinguished.

She held her palm out to the *ifrit,* incised with silver tracery that flared with power. "I am Fatima," she said softly. "Give me the Key."

Zoraya shrieked and ran to the sword Fatima had laid against the wall. She picked it up and held it stiffly out toward Fatima.

Dona Isabel had betrayed her nation when she became the Sultana Zoraya, and the Sultana Zoraya meant to betray her adopted people now. But Fatima was not afraid of her. She almost pitied the woman facing her with a gargoyle mask made of hate and fear. No, it was Zoraya who was afraid of Fatima.

Zoraya did not know what to do with the sword. It was too heavy for her, and she held it awkwardly. Fatima reached for the knife in her bodice and threw it. The blade struck Zoraya's shoulder, and the Sultana screamed and dropped the sword.

Fatima closed the distance before Zoraya could pick up the knife, and then touched the Sultana's forehead with a silvered finger. The traitor whimpered and sank to the floor. The room smelled of burning blood. The *ifrit* was gone.

The Key lay in the center of the chamber. Fatima felt the silver of the talisman in her veins, consuming her body. She picked up the Key and its great weight

did not affect her. She pushed it through the delicate
sandalwood carving of the window over the inner portal. Almost by its own will, it dropped back into the
stone where it had been set when the fortress was
built.

Overcome by weariness, Fatima sat down against
the wall. From a distant minaret she heard the call to
morning prayers. She stared at the protective pattern
filigreed into her flesh, now shimmering only with the
reflected light of the first dawn. She heard soft footsteps at the threshold and looked up. Farid, shimmering like an alabaster lamp, stood in the doorway.

"What are you?" she asked. There was no fear in
her now, nor hope.

"I am a servant of the One," he replied. "I was sent
to teach, and watch, and test. This last was not of my
making, but necessary for the Faithful of Granada."

She shrugged. His words were meaningless to her.
"Then I suppose I am Sultana now."

Farid smiled. "No, not Sultana, not Queen. You
have proven yourself worthy of the title Caliphah, the
Defender of the Faithful."

She rose and motioned him not to follow. She left
the high chamber of the Gate and walked through the
garden. Ruddy light stained the snow on the mountains. Birds sang in the tall cypress and a still pool
reflected the ornate traceries of the Palace portico in
the glowing rose and amber of the early light.

She entered the Palace. From the large terrace framed
by delicate arches and columns, she could see the
mountains and the plain spread out below her. A
cloud of red dust moved to the west, and she knew
that the knights of Aragon and Navarre, Leone and
Castile, were on their way home.

COMMENCEMENT

by Lynne Armstrong-Jones

Lynne Armstrong-Jones—no relation, I assume, to Lord Snowdon, ex-husband of Princess Margaret—is a perfect example of persistence; she has sent me a story every month or so since I started these anthologies. When I was a beginning writer myself, my first husband tried to discourage me from sending too many manuscripts to any one publisher; he thought that seeing my name on so many unusable manuscripts would cause the editors to think of me as a hopeless incompetent, and I would never sell anything because eventually the editors would not even bother to read anything I wrote.

Well, he was wrong; and since becoming an editor, I have "discovered" a lot of writers who seem never to learn from rejection; I reject one of their manuscripts, and they send me another frequently no better than the first, and it's true that I groan when I see yet another story. But I still read it—nothing is impossible; one of these hopeful writers may some day send me a manuscript which I can use. One has to admire persistence, and nothing speaks more eloquently of their desire to succeed.

Anyhow, it was a real pleasure to find this story among the slush; I was pleased to think it was from an old friend who had not been discouraged by many rejections.

As they say in the Bible, "Him that has ears to hear, let him hear."

Amita had packed her few belongings inside of the small sack. There was nothing more for her to do here.

She sighed. She did not wish to leave: the tower had been her place of study for many weeks.

The young woman raised her head in response to the twitters of the birds outside of the small window. She smiled slightly, recalling the joy of watching the nestlings last spring. She crossed to the window and looked outside.

Immediately, she knew that this had been a mistake. How it hurt inside when she thought of never returning!

Oh, it would have been different had I been a success, thought the woman. *I would have been leaving here with the aim of helping people. I would have been thinking of the different ways that my magic might make this world a better place. Now I feel as though I have—am—nothing.*

She bowed her head once more—not thinking, just feeling.

Her head jerked up at the sudden sound behind her. The door had opened.

"I am sorry, my dear, if I startled you." The older woman smiled encouragingly. It was difficult to have to dismiss such a sincere and likable pupil.

Despite her despair, Amita could not resist smiling in return at the sight of the Superior's wrinkled, caring face. *How I have loved learning from you,* she thought. *And how I am loath to leave!*

The moment could not be delayed. She followed the older woman down the winding stairway and accepted the best wishes of her closest friends, who had gathered at the door.

Her dark eyes filled with tears as she mounted the little donkey which would carry her to the nearest town.

The Superior grasped Amita's hands and held them. "Please, my dear, do not despair so! Not every one of us is destined to live her life as a sorceress! Do not neglect to develop further your strengths." Her voice softened. "The importance of magic pales in comparison with intelligence, patience, and kindness such as you possess. Please, dear one, use those blessed traits to make our world better. . . ."

Amita could feel the ring of truth behind the words, but for now she would have preferred to sacrifice some of those traits for the talent which she lacked! She withdrew her hands from those of the Superior and turned away, urging the donkey forward.

She did not look back.

Whatever shall I do now, she wondered.

She could not imagine anything else which would bring her the joy and satisfaction which she knew that the world of magic would—*had,* for a time. She reflected upon her failures—her ability to create illusions and initiate simple spells, only to have them dissipate.

The Superior had said that this happened from time to time. It did not mean at all that Amita was a lesser person than the others, she had said.

Somehow, thought Amita with another sigh, *that does not prevent me from* feeling *lesser!*

She continued to ponder the possible paths upon which her life might now lead her: this was another mistake. None of the options which she could foresee were appealing—or even bearable.

It seemed as though she had no future at all.

It was amazing how her life had turned so completely around. She had felt as though she had had everything until her weaknesses had become apparent.

Now her future could hold *nothing* for her. There seemed no point in going on.

She shook her head in anger. *Is there no peace for me? Now that I realize that I do not wish to continue with my life, I can do nothing about it: for, even though I am no longer a novice sorceress, I feel totally bound still by my oath against deliberately causing unjustified harm.*

Is there no way out?

Her fists were clenched in anger as she urged the donkey to trot more quickly.

Such was her preoccupation with her plight that she did not at first hear nor see the sobbing woman who was shouting for help. It was not until the woman had run to the side of the donkey that Amita even noticed her.

The woman was sobbing something about her husband and begging for help. Tears streamed from terrified eyes. She begged Amita to follow her to her home, turning and beginning to hurry in that direction. This was awkward for her, as she looked to be about midway through her pregnancy.

The desperation of the poor woman touched even the preoccupied Amita deeply. Hastily, she urged the donkey to follow.

She dismounted and followed the woman into the tiny cottage. All appeared to be quite as it should, except for one thing.

The woman's husband stood in the middle of the large room as though he had been turned to stone.

Amita approached, studying the strange sight. It was obviously the work of a magician—and a powerful one, at that.

Amita shook her head. "I am very sorry, but there is nothing that I can do to help—"

Dara was incredulous. "But you are a sorceress! Your cloak is one of theirs, I know it! Please—I do not care if you are novice or not—you must try!"

Amita shook her head once more. "You do not understand. I cannot use spells at all. They would be futile."

She could not make herself heard nor understood over the sobs of the desperate woman. Amita envisioned the likely consequences of any puny attempts which she might make to counteract the sorcerer's spell. . . .

Suddenly, her eyes brightened. She still felt bound by her oath against deliberate harm (to herself, or others), but there was nothing to prevent her from attempting to convince someone *else* to end her suffering for her!

She looked quickly around the room, feeling the air for hints of enchantment. He was here, somewhere.

"Great wizard, where are you? Show yourself."

Silence was the only reply.

"Wizard! Are you coward? Why do you hesitate to make yourself known? Do you fear me?" She asked the last question with just a hint of disdain.

Suddenly, a booming voice filled the room. "And who are you, little one, to speak to me with such disrespect!" It was not a question.

"Only a novice, great wizard—but one with powers which you cannot imagine! I have been schooled much differently from you: I have at my disposal powerful enchantments. I can render you totally powerless. And this I shall do if you do not restore this man to his correct condition!"

The wizard responded by laughing with great disgust.

I must get him angry, thought Amita. "You are nothing but a great bag of wind! You fear to trifle with the likes of me! Set the man free or defend yourself! Move quickly or you shall feel the full force of my anger and power!" Her eyes were wide, her voice forceful: she hoped that she might have angered him enough to kill her.

"You young fool!" The walls seemed to shake as the booming voice began once more. "Do not tempt me, child!"

Amita saw her opportunity. Her eyes flashed. "You are *frightened* of me! Your power is nothing compared to mine."

Suddenly, a great wind seemed to come from nowhere. Bolts of lightning filled the sky outside and seemed to flash from inside wall to inside wall. Amita heard the woman scream—

Amita lay quietly, tuning her awareness to her surroundings. Was this, then, the afterlife?

All seemed very quiet.

She opened her eyes and eased herself into a sitting position, noticing that Dara beside her was doing the same. Dara turned to Amita and began to ask what had happened but stopped suddenly. She hurried to her husband on hands and knees.

She reached her hand to his face and stroked it, as though she could not believe that she was feeling warm flesh once more, instead of the horrid, cold stone. He turned to her, smiling, and the two embraced.

The woman looked to Amita and gasped her thanks.

But Amita shook her head. "I did nothing," she said.

Dara came to Amita's side. "Do not be so humble. It was a wonderful spell!"

Amita still shook her head. "It was no spell," she said softly. Then, in whispered disbelief, she gasped: "I intimidated him!"

The older woman patted the shoulder of the younger. "Well, whatever you magic people call it, it was wonderful. You have given us such tremendous joy that we can never begin to repay you what you deserve. And just think—your lifework as a sorceress is just beginning!"

Amita looked past the woman and through the open doorway. She gazed at the silhouette of the tower in the distance. She thought once more of all the strange and magical things which she had learned there—and of the important aspects of life which they had *not* shown her.

She wondered which of these taught the greater lesson.

She looked once more at Dara, who was again embracing her husband. "Your statement was not quite correct," Amita said. "It is my *life* which is just beginning."

Amita quietly declined their invitation to sup with them. As she climbed once more upon the donkey's back, the older woman touched her hand. "Thank you again, Amita," she beamed. "I want you to know that, should my child be a daughter, she will bear your name. May the goddess bless you on your journey."

Amita bid the pair farewell and moved along the path. She stopped when she heard the trills of the bluebirds. Listening, she began to smile. *Strange*, she thought, *I had not noticed them along this road before*. . . .

A LESSER OF EVILS
by Morning Glory Zell

I sort of expect a story by Morning Glory to be about queer beasties and ecology-conservation; she sold her first story here, a piece about the need for conserving the dragon (would that we could) and in the interval before writing this new story, she went off on a mission to the South Sea Islands to "find the mermaid." What she found, as I suspected she would, was the manatee— an endangered species by now. Maybe if she *had* discovered women with tails, it would be easier to convince various countries to conserve them.

In spite of my belief in the value of this cause, some conservationists *do* go overboard; I think it may have been in one of the New Age magazines that I read a plea, serious I believe, for "conserving" the smallpox virus. I am afraid my ecological conscience doesn't extend quite that far; I'm of the opinion that some species should be exterminated as soon as possible; and so this plea for rehabilitation of the basilisk tends to fall on deliberately deaf ears.

Right now, Morning Glory is working on a *nonfiction* book, to be called something like UNICORNS IN MY GARDEN. Yes, I said non-fiction; how about that?

The Witch listened to the voice of the screaming statue. The wind was its tongue as it whistled and moaned over hollows and crevices in the gleaming white calcium deposits. This statue was a young woman turning to look fearfully over her shoulder; her eyes held the horror she had seen, would hold it now forever. . . .

Well, maybe not forever. Many of the other statues showed the weathering action of rain as well as the everpresent wind. That one over there, for instance, was an old man and he looked truly ancient. Yet farther on, there was another one that was so old that it was no longer possible to determine the sex of the original person. Yes, person. They had all been people once and that was the true horror of seeing them. Worse than the moaning wind and the sense of desolation was the knowledge that once they had all been people going about their business. And what added the final chill was that at any moment here, it could happen to you. She shuddered and her long, loose salt-and-pepper hair rustled against the neck of her green tunic. Slowly she turned to her companion, the swordswoman Valla. "I hope your resolve is firmer than mine at this moment."

Valla answered somewhat slower than her usual quick tongued riposte. "This valley would put anyone's courage to the test unless they were already made of stone."

"Are you starting to have second thoughts about this expedition?" The Witch raised one dark eyebrow.

"Andred, sometimes you ask the most annoying questions!" Valla tossed her red braid back over her shoulder and noted that the eyebrow remained raised. She replied evenly:

"I passed my initiation into the Order of Artemet, and the Goddess accepted my oath to serve Her by protecting the last of Her mythological animals from extinction. This is my first assignment. I knew it would not be easy to capture and relocate a basilisk, but I'm not about to turn around and . . ."

The swordswoman suddenly spun around. Drawing her blade at a sudden small noise, she interrupted herself. "Whew! Nothing but a hummingbird." Valla sheathed her blade with a sigh of relief.

Andred gestured with measured grace and asked obliquely: "Did you notice the profusion of wildlife in this valley? Birds and small animals are all around and seem quite unafraid."

"Good for them," Valla said. "But then I don't see any animal statues about. No little garden bunnies, unless that unrecognizable mass over there was once a bear," she added sardonically. "But why would a basilisk only attack humans?"

It was Andred's turn for sarcasm. "Maybe it's smarter than we think it is."

The two women looked at each other and smiled. Their camaraderie was marked with friendly competition from its contentious beginning. Valla muttered something under her breath about whistling in the graveyard and Andred said, "Now that we have gotten the feel of the place and seen the lay of the land we should get on to Marshby and meet our erstwhile employers."

Her eyes twinkled with contained mischief as she continued, "Usually we have to fight people tooth and nail in order to relocate some unfortunate beast, but for once people are actually paying us to do it."

With soft words and firm hands both women coaxed their nervous horses uphill into the whistling wind and headed toward the pass leading out of the valley, keeping a sharp eye out for motion and giving a wide berth to the visible entrance of a large cave purported to be the lair of the basilisk. Outside its looming entrance, scattered around the deceptively calm little valley, the statues continued to moan their protest.

On their way across the pass into the neighboring valley Andred explained to Valla how basilisks had been created as hybrid magickal creatures by a mad Wizard distant ages ago. They had slain their creator and escaped to breed on their own. Fortunately or unfortunately they remained quite rare.

"What I cannot fathom is why anyone would want such a creature in the first place!" Valla exclaimed with characteristic impatience.

"They have their place in the order of things now. And besides, we want the opportunity to study them in a protected environment. Perhaps we can discover a way to reverse the calcification process and release its victims from their thrall."

"Well, we'd better hurry because that one poor lump would be a sorry sight brought back the way he is now," Valla opined.

As they rode into the town of Marshby, it was as though the fear engendered by the Valley of the Basilisk had followed silently in their shadow; or perhaps there was something tainted about this valley as well. The trees were sickly and drooping and there was an oppressive air about the place. The houses seemed prosperous enough, with high gabled roofs, but many were unoccupied and the empty doors and windows hung accusingly ajar with the slack-jawed look of an idiot. When they came around a bend, they could see more of the valley ahead including a fork of the Ariah River circling around the barely visible marshes. There was a sweet-metallic tang in the air covering a darker smell of decay. Andred looked into the distance, an unfocused gaze in her green eyes, and said softly, "Secrets lie buried here which are better left unknown."

Valla tightened her thin lips but made no answer and the two women rode on in silence.

Guildmaster XXam was an imposing figure of a man; good looking and dignified with an open handed charm. Both women stood up as he entered the dining room of the opulent inn, where he bought them a lavish breakfast. Then he hurried them over to the refinery site where they were shown how the leadium ore was smelted into ingots. "Leadium made this town what it is, and we are blessed indeed by its fortune. We use the purest of the ore for dedication to the gods."

Andred told him, "You are a most pious man." And she wondered why it came out sounding ironic.

The Guildmaster then waxed eloquent about how the mines would prosper by following the vein of leadium into the neighboring valley. "We have suffered greatly. How soon will you be able to move the creature?"

"We had planned to begin tomorrow, after we obtained a few small essentials from the local midwife." Andred informed him.

Master XXam spoke with withering scorn, "The midwife! Why, she is nothing but a superstitious old beldame! The Guild can supply any need you have without resorting to such as her."

"I was told she was trained by the Order of Artemet." Andred said coolly.

The Guildmaster looked pained: "I . . . I meant no offense Lady. Perhaps it is not the same midwife."

"Have you more than one?" Valla spoke up sweetly.

"Perhaps . . ." He became evasive and would not continue.

Outside in the courtyard they admired the small shops along the main streets. They were neatly kept and bursting with goods from all over. Large wooden flower pots were strangely devoid of flowers and other greenery; instead they had been filled with leadium cast figurines and sculpture. It reminded Andred oddly of the screaming statues of the basilisk. Suddenly, a small man wearing a uniform tunic came hurrying up to the Guildmaster and whispered in his ear. Master XXam looked agitated, conferred in an urgent *sotto voce,* then turned to the women: "Please excuse me, Ladies; a most unavoidable emergency has arisen that I must attend to myself immediately."

"Don't trouble yourselves about us, Master XXam. We can find our way back to the Inn," Valla assured him.

"Then if I am permitted, I will join you later this evening for dinner," he said unctuously.

"But of course, and uh . . . Master XXam, could you remember to bring up three bunches of dried rue? We will need it to disarm your basilisk tomorrow." Andred was all charm, and the man inclined his head taking his leave. When he was out of earshot, Valla asked Andred what she thought of him.

"He reminds me of these leadium sculptures: polished, hard and hollow; a likable fellow but not to be trusted."

The Witch and the swordswoman continued to stroll down the shopkeepers' lane, stopping to admire various items. Valla was particularly intrigued with the exquisite figurines of Artemet in Her many breasted form as Mother of the Animals. A shopkeeper hovered obsequiously over their shoulder and said, "The Ladies will note that this figure is of pure cast leadium and has all its properties, including the one of glowing in darkness."

Valla had just purchased it for a surprisingly modest amount, when a small and wiry old woman whom Valla had noticed watching them in several other shops, stepped up and addressed them in a voice harsh as an raven: "You Sisters are all alike! One eye open to the pretties and the other one closed to the harsh world. You would wink at Death Herself if it got you a better bargain on some trifle you fancied."

Valla turned on the crone and flared: "Who do you think you are to pass judgements on our Order with no knowledge?"

The old women sneered. "Why, if either of you was the witch she pretends to be, you'd *know* who I am. Oh, I have knowledge of *your* ways: *'By the Fruit shall you know the Tree.'* And what fruit does your Order bear?" She held up a delicate figurine of Artemet, then flung it into the dirt. "Trinkets and jewels! And what is the price you are really paying? You haven't even got the guts to find out, but I'll give you a clue." Her voice hissed as she moved her face close to Andred's. "Look around you: the price you will pay, that we are all paying here, is death!"

Andred looked around where the woman indicated. The aura of the town itself exuded a veneer of thriving success hiding a deeper layer of decay and despair. It showed itself in the drooping vegetation and the forced artificial smiles of the few people on the streets. And the children . . . where were they? The question popped out of her without volition: "The children . . . where are the children?"

"Well, well, maybe there is more to you than I

thought." The old woman cackled. "But I thought all you cared about was the salvation of exotic magical creatures like your precious deadly basilisk. How could you possibly have any interest in a bunch of ordinary human children?"

"All living are Her children. We speak for those who have no way to speak for themselves." Andred spoke carefully. "What is it you are trying to tell us."

"Tell you! I cannot tell you. But if you believe any of the oaths you swore to the Mother of Life, then come with me and I'll bloody well show you! One look is worth more than a thousand words, they do say," the old woman challenged them.

"We were on our way to see the midwife and get some rue . . . and we're supposed to meet Master XXam for dinner," Valla temporized.

"You'll see the midwife, I promise. Only come with me," the crone insisted and then snickered, "Besides, Master XXam has just had a heap of mining trouble land on his plate and I have a feeling he won't have room for any dinner."

"All right, we will come. Truly all is not well here, and I need to know more before I involve the Order in something we may regret," Andred decided.

The old woman whirled on her heel and disappeared into an alleyway. The two younger women were hard put to keep up with her as she wound through the backside of the village. Her path led into increasingly wilder places and along downhill water courses. A smell that had permeated the valley since they had arrived became stronger and finally almost unbearable. They scrambled under fences and over a broken stonework bridge to drop ankle-deep into stinking mud. And then they saw it.

At first neither woman could believe her eyes. But if eyes could lie, the nose was usually reliable, and their noses delivered the same message: this was death. Death multiplied and death squared so that it lost all meaning. All around them, the marsh and wetlands that had filled the curve of the Ariath River was one vast mortuary. Black stagnant water lapped the dead and dying sedge grasses and scrub willows, leaving ghastly red rings at the water line like festering scabs. Everywhere they looked the sight was awful. Acre upon acre of dead fish and frogs were scattered in piles of decaying feathers that had once been herons and ducks and swans. All were coated where they touched the water with that bloody red pall. Bodies covered the earth like a hideous carpet. Even the scavengers who had come to feast had themselves been victims, from flies and beetles to crows and vultures. Not a thing moved. There was no sound but the drip of water from the blackened snags of former cypress trees.

In a ragged whisper Valla finally spoke: "Is there nothing left living?"

"Oh, if you hunt around you might find something, but I'd hardly call it living." The crone's harsh croak recalled them, "Come on, Ladies, the tour is not yet over."

They followed silent as whipped curs. Presently she brought them squelching along to where a huge black pipe poured red fluid into the dead marsh, spurting like a severed artery. A pool of crimson spread out from it like a bloody wound, fading into invisibility except where it congealed around the water line . . . except where it crept into living bodies with its death message.

"So here is the source, the source of wealth for the Guild and for the town; the source of pain, deformity and death!" The old woman's voice had become a shriek. "Fifty years I've lived with this! I watched it grow into this! I tried to warn the Guild, the townspeople; all they understood was the money. "What about our jobs, what about the trade?" she mimicked fiercely. "Fools! What about your land? What about your lives?" her voice broke finally. "What about your children?"

"But . . ." Andred began.

"Don't say it, Sister . . ." The crone cut her off. "I tried to warn the Order. They dismissed it as the ravings of a lower class student who had a personal feud with the Guildmaster. They never trust anyone who doesn't complete her training."

"Did you offer proof?" Andred asked defensively.

The old woman looked at her with bitter tears forming red runnels down her lined cheeks. "How's this for proof?" she said.

"Let's get out of here." Valla said suddenly into the tension filled silence. "I don't want to die here in this."

"It takes a while, Ladies. It's a cumulative effect. First it goes into the soft tissue, then your organs, and finally your bones. If you eat raw herbs and drink water that is distilled you will leach it out of you and take little harm from small doses. It's living with it daily that destroys you."

They were almost to the road when they heard a shout and looked toward the broken bridge. There were two men with uniform tunics like the ones they had seen worn by guards in the smelter.

"That tears it!" the old woman exclaimed almost exultantly. "Those are the Guildmaster's guards and they've spotted you! Run for your lives! They will kill you before they let you tell what you've seen here!" She ducked into a drainage canal and around a ruined shed. Andred and Valla followed her as best as they could over the gooey ground. The crone was agile and she knew this forsaken spot like a rat knows its sewer. They scrambled and crawled through dead bushes and finally struck a path that led them into the back streets of the village. They ducked into the courtyard of a seedy looking tavern, where the old woman spoke swiftly:

"We haven't got much time and there's much more you need to know. I'm the midwife, Eilethia, in case you haven't guessed it by now." She grinned like a skull. "This is not unanticipated, nor are we alone in our opposition to the Guild. We'll make for a cellar where I have the herbs you will need. We can't go to my cottage or back to the Inn for your things. If the

Guildmaster captures you, he'll give you to the basilisk and you'll become another screaming statue. He must not let this tale get back to the Order. They're the only ones who could really stop the mining here and he'll kill you before he lets that happen. He's done much worse things here, I assure you." She repeated her rictus grin.

"You said there was more we needed to know . . ." Andred began.

"What about the children?" Valla asked at the same time.

"Yes, that's what you need to know." Eilethia spoke with resignation. "But you must follow me now and trust to my plan. I will help you escape, provided . . ."

"Provided . . . ?" Andred asked.

"Provided you will make me a promise when you hear the whole story."

"Only a fool makes blind promises, but we are at your mercy, so lead the way," Andred told her.

They followed her through the twilight alleys. In and out the tireless old woman led them, down garden paths and cobblestone drainways. As they ducked and dodged and rested, she told them the following story:

"I said that I've been watching this thing growing for nearly fifty years; since I was a teenage girl. Oh, and a hot tempered lass I was then! And when I saw the plants and animals starting to go awry I tried warning everyone. But no one would listen. It was about twenty-five years ago now, that the first of 'em were born. A baby girl born to the Whitlows. She had pretty blue eyes, all three of 'em. After that it was about three babies born like that every year or so and finally it's gotten to be only three or four a year that are ever born normal, those that survive at all. When it got so bad that you could no longer ignore it, the Guildmaster came up with the notion of culling the children. So now the normal ones get to stay in the town and go to school and learn to be shopkeepers and such. But the ones that are unlucky enough to be born deformed in some way are sent to work in the mines . . . so their parents don't have to see them ever and be reminded. You see, on the outside the children are the freaks; but it's the parents that have allowed this to happen who are the real monsters!"

When the old woman had finished her tale, Valla spoke up: "Why didn't you ever run away and go for help?"

"Sister, I was the only midwife in a township of hundreds of people, someone had to deliver all those babies, and I had children of my own. XXam let me know that my whole family'd go to the basilisk if I went outside for help. I'd a duty to the babies, don't you see? He'd have had them all killed; mine, too!"

"Perhaps that would have been a blessing, considering the lives they are condemned to lead." Andred said dryly.

"Well, Sister, each of us must do things the way their conscience tells 'em to do, and I did the best I could for those poor forsaken kids. My kids were normal and they're all grown now. My grandson, Dalen, teaches school down in the mines and I'm the only doctor the Guild will let anywhere near the miners. They know what'd happen if other communities got wind of what we've done to our own children. And that's what you must promise. If we help you escape, you must tell the truth about this horror show; pull the curtains on the ones that created this nightmare for a profit!"

"If that is what you want us to promise, then you have our word. We would only have refused you had you attempted to silence us about the death of the marshes," Andred said, her jaw squared with determination.

"After what we've seen, the only way to stop us would be to kill us!" Valla seconded her.

"Well, Sisters, that's the Guildmaster's plan. How'd you think that basilisk came by so many statues? But I think we can figure out something better. The tavern-keeper will dress his daughters in Order tunics and lead 'em off toward the South pass. But you'll go in the direction that'd be the last place in the world they'd think to look . . . into the mines and out through the basilisk cave. My grandson will meet us and take you to the Masterminer, then he'll sneak over the North pass into the basilisk valley and meet you with horses and supplies . . . when you make it through," Eilethia explained cheerfully.

"Don't you mean *if* we make it through?" Valla asked.

"Of course you'll make it! The Order doesn't send out incompetents on a project like this one," Eilethia insisted.

"For a drop-out you certainly have a lot of loyalty," Andred observed.

Eilethia's seamed old face blushed like a school girl. "I was too headstrong for 'em, but I know their worth even if I couldn't measure up to it."

"It seems the Goddess found more important work for you to do," Andred told her gently.

The gibbous moon was tinged yellow with the fog of the rotting marsh, but her light was still strong as it shone on the derrick of the ore processing lift, giving it a skeletal cast as the three women approached.

"Hssst . . ." came a whisper from behind the derrick.

Valla and Andred froze like a pair of hunting cats, but Eilethia hurried over with a sigh of relief. It was the grandson Dalen who awaited them.

"He's the most determined member of our conspiracy, and the apple of his old granny's eye. Aren't you, boy?"

The tall, tense-looking young man hugged the old woman's shoulders. "Granny, you let me take it now. The others are waiting for you at the turnaround."

"This is what we've planned for; these Sisters are going to be our messengers. You all take care of yourselves!" Eilethia reached out and hugged Valla and Andred.

They both murmured: "Go with the Goddess and blessed be."

The amazing old woman scuttled out of sight as Dalen told the two women to step onto the lift. He began pulling on a set of ropes and slowly they dropped out of sight, leaving the bright moon behind them to sail through the clouds.

Deep underground they went, bit by bit, to the creaking sound of ropes and pulleys. Finally, they reached the bottom and the lift stopped moving. It was so black that neither woman could see a finger placed upon her nose, and the silence was deafening. Dalen cleared his throat and both women startled.

"Underhill, the Masterminer, will be here for you in a moment. I signaled him earlier, and he'll guide you all the way to where the basilisk cavern begins. Once through, I'll be waiting for you with the horses."

The silence and the darkness were finally broken by the sound of echoing footsteps and by a bobbing luminous light. A gnarly man with a glowing stick appeared around a bend in the tunnel. Dalen called to him: "Underhill! I knew we could trust you! The Gods witness that we need you now. These are the priestesses . . ."

Briefly Dalen outlined the situation and the Masterminer agreed to help with a gruff toned, "Follow me, Ladies, an' don't get lost."

It seemed like an eternity for Valla, following the will-o-wisp of the dwarf man's torch through the blackness. She stumbled occasionally, as the rush of events had overwhelmed even her considerable wiry stamina. Finally, they could hear the sound of voices and laughter as the tunnel opened out into a hallway where a group of at least fifty people were eating together at long trestle tables.

Master Underhill cleared his throat and everyone looked up suddenly, staring at the two priestesses who tried in vain not to stare back. But it was impossible not to stare because the scene before them was too bizarre for words. The group of mine workers varied in age and gender, but the most shocking variation was in the basic human form. There were faces where the features looked squeezed together; faces covered with hair or scales or completely bald; blind or multiple eyes; double noses or none at all. There was a woman with a hunchback and an extra leg; there was a child with flippers instead of feet. The visual impact of so much deformity was stunning. A hardened swordswoman, Valla felt afraid and at the same time still wanted with all her heart to burst into tears at the sight of so much human suffering.

Andred clenched her hand around the rosey meditation crystal in her pocket reaching for inner calm, then spoke into the tense silence: "Goddess give you greetings, friends. Dalen the Teacher and Master Underhill have told us you have agreed to save us from the Guild. You have both our deepest gratitude and promise of assistance. Your story will be told and your wrongs avenged; we swear it by the blood of the Great Mother."

Her proclamation met with silence. And then a squeaky voice spoke up: "Maybe good, maybe not. Don't try to judge for us—Outsider!" Voices high and low broke out murmuring and squabbling with each other.

The Masterminer's voice rode over them all. "We've had our meeting an' agreed to help 'em. The argument's done now, so shut up an' eat!" And the strange assembly grew silent and fell to their meal, except for one pale, hairless youth who glared at them and muttered into his porridge.

"Don't pay 'em any mind. Ye shouldn't be surprised if some of 'em got shortchanged in their wits as well as their looks. When we discussed it earlier, many o' the lads had reservations about gettin' help from the Outside, don't ye know. It's all very well to speak out about us poor mistreated miners an' all, but the truth is we'd all be treated like a bunch o' freaks anywhere else. We've made a life for ourselves here. It mayn't seem like much to an Outsider, but we're a kind o' family, can ye see that?"

"But what about the children . . . what about *your* children?" Valla burst out.

The grizzled dwarf tugged at his beard in an embarrassed manner:

"Ah, yes; well, it was that which decided us all, Ma'am. We cannot do to our own young-uns what our own folks did to us, don't ye see? Why, we'd be worse'n our parents, 'cause we know what we'd be doin'."

There was an embarrassed but respectful silence as Master Underhill seated the women, supervising the meal as well as the packing of spare rations for the journey. A motley crew assembled itself as dinner was cleared away and Underhill introduced them as the guide party to the basilisk caves. He unrolled a map on the trestle table and explained the route through the twisting tunnels and mine shafts. Valla paid special attention for she had no intention of becoming lost in the bowels of this black labyrinth. Andred seemed more interested in a conversation she was having with a young girl who was not only blind but eyeless as well, and Valla wondered how an eyeless person could be their guide. Later, when the girl, Keelar, settled a general dispute over the choice of a bewildering array of tunnels, the swordswoman decided that eyes did not necessarily give one an advantage for this kind of life.

The trek through the mine was like a strange dream of being entombed alive. The cramped, scuttling gait they had to adopt to navigate the uneven tunnels was tiring. Then there was the amplified silence broken only by the dripping of contaminated water and the unnerving rustle of leathery wings or the mindless chittering of some tiny creature better left unseen. And though she tried to be sympathetic, Valla was unnerved by their grotesque escort; especially by the rasping speech of Blenth, the noseless woman, and the way the legless man, Colly, could appear silently at her side with no sound of a dragging body. She suspected Andred felt the same way but was too proud to admit it.

They knew by the feel of the air when they reached the end of the tunnels. Aloud she asked. "Is this the cavern of the basilisk?"

"It's they back door, Missy, they bein' our neighbors an' all." Blenth sniggered maliciously, knowing the effect she had on the nervous swordswoman.

Inside the cavern, they recovered a cache of glow

torches which were able to provide considerable light. This ennabled them to see several calcified statues of unfortunate miners waylayed by the basilisk.

"They was gettin' water from the pool here. It's the only source o' good water nearby. This be a dangerous place and we go no farther. You Ladies be on your way now alone . . . alone . . . alone." The cavern acoustics made Colly's voice echo weirdly.

The two shouldered their packs and bid their companions farewell. Andred embraced both Keelar and Colly, whispering in his ear and making him blush and laugh. Valla stood fidgeting until the trio were engulfed in the mouth of the black tunnel.

"I could never get used to them somehow . . . What did you say to Colly?"

Andred studied the toe of her boot and then looked sidewise at her friend. "I told him how clever he was to learn levitation. None but fifth-level magicians usually have that skill."

Valla's jaw dropped, "So that's how he managed to be so silent!"

Andred pulled out the map Master Underhill had given them and planted two glow torches in the sand so she could study it better. She opened her pack and took out the carefully stowed bunches of rue. Then she told Valla, "Bring out the shield, Sister."

Valla produced the small round shield that she carried over her shoulder and across her back. Carefully, she removed its soft leather cover to expose the highly polished surface. The shield reflected her sharp freckled features and hair drawn tightly back into a fighting knot. It was an excellent mirror.

"Let's get moving, quick!" Valla vaulted to her feet and gathered up their paraphernalia.

The priestesses followed the map carefully, but they had crawled through endless black tunnels for so long and they were so close to the exit they were seeking that hope must have made them careless. The gallery of the cave they crept into suddenly widened out and it was Andred who kindled another glow torch so that they could see what was ahead. The torch flared up and lit the whole chamber. Suddenly they heard a horrible slobbering and clucking sound and simultaneously they smelled a dreadful stench. They glanced to the left beside a large stalagmite and there was the basilisk. It was as large as a big dog and greenish-black in color. It walked on two legs like a cockerel and had feathers on its neck, but the body was scaled like that of a dragon. It had a bluish-colored comb and wattle that covered much of its face and ran in a ridge down its spine, resolving into a scaly crest. The creature had leathery batlike wings and a scaly tail that curved over its back, with a lethal-looking stinger that lolled about its head. But the most ghastly part was its face, which looked like a temple gargoyle with huge eyes. Oh, the eyes; they were like nothing you would ever want to see! The light in its eyes was like sick moons burning poisonously through the greenish-yellow mist of the dead marsh.

"We mustn't look into its eyes!" Valla spoke desperately. Andred, startled out of her trance, blew the rue bundle alive with flame and the smoke filled the chamber in a choking bitter cloud. The basilisk uttered yet another hissing cry and moved toward them in a menacing, stiff-legged strut. It rattled its crest and waved its stinger in their direction. The two women avoided its baleful gaze by leaning together and deliberately turning their backs to the enraged animal. Both women peered anxiously at the shield in front of them, using it as a mirror to watch the oncoming basilisk behind them. But the basilisk, undaunted by the odd behavior of its enemy, stalked closer. The hairs on the backs of their bodies prickled as the two women maintained their unnatural defensive posture.

If it breathes on us, we will be turned to stone, Valla thought. *It doesn't matter whether we are hypnotized or not.* She looked for a way to run but saw that the path ahead disappeared into one of those infernal holes like those they had often crawled through. The holes probably connected this room with another, yet they couldn't go back either way. "It will have us before we can get away!" She felt the touch of panic as she realized the

Witch's powers were as nullified by the rue as the basilisk's. So now Andred, the friend and teacher Valla had come to rely on, could only fan the rue smoke and pray. Valla could see the creature was almost upon them when she heard Andred call out:

"The mirror—quick, use it now!"

Valla's lightening reflexes whipped the small round shield about directly into the oncoming basilisk's line of sight. The monster rushed to a halt, muttering and clucking as it contemplated its never-before-seen reflection. Andred shoved the rue into her pack and doused it with water. The smoke dissipated rapidly in the drafty cave and the basilisk sank to the floor, eyes glazed, still muttering and clucking to itself.

"Let's get out of here!" Valla cried to her companion. But the Witch had seemingly gone crazy and was striding in the direction the basilisk had come from, stooping down and carefully picking up something from a pile of leaves.

"All right, now we will go," Andred said in her most maddeningly pedantic manner, "But I have just figured out a way we can relocate a basilisk to our Sanctuary for study, while at the same time leaving one on guard here to keep Marshby from spreading to this valley for awhile." She showed Valla a large greenish-black ovoid.

"Eggs! Then it's a female!" Valla exclaimed.

"Yes, and now if we are careful we will have a baby basilisk of our own. I left one behind as well."

"Andred, now let's go!" Valla reminded her urgently. And they fled without further mishap, leaving the enchanted female basilisk to her own devices.

Outside, the day was just dawning and the birds were awake to serenade the emergence of the two priestesses from the cavern's mouth. They heard a nickering sound and saw Dalen standing beside a rock formation with three horses at his side. Valla suddenly thought she had never seen a more handsome man in her life.

And when Dalen said to her as they rode out of the valley, "Granny never doubted you, but I am certainly relieved that you managed to escape the evil of the basilisk." The swordswoman promptly told him in no uncertain terms, that as fearsome as the basilisk was, nevertheless, after everything they had seen in the valley next door, it was a wholesome and necessary influence in this neighborhood. Perhaps, she was only downplaying things as a flirtation, but her voice was strong and sincere as she assured him:

"When all is said and done, I consider basilisks to be the Lesser Evil."

AND SÁAVÜLD DANCED

by Kier Neustaedter

At one of the various autographing parties I attend—
there are so many that I don't remember much about
any particular one—Kier Neustaedter turned up; she
told me then that she wanted to write. Since I hear
that about ten times at every such affair, I wasn't
inclined to take her too seriously; but even so, I told
her I was reading for an anthology, and either handed
her a sheet of guidelines, or told her where to send
for them. Some time later this story came in; and
to my surprise and pleasure it was something I could
use.

Which goes to show that you never know who is
making polite noises, and who really means it when
they say they'd like to write.

Kier Neustaedter describes herself as "31, female,
married," and says she was taken to Mexico to live at
nine years of age and adopted by her mother's second husband. At the age of 27 she came back to the
States to meet her real father, find a good man and
marry him, go back to school, and write; all of which
she has done. This is her first professional sale—but
with this much determination and persistence, it won't
be her last.

Through the sparkling jewels of sun-drenched sea-drops the peoples of Ocëan sported. They threw themselves out of the gaily tossing waves that broke over the mudbeds of Selleffe and flipped in the sea-freshened air, turning and twisting before landing with a splash. The Dolphins chittered as their gray, white, blue, and black bodies outlined clean profiles on the blazing sun or the rich blue sky. The Meären laughed with the deep booming sounds of the depths as they tossed their four-limbed bodies high, showing red and gold and green crosses against the dome of the world.

Farther out the Orcas also disported themselves and still farther could be seen the spumes of the Great Ones, the Whales. In their play, the peoples of Ocëan accomplished their work. Great schools of tuna and mackerel were being chased out of the shallow waters over the mudbeds to the deeper reaches. They swam directly to the waiting Orcas and Whales who ate voraciously.

The mudbeds of Selleffe were lifting inexorably from the sea floor. Already, to the north, extensive lands now stood high and dry. The Meären had brought fir cones, coconuts, fruits, grasses, grains, flowers, and small animals to the ever-growing shores of the northern land. The Four Races of Ocëan watched with interest as the plants and animals adapted themselves to a new life. Once in a while the Great Ones would insist that the Meären trade. Then would the Meären go ashore the great Southern Continent that the land dwellers called Salem. They would carry with them the treasures of the deeps; pearls, coral, enormous fish, and the skins of the northern sea mammals, and trade for some of the larger animals of the land. These would be placed on rafts and carefully pushed north.

Again and again the Great Ones foiled attempts by the land dwellers to send their puny coracles and larger clinker-built boats northward. So often had they been stopped that those of Salem now considered the North accursed and the Great Ones servants of a Sea God, sent to warn them. So the land dwelling men came not to the new continent and it grew and clothed itself in peace, protected by the Four Races of Ocëan.

The Meären themselves had once dwelt upon the land. But for untold generations they had made their home in the bosom of the Mother Sea. They had the tough, thick skin of the dolphins; colored glorious reds, green, blues, and golds. Their feet turned easily at the ankles, forward and backward, but not at a right angle. Their hair had become a pelt, thick and short over head, spine, breasts, belly, and buttocks.

Still, there were some who could walk on land. Coral pink Sáavüld was one. She delighted in her ability to place foot on land without pain. She dived and somersaulted in the sea, at one with her four kindred. Yet, often she would scale the cones, islands just lifting from the seabed. Today her family and friends laughed and encouraged her as she ran from the waves, her pink body softened with sleek white fur that dried and fluffed. They no longer walked on land without pain, their heels were gone and their ankles stiff. But they cheered their sister who danced upon the sands of the little island. She stamped and whirled, jumped and kicked to the tune of the Great Ones sounding in her mind.

Much as Sáavüld loved to dance before her people, she had a place where she practiced alone. On the Northern shore of the continent of Salem, where the cliffs lifted frowning barriers, both to the land and sea-dwellers, there she had found her privacy. Long ago Sáavüld had learned how to throw herself from the waves and catch at the eroded rocks. She took great pleasure in being able to climb the slippery cliff. At the top was a little meadow with sparse vegetation, hedged round with bushes. The soil was harsh and rocky.

Here Sáavüld danced in secret. Here she could practice without her family seeing her mistakes or laughing at her contortions. So she danced. Squatting she pounded the ground with the rhythm of the waves pounding the cliffs she had climbed. She sprang up and jumped, turned and came down slapping broad feet against the ground. Her pelt stood out in the breeze and she leapt over a small bush and checked, stumbled, and stood dumb.

A man of the land dwellers was crouched there, holding his sides and suppressing his mirth. Sáavüld felt her lips pull back, baring sharp teeth in a feral grimace, and she sounded a warning. The man hurriedly stood and shook his head. He was shorter than she; his skin a strange, muddy brown color, his eyes were brown, and his pelt a curly black. It was tied back from his forehead with a band and fell to his shoulders.

He lifted both hands palm up and stuttered, "D–d–don't–t–t, p–p–please. I wasn't m–m–making fun. You just dance well, and, I–I–I didn't want to stop you. . . ."

Sáavüld lost her anger. This frightened boy wouldn't harm her and seemed truly sorry he had offended her. Curiously she reached out a hand and touched his pelt. He started back, like a deer. "D–d–do, do you speak?" he asked, his voice squeaking.

Sáavüld thought this passing funny, herself. With a good humored laugh that echoed the sounding of the waves, she answered, "Of course. I have been to trade in Mareetha and Jendana. Do you not know that the Meären are human? Are we not alike?"

He shook his head and then hurriedly nodded it. "Yes, yes!" he gasped out. "Most extraordinary. My mother is a Sea Priestess, but she has never let me know any of the secrets. Truly we are as alike as male and female can be."

Sáavüld nodded. "What is your name?" she asked.

The man looked like he would bob into ten different pieces. Sáavüld wondered if he were simple or if land dwellers just thought differently. To save him embarrassment she said, "Mine is Sáavüld, it means 'Wave at Sunset.' "

"Ah, ah," gasped the man. "Sáavüld, yes, most nice. I am known as Terrog. Terrog the Terror, as my mother calls me. Do you know your mothers and fathers in the sea?"

Sáavüld thought this was the most extraordinary question. "To be sure. Do not you know yours on land?"

Terrog the Terror sat down on a rock and shook his head. "Not–not the children of the Priestess. She may suspect, or even know, but no one else may."

Sáavüld sat next to him and said, "Can I touch your pelt?"

Terrog looked at her in surprise. "Why?"

"Because it looks so different from mine," said Sáavüld.

Terrog's eyes lit. "So it is," he said cordially. "Maybe you would let me touch yours?"

Sáavüld nodded and put out her pink hand again. This time Terrog didn't jerk back. The soft, silky, oily locks felt strange to her hand. Terrog wiped his hand along the pelt on her head and down her back.

"It feels like the pelt of the animals that you bring from the north."

Sáavüld nodded. "It is alike."

"Just where do you hunt them?" asked Terrog, inching closer.

"Hunt them!" exclaimed Sáavüld. "Never! We only take the pelts of those who are already dead; from storm or something else."

Terrog seemed disappointed at this answer, but Sáavüld wanted to touch the fuzzy pelt on his chest. She raked lightly at the curls and studied the drawers and belt that he wore around his waist and legs.

A bit hesitantly Terrog stroked the pelt over her breasts and belly. Sáavüld caught his hand before it could go farther. "No. We do not touch like that unless we are lovers."

Terrog grinned at her. "Well," asked he. "Why not?"

Sáavüld was startled. "You cannot know if you wish to be the lover of a woman in a few handspans of the sun," she objected.

Terrog laughed, a sudden sharp laugh that reminded Sáavüld of the call of some bird. "Why not? I have seen you dance. You have given me your name. We have touched each other's bodies and named our lines. Why not?"

Sáavüld studied his brown eyes. There was laughter and recklessness in them. The recklessness called to her, called to the reckless woman who scaled unscalable cliffs. Suddenly she decided that she had never found a man amongst her own people. Why not this one whose recklessness called to her?

Her answering smile brought forth another bird-laugh as Terrog caught her around the waist and pulled her to the ground. He quickly stripped away his fine calfskin drawers, throwing them over a bush. Sáavüld had time enough to mark that he was similar in construction to the men of her race, before he took her. She was soon disappointed. Terrog took his pleasure quickly and violently. There was none of the subtlety she had expected. With an internal sigh, Sáavüld accepted that she would have to teach Terrog the ways of pleasure.

Twice more Terrog returned to her, but each time he defeated her aim of teaching him pleasure, mumbling, "Hush up, do. I have enough of bossy women any day."

Silently she withdrew and Terrog stood and pulled on his drawers. He turned to go and Sáavüld made a surprised sound. She stood to follow him, but he turned and scowled, "What do you want now? Isn't it enough that I gave you what you wanted?"

"What *I* wanted?"

"Yes, you!"

Sáavüld simply shook her head. "We are mated," she said. "Will you come and meet my people first or shall we go to meet yours?"

Terrog laughed, the laugh like the black birds make. "Mated? With a monster like you? Not at all. Whatever the customs of your people, they aren't the customs of our people. You weren't even any good!"

She stood, stricken. Terrog turned and vanished through the undergrowth. Sáavüld, daughter of the Four Races, child of Ocëan sat on the cliff and looked at her broken life. No man would take her. The Meären mated for life and she had just mated. But the men of land weren't bound by their customs and he had called her monster! She, Sáavüld, who was called the sunset of the sea!

She stretched out her arms, glowing coral-pink, their skin taut and sturdy with the underlying fat that supported her in the sea. She felt her round face, ruffled her pure white pelt, so different from the mottled ones so many of her people had. Yet, he had called her monster and despised learning the ways of pleasure.

From sundown to sundown Sáavüld sat on the cliff edge. Her hate and anger took on form and intensity. Before her a small pool opened up. In it bubbled molten rock, glowering redly. The glow was hypnotic. By the next morning a fair-sized pool had opened near her. A form took on dimensions over the molten rock.

It glowed, more darkly than the pool. "Well, Sáavüld? Do you wish for revenge?"

"Yes!" she shouted. "Call me a monster, will he! What can I do for revenge?"

The molten form drifted in the air and sighed, a sound like water hissing on hot rock. "Dance for me, Sáavüld, Sunrise and Sunset of the Ocëan. Dance and you shall have your revenge."

"It's no good to just have my revenge. I want to see him suffer!" exclaimed the daughter of the Meären.

"You shall have that," promised the Molten One. "Dance for me, Sáavüld."

The dancer of the Four Races stood. She crouched down and beat a complex rhythm out upon the rocks of the promontory. One—Two—Three! And the ground answered her. It shook and jerked. Sáavüld stood and stamped. Great pieces of the southern tip of the continent broke off.

The woman leapt lightly into the air and twirled and great sea currents flowed down the west, around the south and up the east coast of the continent of Salem. Sáavüld clapped, slapped the ground, and kicked. The entire continent shook. And Sáavüld felt the fear and terror of each human on Salem. In the deep south a poor woman hauled her five goats up, one by one, to

the thatch roof of her cottage, using ropes tied about
their necks. Three survived the operation. The woman
clung to the roof, her face gray with fear. North of her
she could see water from the lakes that had rested in
the high mountains foaming loose.

To the east, the fishing fleets put out, carrying all
the little treasures that people find precious in times of
fear and upheaval. They were caught and whirled by
the northward currents. Few survived. To the west the
fishing fleets were flung back upon land, splintered
and broken, spilling shattered bodies. Here and there,
a lone animal, a small human, someone wise, stubborn, or lucky, would find a seaworthy craft, a roof,
or even a log and the north-flowing current.

Sáavüld suffered, feared, and died with each. The
old woman watched as the water swept down the
mountains and smashed the cottage under her. She
kept a tight hold on the thatch. The roof spun east and
north, buoyed along by the water. Suddenly it came to
the cliffs that gave on to the sea. Sáavüld followed the
woman down the cliffs as she tumbled and was broken, dying before she reached the salt waves.

With an effort Sáavüld wrenched her mind away
and sought out Terrog. He was crouched in the Temple of the Sea. His mother was giving quick orders to
the terrified populace. Sáavüld heard her say, "No,
no, I have no idea what we did to offend the Sea
Gods. It must have been something terrible. Go take
to the boats. Follow the great sea currents and pray
for forgiveness. I and mine shall stay here as a
propitiation."

Sáavüld could feel Terrog's refusal. It availed him
nothing. His mother tied him to the Temple pillars. As
the Sea Priestess spoke, Sáavüld realized that he had
lied to her. His name was not Terrog. He had simply
been afraid of her telling his mother later what he had
done. Amazed, Sáavüld probed into his mind. She
found little remembrance of herself. She felt his mother's
mind and learned that she considered him a ne'er-do-
well. His sisters came and despised him also. They
stood with their mother and willingly offered their

lives in propitiation for the wrong that must have been done to anger the Goddess so. But Terrog cowered, screamed, and tried to loosen his bonds, even as he slipped and slid and the earth convulsed.

Angered anew at his puerile attitude, Sáavüld danced harder. Salem crumpled, the floor of the world sank. To the north, the seabed lifted and many of the Four Races were stranded high and dry. The Meären struggled with their handicapped feet, rescuing those they could.

In Salem, the continent sank so suddenly that Sáavüld was left hanging in the air. She came down, drifting like a feather. The waves roared up and around and caught her, still in mid-flight. She tumbled and rolled in the waves. Far away, Terrog, the Terror cried in fear as the white-capped water swept down upon him. Beside him his mother and sisters lifted their hands to the waves and offered their lives to appease the angry Goddess.

Sáavüld surfaced and found the pool of lava still steaming on a sodden islet. The form still hovered around it and she pulled herself up on the land. Exhausted she fell to her knees. The Molten One asked, laughter like the crackle of flames in a forest fire, "Satisfied, my little one?"

But Sáavüld shook her head. "He never knew why he died. He learned nothing. He never even thought of the injury he did me. And all those others have died, too."

The Molten One laughed again. "Then, you are not happy with your revenge, little mortal?"

The Meären woman shook her head. She could still feel her people working to save the members of the Four Races stranded by the cataclysm. "I didn't get revenge. He never knew why he died and so many more died besides him." In her heart burned the despair of many people, dying senselessly and brutally. Without pause for more thought the woman flung herself forward into the pool of lava.

The Molten One laughed, his laughter ringing out, like boulders pelting down a mountain side. From the pool rose the fiery-red form of Sáavüld. Her spirit asked in dismay, "What has happened?"

The Molten One chuckled. "You are mine, little pet. You shall dance at the earth's core to remind me of the time when the earth fell."

The spirit form of Sáavüld hovered motionless over the islet for many moons and seasons. But in time she forgot the past and even her original form and danced with pleasure in the molten waves at the core of the earth.

STONE OF LIGHT
by Linda Gordon

Linda Gordon has made two sales; this is her second appearance in one of these anthologies. She says that "since my husband feels I no longer need to punch a time clock, (God bless him)" she will do some more writing. She has also been awarded a certificate of Honorable Mention from the "Writers of the Future" contest.

Good luck to her; I remember when it was all right to say that the one thing a writer needed was a working wife. Well, a working husband made all the difference to *me*, enabling me to learn my craft. At that time, and for several years thereafter, my marketable skills were a minus quantity and writing a nice hobby for a person with no other talents.

"A small piece of witch-glass will do me." Tanid held Silkwyk's essence-stone on outstretched palm. Sunlight danced through the stone's purple depths, casting brilliant red and violet rays across his flesh.

Silkwyk wanted to grab the stone but folded hands in front of her. She had dealt with men before. "I will hand the glass to you as soon as you give me my stone." To entice Tanid to do her bidding, she pulled a glittering object from a pouch at her side.

Tanid gasped, eyes bright with the hunger of greed.

The witch-glass dangled from a knotted silver thread, its shape a large tear drop, its boundaries formed in such a way that fire seemed to nip at its edges. The glass danced in the breeze, rainbows of color sparkling from its clear flat center.

Tanid's eyes widened. "It was difficult to be generous," he whispered, "but now I see the worth of it." He stepped toward Silkwyk.

Silkwyk moved the witch-glass away from him. "Your generosity was forced?" *That was not good,* she thought without surprise.

Tanid closed his hand around her essence-stone. "We both know what the glass requires of us." He tilted his chin upward and smiled. "Do you think me daft, woman?"

Silkwyk's eyes narrowed. "Perhaps all who have learned of the powers of the witch-glass have also heard of its requirements." The corner of her mouth turned up. "But do you truly understand?"

Tanid chuckled. "I know the power that awaits me." He raised a clenched fist. "Through the glass, I will know what new day brings before its arrival."

Silkwyk nodded.

"The God of Good Fortune will smile upon me." His gaze seemed to sparkle with an inner fire. "Riches and fame, all else I desire, just for the asking. The glass will show how the Gods favor me."

"What if the favors are not what you expect?" The Gods, she knew, had a frightening way of gazing upon mortal life.

Tanid was taken back for a moment, brow furrowed. "I had not thought—" He studied Silkwyk through slitted eyes, then threw his head back and laughed. "Do not attempt to trick me." He briefly paced while he watched her. "I have earned the glass. I have shared my stores of grain, given shelter to those without, sent my soldiers to assist the farmers in planting, and," he paused and sighed, "have done other such deeds. I have earned the glass," he repeated.

"The witch-glass will know of your actions." She smiled inwardly and glanced at the edge of her essence-stone which was still inside his fist. "Are you prepared for whatever the glass may bring?"

"I have been kind and generous in exchange for the glass. Let us speak no more of it."

"Once I give you the glass, you cannot part with it."

"Why would I want to?"

"You will be one with it for all time."

He shrugged. "To have such power a part of me is most desirable."

"Very well." Silkwyk held hand out. "My stone."

He tossed the purple rock to her. "The glass."

Silkwyk held the glass up and chuckled. "If you had not truly earned the witch-glass, I would be tempted to keep it and my stone."

He looked surprised as if it had not occurred to him that she would do such.

Silkwyk handed him the knotted thread, the glass sparkling at thread's end.

Tanid snatched the glass and moved away from her. He studied its flat surface and laughed as it clouded with faint images.

Silkwyk ignored the man's giggle of pleasure and wrapped her hands around her essence-stone. With eyes closed, she concentrated on the warmth that radiated from the object's outer skin at her touch.

Already the stone was smooth and pliable like a shelless egg boiled too long.

Inner fires sparked to life, and a force charged through her body. The intensity increased, twofold, threefold; then a fire ignited deep in her chest, a fire that reached out until the small hairs on her flesh rose with chill. A deep red colored her face, neck, and upper torso.

The essence-stone shivered in her hands, its now pulpy substance steaming.

Her skin prickled as if thousands of tiny knives touched point to flesh, then the essence-stone evaporated, her body absorbing the stone's vapor. She opened eyes, a mild lavender sparkle showing in green depths, moisture glistening on forehead. She wiped sweat away and turned toward the man.

Tanid held the witch-glass in his cupped hands, dark gaze studying the scenes that flashed on the glass face. Suddenly he gasped, countenance twisted into a mask of horror.

Silkwyk was sure he now saw part of his future.

"No!" A strange grin crossed his face, then a sound escaped his lips; a chortle made by someone on the edge of madness. "It cannot be," he whispered. He tried to drop the witch-glass, but it held fast to his hands. "By the Gods," he cried out while stepping backward.

"A part of you always," Silkwyk reminded him.

"No!" Tanid whirled to face her, eyes filled with question. He flung his hand to dislodge the leechlike object, but the glass remained as if sewn there. He paled and his terror-filled gaze latched onto Silkwyk. "What is happening to me?"

"You have seen such in the glass."

Tanid did not hear her reply. All at once his body began to shake, then he involuntarily moved in circles like an animal after its tail. His tail chasing changed to spinning, faster and faster, until the momentum whirled him into a blur. As he became a whirlwind, a red glow appeared at his feet. Just before he changed completely, he cried out, his voice faint as if coming from a great distance. "I did all I—had to—do—for the glass—did I not?"

The whirlwind faded into a small dust devil, then vanished completely. An irregular-shaped chunk of glass, deep wine in color, now lay on the ground.

Silkwyk retrieved the changed glass and held it up to the sun. Rays of red, orange, and wine lanced outward across her hand as she slowly turned the transparent stone. "I warned you that the glass would know of your actions."

A smile turned the corners of her mouth as she

studied the red object. "You are both frightened and angry now, but you will earn your freedom, as I have. And by then your heart will speak louder than your mind." She dropped the red essence-stone into the pouch that once held the witch-glass and left the clearing, paying little heed to the rays of color that, even through the pouch, danced out from the stone.

CHANGE OF COMMAND
by Nancy Jane Moore

Nancy Moore has two major interests; the obvious one is writing and the other is karate and the martial arts, which she feels give her the discipline and confidence to be a writer. Born in Texas, and a graduate of Texas University, she still considers herself a Texan, though she now lives in Washington, DC, and likes it there.

I always say Texas isn't a bad place to be from— preferably as far from as possible! No offense meant; I myself was simply too miserable in Texas to be fair to it.

S he had just enough time to scream "Retreat" to her troops before the impact of the arrow hitting her chest knocked her to the ground. It took her a couple of seconds to realize she wasn't dead, and by then arrows were flying all around her. The arrow must have hit something in her inside pocket. She pulled it loose as she rolled to her feet and took off, half running, half stumbling toward the relative safety of a nearby grove of trees.

The unaccustomed sword at her belt caught on the underbrush, almost tripping her. As she steadied herself with her halberd, someone said in an undertone, "Faris." She moved toward the sound, joining her soldiers who were hunkered down among the trees. There were no more arrows.

"Did everyone make it?" she inquired.

A young man—really only a boy—shook his head. "Grimm went down."

The young woman next to him asked, "What now, Faris?" And everyone looked at her expectantly.

It was a good question, and she didn't have a good answer. Damn Shaw for dying, she thought, and for leaving her with the lives of these fourteen people. No, it was thirteen now. Gods, she'd been in command only half an hour, and she'd already lost one. Down to thirteen from an original troop of thirty.

The squad leader's sword—Shaw's sword—dug uncomfortably into her ribs, and she tried to adjust it. The only thing she knew about command was something Shaw had said to her one night when they had sat up drinking after the others had gone to sleep.

"How do you make them follow you?" she had asked, marveling at the way that Shaw had integrated the inexperienced volunteers into their troop so quickly.

And he had replied, "I act like I know what I'm doing."

She had looked at him wide-eyed, and said, "But you do, don't you?"

He had laughed then, and taken another drink of wine.

She pushed the offending sword sideways and knelt on the ground, drawing the others closer. "We won't be safe here for long," she said. That was certainly true. The farmers who had settled this valley had apparently left these trees as a source of wood; the remainder of the area now being used as a battlefield had been cleared for planting.

"It's only a matter of time before some of the invader forces take cover in these trees. Now that we know there are archers in the hills to the south, we'll have to take another direction."

Cut off from the main body of the army of the city of Escarpan, they had been making for the hills, hoping to get behind most of the invader forces.

"What do you suggest now, Faris? Straight through the battle back to the city?" There was a sneer in Garon's voice. Like most of the troop he was an inexperienced soldier, a volunteer who had joined the army when word had reached Escarpan of the steady fall of the cities in the south to the invaders. Though young, he had built up a promising business, and had a high opinion of his own abilities. Even Shaw had had difficulty teaching him to obey orders.

"No," she said simply. It would not be useful to take offense at Garon's tone. "That would be suicide. We'll move to the east. There are fewer invaders to that side."

"But the cliffs, Faris. What about the cliffs?"

"We climb them."

A number of voices protested loudly.

"Quiet," she hissed harshly. The noise subsided. "We climb them and then we circle back around to the city." The cliffs made up the eastern wall of Escarpan.

"Faris, we'll be sitting ducks for archers climbing those cliffs."

"It'll be dark soon. There's no moon tonight."

There was more noise. One voice said clearly, "You want us to climb them in the dark?"

Another chimed in, "We don't even have any ropes or equipment."

That was true. The provisioning of the army had been spotty at best. They each had a halberd, a long staff with a short sword blade on the end, plus knives, water containers, and uniforms of a sort. They carried no other supplies. No one had expected them to be out of the reach of the city.

Garon's voice carried, "Might as well die fighting through the battle lines as falling off a cliff."

She wanted to scream out, "You have a better idea?" but she didn't. Instead she said, quietly but firmly, "We'll make do with what we've got. It's our best chance. Let's start moving."

It surprised her a little that they did, with a minimum of grumbling. Cautiously they worked their way to the eastern edge of the woods.

She had some qualms as she assigned Jian to lead, with the rest of the troop following in a v-shape, like a flock of geese. Jian was perhaps her best friend in the troop, a smart, hard-fighting woman who was now the second-in-command. She assigned Jian to lead just as Shaw had always sent Faris to the front. She was beginning to understand why Shaw had always held himself a little aloof from everyone.

She brought up the rear on the southern flank herself; another of the four veteran soldiers was on the northern end. They moved cautiously out into a cornfield, the plants still high in the late summer, with late corn ready for harvesting. She passed the word up for everyone to take a few ears; it would be dinner if they could find a safe place to rest.

They moved through the corn, unnoticed, though she saw with annoyance that several of her people were not stooping as she had instructed; their heads showed above the plants. If an alert archer was watching . . . but apparently no one was.

Presently they came to a fence with wheat growing on the other side of it. The message was passed to crawl, and they did, more or less. There were several more fences, and several more fields of wheat. Their legs were growing cramped. It was growing darker.

Suddenly, they had stopped, and the message came back from Jian: enemy encampment ahead, and they looked to be setting up camp for the night. Faris cautiously made her way to the front.

Campfires were being lit both to the north and south of them. In the clearing just ahead, on both sides of a barn, there appeared to be two troops setting up camp. She guessed them to have maybe fifty soldiers each, and noted that the officers appeared to be settling into the barn.

She drew the troop around her, squatting in the wheat field. "We'll set the barn on fire," she said, "and then slip through the camp in the confusion."

"Why not just walk up and tell them we're here?" whined Garon.

She ignored him. "While they're struggling with the

fire, we'll split into two groups, go around on either side of the firefighting." And then, not wanting to do it, but knowing that she had to make a decision, she turned to Liam, "You will fire the barn. We'll meet up with you at the sentry's cabin at the cliff wall. You know where that is?"

He nodded, as she had known he would. No one mentioned that he was unlikely to make it. Perhaps she should have asked for volunteers, but she knew he would have been one of them. And he was the best choice, the sneakiest of the lot, the one most likely to actually get the barn set afire, the one with the best chance of getting through alive.

"Jian, you take those five and go north; I'll take the rest to the south. We take off as soon as the fire starts."

Liam gave her a half-salute, half-wave, and took off, veering this direction and that down toward the barn. They soon lost sight of him. Some of the soldiers began to murmur about the cramps in their legs. Garon's voice was the loudest.

"Hush," she hissed, but the murmurs continued. "Your voices carry," she admonished. A sentry appeared out of the deepening gloom, peering into the wheat, trying to find the source of the noise. Faris stood up, ignoring the cramps in her legs, halberd held across her chest in a ready position.

"Halt," he yelled, but that was his last word. Jian had moved behind him, and stabbed him in the kidney with the end of her halberd blade. Faris moved quickly up to cut his throat to stop any dying moans. Now they had only as long as the time before the sentry was to report to another—not long in a battlefield camp.

The smell of smoke came drifting over, and the beginnings of flames shone at the barn. They quickly engulfed the barn, which was probably full of early hay at this time of year, dry enough now to catch quickly.

The troop scurried out, half to one side, half to the other. There was a small creek that ran somewhat south of the barn, and the enemy would be running for it for water for the fire. She led her half of the troops to the other side of it, fording it easily as it was only a few feet wide now; it would gush in the spring. Moving along the scant treeline that bordered the creek, they could see frantic soldiers running back and forth with buckets.

A group of enemy soldiers from south of the creek were running up to see what the confusion was all about. Suddenly, Faris and her soldiers were face-to-face with the enemy. She sliced her halberd blade through their leader's neck before he had time to bring up his own weapon, then spun around and hit another enemy in the face with the butt of her weapon. He also went down, though probably not for good, and as she moved to finish him off, a third soldier was there, this one large and burly.

He cut toward her neck with his halberd, and she blocked. Her block deflected his blow enough to spare her, but it was weaker than his strike. She tried bringing the butt of her weapon up between his legs, but he moved nimbly to her left side and struck again. She blocked once more, stopping his blow, but feeling the staff of her halberd break in the process. Dropping it, she jumped just back out of range and drew the unfamiliar sword. As he came in again, clearly expecting her to keep backing up, she dove suddenly forward, ducking under his cut to her head and bringing her blade across his stomach with a slicing motion. He brought the halberd back toward her even as he fell, dying, but the strength was gone from him, and she blocked it with her sword arm. The weapon fell from his hands, and she picked it up, looking around the area to see her next opponent.

There wasn't one. There were three other people left standing, all of them hers. The enemy lay around them, dead or dying. "One of them ran for help," Garon informed her.

She nodded. "And the rest of our people?"

"This one is dead." He indicated a body behind him.

"And the other boy?" she asked. No one knew. She

heard a weak voice over to her left, and moved that way. A young man lay there, his abdomen sliced open.

There was nothing she could do for him except to make his dying faster. She raised her sword, met his eyes. There was fear there. Not really a soldier this one; a shopkeeper's assistant, still almost a child. She hesitated, but there was nothing else to do. Quickly she sliced through his jugular vein, and he lay still, eyes still wide open with fright.

She tried to shake the blood from her sword as she had seen Shaw do, but it didn't come clean, and she knelt and wiped it on an enemy's uniform before sheathing it. "Let's move on," she ordered, and the others followed.

They made it to the sentry's cabin without further incident. Jian and her people had beat them by a few minutes. Faris counted five and waited. "We lost our last man. One of the enemy saw him and jumped him; he was wounded but managed to kill the enemy. By the time I got back to him, he was dead."

So now they were nine, ten if Liam made it. The fire burned brightly to the west; it showed no sign of being put out. Behind them loomed thirty feet of cliff, imposing enough in the day time, but even more ominous in the dark.

"Can't we camp here, Faris?" someone asked.

She looked at the speaker incredulously as someone else muttered about being hungry and tired.

"We'll rest about fifteen minutes, wait for Liam, and then we'll tackle the cliff."

"Faris, it's been a very long day," Garon argued in the manner of a man who was used to getting his own way.

"And it's going to be longer. Once they have that fire under control, they're going to be looking for us. The only place we can safely camp is up there."

"Most of us haven't had much experience in climbing," he went on. "There must be something . . ."

She didn't let him finish. "We rest fifteen minutes, then we climb," she said in an icy voice.

Garon started to say something else. She put her

hand on the sword handle. "Pick your words carefully, Garon. They'll be your last ones."

Their eyes met for somewhat less than a minute. Then he turned away and moved over to sit by another soldier. Everyone breathed again. She turned and walked away, realizing that her hand was shaking as it still gripped the sword handle.

Just as she was about to give the order to start climbing, Liam came strolling up, almost casually. He was sooty from the fire, but he was in one piece. "Had to hide out while they ran around trying to find water."

"Good job, Liam," she said, trying to imitate the relaxed way Shaw would have said it, trying not to show how glad she was that he was alive.

"Piece of cake," he shrugged off the compliment. "You ready to climb this thing?"

"Yeah. You'll lead one group up on that side." He nodded. She turned to Dylene, one of the volunteers who had impressed her before as having a lot of common sense. "Have you ever climbed?"

"A little."

"Good. Then you'll lead up this side. Jian, you bring up the rear on Liam's side; I'll do it over here. Any questions?" she added in a voice that gave notice that there had better not be any.

She slung her halberd onto her back, fastening the carrying straps that were there to hold it on. The others followed suit, and Liam and Dylene began the climb.

While the cliff looked sheer, it actually held a number of hand- and footholds. She and Liam had both climbed it without ropes. But of course, most of these people had never climbed. She heard Dylene speaking quiet words of encouragement to the soldier just below her, telling him to touch her foot, then put his hand in the hole where it was.

Another soldier started up the wall. Garon would be next, then her. She noticed that he was sweating; he was probably frightened of heights and she would have to talk him up, probably threaten him up. It was his turn now. He turned and looked at her, saw no compromise there, and reached for the rock.

"Make certain that you have a good grip, then move to the next hole. Use your legs as much as you can."

He started up cautiously, but not as amateurishly as she had feared. When he was several feet above her head, she began to climb. She looked up. Dylene was almost to the top, but the soldier below her was holding fast in one place, sobbing, "I can't, I can't."

Dylene climbed back down a little way, trying to talk to the terrified man. "There's a hold here," she instructed him. "Let go with your left hand and reach for it. You can make it."

He protested; she encouraged him. Suddenly he tried it, in a pitiful burst of courage, and lost his balance. Screaming, he grabbed wildly for something and ended up with Dylene's leg, pulling her loose and bringing both of them down the side of the cliff.

"Keep climbing," she snarled to the two above her, as she moved back down the few feet to the ground to see what she could do. The other soldier was dead from the impact. Dylene lay with one leg sprawled on top of him, conscious but in obvious pain.

"Can you move?"

"I don't think so. I think my back is broken."

"Try to stand up. I'll help you climb."

"I can't even feel my legs, Faris. And I'm probably bleeding inside." The blood that ran from her mouth as she spoke made that very likely. Even if they could get her to the surgeons back in Escarpan, she was unlikely to live.

"Try," she insisted, her heart about to break. She didn't want to lose anyone else, and especially not this one.

But the calm expression in Dylene's eyes was of someone who knew she was dying and had accepted it. "Don't leave me here for them, Faris."

Faris knew what she meant. She drew the sword to take the life of one of her own for the second time that day, and hesitated.

Dylene said, "Please," and she struck as quickly as she could, then shook out the sword with a brutal snap that did clear it. She sheathed it and returned to the wall.

Garon and the other soldier were frozen where they had been, looking down. "Climb, damn you!" she screamed at them, and climb they did. They all made it to the top this time. Eight of them now.

She ordered them to move away from the edge, along the top of the plateau. Then, exhausted, they sat and made a sort of camp. There were stubby trees on the top of the plateau, and they used some of the wood to build a small fire and roast the ears of corn they had brought. There was nothing else to eat; a couple of people produced whiskey flasks, supposedly forbidden, but shared around in gratitude. Faris sat off to herself, eating a little corn because she knew she needed something, but only out of duty, out of discipline, not out of any desire for food. They left her alone.

She took first watch, sitting there staring into space as the others slept. When Liam came to relieve her a little past midnight, she stayed sitting beside him. She was unable to sleep.

A little before dawn, she roused them to move on. "We'll head up to the edge of the city, then climb down the wall and reinforce the defenders."

"A lot of good eight more soldiers will do," Garon groused.

"It's eight more than they have now," said Liam, quietly.

They could see the battle start up anew as the sun came up. The valley was a panorama below them, and while the people fighting below looked like ants from this view, they knew it was real. And they could tell that the invaders were moving in closer and closer, and that their own troops were in retreat. It was beginning to look like the best Escarpan could do was to try to withstand a siege. And, since it was not yet fall, most of the food was still in the fields outside the walls. Faris had seen what happened to under-provisioned cities in sieges; she had little hope that Escarpan could last long.

She knew that she was leading them back into the city where death almost certainly awaited them. But there was nothing else to be done. They were soldiers and their city needed them, if only to die for it.

After about an hour's walk, they came to edge of the cliff where it met the city walls. Faris and Jian moved toward the edge to look over. Behind them, a soldier said, "Look." She pointed toward the city gate.

They looked where she pointed. A white flag of surrender was being raised at the front gate. As they watched, the gates were opened and they saw the high commander walk out with several of his chief advisors. The battle was over. They had lost.

The seven remaining soldiers turned to her again, "What now, Faris?" one woman asked for them all. And they looked at her, confident that she had an answer.

"We get out of here. There's nothing more we can do down there," she said, heavily.

"What do you mean?" cried Garon. "Our homes and our families are down there."

She looked at him in surprise—was this the same man who had grumbled about going back there to fight?

"There's nothing we can do for them now. Our leaders have surrendered; the streets will be full of invaders in the next hour. Nothing that was yours will still be yours."

"I cannot leave without my family," Garon insisted.

"Nor I," echoed one of the other men. A woman nodded her vigorous agreement.

Faris looked down at the city. She could see a number of fires burning; they had probably used fire arrows in the attack, arching them over the city walls. Over by the gate she could see the invader generals marching to meet the city command. She had no family, but she understood. She nodded.

"Those of you who want to go had best go down now, before the surrender takes place. It will give you a little time to help your people, though maybe not enough. Don't stay there with them; climb the cliff and bring them out. No one is safe there."

"You don't think they'll honor the surrender."

She laughed, bitterly. "They didn't at Gathos or at Lytalia, or so the messengers said."

"I have to go," said Garon. He moved to the edge of the wall and let himself over. Two others followed him.

"Good luck," Faris offered softly behind them. She turned to the four who remained. "None of you going down?"

"I don't have any family," shrugged one man. A young woman nodded her agreement.

Liam and Jian, professional soldiers like herself, looked at her. Jian said, "It's like you said. There's nothing we can do down there now. Better to live to fight another day."

"So where are we going?" someone asked. And once again everyone looked at Faris expectantly. She was beginning to get used to the idea.

The answer suddenly popped into her mind. "We'll make for Athely," she said.

"Athely? But we've been at war with them off and on for the last ten years," Jian protested.

"Yes, we have. All of the cities have been at war with each other for as long as any of us can remember. That's why the invaders have found such easy targets. We go to Athely and try to warn them, and perhaps—just perhaps—they will make truce with the cities beyond them and unite to fight the invaders. And in any case, there will be work for soldiers there."

By sunset they were out of range of their city and the invaders; no one seemed to have followed them, and they risked a fire. They sat around it, making dinner out of herbs they had collected and a couple of rabbits which had strayed into their path.

Liam said to Faris, "Yesterday, when you took that arrow in the chest, I thought sure you were dead. What happened?"

"I'm not sure. It must have hit something in my pocket," she replied. "I had forgotten about it." She reached into her inside pocket and pulled out a small box. There was a hole through it where the arrow had struck. "My cards," she exclaimed. "My playing cards saved my life." She kissed the box. Everyone laughed. "I'm afraid we won't be able to play cards tonight. I'll have to get a new deck in Athely."

"One that isn't marked," said Jian, who had played cards with her before.

"Are you calling me a cheater, Jian?" she replied in mock anger.

"Just awfully lucky, Captain," Jian grinned.

Faris started to reply to the banter, then stopped short. "Captain?" she said.

"You're the captain now. You've done the job."

She thought of all the things that had gone wrong, and part of her still wanted to cry out, "No, I'm not in charge, it's not my job, I can't do it." But she had done it, done it as well as it could have been done under the circumstances. And as the captain, she no longer had the luxury of telling them she was afraid, or not qualified. She had to continue being responsible.

"I guess I am," she said.

THE STARRY KING

by Vera Nazarian

Vera Nazarian started writing (and selling) while still in high school, and will soon begin a new job as Russian Language Resident at Pomona College. This is her second sale to *S&S*. She's also "doing a lot of writing." She should make it; almost anyone who continues writing and selling while holding down a full-time job has what it takes.

By the bye, she says "The Starry King" is "dedicated to D.L.K."

It was on one of those nights when stars reveal their true nature as naked living souls that the woman came walking through the sleeping town. She walked with an apparent lightness, an infinite poise in her statuesque figure. And yet, though none would know it, each step she made was like a burden of lifting up a world.

At first glance she was young—slender like any girl of twenty winters, if only taller. In the first tavern she entered, they noticed, under the cheap illumination, that her clothes were masculine and modestly threadbare. Her face and hands, it was observed, were pale as a smoky dream, colorless, lifeless, drained of everything that was of the soul. It was only the heavy look of her blue eyes that spoke not only of a great life-will, but of burdens unspeakable, and of power even beyond.

And thus they all noticed her.

As everything happens in such intimate towns as this, rumors spread fast. Some said she was a great noblewoman, masquerading for her own private reasons. Others, after discerning the deadly-beautiful blade among the folds of her cloak, spoke of warrior women from the East. She dressed, indeed, as some former aristocrat who'd seen better days. Yet, others claimed, there was gem-light of rings about her fingers! She could have bought the whole town with them, if she tried.

The woman had old eyes. It was, if anything, the heavy expression which made them appear thus. No one she had to deal with quite fathomed these eyes since none met her gaze longer than necessary.

And then, one day, someone had seen her take the hood off her hair, and this was when rumors went mad. Her hair, like long filaments of exquisite satin, was white as death.

She said that her name was Nellval, and she was looking for the starry king. At this point, many laughed in her face, while rumors also quieted, seeing before them only a madwoman.

As children, all had been told the tale of the "starry king," and as adults, could only scoff at any who might even suggest a belief in such things. Who, being sane, would credit as history the story of an ancient king's son loving his bride to the extent of interring her dead body with himself in a stone tower? Who could believe that he stayed alive with the lovely corpse for more than a month, without food, or water? Legends said that for over three months his sobs and moans resounded through the tower, as he tried to breathe life into her, until remnants of his own left him slowly and with placid cruelty.

And then, when the moon waxed and waned thrice over, they said, and his soul departed the grief-wrecked body, there were odd occurrences all throughout the land.

The sun rose one morning, redder than a rose. The great river that flows to the sea, changed its course— yes, verily!—and branching, gave birth to a twin. Far West, snow, like silver, fell prematurely over the tall mountains. And one night, when people looked up, they saw a new constellation formed in the heavens, stars sprinkled over the black abyss of sky in the shape of a man.

The Starry King, they called it. The man-shape wrought of pinpoint lights had its one arm outstretched in silent longing, a circlet-crown of greater stars traced his brow, while his eyes, yes, the eyes of the starry king, seemed to weep—sadly the two eye-stars flickered, in semblance of fluid motion. They looked down at the world, and old folk said that the Starry King's great love had, through its suffering, taken in and contained the burden of primeval sorrow that was originally fated for mankind to bear. He, the starry king, had not died, they said. And if one could but find him, somewhere in this world, then one's sorrows and burdens would depart, a cleansing. . . .

"A pretty story, is it not?" a tavernkeeper said after lengthy recounting, to Nellval, feeling sorry for the mad one. "Almost makes you wish you had lived in those days, when people made up such things. And believed them, too."

Old-young eyes met his. And the tavernkeeper also never quite fathomed that gaze. "Would you like to hear more?" he asked, pitying her, and thinking of gold.

She shook her head negatively. "I would like, but I have no time, my friend. I must go on." She spoke softly, kindly, and then left his tavern. Several blank or mildly charitable eyes turned in her wake.

Nellval went to see an old sorcery-woman of the town. "How can I find the starry king?"

The expedience-inclined hag did not even blink (although she, too, had heard of this mad one's search). "How much are you willing to sacrifice of yourself, to obtain this meeting?" she said harshly, her black eyes like sharp agates, and gold dangling about her gypsy-hands.

But when the younger woman raised her heavy eyes, and threw the hood off her white hair, the black agates narrowed in sudden understanding of the uniqueness of these circumstances.

"The Starry King . . . does not take all burdens indiscriminately," she whispered in a different intimate voice, "He also has a limit, a price. . . . Do you really think you can—"

"Enough. What is *your* price, old one?"

"What is your burden?"

Nellval got up then and shrugged. She turned to leave.

"Wait!" said the woman, eyes lusting after the precious rings on her fingers, "No questions, my pretty, no more. That blue stone—give me—"

With utmost indifference Nellval removed the ring, dropped it in the wrinkled clutching palm.

"A–ah," the sorcery-woman cackled, fingers closing over the thing, "What you search can be found but in a graveyard under a full moon, when the white star-flower blooms."

"Indeed . . ." For the first time, something almost like sarcasm came through Nellval's tone. "But—I believe you."

When that month's cycle came to the moon's apex of fullness, Nellval set out in the early evening (accompanied at first by careful crowds of tentatively cruel laughing urchins, for she was an object of peculiar half-mockery) to a nearby old graveyard on the outskirts of the town. Soon, with the coming twilight, the children dropped away, and she continued unaccompanied, along a winding path, among hills, birdsong, and rhythmic cicadas. The graveyard lay in a clearing, old tombstones half-sunken among wildflowers and brush, and overhead the sky streamed endlessly outward, lightly hued with silver on the horizon, and black as ink at the zenith.

Nellval stood among the gravestones. Then she be-

gan to pace, limber as a shadow, yet tall with her
mysterious power. She continued to pace thus, her
soft boots marking the anemic grass, as the moon
floated at last over the horizon's rim, round and bright
and perfect, like the sun's shadow.

It was then that the sunken earth all about her
started to move and quiver, like waves on a high sea,
and the gravestones began shifting. Pale lotus-hands
thrust through the dark earth, reached out, followed
by waxen faces with vacant or feverishly burning red
eyes. The dead were emerging, with moans like siren
song. And they reached out to her, inevitable in their
approach.

Only, Nellval brushed the pallid hands away with the
firm leather of her boot, blankly, almost disdainfully,
and with some secret pity. If *they* continued, insistent,
then she bared her sword blade, and had but to touch
the dead flesh with its radiant sharpness, for *them* to
give way. But most often, it was only the look of her
heavy eyes, that made the burning red ones cringe,
look away, and conceal themselves back in the abys-
mal earth. And thus Nellval quietly paced among the
graves and silver grasses, and the softly wailing dead.

When the moon-disk soared straight overhead in a
dome of night covered with a trillion stars, a shadow
of silver came to stand like a haze over the earth.

Nellval looked about her, and her gaze swept the
ground. She saw small pale blossoms opening their
hearts to the moonlight, at the very precise moment of
the moon's zenith. The cicadas grew silent, and the
last night bird held its breath. Even the dead sank
away once more into oblivion.

The star-flowers growing among the graves, tiny,
delicate as gossamer, seemed to reflect in them identi-
cal shapes, the lights of each individual star.

Nellval felt something equally delicate snap within
herself, deep, as she watched the stars and their shadows, star-flowers, begin an interplay with moonlight,
so that after some moments, her honed, tense vision
began to *perceive*. She saw lines, or rays of silver
moon-form, reaching from each one flower to each

single star, a bond of one-on-one, spanning the limit-
less airy expanse of night.

And suddenly, she began to make out a solidifying
outline of a constellation in the sky, a man-shape with
a crown. The stars congealed about *him*, adding features and light to the form, and the eye-stars were now
supernovas.

There was a feel of many souls, of power in the air,
and a tingling in her blood. Throwing back the cloak,
so that her white hair billowed like nebulae, she turned
her pale face to the skies, and looked in *his* eyes.

"O, starry king!" cried Nellval, a hollow empty
voice, then whispered, ". . . starry king . . ."

She blinked but once (or was it the moistening in
her eyes), and a man stood before her, on the human
grass.

He was half-corporeal, half-night. His outlines were
of moonlight and starlight, and like an exquisite ghost,
tall and majestic, he wore garments of ancient glory,
wrought now only of mist.

He took a step, shadows shifting all about, in liquid
silver. Nellval watched the dully gleaming crown on
the light silk of his hair, the haunting face.

Surprisingly, he had a deep voice, solid and ringing
with power, as a mortal man—a lord among them.

"I am he. What would you have of me . . . ?"

The words were kind, yet they echoed inhumanly
with the emptiness and eternal expanse of night. (His
face, oh, the beauty of his face!)

Nellval looked at him, and her lips quivered. "Starry
king," she said, oddly passive, "look in my eyes. . . .
What do you see there?"

Eyes of shadows and stars met mortal eyes of pain.
For an instant, only.

"Bitterness," he said. "Blood and death—on your
soul. Anger, burning within you, a cauldron of boiling
poison-hate. That, deep under the surface of your
placid outer shadow. You are but a shadow, woman,
nothing any longer touches you. An outer husk you
bear, of soft-spoken apathy."

"Hah! My greatest burden, you have guessed it—

apathy!" Nellval cried, in a suddenly sarcastic, ago-nized voice turned hoarse by a lack of breath, so that her own heart jerked at the hysterical sound of it. She faced him who remained unperturbed. "What else do you see, starry king? How deeply *have* you looked? My eyes—" and she took a step forward, almost touch-ing the ghostly man (but he was so solid, so real). "Do you see my parents, my brothers, among the ravaged dead? And what of my child, whose *beheading*—a foul mockery of the word—I have seen myself, powerless to stop the madmen? Or," and her eyes now flashed, "the eyes of the man that I had loved, cold and indif-ferent, as he turned to love another? And the convuls-ing hands of the hanged man who had fought at my side as my brother? Or the beggars on the filthy town-streets, who always raise their hollow martyr eyes at me, when I hopelessly drop a coin into an emaciated palm?

"And what of the *pain,* the *horrible pain* of those I myself have killed, or hurt in any other way? It is *their* eyes I remember, their cringing. . . . The eyes of the king I—betrayed. And—just as *he* had cringed, whom I loved and pursued—in my damned possessive obses-sion, his fear, his eyes—"

"Enough," said the one called the starry king, and there were no words to describe the nature of the understanding that had passed them. And he added, "Your hair is white as a dream. . . ." And suddenly, then, his voice was but a whisper.

Nellval looked at the face that was neither old nor young, neither of the fancy, nor truly corporeal. She, too, whispered urgently: "You understand, then, what my burden is."

In answer, waxen lips smiled with gentle sorrow.

"Will you . . . cleanse me, Lord of Stars?" said Nellval.

A pause of silence then, as all the night waited for the *answer.*

His lips moved.

"First—take the seal of silence off your heart. Weep . . . O woman."

She shuddered, letting in a sudden flash of memory of *something* so far gone, so far. . . . "I can't. It—it would *hurt* too much," she concluded, knowing the stupid helplessness of her words. "I don't—cry anymore. I—don't feel."

"I cannot take your Burden, if you do not bare your soul!" rang his words now, like thunder. And the night resounded, and the stars trembled.

"Yes . . . I suppose you must open an infected wound to cleanse it. Or an infected soul. Well, then." And for the first time in many years, Nellval (who had been so many things, her previous "lives" involving the pain of so many, and now but a tangled skein rolled tight in her deepest depths) allowed herself to remember. Doing so, she looked into *his* eyes, the fathomless eyes of the starry king, and—drowned.

She was swimming in the Sea of Pain of all Humankind. For one instant only, she knew the unspeakable *agony* that one mind cannot conceive. And the next instant, like a bubble of air, she burst forth out of that Sea, for her life. . . .

Gasping, she found herself looking at the hazy surface of his placid otherwordly eyes (no longer two pits giving way before her). "Who are you, really?" she asked, "*What* are you?"

"Who am I? I am you," he said. And then the eyes cried.

There was an odd stillness to the silver night, as it listened to the silent weeping of the starry king. Several large tears (containing in them reflected starlight) rolled from his eyes, inevitable, like the passing of seasons. Yet, not a single twitch came to the face. Its absolute lack of tension spoke of strange acceptance of all things.

His tears stopped. Again, silence.

And then Nellval felt a great *thing* lifted off of her, a great weight gone from her soul. (And she noticed that the locks of his hair were now even whiter than her own—or, were they of the same infinitely pale shade, had they always been thus?)

She was free. A nothingness now filled her, a great

empty bubble of air and nothing, of hazy moonlight musings, and thoughts calm as silk.

The starry king said: "I have taken your Burden." And then began to shimmer, gossamer-fine, and fade away.

"Wait!" cried Nellval (blood pounded at her temples), "Wait, Lord of Stars! You have taken away not only my Burden of suffering and pain, but also my memory of the self. . . ." Her voice grew small (in the stasis of the night). "I have—nothing."

"Such is the price," came his dwindling voice.

But Nellval reached out with her pale strong human hand, and grabbed the shadowy fading being, took hold of him, and they *struggled,* in a weird instant of timelessness. In her embrace she held a universe of silver and stars and night, and it was a touch so ardent, yet so oddly sweet, so gentle, that as she fought him (so oddly familiar), she found herself instead caressing him. And she suddenly inexplicably began to *know* who and what he was, had been, and to *remember.*

. . . Birds sang outside the ancient tower. The King, young and emaciated, lifted his red sunken eyes from the lily-white corpse of a young woman, covered by rose petals and her own fragrant hair, like rust. Death.

He could do nothing. Absolutely nothing. Here before him was a fact. Death.

He had no more tears left. The Sun had been shining the same way now, for the third month (During the second, he had forgotten the meaning of *sun* and *day,* and perceived only shadows).

How could she no longer be? How, O gods! She hadn't even been beautiful. Or exceptionally lucky, so the gods had no reasons to envy her and punish. . . . Or him. He had been humble. Yet—a humble king.

Why? O gods!

When his moment of crisis had passed, he was left with a sense of nothing, an emptiness of soul. And when he looked again at the once-dear body of a once-living woman, he suddenly realized that it, too, the body, the *thing,* it did not matter.

Nothing any longer mattered (He saw that flies came

to sit on the corpse. And the definite beginning stench—or had it been thus for some time now?).

And the king, or the one who had once been king, lay down on the cold clean stone of the floor and then began to watch the day outside the window, calmly, relearning every nuance of the coral-gilded dawn and sunset, every shifting of things, and accepting them within his empty, dying heart. . . .

"That was but another life. . . . One life that I had lived, of so many," spoke the starry king to Nellval, in the instant of their struggle-embrace.

In answer, suddenly she began to weep, shuddering sobs rending her body, still holding him tight as a dream. And his gentle shadow-hands tightened about her, as he continued: "Yes, it is the futility of things, and consequent apathy, that had first killed me, and then made me see things in a different way, and to *care*."

"But you have cared for so many!" she sobbed, the young-old white-haired woman with a once-black soul. "I have seen it inside of you, and they had all been just like me, not better off at all, all hurting—"

"We are but one thing ultimately. One thing of pain."

"And you, are you then but a starry vaporous ghost, the magical yearning of my dreams? My conscience? You, who have 'taken' my burden and hate away, and then gave back *new* memories of things?"

"No, not a dream," he said, "I have been once a man. And now, I no longer know. For the moment, you might say, I am—you."

Nellval continued to weep. "You have taken so many Burdens on yourself!" she repeated, "so many Burdens!"

And his placid eyes were on her, and they had ceased the struggle.

"So many Burdens, starry king . . ." she whispered. "And what of your own?"

Was it surprise that flickered in the haunting immortal eyes? He then *looked* at her. "*My* Burden? What of it? I no longer have a Burden to call my own. Don't you understand, it is the things that *you* cannot bear, that I take from you? And the things that the others could not bear, they constitute my Burden now."

"But—how can you contain so much within you?"

"How can I not? Who else is there, what god or gods," laughed (yes, laughed!) the starry king in gentle sorrow, "that can, or is willing to bear *my* Burden?" And his voice echoed out into the sky and stars of night.

Nellval thought only for a moment. "I have nothing now, really, nothing—to live for. And I have learned of myself. Go, for once in your own peace, you who were once a man—I will bear your Burden."

And before a whisper of protest came from him, she reached with her hands (her fingers incidentally touching the silk of his locks, oh, the strange sweetness of it!) and took the dull crown of stars from his brow (it burned her like agony), placing it on her own white head.

As she did thus, there was a fire inside her mind, and the shadow-man standing before her without a crown, gifted her with a look of such empathy and awe and at last recognition, that her heart (having so many fatal cracks of pain in it) broke at last.

Who knows if she died or not then, but she was *changed*. He, too, was gone now, truly, a smoky dream. Nellval *stood* alone in the night, among dark old graves and silver star-flowers, and the sleeping dead. The moon had dipped to the nadir, close to the horizon, and the heavens were filed with only a trillion stars.

Nellval once again carried her old burden within her. And with it, somewhere deep, she knew somehow there were others. And yet—

Nothing was quite the same. And the Burdens of the World, odd as it seemed, were not at all difficult to contain. Indeed, they seemed light as a feather, as night vapor. . . . Like a load of stars from the sky, ringing, light and silvery. For, there was now that ever-present "feel" of the Crown about her head, a sensation of agony so close yet so far away, and never quite touching her, that allowed her to Bear. Only at once instance could it touch her, Nellval knew—not when she remembered her own (already receding) burdens of death and unfulfilled love and betrayal, no. It, the agony, would burn only when she momentarily recalled (with such longing . . .) the hazy dream-memory that the starry king had given her, of his own past, and of the one life (the last) in which he had loved a woman with hair like rust. For when (so long ago, it seemed) Nellval's own white hair had color, it was thus, *rust*. And Nellval had recognized, in that silent woman's corpse, many lives ago, herself. . . .

But now, that was all irrelevant. She stood, and the world was once again before her. She had freed him.

The Starry Queen.

MIRROR IMAGE
by Nina Boal

Nina Boal is no newcomer to writing; she has published a Darkover fanzine, *Moon Phases*, and was briefly an editor of *Fighting Woman News*, along with Deborah Wheeler and Nancy Jane Moore. She says, "I was a bit spoiled in the writing process, as my first story *ever* sold to FREE AMAZONS OF DARKOVER" ("The Meeting"), but since then she has gotten her share of rejection slips (if you can't handle rejection, you're in the wrong business) and "now feel as if I had graduated from writing about Darkover to writing in my own universe." She is also—like most writers—working on a novel.

She has been teaching math—better her than me—in Chicago, and will move soon to the Baltimore public school system. She adds, "I also have my cats—but fewer of them and they're all neutered and spayed; I no longer have the time to breed them."

Lady Halaine Eden stared at the veiled figure who inched forward on hands and knees. One more supplicant needed help. One more crouched before Khedainie's ruling Lady, seeking respite from illness.

Halaine's shoulder muscles complained from exhaustion. Twenty people she had healed that day, twenty-one the day before. An uncountable throng had crossed the Fire-Goddess' hearth during her five years of rule. Arduously, Halaine had worked on every single one; either to cure their diseases or ease their path to the next life. Guiding her people, tending to their ailments—these were her reasons for arising each morning.

Suddenly a knifing pain split her head. Shadows flickered before her. *The dream . . .* A stark image began to form, but she slammed her mind against it.

Her stomach churned. The nightmare, which had invaded her sleep the past week, was intruding into her waking hours. *Why?* Her anguished questions clamored within. *How much longer must I bear this?* She could never recall the dream's image; her mind always raised protective barriers. *I've healed thousands. Can't I heal myself?*

She rallied her strength, stilling her body's trembling. *Careful,* she told herself. *Take control. You are tired.* She took several deep breaths. *I can examine myself—later.* Her present task was to examine this one last supplicant.

The orange flames gently played in Shal'lu's sacred fireplace. Halaine reached into one of the deep pockets which had been sewn into her crimson wool gown. *Just this last one,* she told her still-pounding head. *Then a hot, steaming bath . . .* She pulled up her cramping shoulders, then released them. She drew a brown leather case from her pocket and untied it. She held up a tiny, round mirror.

Halaine whispered a prayer as she faced the mirror toward the Goddess' hearth. This was her own Healing Mirror, which Shal'lu had given her many years ago. As the Fire-Goddess' lights touched it, a blue flame danced and crackled along the mirror's edges. Brief images of some she had helped that day ran through her mind—an old man whose body had been reduced to bones by the Wasting Sickness, a young singer whose clear soprano had been racked by a rasping cough, a blue-faced infant whose imperfect heart struggled to beat. Their thanks and the music of their laughter echoed in her mind. They would chase away the nightmares, wash the fatigue from her. *Just this last one,* she told herself once more.

Halaine turned to face the supplicant, who crouched piously under a coarse veil. "What is it you wish from me?" she asked gently.

"I am only a freelancer," a woman's voice spoke, muffled by the cover. "I suffered a war-wound from my last job. I once thought it would heal by itself." The voice paused. "But it now seems that I need the Goddess' help." Bitterness crept into the voice. "There is an infection which festers . . . and festers."

A flood of pity flowed into Halaine as she gazed at the supplicant. What reversal had forced this dispossessed warrior to eke out a living, selling sword and prowess in these times of relative peace? Halaine, as a child of the ruling family, had learned sword-arts. Now she rarely used them as she had an army at her disposal. She had dedicated her life to statesmanship and the Fire-Goddess' craft of healing.

Halaine spoke softly to the mercenary. "To attain healing, I must look at your soul as well as your body."

Again, the knifing pain split her head; she staggered momentarily. The dream crawled into her mind, struggling vainly to form its picture. Desperation clawing at her, she dammed her mind once more against the dream. She clenched her jaw, forcing herself to continue the ritual. "If a soul ails or carries a weight inside, the body cannot be mended," she intoned. "You will unveil yourself and look into Shal'lu's Mirror."

The warrior lifted the cover off her body, keeping her eyes downcast. Halaine's eyes fell on the once-fine breeches and tunic, now patched and encrusted with old dirt. The tunic's left sleeve was stained with blood. A new discomfort crept in. *Something is familiar about this warrior. I can't place it.* Halaine centered herself, holding Shal'lu's mirror in the palm of her hands. She placed it beneath the warrior's downturned eyes. "See yourself in this mirror," she murmured.

The mirror's flame flared and crackled. A dense

smoke covered it, then an image arose—an image of one exiled, a dark-haired woman driven far from her home. She had to sell her sword; she had no other skills. Jobs were few and far between. Other images appeared—at a tavern, a swordswoman drinking merrily with a young red-haired man . . . a tiny wood hovel, the wind screaming through its walls, a child at the warrior's breast, whose scream of rage turned into a whimper—the breast had no milk. Then a tiny still figure, wrapped in a cotton rag, was placed into the Earth. . . .

The warrior looked up. Her midnight eyes gazed at Halaine, trapping her in their pools. A shudder of rage emanated from them. "Yes, I am familiar to you," the cracked voice spoke. "I am Danlyn, your twin sister." She smiled. "Though it has always been said that we are as different as night and day."

Halaine twisted away from the dark eyes. *My sister* . . . Blazing anger, mixed in with a strange fear, seethed inside her. *How can she dare to come here like this, invading my home!* "You were justly exiled for your crimes!" Halaine cried out hotly. "It is death for you to return here."

"*Whose* crimes?" Danlyn's hoarse voice demanded. "Yes, I know I bore a son and allowed him to starve," her voice trailed. "But someone committed the original crime—for which I was exiled." Her voice had the knife-edge of old wounds. "For my son's sake as well as my own, I've come back to Shal'lu's hearth to find out." With lightning quickness, Danlyn reached into a worn leather bag which hung from her belt. Halaine could only stare in frozen amazement. "Shal'lu gave me one of Her gifts, too," Danlyn continued. "Don't you remember? She gives Her gifts to any who can withstand Her training. I was given mine the same day yours was given—we are twins, are we not?" Danlyn paused, breathing hard. "Look into my mirror."

Blue-green flames flickered around the mirror which Danlyn held. Something forced Halaine to gaze into the mirror, even as her mind vainly wrenched itself to and fro. She had forgotten that Danlyn possessed a mirror. *No!* Her mind fought a new blank terror. *This isn't the time or place.* . . . The merciless force gripped her in steel. It compelled her to lay her own mirror—now a black, dead object—on the floor in front of her.

Dense smoke covered Danlyn's mirror as Danlyn knelt before her. Halaine's eyes were reflected, as pale as Danlyn's were dark. Images, buried deep—poison from an old, untreated wound—began to trickle out. She saw herself, Danlyn's twin, surpassing Danlyn, both in swordplay and book-learning. The flame of her Healing Mirror seemed to flare more brightly than her sister's. Yet Danlyn had come out of their mother's womb first. Danlyn, not she, was the Heir. Danlyn would be the one who would rule Khedainie. A petulant, childish voice cried out. *It is not fair!*

The smoke shifted slightly. A blond girl of fifteen was in the castle treasury's storage room. She grasped rubies out of a jewel-box, letting them run through her fingers. *If I were to take these,* the girl thought, *accuse Danlyn of the robbery, convince my father at the Judgment hearing* . . . She laughed, foreseeing her final triumph. Danlyn would be declared unfit to rule and Halaine would be named Heir. *I am the most accomplished,* her thoughts pounded, echoing each other. *Both Khedainie and I deserve it. Only an accident of birth separates me from rule—and now that damage will be repaired.*

The mirror's smoke curled. The blue flames flared orange. Another figure appeared. A maidservant pattered into the room to dust the castle's treasures. Blank terror sized Halaine. *She* would be caught with the jewels in her hands; she would be severely punished. With a trembling hand, she picked up a brass candlestick and hurled it at the servant. The girl lay still, in a pool of blood.

A raging bonfire roared inside Halaine's head. "NO!" she screamed. "I didn't mean to kill her, only to knock her out! I am no murderer!" The fire turned into a screeching whirlwind as smoke-gray fingers reached out, choking her, pulling her down its passageway. More familiar images crawled to her mind's surface. *My dream!* her mind gasped out. But a final image lay shrouded in a thick, smoky veil.

Her reason fought back against the dream; her thoughts sang their song against the maelstrom. *I've paid back for that death. I've healed so many of my people's wounds—every day I treat more.* She bore her eyes into the fiery mirror. *Who would take care of them if I were to be exposed and condemned?*

"Who?" Halaine's rasping voice hammered against the curling haze. "Tell me, who would take my place? Who?"

Her mind's door clanged shut, locked tightly against the mirror—against her own nightmare. Her final assertion rang out shrilly. "Thousands of my people would surely die without me!"

The room held a deafening silence. The flames of Danlyn's mirror had stilled.

"So that's why I was exiled," Danlyn whispered. "I never knew the truth until now—although I had begun to suspect." She leaned back on her heels. "All I've known for sure is that some criminal carefully arranged it so I would be blamed for a dreadful murder. I could not clear myself at the Judgment hearing— even our parents refused to believe in my innocence. I thought—I've *wanted* to think, through all the years of my exile—that an especially clever thief had done it." A single teardrop edged out of her midnight eyes. "It really *was* my own twin sister."

Flames of righteous anger swept through Halaine. "You've gazed at my inner depths. You've seen my nightmare. Now look at me again. Look at all the good that I've brought to Khedainie. I've brought prosperity. Wars do not rage here. And," she lifted her chin, "I have brought my healing gift to my people, to any who would die of illness—even to you. One need only come to my castle—to Shal'lu's own hearth." Halaine stared down at Danlyn's rags. "Do *you* expect to replace me? What do you know of healing, you who have killed for hire all these years? Or would you bring war and destruction to a peaceful land—just for your own vengeance?"

Danlyn looked up at her sister, her eyes two calm pools. "I have no desire to take your rule," she said steadily. "I've learned a few things as a sell-sword. I've learned to use my mirror instead."

Her eyes danced around the brick walls. "I guess I still wanted revenge when I came seeking you," she mused absently. "I thought revenge would cure my wound and bring repose to my son's soul."

She shrugged. "Now that I've seen your side of things, I no longer need vengeance. My son's soul will rest as all other souls do, then attain its new body." She wiggled her left arm and smiled gently. "My shoulder is well—the wound no longer festers. Shal'lu is truly a healing deity." Her mirror flashed brightly as she replaced it in its pouch. "She has given me my peace." She looked directly at her twin, her eyes filled with pity. "I can only hope you can find yours."

Halaine's body trembled in fury at Danlyn's pitying glance. *How dare she make such a mockery of Shal'lu and her gifts?* "I, as Lady of Khedainie and guardian of this hearth, order you to take leave immediately!" she shouted fiercely. Her heart pounded against her chest, while something buzzed and scraped inside her head. She fought against it—an image which strived to unveil itself. If only her own determination could still the roaring within her.

"Farewell, sister," Danlyn rose and bowed. Turning on a booted heel, Danlyn left the room. Her footsteps echoed down the long hallway which led to the castle's exit.

Halaine bent down to pick up her mirror from the floor. Cold shivers reached icy fingers around her. Her dream's final image was unveiled, clearly etched on the floor. Her mirror, the one Shal'lu had granted her for healing, lay on the carpet. It had shattered into thousands of tiny pieces.

SLEEPING DOGS
by Jennifer Roberson

Since the introduction of Jennifer Roberson in the first of these anthologies, she has had a great deal of success; she has had seven of her Cheysuli (shape-changer) novels published, and three of the *Sword Dancer* series—for which we had the honor of introducing the protagonists, Tiger and Del, in the second of these volumes.

In person Jennifer is slender, soft-spoken, and fine-boned, nothing less like a swordswoman would be possible for me to imagine. She is married, and I believe she has also written a couple of romances. However, that's forgivable—as long as she continues to write us this kind of fantasy.

He did not so much as knock, or call out to be beckoned in. He simply kicked open the door.

It set the dogs to barking, all three of them, and the newest litter of pups to squeaking and squawling as the bitch sprang up from her nest before the hearth. Most of the cats paid no mind at all, save to stare balefully at the intruder; one or two of them fluffed tails and keened a warning, but their small noise was lost in the clamoring of the dogs.

"Sit you down, sirs," I told two of them. "And you, lady, tend your pups; I will tend this man."

I waited. The males settled. The bitch lingered longer, hackles erect, then returned to her pups. She cleaned each and every one, tumbling them like oracle bones, then lay down with a final growl. All six fastened themselves to damp nipples with manifest contentment.

I turned my attention at last to the man. "It wasn't locked, the door."

"I need you," he said. "At once."

"It wasn't locked," I repeated.

He made an impatient gesture. "Now, if you please."

I looked past him to the threshhold, to the darkness beyond, searching for companions; surely he had some, being who he was. And yet he was unattended, save for the storm; rain slanted into my hut. It beat against his cloak and soaked through dark hair to his head, exposing the shape of his skull.

The cloak spilled water. A widening pool crept across the flagstones by my door to the hand-loomed carpets I had labored over too long in an effort to make the hut home. Then, it had been makework. Now part of my life.

"What is the trouble?" I asked.

"Prolonged labor." He was terse. "You are the sorceress; I want you to stop the pain, so she may deliver safely."

Sorceress. I sighed. "Wait outside," I told him.

He stared in disbelief as water ran from hair and cloak. "Outside—?"

"And shut the door behind you."

In poor light, his eyes were black. He was wet, cold, worried, too distracted to make proper protest. He simply turned on his heel and went out, shutting the door behind him.

My lap was heavy with cat. I stroked the black silk of her spine and apologized for the upheaval, then gathered up her warm bulk and placed her on the rug with her daughter, who had kittens of her own. No one protested. The night was cold and wet; they were snug and warm.

It took but a moment to shroud myself in my cloak, to gather up my bag, and then I went out the door.

The latch, I discovered, was broken—he had been overhasty—and to keep the door closed I was required to set a rock against it.

He waited nearby with two dark horses, both standing with rumps to rain, heads hanging, eyes closed. Breath steamed in the air. He had ridden hard.

"Here." He handed me rein, turned to his own mount and swung up, kicking rain-soaked cloak aside. Dim fireglow from my window sparked briefly on a spur. Graceful for a man, even in urgency. A horseman born and bred; the mounts were exceptional.

With less grace, I snugged a foot in the stirrup and mounted, gathering slick wet reins. "I am surprised you came yourself. Have you no men to send?"

"I have men," he answered stiffly. "I came myself because she is worth it, and I wanted to waste no time."

"Commendable." And unlike him, or so they said; his reputation was for fecklessness, not solicitude.

"She is worth it," he repeated, and turned his horse from me.

Iron rang on ironwood as we rode across the drawbridge. The moat, in the rain, was gray, freckled by slapping drops. Torches hissed and guttered as wind licked into cressets. He had said nothing of the rain, but I knew it could not please him. A nightstorm was not a good omen for the birth of the king's first child, bastard-born or no.

A horse-boy came running out of darkness to catch the reins to our mounts. When he saw me, he stared; he was far too young to have known me, but my story is harper-fodder. The old king had made it so to justify his actions. The young one, now dismounting, said little on his own, but denied nothing the father had claimed. I could not say if it was out of respect for the dead, or merely a form of agreement. At best, it was indolence; he gave little thought to others.

The horse-boy clutched at reins as I climbed down from the royal mount. His eyes lingered on my face; on the mark branded into my flesh, high on my left cheekbone. The king had ordered it done before he ordered me out of the castle.

No man, seeing me, could not know what I had done. To the castle, I was outlawed; yet now I was brought home. Without honor, perhaps, and certainly lacking fanfare, but nonetheless I was *home*.

The horse-boy led away the mounts. The young king, the new king, knitted black brows at me. "Come," he said impatiently. "Will you gawk in the rain all night?"

Gawk. Indeed, I gawked. Twenty years beyond the walls, and I had forgotten nothing. Neither had anything changed.

Except the old king was dead, and his orders were no longer obeyed.

I touched a fingertip to my cheek, then drew my hood closer, as if to keep out the rain. Instead it kept in the tears.

"This way," he said.

Mercifully, he did not take me into the Hall. That I could not bear, even after so many years. Instead he took me through a side door and a quiet corridor, avoiding sycophants, and stopped at last at a door in a corner of the castle.

I went in as he lingered, holding open the door, and stopped almost at once. "I thought—" But I broke it off as he crossed the room and knelt by the bed, crooning to the occupant. Not in the way of a madman, or a man far gone in his cups, but in a way I knew so well, having my own share of the Gift.

He turned his head and stared at me, daring me to challenge his right to do as he did, to question his priorities. I dreamed of doing neither, understanding too well.

So. Not woman at all, but wolfhound. Yet worth saving all the same.

He tensed as I came to the bed. In his eyes was the fear I might startle the bitch, but the fear died as he saw the mark on my face. Something else lit dark eyes: memory and acknowledgement.

And yet he spoke of neither. "She is the best," he

said tautly. "All of twelve years in the breeding, and the only one worth the time. I culled her littermates for temperament, and the sire died last year. If she dies, the line is lost."

"This is her first litter?"

He nodded. "Second cycle, of course, so as not to taint the pups. But—you see how she is."

Indeed. She was exhausted, and no puppies to show for her time. "Her name?"

"Ceara."

"Spear." I smiled. "A proud name for a king's hound."

"Deserved," he said curtly. "I will pay you well if you save her."

"We will speak of payment later." I set down my bag, stripped out of my wet cloak and dropped it, then moved close to the bed. Crooning much as he had.

The bitch rolled a dark eye in my direction, but made no sign of protest. She was clearly too weary to expend any effort past that of trying to pass her puppies.

"What will you do?" he asked intently.

"It might be best if you left," I told him quietly. "If you are here, she will think of you; she would do better to think of the task."

It whispered in his tone: dreadful fascination. "Will you use sorcery?"

Deliberately, I faced him. "How much do you want this litter? How much do you want this bitch?"

I saw the answer in his face; he saw acknowledgment in mine. He left the room in silence save for the wet slapping of his cloak, the ring of a silver spur, the click of the closing door.

The bitch whimpered. I turned to her at once, knowing it would not be a simple task to bring forth live puppies or to preserve the hound. She had spent too much time already; likely, all were dead.

I sang to her softly, giving her the history of the realm for want of a better thing. It is tone that counts, not content; she heard my voice, my promises, and listened, allowing me to soothe her. Such is the work of my sorcery; a man with patience and compassion can do as much, but few are willing to try. Midwifery, they claim, is woman's work, be the mother human or animal.

"Bright, bold girl," I whispered, putting gentle hands on the wolfhound. "Bred of kings and queens to serve kings and queens . . . huge of heart, bright of spirit, unflagging in loyalty. And bought so cheaply, too—a kind word, the touch of a hand, the glint of pride in a man's eye—" But I broke it off, knowing I was treading too close to things better left unsaid.

Long of leg, big of bone, well-fleshed and tautly muscled. Standing, her shoulders would reach my hips. Rearing up, hooking front paws over shoulders, she would look a man in the eye. Running against the wind, she could strike a pace to rival a horse's.

Warhound, hunter, companion. The consummate defender, capable of taking down elk, wolf, man. Bred for the first two, trained to the third.

But now she did none of those things, being confined to the bed. The coarse silver-gray coat lacked the luster of health. The tail, thick as a tree limb, lay limply across the bed.

"The last of your line," I said. "Such a waste of blood and heritage, spilled out for a man's pride."

She stirred, whimpering, as I gently slipped my hand inside and felt for the first puppy. And I found it, turned it, urged it out into candlelight.

Stillborn. And the next, the next, the next. Five of them, dead. The bitch whined, whimpered, strained, and passed a final puppy. As I had with each, I tore the sac at the head, carefully worked it backward, then freed the puppy entirely. Quickly, gently, I cleaned mucus and fluids from the mouth and nose, then began briskly to rub it dry with a piece of sacking. And this one began to breathe.

Too soon to rejoice. I tied the cord, cut it, dabbed an herbal paste upon it. Rubbed again, mimicking as best I could the bitch's tongue with the sacking. The puppy squirmed, whimpered, lifted a blind, seeking head.

"One pup, Ceara." I said softly. "Surely you have milk enough for one."

The bitch whined and craned her head toward me. I put the stillborn pups aside, then placed the puppy at the warm, taut flesh of her belly. Her tongue replaced the sacking, urging the pup to suck.

I heard the door open. Spurs rang. He had come to see the results of all his years of careful breeding.

"She is weary, but should do," I told him calmly. "She passed the remains easily enough, and the last puppy. But all the others were stillborn."

"One," he said sharply.

"One. A male."

"Well, that is something." He moved close to the bed, mouth relaxing, and spoke quietly to the wolf-hound. She gazed up at him briefly with pronounced weariness and pride, then set tongue to pup once more.

"He should thrive," I told him.

The royal mouth tautened again. Dark eyes black-ened. One hand stabbed toward the puppy, but I caught him by the wrist. He stared at me angrily. "*You* did it," he accused. "You put a changeling in its place!"

"Changeling!" I stared as he snapped his wrist free of my hand. "Are you mad? She bore that pup but a moment before you entered. That is no *changeling*."

"Look at her." One finger indicated the bitch. "Ceara is of the finest line of wolfhounds in this realm. She was bred to a half-brother of the same line. Do you stand here and tell me *that* is a wolfhound puppy?"

I looked at the pup. He was short-haired, pale fawn, edged with black at muzzle and legs, tipped on ears and tail. And I hid a smile with effort; no changeling, he. No shapechanged puppy. Merely the offspring of one of the king's mastiff guard dogs.

"No," I said quietly. "I would suggest you tend your kennels more closely. Or hire men who do; your bitch has borne you a halfling."

"Changeling," he hissed. "Do you know what this means?"

I sighed, holding onto waning patience with effort. "It means, no doubt, you will have this puppy killed and tell others interested in her litter that all were stillborn."

"Of course. How else is the line kept pure?" He was impatient. "It is best to do it now, before she grows too attached . . . I will have her bred again next cycle—" His face was grim. "And I will order beaten the kennel-boy who allowed this to happen."

"Of course." I kept my tone neutral. "You are the king, and her master . . . you may do as you see fit."

He frowned. "You make no protest? I should think that being a woman—"

"—I would beg you to spare the pup's life?" I shrugged. "Would it do any good?"

He stared at the bitch, carefully tending her only living puppy. He scowled at the puppy, so clearly sired by a dog who was not a wolfhound. And something warred in his eyes. There was, I thought in surprise, a trace of humanity in him after all, and compassion, perhaps even tenderness; whatever else he was, he had his father's talent, and his mother's Gift.

He looked at me uncertainly, shedding arrogance like a cloak. "He would have to be castrated if I were to let you take him. I could not have it said he was Ceara's pup, nor allowed to sire mongrels on wild bitches."

Inwardly I rejoiced. "When he is old enough, I will see to it."

He chewed his bottom lip. "You must swear."

"Of course."

Dark eyes narrowed. Uncertainty was replaced with suspicion. "For a sorceress, you are overaccommodating."

"Am I? What do you know of sorceresses? What do you know of me?"

Brows snapped together. "All I need to know. They tell tales of you, madam. How anyone with a sick or injured animal need only take it to you, and you cure it with sorcery."

I lifted one shoulder. "If that is true, would you not agree it is a benevolent power?"

He looked again at the wolfhound and her offspring. The arrogant mouth tightened. "I said I would pay you for the safe delivery of my bitch. Sorcery or no, I keep my word."

I laughed. "I am no more a sorceress now than I was when I bore the king a son twenty years ago."

His head snapped up. "We do not speak of that here!"

"Do we not?" I lifted brows. "Then you are deaf, my lord—or do you simply conveniently choose not to hear the harper ballads, the whisperings of your servants, the tales in the village—"

His color was bad. "My father told me the truth, madam. How you were barren until you turned to sorcery. How your spells conjured a son without benefit of bedding."

I drew in a quiet breath. "If that is true, what does it make you? Demon-begotten, conjured man, witch's poppet come to life?"

His hand flashed out to fetch me a blow across my cheek. A ring caught flesh, tore it; blood spilled down my cheek.

He stared. Dilated eyes were fixed on the blood, and on the mark branded into my face. "He said you were a *sorceress.*"

"What I touch, I heal. It is a true Gift, and I use it; call it sorcery if you like."

"He said—"

"—many things, I am certain, and with good reason." Something twisted inside. "He came to resent my Gift, because it could not heal him."

"Heal *him!*" He stared. "What do you mean, madam?"

"I mean that in one thing, my Gift failed. I could not heal him." Blood trickled down to my chin. "He was incapable of siring a child. A spear wound, festering, rendered him unable. It was a secret between us, and never spoken aloud. But the time came when he required a son. And so his lady wife, desiring to give her lord that son, turned to—"

"—sorcery."

"No." I shook my head. "My Gift had failed, so I sought another way. I turned to another man."

Color flamed. "Harlot."

"No more that than sorceress." Weariness descended upon me so suddenly it was frightened. "An old tale, my lord, and not worth the hearing. Now, if you will give me leave to go, I will take Ceara's misbegotten son and return to my home."

"That hovel."

I bent, retrieved my wet cloak from the floor, slipped it over shoulders. The pup I would wrap in sacking and carry in my bag; the ride was not so far.

His tone was steadfast. "You were turned out for *sorcery*."

"I had to be turned out for something."

Breath hissed through his teeth. "Then why not for the *truth*?"

I hesitated. "You are perhaps too young to understand, having no woman of your own, but the king loved his queen. She was innocent of men when they married, and loved him as much as he loved her. When he was no longer able to bed her, she swore it did not matter; that it would change none of her feelings for him." I swallowed with difficulty. "And it did not; in that she told the truth. But he required a son. It was destroying him, as king and man, that he could sire none. And so his lady wife, seeking to assuage his anguish and fulfill his needs, gave him that son."

He sat down awkwardly on the bed, spurs tangled together.

"An adulterous queen is executed," I told him. "He loved me too much for that."

"And—so—" He shivered. "He named you sorceress and cast you out."

"Everyone knew I was a healer. Healers, when patients die—or others sicken—are often accused of sorcery." I sighed. "It was a greater kindness than having me executed."

His eyes locked on the bloodied brand. "But if they thought I was begotten through sorcery—"

"No. Not that. The charge of sorcery came for the healing, not your conception—there could be no taint cast upon your birth, or your worthiness questioned."

"Then why did the king bother with this mummery?"

"Ambition," I said quietly. "The head kennel-keeper wanted more than he had, having bedded a queen. And so he sold the truth to a high-ranking nobleman who also desired more power, and knew how to go about getting it."

"*Kennel*-keeper!"

I nearly laughed. "You would prefer nobility? Ah, my apologies, but I knew him best of all. I spent much of my time in the kennels, training the hounds. I bred your Ceara's great-granddam."

But Ceara was not, at that moment, his concern. "And so the king accused you of sorcery, to turn attention from the truth."

I caught a drop of blood on my fingertips. "The truth could have fueled the fires of rebellion. To put down rebellions, kings make sacrifices."

His tone was colorless. "You."

"As I made my own: *you.*"

Dark brows knitted. His hair, like mine, was still damp but drying, curling against his neck. He had my coloring, but his father's bones, strong and bold and striking. "What happened to him? My—" He paused. "The kennel-keeper."

"He was murdered."

His mouth opened in outraged shock.

"Not by the king. By the nobleman who paid him gold for the truth; having spoken, he offered no more."

The mouth closed slowly. His eyes were full of memories, recalling a childhood of safety and security; the promise of eventual power. Now he had it. And now also the truth.

"Did it hurt?" he asked.

I made a move to touch the brand, withdrew my hand when I recalled the cut. "It healed. So will this."

His tone was steady. "No. I meant, did it hurt to give up your title, your place, your life? All for a lie?"

"Not so much as it hurt to give up my son."

He flinched, recoiling from comprehension. He hid himself behind a veil of dark lashes, masking himself to me.

Then at last he rose, speaking forcefully. "I will have you back. Too much time has passed; no one remembers."

"Everyone remembers." I shook my head. "If you recall me to the castle, all the songs will be sung, all the tales will be told. And the truth will do its damage by stripping you of your title."

"I am king, madam. Bred and trained for it, as a hound is bred and trained."

"You are the son of an adulterous queen, called sorceress, and the king's kennel-keeper," I told him plainly. "Noblemen are not impressed by such. The truth will affront them and everything they uphold; you will damage fragile self-importance and nonexistent honor. Mongrel, they will call you, baseborn son of a tender of hounds—" I drew in a breath, made myself speak more quietly. "They will haul you down from the throne and cast you out. They will cull you as a *mongrel*—and replace you with the nobleman who survives the battle for power. Is that really what you want?"

Fiercely, he answered, "I want things put right."

"They are as right as they can ever be, after so much time. After so much anguish." I forced a smile. "Sleeping dogs, left to lie, never bite their master."

He was king enough to know it, and to acknowledge it. But now, after so many years, more than merely king. He was also a mother's son. "Did you mean never to tell me?"

"It was for you to come to me."

A muscle ticked in his jaw. "I came for Ceara's sake."

"It brought you. Does it matter?"

"I may come again. For my sake, now."

A soft flutter filled my chest, of hope and anticipation; of gratitude for all the petitions answered. "The hovel will welcome you."

He smiled. It was the first of his I had seen, and so reminiscent of his father, whom I had not loved, but liked, for his empathy with the hounds. "Then you desire no change in your lifestyle."

"Sleeping dogs, my lord."

Ceara shifted on the bed. The pup, sated, slept snugged against her belly. She looked at her master, whined, slapped her heavy tail against the coverlet. It brought him to her at once.

He bent to thread fingers through the coarse, wiry coat, to stroke her head and scratch her ears and find the place at her throat that dropped lids over her eyes and transformed her to slack-jawed satisfaction.

He touched the puppy gently, stroking the velvet fawn-and-black baby coat. In the silence of the room I heard the muffled grunt.

He turned abruptly to face me. "I will keep the pup," he said firmly. "For Ceara. But also for *you*."

"For me?"

Fierceness returned, accompanied by self-condemnation. "Why strip him from her, or ask her to give him up merely to placate a man's pride and sense of self?" He came forward and touched the blood on my face, smiling faintly. "I am old for lessons, madam, but I think you will teach me many."

"Old dogs, young men." I pulled my cloak closed. "Come whenever you can; when the noble dogs lie sleeping. And bring the pup, as well. It will be interesting to watch what he becomes."

My son grimaced disgust. "With *that* breeding, who can say?"

"Mongrels are often the best," I told him serenely, "in dogs *and* kings."

It was the only gift I could give him, after so many years. But as he laughed aloud, I knew it was enough.

SHADOWLANDS

by Elisabeth Waters

Anyone who knows me knows that I have one over-powering interest, and that is opera; and that anyone who lives with me either gets to like (or at least tolerate) opera. One evening last winter, Lisa (Elisabeth Waters) and I were watching one of my favorite opera tapes; the performance, with Dame Janet Baker, of *Orpheus and Eurydice*.

In my opinion, Baker is one of the world's greatest artists—it was a very special performance; and we had gotten caught up—or at least I had—in the familiar story of the spouse who went down into the afterworld, and pleaded for the release of his beloved. Lisa made what I thought at the time an offhand remark—that perhaps this—dragging someone back from heaven—was not altogether the act of a loving spouse. A few weeks later, the first draft of "Shadowlands" lighted on my desk. As I have said before, there is only one advantage to living close at hand; I usually either accept or reject—because of time pressure—I very seldom send anything back for a rewrite; but the potential of "Shadowlands" seemed so great to me that I asked for a total of four rewrites before it became what I had known it could be. I'll probably never watch *Orpheus* again without thinking of this story. We'll bet you won't either.

Oriana confronted the household priest over her husband's body, which lay on the bier in front of her. "No, I will not agree to hold the funeral at first light tomorrow! Why are you in such a hurry to put my husband underground?"

The priest sighed. He had been in the chapel with her and the body for several hours now, it was late, and he was tired. "My lady, why do you insist on delaying the funeral? This refusal to accept the situation avails you nothing."

Oriana simply stood there, a silent column of black. Her sole concession to her husband's death had been to put on mourning robes: a loose black gown, tied at the waist with a plain black cord, covered with layers of black veiling, enough to hide her pale face, her dark hair, and anything of the slender body the garments might conceivably have revealed. She felt like a walking shadow, and everything seemed distant and unreal.

The priest gathered what remained of his patience and tried again. "You are overwrought," he said gently, "and it's late. Please, my lady, go to your bed; sleep, and things won't seem as bad in the morning."

That argument she had heard before. "No," Oriana said firmly. "I did as you ask last night, and I assure you *nothing* was the slightest bit better this morning."

"Healing takes time—" the priest began weakly.

Oriana ignored him. "But, as you say, it is late, and I am sure you are tired. You have my leave to retire; I shall stay with my husband. I'm not as ready as you to consign him to the lands of the dead."

The priest opened his mouth to protest, decided it wouldn't help, and left, shaking his head.

Oriana knelt at her husband's side, the perfect picture of a devoted widow—no, wife; she absolutely refused to think of herself as a widow—and listened to the priest's footsteps fade away into the silence. It was nearing midnight, and the rest of the household had gone to bed long since.

Oriana looked steadily at the face before her. Quaren

looked magnificent. He had always worn his age lightly, even in life. Oriana had never thought of him as old, even though he was twice her age. Now, with his body at rest and his face peaceful, he looked even less than his forty years. The few threads of gray in his dark hair seemed to be nothing but a trick of the flickering light cast by the candles about his bier reflecting off the silver embroidery of his dark green tunic. She still expected him to open his eyes and speak to her at any second.

He'd never been ill a single day in the six years of their marriage. It was totally inconceivable to Oriana that he could be gone so suddenly, in a single hour. The huntsmen who brought his body to her spoke of an accident, a bad fall with his horse, which had landed on him, but it made no sense to her. Her husband lay on the bier before her, but he just *couldn't* be dead.

And if he was, she was going to bring him back.

The house was still now; even the priest had gone to bed, and there was no one about to interrupt what she was about to do. Quaren might yet benefit from the things he had taught her. Of course, every minstrel knew the song of Orfeo, who had gone to the lands of death to bring back his wife, but very few people knew how to make the journey in truth. Such studies had been a hobby of Quaren's, and he had taught Oriana everything she could absorb. She rose silently to her feet and crossed the room to the door standing open between the chapel and the rest of the house. Quietly she closed the door and locked it. Then she returned to the bier.

From its hiding place in the long sleeve of her undertunic she pulled a small silver dagger, Quaren's ritual knife. The household priest didn't know about all of the rituals performed in the chapel. This would not be the first ritual she had done behind locked chapel doors, even if it was the first one she had tried to do alone. She could only hope that Quaren had taught her enough.

Using the dagger, she cut a lock of his hair and two

locks of her own, braided them together and wound them around the hilt of the dagger. Now the dagger would tie her spirit to her husband's and help her to find him. She circled the bier, blowing out the candles, until the chapel was absolutely dark. Then she lay down on the bier, draping herself carefully across Quaren's body, and shifted into trance state.

She was in a narrow rock passageway, filled with billowing fog. Everything around her was a very dark grey, but as she went forward down the sloping tunnel, it widened and became lighter. Soon she could see quite well. She needed to be able to see here, for this was the place of the recently dead, the spirits not yet detached from the world and its concerns. Quaren should be here, if she was lucky.

The fog had slacked off to the occasional wisp by the time she reached the gates. There were two sets of them, made of round iron bars the size of her arm welded together into giant lattices. One could climb them easily, as many of the forms on the far side of them were doing, but since they went right up to the ceiling, they couldn't be climbed over.

Oriana walked up to the first gates, the ones that didn't have whoever they were crawling all over them. The gates were latched on the other side, but they didn't fit together snugly and it was easy enough for Oriana to slide the blade of the dagger through the crack and lift the latch. Opening the gates was much harder; she had to lean on one of them and push with all her might before it opened wide enough for her to slip through. It fell shut with a loud clang as soon as she released it, but by then she was safely through. Holding the dagger tightly with both hands, she approached the second gates.

The forms on the other side proved to be people—more or less. They wore no clothes, and their bodies lacked the sharp detail of a human body, rather they were pale brown human-shaped manikins. But their faces were definitely human, as were their voices.

"Who are you to walk through the dark mists before Death has summoned you?" one of them demanded.

"This place will fill you with horror and drive you mad!" said another form. It was not a friendly warning; the voice sounded gleeful at the prospect.

"You will be trapped here forever—unless Death deigns to release you!"

Oriana looked from face to face. Their threats didn't terrify her; if she couldn't save Quaren, she didn't care what happened to her. But his face was not among the ones around her.

"Why have you come here?" one of the spirits challenged her, facing her through the gates.

"I am looking for my husband," Oriana replied steadily.

"Husband!" The spirit laughed. It was not a happy sound. "Do you see him here?"

"No," Oriana answered.

"Perhaps he is on the Isle of the Blessed," one of the others said sarcastically. Oriana started; the voice sounded very much like that of her eldest sister, who had almost invariably used that tone when talking to her. Well, she knew how to deal with sarcastic bullying.

"Perhaps he is," Oriana agreed quietly.

"And do you plan to go all the way there to look for him?" This spirit also seemed to have been female; its face reminded Oriana of the way her sisters used to look when they teased her.

"Yes," she said firmly, "I do."

This produced a great burst of hilarity, and the spirits pulled open the gates and bowed Oriana through—or perhaps they were simply doubled up with laughter. Oriana walked quickly past them, glad that Quaren wasn't there. Even for the sake of finding him easily, she wouldn't wish him condemned to such company. But it was odd that he could have gone so far so quickly. Was he truly already on the Isle of the Blessed?

The mocking laughter faded into the distance behind her and was replaced by the sound of water lapping sluggishly against the shore. Oriana knew this landmark well. The river had many names, but everyone knew one had to cross it to get to the Isle of the Blessed. Some people said there was a ferry across it and buried their dead with coins for passage money. Oriana had always thought that story rather fanciful, and certainly she saw no sign of a boat or a landing for one now.

She looked down at the dagger in her hands; it was glowing faintly. She took a few steps downstream and the glow faded, brightening again when she returned to her original position. When she continued walking upstream, the glow got even brighter. She watched it carefully and stopped when it started to fade again. Obviously this was as close to Quaren as she could get on this side of the river. He must be on the land opposite her, which she could see dimly through the thin ghostly river mists. The river was eerie, but the current wasn't particularly swift and Oriana had never been afraid of getting wet. Still, she knew she had better get across this water as quickly as possible; one of the names for this river was Oblivion.

She stepped in and gasped. The water was colder than anything she'd ever felt in her life—*probably,* she thought, *colder than anything* anyone *ever felt in their life.* Gritting her teeth so they wouldn't chatter, she slogged on. *Step, step and another step. Come on, you can do it,* she admonished herself. *Remember to keep the dagger dry. Step, step, step . . .*

She sat in the grass, under the trees. She was wet up to her breasts, but it didn't matter; she'd dry fast enough in the sun, which was making lacy patterns as it shone through the leaves. It was so peaceful and so beautiful. She was perfectly content to sit there and watch the play of the light and listen to the rustling of the leaves. The birds were singing, the squirrels were chattering; it was the kind of morning that made one glad to be alive.

Alive. For some reason the word bothered her. *But why? What's wrong with being alive?* Her fingers, idly tracing the dagger in her lap, touched the braid of hair around the hilt, and her memory returned with wrenching suddenness. *Quaren. My husband is dead, and I came here to save him.*

She stood up and pulled at her wet robes, which seemed determined to cling awkwardly to her body. She started to remove the layers of veiling, but stopped after the first two. The light about her was getting too bright to bear without veils. Obviously the living were not meant to wander unveiled in the land of the dead. *Is this why widows wear veils? Has someone before me done this, and succeeded?* She tucked the extra veils under her arm and started through the woods, trusting that the faint pull from the dagger was a true guide.

She was concentrating so hard on the dagger that she nearly tripped over the boy. He appeared to be about eight or nine years old and he was lying against a tree trunk, turning a leaf between his fingers. He wore a short silver-blue tunic which matched both his eyes and his hair, and his skin looked so pale as to be true white. Oriana apologized automatically, and he looked startled, as if he hadn't noticed her presence before.

"What's wrong with you?" he asked with the directness of childhood. "You're so faint I can barely see you."

Oriana thought about it. She looked normal enough to herself, but she had to admit that he looked somehow more solid than she did. "I guess it's because I'm not dead—at least I don't think I am." She looked down at the braid on the dagger. The hair was still dark, except for a few strands of silver in the hair that had come from Quaren, and Oriana felt somehow certain that it would look different if she were dead.

"You're alive? Really?" The boy seemed to find this a strange idea. "What are you doing here, then?"

"Looking for my husband."

"Oh." He frowned, puzzled. "Aren't you supposed to wait until you're dead, too?"

Oriana smiled for the first time in several days. "Maybe that part of my education was neglected. Did your parents teach you proper etiquette for the Shadowlands?"

"My parents didn't teach me anything," he said matter-of-factly. "I was only a baby when I died."

"I'm sorry," Oriana said.

"Why? Lots of babies die. And I'd rather be here anyway."

"You'd *rather* be dead?" Oriana asked incredulously.

"Of course." To him, this was obvious. "Look, isn't this leaf beautiful?"

The leaf was indeed beautiful; in fact, everything around them was beautiful, which surprised Oriana. She had always thought that the Shadowlands were dim and dull, not at all like this—filled with a bright beauty that hurt mortal eyes. For a moment she almost wished that she were dead, too, so that she could enjoy it freely, but her sense of duty and love toward her husband drove her to press on in her search. She duly admired the leaf and continued on her way as the boy returned to his contemplation of the beauty of unnatural nature.

She found Quaren in a stone-flagged courtyard. He was sitting on a marble bench with two other men, all discussing some terribly abstract philosophical theory. All three of them wore pale blue tunics like the boy's, and the two other men had the same silver-blue hair and eyes. Quaren's hair and eyes were still dark, but the gray that had been in his hair was gone. He looked much younger than he had in life, and his face glowed with the intellectual joy a good problem had always given him. But Oriana had never seen him look quite so happy before.

The sight of him made her heart turn over within her, and she wanted to walk over to him and fling her arms around him. *Did my trip through the river make me forget how much I love him?* she wondered. But for the moment it was enough just to see him again. She sat down on another bench in the courtyard and watched him as the men continued their discussion, content just to be in his presence and to see him happy.

Presently the discussion wound down and the other men left. Quaren sat quietly, lost in thought. Oriana walked over and sat next to him.

"Quaren?" He didn't seem to hear her. "Quaren!" Now he looked puzzled, as if he could hear a faint sound but could see nothing that could have made it.

Am I fading away? Oriana wondered anxiously. *Maybe I'm just invisible in direct sunlight—the boy was in shadow and still had trouble seeing me.*

She took one of her extra veils and draped it over his head. Yes, now he seemed to be able to see *something* when he looked at her. She added the other veil.

He blinked and looked at her. "Do I know you?"

Oriana found herself grinding her teeth. This was not the welcome she had envisioned. After all the effort she had gone through to come find him, he ought to least to remember her. "I'm your wife," she said. She took his right hand and placed it on top of her left hand, with the dagger held between their palms.

It worked; his face cleared. "Oriana." Then he frowned. "But you're not dead. What are you doing here?"

"I came to find you," she explained, "and take you back."

"Oh." Quaren didn't seem to feel any particular enthusiasm for the idea; in fact, he looked rather blank and dazed.

Probably due to the veils, Oriana thought. *Best get him out of here as quickly as possible. The legends hint at all sorts of things that can go wrong now.* She tugged at his hand, and he rose obediently and allowed her to lead him back toward the shore.

This time there was no one in the woods. The walk was silent except for the rustling of their veils. It wasn't until they reached the shore that Quaren spoke.

"Of course. The river. I don't remember coming

this way before, but then I'm sure I'm not supposed to."

"I remember it," Oriana said. "It's cold!"

He chuckled softly. "When you're dead, you don't feel it. By the way, how did I die? I don't remember that part either."

"Your horse fell on you. It all happened very quickly."

"Poor Oriana." He patted her shoulder gently. "It must have been a dreadful shock for you."

Oriana found that her eyes were suddenly full of tears and her throat was tight. "It was awful! I can't live without you!"

"Your heart will suddenly stop beating perhaps?" he chided gently. Oriana knew the tone well; it was the one he always used when she made a statement not fully supported by verifiable fact. He sighed. "I must not have taught you as well as I thought."

"Of course you taught me well!" Oriana protested. "How do you think I got here? Do other men's wives come here seeking them? Do you think it was easy?"

"No," he said sadly. "Not easy. Easier."

"Easier than what?" Why did he sound disappointed in her? You'd think he'd be pleased that she loved him enough to come seek him in the Shadowlands and that she had the courage and determination to find him.

"Easier than your alternatives."

"Well," Oriana mused aloud, "it probably would have been easier to stab myself—but that wouldn't have brought me here, would it?"

"No!" he said quickly. "Killing yourself would you leave you still bound to the world until the time you should have died." He put his other hand over hers. "Don't do that, Oriana."

Oriana thought of the spirits in the rock tunnel and shuddered. "I won't," she said definitely. "Not ever." She clung to his hand. "But I don't want to live without you!"

He smiled at that. "That's better."

"What?" Oriana realized what she had said. *Don't*

want to instead of *can't.* "So my choices now are to take you back with me—I *can* do that, can't I?"

"Yes," he said flatly. "You can. Even against my will."

"—or to leave you here and go back alone." She felt her stomach clench at that thought, but forced herself to think it through. *The incredibly cold river that numbs the mind, and beyond that the tunnel, and those awful spirits—and I can well imagine what they'll say if I come back alone. . . .*

She contemplated the water in front of her. It was clearer here than it had been on the other side, and it glistened jewellike in the sun. The grass was a purer green than anyone alive could imagine, and each blade of it seemed to be full of energy. Oriana suddenly felt out of place, like a smudge on the page of a book, a dark spot on the landscape. The veils she wore seemed intolerably heavy and dark.

She remembered the boy she had met in the woods, and his mater-of-fact acceptance of his state. He'd rather be dead than alive—did everyone in the Shadowlands feel that way?

She turned to face Quaren squarely. "You'd rather stay here than go back to life again." It was a statement, not a question, but he nodded anyway.

"Wouldn't you?"

Oriana looked at the trees, glittering brightly green in the pure otherwordly sunlight. She knew exactly what he meant; more than she had ever wanted anything in her life she wanted to stay in this bright land. But she was only a shadow here, and the light, for all its beauty, was painful to her. "I wish I could see it all properly. Why do they call it the Shadowlands when it's so bright here?"

"You'll be able to see it in time."

Oriana nodded, choking back the sob caught in her throat. "When my time comes." Even through her veils she could see rainbows as the sun caught her tears. "But that could be years and years!" she protested.

Quaren's reply was no comfort. "Yes. It could be."

"And I'd have to go through it all alone—I don't want to do that!"

"Would you rather drag me back, so that I can die again, possibly of some long lingering illness which would have both of us wishing I'd stayed dead?"

"You're just afraid to go back!" she accused him.

"Not afraid," he said calmly. "I know what's back there and what's here. I died, Oriana. My place is here now. You can take me back to the outer world with you, but, now that I've been here, part of me will always remain here."

Oriana burst into tears, knowing now that what he said was true. She could take him home with her, but for the rest of their lives together she would be living with a husband who wished to be elsewhere. It certainly cast a new light on the legends. Perhaps Orfeo's loss of his wife on their journey back to the land of the living had not been a mistake after all.

It would be hard enough for her to live contentedly in the world now that she knew what lay beyond; for Quaren, knowing that he truly didn't belong among the living, it would be worse. Unhappy as she would be without him, she couldn't take him back against his wish.

"You're right," she sighed. "It's not the act of a loving spouse to drag you back." Her fingers clung convulsively to his. "But oh, I'll miss you."

"You'll know where to find me."

She forced a smile. "On the terrace, debating philosophy." She reached out with a shaking hand to pull her veils off him. "Just remember that I love you." She leaned forward to hug him convulsively with her free arm, then deliberately released him and lifted the dagger out of his hand. For a moment he glowed, even more brightly than the sun.

Then everything was gone.

It was dark, and cold, and the stone under her was hard. Gradually, as her eyes adjusted, Oriana made out her surroundings. She lay on the floor of the chapel, across the room from the bier which still held

Quaren's body. Her face was wet with tears, her veils were scattered about the room as if blown by a strong wind, and Quaren's dagger was gripped tightly in her hand.

She sat up, mopped her wet face with her skirt, and walked over to the bier. Was it her imagination, or was there a peace on Quaren's face that had not been there before? She looked at the dagger she still held. Two parts of the braid around the hilt were brown; the third was a brilliant silver-blue. She smiled as she placed it between his clasped hands. Then she gathered up her veils and unlocked the door of the chapel. The priest would need to get in to prepare for the funeral.

THE MAKING OF A LEGEND
by Mercedes Lackey

"Misty" Lackey has been about as successful as any of the writers who made her debut in this anthology; ever since the first appearance of Tarma and Kethry in "Sword Sworn," in the third of these anthologies, their every reappearance has been greeted with enthusiasm. A few years ago, she made her novel debut at DAW with ARROWS OF THE QUEEN and its two sequels, combining sorcery with another fantasy element common to young women; a race of sentient horses. It's an enthusiasm I have never understood, perhaps because I, growing up on a farm, simply knew too much *about* horses; but I'm in a minority, as the success of her novels about the Heralds of Valdemar and their Companions has shown. Swordswoman Tarma and sorceress Kethry appear in THE OATHBOUND and OATHBREAKERS, which takes them up right after "Sword Sworn." And Misty has now completed another trilogy, as well, which takes place in an earlier age of Valdemar—The Last Herald-Mage. I feel a certain motherly pride in these books, as I do in the many, many books by young writers who made their first appearances in these pages—and all those to come.

Brown-gray and green-brown landscape, and a coating of dust all over everything, a haze of dust in the air, a cloud of dust hanging behind them where Tarma and Kethry's tired mares had kicked it up. Fields, farmholdings, trees. More fields, more farmholdings, more trees. Not wild trees, either; trees tamed, planted in neat little orchards or windbreaks, as orderly and homebound as the farmers who husbanded them. A tidy land this; carefully ruled. No calling *here* for outland mercenaries.

All the more reason to get through it as fast as Hellsbane and Ironheart could manage.

On the other hand, the White Winds sorceress Kethry reflected, there was no use in night-long riding when they were in civilized lands. No telling when they might see a real bed once they got into territory that *did* need their spells and swords.

Kethry wiped her forehead with her sleeve, adjusted the geas-blade Need on her back, and blinked the road dust out of her sore eyes. The sun sat on the horizon like a fat red tomato, seemingly as complacent as the farmers it shone down on. "How far to the next town?" she asked over the dull clopping of hooves on flint-hard earth.

"Huh?" Her companion, the Shin'a'in Swordsworn Tarma, started up out of a doze, blinking sleepy, ice-blue eyes. Her granite-gray mare snorted and sneezed as the thin swordswoman jerked alert.

"I asked you how far it was to the next town," Kethry repeated, raking sweat-damp amber hair with her fingers, trying to get it tucked behind her ears. In high-summer heat like this she envied Tarma's chosen arrangement of tiny, tight-bound braids. It may not have *been* cooler, but it *looked* cooler. And Tarma's coarse black hair wasn't always coming loose and getting into her eyes and mouth, or making the back of her neck hot.

"Must've nodded off; sorry about that, Greeneyes," Tarma said sheepishly, extracting the map from the waterproof pocket on the saddle skirting in front of her. "Mmm—next town's Viden; we'll hit there just about dusk."

"Viden? Oh, hell—" Kethry replied in disgust, rolling the sleeves of her buff sorcerer's robe a little higher. "It *would* be Viden. I was hoping for a bath and a bed."

"What's wrong with Viden?" Tarma asked. To Kethry's further disgust she didn't even look *warm;* there was no sheen of sweat on that dark-gold skin, and that despite the leather tunic and breeches she wore. Granted, she *was* from the Dhorisha Plains where it got a lot hotter than it was here, but—

Well, it wasn't fair.

"Viden's overlord is what's wrong," she answered. "A petty despot, Lord Gorley; hired a gang of prison scum to enforce things for him." She made a sour face. "He manages to stay just on the right side of tolerable for the Viden merchants, so they pay his fees and ignore him. But outsiders find themselves a lot lighter in the pocket if they overnight there. Doesn't even call it a tax, just sends his boys after you to shake you down. Hell*fire*."

"Oh, well," Tarma shrugged philosophically. "At least we were warned. Figure we'd better skirt the place altogether, or is it safe enough to stop for a meal?"

:*For a short stop I misdoubt a great deal of trouble with me at your side.*: the lupine *kyree* trotting at Ironheart's side mindspoke to both of them. Kethry grinned despite her disappointment. Seeing as Warrl's shoulders came as high as Tarma's waist, and he had a head the size of a large melon with teeth of a length to match, it was extremely doubtful that any one—or even three—of the Viden-lord's toughs would care to chance seeing what the *kyree* was capable of.

"Safe enough for that," Kethry acknowledged. "From all I heard they don't bestir themselves more than they can help. By the time they manage to get themselves organized into a party big enough to give us trouble, we'll have paid for our meal and gone."

The dark, stone-walled common room of the inn was *much* cooler than the street outside. Bard Leslac lounged in the coolest, darkest corner, sipped his tepid ale and congratulated himself smugly on his foresight. There was only one inn—his quarry would *have* to come here to eat and drink. He'd beaten them by nearly half a day; he'd had plenty of time to choose a comfortable, out-of-the-way corner to observe what *must* come.

For nearly two years now, he had been following the careers of a pair of freelance mercenaries, both of them women (which was unusual enough), one a sorceress, the other one of the mysterious Shin'a'in out of the Dhorisha Plains (which was unheard of). He had created one truly masterful ballad out of the stories he'd collected about them—masterful enough that he was no longer being pelted with refuse in village squares, and was now actually welcome in taverns.

But he wanted more such ballads. And there was one cloud on his success.

Not once in all that time had he ever managed to actually catch sight of the women.

Oh he *tried*, right enough—but they kept making unexpected and unexplained detours—and by the time he found out where they'd gone, it was too late to do anything but take notes from the witnesses and curse his luck for not being on the scene. No Bard worth his strings would ever take secondhand accounts for the whole truth. Especially not when those secondhand accounts were so—unembellished. No impassioned speeches, no fountains of blood—in fact, by the way these stupid peasants kept telling the tales, the women seemed to go out of their way to *avoid* fights. And that was plainly *not* possible.

But *this* time he had them. There was no place for them to go now except Viden—and Viden boasted a Wicked Overlord.

Leslac was *certain* they'd head here. How could he not? Hadn't they made a career out of righting the wrongs done to helpless women? Surely some of the women in Viden had been abused by Lord Gorley. Surely Gorley's Lady was in dire need of rescue. He could just imagine it—Tarma facing down a round dozen of Gorley's men, then dispatching them easily with a triumphant laugh. Kethry taking on Lord Gorley's sorcerer (surely he had one) in a mage-duel of titanic proportions. The possibilities were endless. . . .

And Leslac would be on hand to record *everything*.

Tarma sagged down onto the smooth wooden bench with a sigh. *Damn, but I wish we could overnight it. One more day in this heat and folks'll smell us coming a furlong away. Wish I just dared to take my damned boots off. My feet feel broiled.*

She propped both elbows on the wooden table and knuckled the dust out of her eyes.

Footsteps approaching. Then, "What'll it be, mi-ladies?"

The deep voice to her right sounded just a shade apprehensive. Tarma blinked up at the burly innkeeper standing a respectful distance away.

Apron's clean—hands're clean. Table's clean. Good enough. We can at least have a meal before we hide out.

"No ladies here, Keeper," she replied, her hoarse voice even more grating than usual because of all the dust she'd eaten today. "Just a couple of tired mercs wanting a meal and a *quiet* drink."

The slightly worried look did not leave the innkeeper's shiny, round face "And *that?*" he asked, nodding at Warrl, sprawled beside her on the stone floor, panting.

"All *he* wants is about about two tradeweight of meat scraps and bones—more meat than bone, please, and no bird bones. A big bowl of cool water. And a half loaf of barley bread."

:With honey.: prompted the voice in her head.

*:*You want honey in this *heat?:*

:Yes.: Warrl said with finality.

"With honey," she amended. "Split the loaf and pour it down the middle."

:You're going to get it in your fur, and who's going to have to help you get it out?:

:I will not!: Warrl gave her an offended glance from the floor.

The innkeeper smiled a little. Tarma grinned back. "Damn beast's got a sweet tooth. What's on the board tonight?"

"Mutton stew, chicken fried or stewed, egg'n'onion pie. Cheese bread, or barley bread. Ale or wine."

"Which's cooler?"

The innkeeper smiled a little more. "Wine. More expensive and goes bad quicker, so we keep it deeper in cellar."

"Egg pie, cheese bread, and wine." Tarma looked across the tiny table at Kethry, who was trying to knot her amber hair up off her neck and having no great success. Kethry nodded shortly. "White wine, if you've got it. For two."

"You be staying?" The apprehensive look was back.

"No," Tarma raised an eyebrow at him. "I don't like to slander a man's homeplace, but your town's got a bad name for travelers, Keeper. I don't doubt we could take care of anyone thinking to shake us down, but it would make an almighty mess in your clean inn."

The innkeeper heaved a visible sigh of relief. "My mind exactly, swordlady. I seen a few mercs in my time— and you two look handier than most. But you dealin' with Gorley's bullyboys would leave *me* out of pocket for things broke—more than losin' your night's lodging is gonna cost me."

Tarma looked around the common room, and was mildly surprised to see that they were the only occupants other than a scruffy, curly-pated minstrel-type tucked up in one corner. She dismissed that one without a second thought. Too skinny to be any kind of fighter, so he wasn't one of Gorley's enforcers; dark of hair and dusky of skin so he wasn't local. And blinked in a way that told her he was just a tad shortsighted. No threat.

"That why you're a bit short of custom?" she asked. "Not having travelers?"

"Nah—it ain't market day, that's all. We never was much on overnighters anyway, only got three rooms upstairs. Most folk stop at Lyavor or Grant's Hold. Always made *our* way on local custom. I bring you your wine, eh? You want that pie cold or het up?"

Tarma shuddered. "Cold, cold—I've had enough heat and dust today."

"Then it won't be but a blink—"

The innkeeper hurried through the open door in the far wall that presumably led to the kitchen. Tarma sagged her head back down to her hands and closed her eyes.

Leslac frowned. This was *not* going as he'd expected.

The women—he'd expected them to be taller, somehow, especially the swordswoman. Cleaner, not so—shabby. Aristrocratic. Silk for the sorceress, and shining steel armor for the swordswoman, not a dull buff homespun robe and a plain leather gambeson. And in his mental image they had always held themselves proudly, challengingly—shining Warriors of the Light—

Not two tired, dusty, slouching, *ordinary* women; not women who rubbed their red-rimmed eyes or fought with their hair.

Not women who avoided a confrontation.

He studied them despite his disappointment—surely, surely there was *some* sign of the legend they were becoming—the innkeeper had seen it. He'd been concerned that they *could* take on Lord Gorley's men and win—and wreck the inn in the process.

After long moments of study, as the innkeeper came and went with food and drink, Leslac began to smile again. No, these weren't Shining Warriors of the Light—these women were something even better.

Like angels who could put on human guise, Tarma and Kethry hid their strengths—obviously to put their targets off-guard. But the signs were there, and the innkeeper had read them before Leslac had even guessed at them. But—it showed; in the easy way they moved, in the hands that never strayed too far from a hilt, in the fact that they had not put off their weapons. In the way that *one* of them was always on guard, eyes warily surveying the room between bites. In the signs of wear that only hard usage could put on a weapon.

Undoubtedly they were *intending* to remain here—but they didn't want Lord Gorley alerted by staying in the inn.

Leslac mentally congratulated them on their subtlety.

Even as he did so, however, there was a commotion at the inn door—and red-faced and besotted with drink, Lord Gorley himself staggered through it after colliding with both of the doorposts.

Leslac nearly crowed with glee and pressed himself back into the rough stone of the corner wall. *Now* he'd have what he'd come so far to witness! There would be no way for the women to avoid a confrontation!

Tarma was sipping the last of her wine when the drunk stumbled in through the door and tripped over Warrl's tail.

Warrl yelped, and sent out a mindshriek that was comprised of more startlement than pain. But it left Tarma stunned and deafened for a moment—and when her eyes cleared, the sot was looming over her, enveloping her in a cloud of stale wine fumes.

Oh, Lady of the Sunrise, I do not need this—

"Ish shish yer dog?" The man was beefy, beef running to fat, nose a red lacework of broken veins that told a tale of far too many nights like this one—nights spent drunk on his butt before the sun was scarcely below the horizon. His wattled face was flushed with wine and anger, his curly brown hair greasy with sweat.

Tarma sighed. 'Insofar as anyone can claim him, yes, he's mine," she said placatingly. "I'm sorry he was in your way. Now why don't you let me buy you a drink by way of apology?"

The innkeeper had inexplicably vanished, but there was a mug or three left in their bottle—

The man would not be placated. "I don't like yer dog," he growled, "An' I don' like yer ugly face!"

He stumbled back a pace or two—then before Tarma had a chance to blink he'd drawn his sword and was swinging at her.

Wildly, of course. She didn't have to move but a hands' breadth to dodge out of his way—but that only served to anger him further, and he came at her, windmilling his blade fit to cut the air into ribbons.

She rolled off the bench and came up on her toes.

He followed, so closely on her heels that she had only time to dodge, drop to her shoulder and roll out of his way again, under the shelter of another bench.

As he kicked at her shelter, she could see that Warrl was beneath the table, grinning at her.

:You mangy flea-monger, you started this!: she thought at him, avoiding the drunk's kick, but losing her shield. She scrambled to her feet again and dodged another swing.

:I did no such thing.: Warrl replied coolly. *:It was purely accident:*

She got a table between herself and the sot, but the drunk swung, split the table in two, and kept coming.

Lady's teeth, I daren't use a blade on him. I'll kill him by accident, she thought. *And then I'll have the townsfolk or his friends on our backs.*

She looked about her in a breath between a duck and a dodge. In desperation she grabbed a broom that was leaning up in a corner by the kitchen door.

Since he was flailing away as much with the flat as with the edge, and since *she* could pick the angle with which she met his weapon, she was now effectively on equal footing. Mostly.

He was still drunk as a pig, and mad as a hornet's nest. And *he* wanted to kill her.

She countered, blocked, and countered again; blocked the blade high and slipped under it to end up behind him.

And swatted his ample rear with the business end of the broom.

That was a mistake; he was angered still more, and his anger was making him sober. His swings were becoming more controlled, and with a lot more force behind them—

Tarma looked around for assistance. Kethry was standing over in the sheltered corner beside the fireplace, laughing her head off.

"You might *help!*" Tarma snapped, dodging another blow, and poking the drunk in the belly with the end of the broom. Unfortunately, the straw end, or the contest would have finished right there.

"Oh, no, I wouldn't think of it!" Kethry howled, tears pouring down her face. "You're doing so well by yourself!"

Enough is enough.

Tarma blocked another stroke, then poked the sot in the belly again—but *this* time with the sharp end of the broom.

The man's eyes bulged, and he folded over, dropping his sword and grabbing his ample belly.

Tarma ran around behind him and gave him a tremendous swat in the rear, sending him stumbling across the room—

—where he tripped and fell into the cold fireplace, his head meeting the andiron with a sickening *crack*.

Silence fell, thick as the heat, and Tarma got a sinking feeling in her stomach.

"Oh, hell." Tarma walked over to the fallen drunk and poked him with her toe.

No doubt about it. He was stone dead.

"Oh, *hell*. Oh, *bloody* hell."

The innkeeper appeared at her elbow as silently and mysteriously as he'd vanished. He looked at the shambles of his inn—and took a closer look at the body.

"By the gods," he gulped. "You've killed Lord Gorley!"

"Your husband may not have been much before Lady. But I'm afraid right now he's rather less," Tarma said wearily. Somewhat to her amazement, the innkeeper had *not* summoned what passed for the law in Viden; instead he'd locked the inn up and sent one of his boys off for Lady Gorley. Tarma was not minded to try and make a run for it—unless they *had* to. The horses were tired, and so were they. It *might* be they could talk themselves out of this one.

Maybe.

The Lady had arrived attended by no one—which caused Kethry's eyebrow to rise. And she wasn't much better dressed than a well-to-do merchant's wife, which surprised Tarma.

It was too bad they'd had to meet under circumstances like this one; Tarma would have liked to get to know her. She held herself quietly, but with an air of calm authority like a Shin'a'in shaman. A square face and graying blonde hair held remnants of great beauty—not ruined beauty either, just transformed into something with more character than simple prettiness.

She gazed dispassionately down on the body of her former Lord for several long moments. And Tarma longed to know what was going on in her head.

"I'm afraid I have to agree with your assessment on all counts, Shin'a'in," she replied. "I shan't miss him, poor man. Neither will anyone else, to be frank. But this puts us all in a rather delicate position. I appreciate that you could have fled. I appreciate that you didn't—"

"No chance," Kethry answered, without elaborating. She'd signaled to her partner that her damned ensorcelled blade had flared up at her the heartbeat after Lord Gorley breathed his last. Plainly his Lady would be in danger from his death. Just as plainly, Need expected them to do something about this.

"Well." Lady Gorley turned away from the body as a thing of no importance, and faced Tarma. "Let me explain a little something. In the past several years Kendrik has been more and more addicted to the bottle, and less and less capable. The Viden-folk took to bringing *me* their business, and when Kendrik hired that gang of his and began extracting money from them, *I* began returning it as soon as it went into the treasury. No one was hurt, and no one was the wiser."

"What about—" Tarma coughed politely. "Begging your pardon milady, but that kind of scum generally is bothersome to young women—"

She smiled thinly. "The men satisfied their lust without rapine. Kendrik knew *I* wouldn't stand for that, and *I* was the one who saw to his comforts. One week of doing without proper food and without his wine taught him to respect my wishes in that, at least. And the one time Kendrik took it into his head to abscond with a Viden-girl—well, let us just say that his capabilities were not equal to his memories. I smuggled the girl out of his bed and back to her parents as virgin as she'd left."

"So that's why—"

"Why none of us cared to see things disturbed," the innkeeper put in, nodding so hard Tarma thought his head was going to come off. "Things was all right. We'd warn travelers, and if they chose to disregard the warnings—" he shrugged. "Sheep was meant to be sheared, they say, and fools meant to share the same fate."

"So what's the problem?" Tarma asked, then realized in the next breath what the problem was. "Ah—the bullyboys. Without Kendrik to pay 'em and to keep his hand on 'em—"

Lady Gorley nodded. "Exactly. They *won't* heed me. I would be in as much danger from them as my people. We're farm and tradesfolk here; *we* would be easy prey for them. It will be bad if I keep them, and worse if I discharge them."

Tarma pursed her lips thoughtfully. "Your respect, Lady, but I've got no wish to take on a couple dozen bad cases with just me and my partner and less than a day to take them out. But maybe if we put our heads together—"

"You've got until moonrise," Lady Gorley said, handing a pouch up to Tarma that chinked as she looked inside before stowing it away in her saddlebag. Light streaming from the back door of the inn gave Tarma enough illumination to see that more than half the coins were gold. "That is really all the time we can give you. And I'm sorry I didn't have much to pay you for your discomfort."

"It'll be enough," Tarma assured her. "Now—you've got it all straight. At moonrise you raise the hue-and-cry after us; you offer fifty gold to the man who brings back our heads, and you turn the lads loose. They're going to hear the word 'gold' and they won't even stop to think. They'll just head out after us. You do realize this is going to cost you in horses. They'll take very good mounts in your stables."

Lady Gorley shrugged. "That can't be helped, and better horses than lives. But can you lay a trail that will keep them following without getting caught yourselves?"

Tarma laughed. "You ask a *Shin'a'in* if she can lay a trail? No fear, Lady, by the time they get tired of following—those that I don't lose once their horses founder—they'll have had second and third thoughts about coming back to Viden. They'll know that *you'll* never keep them on. They'll think about the King's men you've likely called in—and the good armsmen of your neighbors. And they'll be so far from here that they'll give it all up as a bad cause."

The innkeeper nodded. "She's right, Lady. They drifted in; they drift out just the same with no easy pickings in sight."

"What about that little rhymester?" Tarma asked, nodding back at the tavern door. They hadn't noticed the minstrel trying to make himself a part of the wall until it was too late to do anything about him.

"I'll keep him locked up until it's safe to let him go," the innkeeper replied. "If I know musickers, he'll have a long gullet for wine. I'll just keep him too happy to move."

"Very well—and the gods go with you," Lady Gorley said, stepping away from the horses.

"Well, Greeneyes," Tarma smiled crookedly at her partner.

Kethry sighed, and smiled back. "All right, I'll geas them. But dammit, that means *we* won't be seeing beds for months!"

Tarma nudged Ironheart with her heels and the battlemare sighed as heavily as Kethry had, but moved out down the village street with a faint jingling of harness. "Greeneyes, I didn't say you should geas them to follow *us* now, did I?"

"Then who—"

"Remember that loudmouth, Rory Halfaxe? The one that kept trying to drag you into his bed? *He's* in Lyavor, and planning on going the direction opposite of this place. Now if we double back and come up on his backtrail—think you can transfer the geas?"

* * *

Leslac slumped, nearly prostrate with despair. His head pounded, and he downed another mug of wine without tasting it. *Oh, gods of fortune—do you hate me?*

He couldn't believe what he had seen—he just *couldn't!*

First—that—*farce* with the broomstick. He moaned and covered his eyes with his hand. How could *anyone* make a heroic ballad out of *that?* "Her broomstick flashing in her hands—" Oh, gods, they'd laugh him out of town; they wouldn't *need* the rotten vegetables.

Then—that Lord Gorley died by *accident!* Gods, gods, gods—

"This can't be happening to me," he moaned into his mug. "This simply cannot be happening."

And as if that wasn't enough—the collusion between Gorley's widow and the other two to lure the bully-gang away without so much as a single *fight!*

"I'm ruined," he told the wine. "I am utterly *ruined.* How could they *do* this to me? This is *not* the way heroes are supposed to behave. What am I going to *do?* Why couldn't things have happened the way they *should* have happened?"

Then—*the way they* should *have happened—*

The dawn light creeping in the window of his little cubby on the second floor of the inn was no less brilliant than the inspiration that came to him.

The way they should *have happened!*

Feverishly he reached for pen and paper, and began to write—

"The warrior and the sorceress rode into Viden-town, for they had heard of evil there and meant to bring it down—"

BURNT OFFERINGS
by Mary Fenoglio

One of the simplest ways to make a sale to this anthology is to provide a break from the general humorlessness—not to say grimness—of most sword and sorcery fiction (and I read all the bad ones, as well as the ones I bring to you). This story, for some reason, touched my funny bone—thus giving the lie to all those people who say I have no sense of humor. My funny bone is hard to reach—I don't much care for slapstick—but it's there.

Mary Fenoglio says she, "has survived the wedding of a daughter," and is now a fifty-year-old mother-in-law. Her ambition is to become a member of SFWA, and, "after that I'll think of something."

Kallina's first sensation when she regained consciousness was pain; she hurt all over. It hurt to move, and breathing was an effort. She lay still, trying to remember where she was and how she got there. Her cheek was pressed against rough straw. The fetid odor told her that it wasn't clean stable straw, but a moldly layer of stuff which thinly covered the cold stone floor. She struggled to sit up and the world swirled eerily about her; sick and dizzy, she lay back down and closed her eyes. Pain gathered itself and concentrated into a solid throb in her head, and her tongue felt thick and dry. She thought longingly of clean, cold, flowing water, and managed to push herself to a sitting position against the wall, every muscle in her body screaming protest. Sitting with her eyes closed, she heard the click of a key in the iron lock and footsteps approaching. Men, from the sound of the steps; one man big but light on his feet, the other one big but clumsy, his feet shuffling on the stone floor. She kept her eyes closed.

"Is this the one?" A rough and unfamiliar voice, a hard hand gripping her face and turning it up, hot breath rankling in her nostrils. Kallina opened her eyes suddenly and they blazed blue-white into the sly eyes of her jailer. At the same moment she heard another voice reply. Her heart leapt with joy, for this voice was familiar. Lanzal!

"It could be. She's certainly dirty enough to be the one. Hard to say. Still, if she had my horse there can't be much doubt, can there? She seems a bit the worse for wear. What happened to her?"

"Fought like a wildcat, she did. Took me and two others to hold on to her. But I knew some gent 'ud come lookin' for that horse and the thief who took 'im, and there'd be a reward, no doubt."

"No doubt," said the big man in a voice like dry leaves. "Is that in addition to the reward you helped yourself to out of my saddlebags?"

"What reward is that? What saddlebags? I can't imagine what you mean, sir! If there's aught missing, here's your thief! Take it out of her hide, but don't look to me. I've done you a service, so I have—"

"Spare me your indignation. I'm in a hurry. Let's have her out." His eyes were dark and dangerous beneath his tousled auburn hair.

Kallina had climbed to her feet and stood swaying, eyes bright in her little pointed face. She lifted her chin imperiously and spoke grandly to the jailer.

"Yes, let's have me out."

"You'll be quiet, you piece of trash!" snarled the jailer, and sent Kallina spinning against the wall with a casual backhanded blow. The next instant he was thrash-

ing and gurgling, his eyes distended and his arms flailing helplessly as Lanzal's iron arm inexorably cut off
his wind.

"Have a little care," Lanzal growled. "She's but a
child, and a spindly one at that. Can you move?" This
last was addressed to Kallina, lying inert against the
wall. She heard, nodded, and struggled to her feet.

"Come on, come on, we haven't got till morning!"
snapped Lanzal, giving the wheezing jailer a final
squeeze that put him on the floor. "Here, let me carry
you." Kallina struck away the hands that reached for
her and staggered toward the door. Shaking his head,
Lanzal followed.

"Gazir is just outside," he said, coming up behind a
weaving Kallina as she stepped outside. "I trust you
can mount unaided?" So saying, he took up the reins
of the big bay horse and swung lightly into the saddle.
He looked down at a fuming Kallina. She was far too
sore and stiff to swing up behind him and he knew it.
He reached a big, hard hand down and closed it over
her hand and forearm. She came up light as chaff in
his grip and settled behind him. It felt natural and
good; they had traveled many miles like this.

The bay horse was eager to go. His long, ground-
eating stride unraveled the miles and Kallina dozed
against Lanzal's broad back, lulled to sleep by Gazir's
easy gait. When at last they stopped, she rolled limply
to the ground and lay there. Alarmed, Lanzal leaped
down and lifted her slight body, carrying her to a
sheltered place underneath some trees. She slept like
the exhausted child she was, and he covered her with a
blanket and made camp. She woke to the smell of
food, but more than that the sound of running water
drew her. Though she had drunk from Lanzal's
waterskin, she burned for cold fresh water, and she
followed the sound.

"Ho, she lives!" Lanzal said cheerfully from his seat
by the fire, watching her stagger back from the river.

"Just barely," Kallina replied. "I'm so sore, and I'm
starving, and I want to get rid of these filthy clothes,

but I haven't any others." She looked at Lanzal plaintively and he grinned.

"I can't help your aches much; you must have taken a real beating. But there's food, and I think I can help with the clothes. Come and eat something, then we'll see."

While she ate the good plain food, scarfing it down like a starving street waif, Lanzal watched her. She was small and delicate, her eyes brilliant blue in a face as pointed and sharp as a kit fox cub's. The wild mane of hair that bloomed around her head was so matted and filthy that its color was obscure, but her grimy hands were slender and fine and her carriage bespoke one who was accustomed to deference from those around her. She had offered no explanation for being with the band of traveling gypsies from which he had rescued her. He had come along just in time to save her a beating from their chieftain, but she would not even answer his direct questions. She was stubborn and disobedient, and had stolen his horse at their third camp and left him afoot to follow as best he could. Had he not appeared at the jail where she was being held as a horse-thief, she would have been sent to prison or worse, and she still wasn't talking.

"Are you ready to tell me who you are, and what you're doing out here all alone?" Lanzal demanded suddenly. His dark eyes bored into hers; plainly, he had had enough of mystery.

"Why are you deviling me with questions?" Kallina mumbled. "Haven't you known me long enough to trust me?"

"Trust you!" Lanzal exploded. "Trust a girl who had a whole tribe of gypsies chasing her with blood in their eyes, who stole my horse and left me afoot the first chance she got, and who hasn't told me anything except her name since we met? And even after I saved you from jail and a life that promised to be unpleasantly short, too. Trust you?"

"I see what you mean," Kallina said, putting down her plate. "But listen, you wouldn't believe me if I told you who I am. I promise you. I'm no thief or criminal. I just have to get back home, and then I can tell you everything. But until then you'll just have to trust me. I will tell you this; if you help me to get home, you won't be sorry." She gazed at him earnestly, her bright eyes pleading.

"I could have told you that!" Lanzal snorted. "I'll be glad to see the last of you, that's for certain. As for the rest of it, I'm tired of trying to pry it out of you. As long as we're traveling in the same direction, we'll travel together. If our paths take different ways, you'll take your path and I'll take mine. Agreed?"

Kallina nodded vehemently, her brilliant eyes sparkling. *Your path and mine are the same, my friend,* she thought. *You just don't know it yet.*

"—least you can do is clean up," Lanzal was saying. He stretched his long body out on his blankets and was almost instantly asleep. Kallina looked around at the untidy camp, the cooking mess and the scattered gear, and made a face.

"Bother!" she whispered to herself. "I want a bath in the river, and I haven't time to spend on this." She murmured a few words softly and things began to happen among the half-unpacked saddlebags; the strewn clothes and gear tucked themselves neatly away and the pans and plates came shining clean to rest in their panniers. The only things left out were a soft linsey shirt and a bit of soft soap from Lanzal's pack. Kallina smiled in satisfaction, cast a glance at the warrior who had begun to snore softly, and made her way at last down to the swift, cold current.

Lanzal woke with a start; he made it a practice, no matter how exhausted he was, not to sleep so soundly. A quick glance showed him no sign of Kallina, and he sat bolt upright with a curse. Gazir grazed peacefully nearby, and that relieved Lanzal somewhat, but he stood up to look anxiously around. Kallina had cleaned everything up beautifully, he saw; she hadn't taken off in haste as soon as he slept. Just before he began to call her, he saw a slight figure toiling up the slope from the river. A westering sun was behind it, but Lanzal didn't think it was Kallina; the wild mop of hair that floated around her head was missing, and there were no filthy rags fluttering about the thin body. Still, there was something about the carriage, the way the head was held—

"Kallina!" he called, and the small figure lifted an arm in acknowledgment. As she drew near, Lanzal realized that she wore one of his shirts; it hung nearly to her knees. As for her hair, she had haggled it off with his knife and it lay in tattered ruins. Her well-scrubbed face had a dusting of freckles showing under the redness left from the cold water and harsh soap, and she looked even younger than he had thought her to be. She stood before him, lost in his shirt, and smiled.

"I feel better now," she announced, "and quite fit to travel."

"Well, I don't," Lanzal replied gruffly. He half-turned away to hide the pang he felt at how young and vulnerable she looked. What circumstances could have led to a child like this being so far from home, and so alone? The last thing he needed was to be saddled with someone else's responsibility! "Gazir is tired; he needs rest and grazing. He doesn't go until I say so— understood?" Lanzal held Kallina's eyes with his own intense gaze until she nodded sheepishly.

"Now that we're traveling together, I won't try to take him again. It's just that I have to get home, and I haven't much time to do it," she said. Lanzal's brows quirked in a curious expression.

"Not much time?" he asked. "Why would there be a time limit on your getting home?"

"I can't tell you that now," Kallina said with an apologetic smile. "But I really haven't much time left."

"Well, the time we have now should be spent in resting," Lanzal said sternly. "Into your blankets and sleep; we'll be on the road early."

"I'll never sleep now," said the girl pleadingly. "I've slept already. I'll just sit by the fire awhile."

"Do as you like. Just do it quietly, for I mean to sleep." Lanzal rolled his back to her and was immediately asleep. He woke in the dark early morning to see

Kallina sitting hunched against the cold before a very dead fire, sound asleep. Snorting irritably, Lanzal struggled up, took up the sleeping girl, and laid her into her blankets. She smiled in her sleep and murmured something, but never woke.

Kallina opened her eyes to a dim gray morning; mist rose from the river and swirled about the base of the trees. Gazir was a ghostly shape stirring great eddies of fog about him as he moved, grazing placidly nearby. Birdsong came muted by the mist, though a pinking in the east promised a fair day. Kallina sprang up and her sore body reminded her not to move so quickly; she wanted to cook breakfast to prove to Lanzal that she could pull her weight. Taking up the flint and tinder box, she began to work on starting the fire. It had looked so easy when Lanzal did it, but she soon began to regret letting it go out the night before.

"Bother!" she muttered. "He'll be awake soon. I didn't know it was so hard to start a simple fire. This is stupid!" She cast a careful look at Lanzal; his tousled auburn hair stuck out from the blankets and nothing else showed. Kallina stood up and drew several deep breaths. In her mind she repeated the firestarter and then holding out one slim little hand, she spoke the words aloud. Her forefinger pointed at the dead ashes and a spout of flame roared up hot and bright. She nodded, satisfied. "Now that's more like it," she said to herself, and busied herself among the pots and pans.

"In the name of all that's holy, what is that smell?" roared Lanzal, coming out of his blankets in a rush. Kallina stood over the biggest campfire Lanzal had ever seen, a smoking pan in each hand and a bewildered expression on her flushed and sweating face.

"Your breakfast!" she snapped. "That's if I can figure out how to keep everything from burning. I never knew cooking was so complicated. It looks easy enough; I don't know what went wrong."

"Best to dump that mess in the river," Lanzal said, looking at the sorry contents of the smoking pans, "and hope it doesn't poison the fish."

"And then what do we eat?" Kallina demanded. Her healthy young appetite growled in her belly.

"Jerky, in the saddle," Lanzal snapped, and began to break camp. After Kallina had scrubbed the pans, chafing under Lanzal's watching eyes, she put them in the panniers, swung up behind him on Gazir, and they set out. Chewing morosely on the rough dried meat, she promised herself to do better next time. After all, no one had been concerned with teaching her to cook once they found out what she was capable of in other areas. Given all the things she could do, she was certain that it was only a matter of time until she was a great cook.

They rode most of the day; each was absorbed in thought and neither one had much to say. In the late afternoon Lanzal called a halt.

"We're not far from my home," he said as Kallina slid to the ground and wobbled around, trying to get circulation back into her legs. "I want to go in quietly, and in the dark. Rumors followed me all the way down south about a certain fellow who's been out to get me for some time. He wants my lands and holdings, which are considerable and lie next to his, and he thinks he's found a way to do it, so I hear. He has taken advantage of my absence to buy favor with the local officials. I need some time to scout the situation and formulate a plan of action before I confront him."

Kallina nodded absently, absorbed in her own thoughts. If Lanzal was about to become involved in a landowner's squabble, she might not get home within the prescribed time limit, and her whole ordeal would have been fruitless. Perhaps he would lend her a horse and send her on her way, yet even as she thought about it, she knew it wasn't likely. He thought she needed taking care of. If he knew what she'd already been through—well, she had stolen a horse once before; she could probably do it again. There was always a way, if one set one's mind to it and looked hard enough. Feeling more cheerful, she took out the cooking things and got to work. Lanzal, returning from a nearby stream with water, was astonished to see a blazing fire and a busy Kallina.

"You're some firebuilder, I'll say that for you," he said. "But you don't have to cook. I've been cooking on the road for a long time. I'll have supper ready before you can get started."

"I have gotten started," Kallina replied peevishly, "and I'm doing fine. There's just a little knack to it that I—oh, bother!" For the fat in the pan had caught fire and blazed up, threatening her hands and face, and she hurried away from camp to dump it out on a sandy mound and scuff dirt over it.

"Are you singed?" asked Lanzal anxiously. When he saw that she wasn't, he continued mildly, "Lucky you'd cut your hair or you'd have been in trouble. I think I'd better cook from now on. How is it that a girl as old as you hasn't the faintest idea of how to start a meal? My sisters all could cook by the time they were as old as you; at least they knew their way around a kitchen and could direct the scullery maids."

"And you think I look like a scullery maid?" Kallina asked hotly, scouring out the pan savagely.

"I don't know what you look like, unless it would be a lost kitten," Lanzal said. "You've chosen not to tell me who or what you are, but well-bred you are, for certain. Used to giving orders and not used to following them. Spoiled and headstrong. That's all I know."

"I'm no scullery maid," Kallina said grimly. "And I'm not spoiled and I'm not headstrong, and I will learn to cook. Nobody ever expected me to, that's all. I can do anything I set my mind to, and that includes a simple thing like cooking."

"All right," said Lanzal, seeing the determination stamped on her face. "Some women never get the knack of it, though, or so I'm told. Who never expected you to learn to cook?" He was not favored with a reply; Kallina's brow was wrinkled in concentration as she struggled to get the meal together. In due time she did so, and called Lanzal to come and eat.

"All that time and effort, and this is what came of

it?" he asked plaintively, surveying the plate she handed him. "I'd like to be a horse just now, and share Gazir's supper." Kallina threw him a withering glance and took a bite of her food. Astonishment, disappointment and disgust chased each other across her mobile face as the food hit her taste buds; she chewed briefly, swallowed hard, and managed a sour smile.

"Delicious," she croaked. Lanzal looked at her in silent awe, dumped his plate back into the pan, and took jerky and a piece of hard bread out of the pannier. Kallina downed half of her plateful of food, declared it tremendously filling, and left the rest to the wild things.

"That seems cruel to innocent animals," Lanzal remarked. "Perhaps we should have buried it." Before she could reply, he added hurriedly, "I'll wash up." They lay down to rest for a while before making the last leg of their journey.

Lanzal slept more deeply than he'd intended. Kallina always slept hard, her tired young body renewing its energy. So it was that neither of them heard the approaching horses, their hooves muffled in rags. Gazir scented them. Raising his head, he whickered softly at the smell of familiar men and horses. Here were no unknown enemies; he took no alarm when a man approached him and fastened a hand firmly over his nostrils, pinching off any further sound. Three other men crept into the camp, lit by a most peculiar fire that blazed evenly but seemed to consume no wood, and fell upon the two sleepers. Lanzal they clubbed into silence; Kallina they rolled out on the ground and stared at.

She stared back, as fluffed out and ruffled as a banty hen kicked off her nest. Her ragged hair stood out all over her head; Lanzal's shirt, worn belted with a leather thong during the day, swallowed her sparrow-thin little body. Ice-blue eyes blazed imperious and unafraid at the dark, silent men who ringed her. She put her hands on her hips and looked at each one in turn.

"What this, now?" one of them asked uneasily.

"There wasn't no mention made of no girl. What's we to do with 'er, now?"

"That's right," agreed another. " 'Twas only Lanzal we was to take. This here is trouble, no mistake."

There was a general head shaking and muttered conference, and almost before Kallina knew what was happening, they had thrown Lanzal's limp body across a shying Gazir and thundered off into the darkness, leaving Kallina alone with Lanzal's gear and the roaring fire.

"Now what?" she thought desperately. "If ever I was tempted—just one little spell—but I can't. I won't give in when I'm so close. There has to be another way. I just have to think of it."

She stowed the saddle and gear in the hollow of a great tree, keeping only a little packet with the last of the jerky and the waterskin, and set resolutely off in the direction the men had taken. Toward dawn the rumbling of a wagon coming up behind her sent her kiting into the bushes; peering out, she saw an old farm woman perched on the high narrow seat of a rickety cart drawn by an equally rickety old horse. It looked safe enough; Kallina ran out and flagged the old woman down and gave her such a sad story about running away from a brutal mistress that she soon had a ride into town. She shared the back of the cart with a squealing pig and several chickens going to market, but at least she made a little better time.

As they came into the first narrow streets, Kallina slipped out of the cart and made her way toward the square, trying hard to be invisible. When she arrived, she instantly knew where Lanzal was being kept; a small crowd of people milled about in front of a grimy building; gray and forbidding, it had only slits for windows and a heavy oaken door. It was still so early that the market hadn't opened, and anyway the mood of the crowd was wrong for a market crowd. Kallina saw dark faces and grim mouths among the men who gathered into little clumps, broke up and reformed, talking seriously together. She knew it must be Lanzal under discussion, and from their expressions it didn't look good for him.

Bother! she thought. *I'll never get home at this rate. He's gotten himself into real trouble, that redheaded giant. What am I supposed to do? I've got my own troubles. And he was helping me with them,* she thought guiltily, *when he got caught. This trouble isn't of his making. He took care of me, whether I wanted him to or not, and I owe it to him to help him now. Only how?*

One man standing near her spoke aloud to no one in particular, and Kallina looked around, startled.

"He's a good man, is Lanzal. He's fought many a battle for us in this town, and done a lot of good. It's not fair, what they're doing, and that's fact!"

"What are they doing?" asked Kallina apprehensively, and the man looked down at her in surprise.

"Why, they're goin' to hang him, little miss, tomorrow. 'Hang him for what,' says I when I heard it. 'For treason and crimes against the king,' they says. 'Hogwallow!' I says. There never was no hint of treason about Lanzal. I've knowed him all his life, and I know that!"

Kallina's blood had frozen in her veins at the man's first words, and she went so pale that he reached out a hand to her. But she stiffened regally and regarded him with cold blue eyes.

"Are you a friend of his, sir?" she asked quietly.

"I am that, and don't care who knows it!" he declared.

"Then will you help me to get him out of there before they hang him for nothing?"

"I will, and there be others who will help as well," the man replied eagerly.

"Good!" said Kallina decisively. "I think I have a plan. Is there somewhere we can go to talk?"

"Aye, my place is just a step up the street here. No one will bother us there."

They went into the little house together, and neither emerged for the rest of the day. Comings and goings there were, swift and furtive, all manner of men slipping in and out, but Kallina didn't reappear until evening. When she did, she bore a great tray covered with a clean cloth; the clink and rattle of dishes proclaimed it to be a supper tray. Her new found friend stood in the doorway of his house, a bemused expression on his face, as Kallina, laden with the tray, staggered and wove her way down the street to the jail.

"Ho, girl!" the burly guard challenged her sharply at the door. "Where do you think you're going?"

"I'm bringing Lanzal his supper," she said demurely.

"Supper, is it? And who might you be?"

"His niece, that's who. We've been traveling together, and I'm all he has to bring him supper on his last night." Her eyes filled with convincing tears; they were only partly faked. The guard flipped back the cloth with a grimy hand and his eyes brightened greedily.

"And what a supper you've brought!" he said. "Might be from the king's own kitchen, it looks that good."

"Do you think so?" Kallina dimpled prettily. "I'm sure there's enough for you and—anybody else who's in there." She peered around him curiously and saw two more big guards sitting inside the jail dicing. "Or maybe you've got supper coming. Something much better than this."

"No, no, one of us was going over to the inn later to get some stew. It's stew they have mostly, over there. At least, that's all we've money for. But if you've enough here for three more— "

"I made a lot," Kallina said. "And anyway, you could take it from me if you wanted, and Lanzal would never get a bite of it. I know that. So have some, and welcome."

"Aye, there'll be enough," came a rough voice from inside the room. "Not much appetite in the back cell, I shouldn't think." The three laughed hoarsely and Kallina's face pinked dangerously, but she held her tongue.

The three guards divided out the steaming food onto wooden plates produced from somewhere in the back and fell to hungrily. Kallina slipped down the short, narrow hallway to the cell where Lanzal lay disconsolately on a wooden shelf hung from the wall by a chain. He roused instantly when he saw her and came to the door swiftly. His big hands clenched on the bars as he brought his face down to her level; his eyes shone and a grin split his face.

"If it's not the little one!" he cried delightedly. "I'm glad to see you're all right. I've been lying here wondering what could have become of you, left all alone out there in the dark."

"I'm not afraid of the dark," she said pertly. "I've told you over and over, I can take care of myself. I didn't know I'd have to take care of you, too."

Lanzal straightened and frowned at that.

"Your tongue's as sharp as ever, I see," he said darkly."How did you get in here, and why did you come?"

"I've brought your supper," Kallina said in a loud voice "I worked on it all afternoon; I wanted it to be special, since it would be your last." She leaned closer to Lanzal and said softly, "At least, they think it will be your last."

Lanzal had lifted the cloth and was staring at the tray she held.

"And so it would, if I ate it," he muttered. "What is it, anyhow?"

"Mutton, potatoes, and onions," Kallina said indignantly. "And they have some, outside, and they love it."

"I can only wish it would poison them," Lanzal said wickedly, "and then you could get the key and I could—" The look on Kallina's face stopped him cold. "Kallina! You didn't! You'll hang with me for certain if you—"

"Poison? Me? Poison is the tool of the assassin," Kallina said in an offended tone. "Do you want your supper or not?"

"Thank you, no. I've trouble enough without weighting my belly with that. Are the guards really eating that—"

"Shhh!" Kallina hissed. "Yes, they are. And in a few minutes you're going to walk out of here with me, get on Gazir, and be gone."

"You mean it will make them sick that fast?" grinned Lanzal. Her ice-blue eyes burned into him.

"Is that the thanks I get?" she demanded.

"You'll get thanks in plenty," he assured her, "if your scheme—whatever it is—works and you can get me that key."

"Key? We don't need the key," Kallina said off-handedly. She stepped back from the door, put the rejected tray down on the floor, and closed her eyes for a moment. She spoke some words so swiftly and softly that Lanzal couldn't catch them, and then took hold of the door and swung it open. It creaked mightily, and the two of them froze, but there was no outcry from the guards. Stealthily they crept to the door and peeked into the outer room.

The three guards sat where Kallina had left them; one had his fork raised midway to his lips, one sat staring at his plate, and the other smiled bemusedly at the empty air in front of him.

"What's wrong with them?" asked Lanzal incredulously. "They look bespelled by something—or someone—" He looked down at the young girl beside him as if seeing her for the first time; looked past the thin young face and the haggled hair, deep into the startling blue eyes. "Who are you?" he asked quietly, and the manner of his asking was different than it had been.

"We haven't time now," Kallina said urgently. "It won't last long, and they'll be mad as hornets in a shaken nest when they come out of it. I'll tell you what you want to know as soon as I can, truly."

They hurried out the door; it was dusky dark, and the poor light fooled the eye. Gazir stood under the shadow of the jail, and at his head stood Kallina's collaborator with two or three other men. A quick handshake all round, a whispered promise of return and retaliation, and Lanzal was mounted, swinging Kallina up behind. He squeezed Gazir gently and the big horse eased out into the street; their passage went unnoticed since it was the supper hour and most folks were indoors. Once out of town, Lanzal pulled up and half-turned to face Kallina.

"You choose the way, little one," he said. "I said you'd have thanks in plenty, and the best thanks I can think of is to take you home."

"North," she said, leaning against his back comfortably. "North is home."

He nodded, turned Gazir's head due north, and squeezed him gently. The bay horse set off with his easy, rocking gait and Lanzal was silent for a time. Then he cleared his throat and spoke hesitantly.

"I'll find out who you are, sooner or later, I'm sure. I can bide my time. There is one thing, though. On the rest of this journey—I'll do the cooking."

Kallina grinned against the broad back.

"I was getting tired of doing it, anyway," she said.

RATSBANE
by Dorothy J. Heydt

Dorothy Heydt made her *S&S* debut in the second of these anthologies, with a story about the ancient world and the classical Greek sorceress Cynthia; since then there have been three or four Cynthia stories and judging by the mail I get, there ought to be a lot more.

Sooner or later, I suspect, these stories will make it into a novel; I at least will be glad to have them collected in one place.

Like most of our writers, Dorothy combines writing with raising a couple of articulate and brilliant kids; they are being brought up the right way; as compulsive readers, and science fiction fans.

"Open the window," Cynthia said.

"No, don't," the alewife said. "You'll let her spirit escape."

"It's escaping anyway," Cynthia said. "We'll let it go freely, and not linger in this stench."

The boy unlatched the shutters set into the outer wall, and pushed them outward. There was a grating sound of wood against the rough brick, and light poured in: the tarnished golden light of late afternoon. It was not long till sunset. The smell of seaweed and rotting fish began to overlay the smell of death.

"Ah, that's better," the old witch said. "Farewell,

Cynthia. I wish we could have known each other longer; I'd have taught you more. Still, I've taught you what I could. You practice, eh? I've given you the fire-starting, and the ink-bowl, and the shape . . ." Her voice stopped. Her expression did not change, except that there was nothing left behind it. Cynthia closed her eyes. The alewife, who was her daughter, began to cry.

"Goodbye, Xanthe," Cynthia said, and sighed. They had begun as enemies, ended as friends, but to lose enemies and friends alike was the way of the world. *What are we? What are we not? Man is only a dream of a shadow*. "Come," she said aloud. "If you'll bring water and linens, I can help you lay her out before I go. I have other patients to see this evening."

They washed the fragile old body, and wrapped it in a linen sheet that Xanthe's daughter fetched from her chest: part of somebody's dowry once, maybe, or (equally likely) the remnants of a successful theft.

"What's the time?"

"Sunset," Cynthia said. Red light was pouring in the window. "Isn't it? Surely we haven't been here all night."

"And the moon's in the last quarter," the alewife said. "She'll go out with the turning of the tide."

"Go where?"

The alewife shrugged, and smiled crookedly. "She never told me things like that."

The boy Perikles, Xanthe's grandson, followed Cynthia down the rickety steps that led to the inn's common room. "You're not going out now, are you? It's getting dark."

"Don't worry," she said. "I've been coming down here every day; the people know me. Half of them think I'm a witch, the other half, a physician; nobody's going to meddle with either one. I haven't any money, and nobody's going to strike me down for my beauty."

"Don't be so sure," Perikles said with a grin. He must be thirteen or fourteen now, small for his age but clever. "When you smile—and I've seen you smile— you're not nearly so bad as you think. If you insist on going out, I think I'd better teach you how to use a knife."

"I've used one," Cynthia said. "Don't worry about me." She found she was leaning against the door frame, her eyes closed. "Sorry," she said, brushing a wisp of hair out of her face. "It's all right, Perikles. I'm just tired. I'll see you tomorrow maybe."

She made her way into the common room. Xanthe's son-in-law broke off a long shapeless discussion with a couple of Neapolitan sailors to offer her a beaker of wine, and refuse the coin she offered as payment.

The room was close and dark, and could have benefited by having its own shutters opened—but most of the clientele would have objected. They were here having, as it were, their breakfast, preparing for the night's day that was dawning: footpads, night-climbers, street-walkers of every shape and kind. They paid no attention to Cynthia, nor she to them: as she'd said, they knew her.

It was because the man was looking at her that Cynthia noticed him, caught the bright gleam of eyes in the corner of her own eye. She shifted her position slightly, and contemplated the man without really looking at him.

A dark-haired, black-bearded fellow with a squint, maybe forty years old. Staring at her, with a little smile. Somebody she knew? As a child she'd spent a lot of time on Alexandria's waterfront, playing with the boys as a boy, her hair bundled up under a turban, until time and sudden growth had made that impossible. And her unrecognizable, she would have thought; so where did this man know her from? If he did?

(A dark squinting fellow with an irritating little smile, wrapped in a cloak that was dirty now, and nibbled around the edge by rats, but once had been expensive. Something glinted at his throat—)

She finished her wine and set the beaker down. "No, no more, thank you. I have other patients to see." She turned to go. (The smile widened. The fellow had long yellow front teeth, and he thought something was funny. That shape at his neck was a piece of hammered copper, cut out into a circle and a triangle, a shape she'd seen: it was just at the edge of her memory.) She gathered her cloak round her and left the inn.

Outside, the shadow of the western mountains had fallen over the island, and Hesperus was bright overhead. She would go to see Daphne next, whose longshoreman husband had fallen to the plague and would die tonight, or tomorrow. The house was not far away: she had the choice of going directly there, through an alley favored by rats, or round three sides of a square, along the docks. Here were two houses, each leaning to the right, so that Cynthia must do the same to go between them; and here was a pair of steps that looked rotten but weren't, and here was the waterfront.

There was a ship in, that hadn't been in this morning. Long nose, graceful lines, an Alexandrian ship maybe? (Maybe that ratty-looking fellow in the inn *had* been someone she knew!) She walked up alongside it, where the slatted gangplank stretched from ship's side to dock. Men were filing up and down in two steady streams, offloading amphorai of wine and ingots of copper and raw glass.

Oh, yes, it was an Egyptian ship for sure. Crouched on the gunwale, licking its paw and rubbing its ears, was a cat.

"Hello, cat," Cynthia said, and the cat looked at her and stretched itself into half again its length. "Pusht, pusht," she coaxed, and the cat leapt onto the gangplank. It slipped between the men's busy feet, and came down to have its ears rubbed, purring with a rumble deep as the wheels of a cart going by in the next street.

Cynthia hadn't seen a cat in years. In the old days, before Alexander's conquest, the cats had been sacred to the old gods, and to take one out of Egypt was punishable by death. Even now, under the enlightened rule of the Ptolemies who cared not what business you did so long as the royal treasury got its cut, not many cats had made their way to other countries, not yet.

Its tawny fur was tinted red by the last rays of the

sunset, and there was a thin black line all the way around its mouth. When it yawned, its mouth opened wide, showing an impressive collection of fangs and looking like a tiny lioness.

"Good evening," said the shipmaster from the rail above. "What brings you here?"

"I'm a physician," Cynthia said. "There's sickness hereabouts."

The shipmaster made a sign against evil. "What kind?"

"I don't know," she said. "I've never seen it before this month, down here on the docks. A waterfront is a bad place for illness, you know that; there are the ships bringing in new diseases from elsewhere—no offense to your vessel, sir; you've just arrived—and then the people live cheek-by-jowl and catch everything from one another. And this is something new. The black spots in groin and armpit, the stiff swollen joints—I've never seen it before, nor read about it either."

"And do they recover? or do they die?"

"Mostly they die. I've had only two survive so far, both healthy young women without children. They're helping me nurse the rest."

"Ah," the shipmaster said. "Here's something you should know. There's talk in the ports that the men of Carthage are bringing force against the Hellenes of Sicily, trying to make them give up some of the disputed cities between here and Lilybaion. And men say—mind you, this is only tavern talk—men say they've got a he-witch to cast spells for them, to bring about by magic what they can't achieve by war."

Cynthia stood very still. "Is there anything said as to what the man looks like?"

"None."

"But he's one of their own? a Phoenician?"

"I believe so."

That was what she had seen in the tavern, around the neck of the rat-faced man: circle for head, triangle for gown, and hidden among his chest-hairs the little stick-fingered arms. The sigil of Tanit, charmless queen of the Phoenicians' sourfaced gods. "I think I've seen him. Thanks for your news, shipmaster. Goodbye, puss." She gave the cat's ears another rub, for luck, and turned back in the direction of the tavern.

"Good fortune," the man called after her.

She stopped short in the shadow of the skewed house. The tavern's door was open, and three men were coming out. Two went one way, one the other: and he was the rat-faced Carthaginian. He was smiling still, and he vanished into the alley without taking any notice of Cynthia. Silently she followed.

There was a place between the roofs of houses where the sky showed, and the last of the sunset cast a square patch of red light on the ground. The man stood there, stripping himself naked; he folded his clothes into a little bundle and tucked the medallion with the sign of Tanit into the midst of it. He put the bundle next to a wall, out of the skylight and out of the way of traffic. He looked up into the darkening sky, and kissed his hand to it, and murmured a few words. And vanished. There was nothing alive in the patch of dim light but a long-tailed rat.

It was bigger than any rat Cynthia had seen, and lighter in color (though it was hard to tell in the ruddy light). It ran its forepaws briefly over its whiskers, and switched its tail back and forth. Then it scuttled out of the light, through a hole in a wall and out of sight.

Shape-changing, Cynthia thought. Xanthe had taught her the words, if she could but remember them. The words were the same for any act of changing; you had to fix your mind on the shape you wanted to take. A terrier, she thought, would do nicely: about two years old, with nice sharp teeth, small enough to follow through the hole in the wall, big enough to put paid to the rat. She thought of a terrier, and said the words.

And nothing happened. Cynthia bit her lip. Had she misremembered something? She thought not. Xanthe had drilled her carefully, seeming to hold no grudge that Cynthia had defeated her—

Defeated her with the aid of Arethousa's ring. That was the answer! The gift of the nymph, patroness of

Syracuse—it had faded from its original black to a
silvery color that reflected her skin and made the ring
very hard to see—it shielded her from the effects of
others' spells, why not her own? She twisted it off her
finger, laid it between her feet, and said the words again.

A day or so after she came to Syracuse, she had
come down with a flux that had melted all her inward
parts into glutinous mush, bubbling slightly (over a
low fire, so to speak) and threatening to slosh over the
sides of its container. Now her whole body seemed to
flux, arms and legs and trunk flowing like water, and
she could feel her back stretching out like dough in the
baker's hands, stretching out into a long supple tail.

Her face was in shadow, she could not see. In mo-
mentary panic she clawed at whatever it was, and
scrabbled for a way out. Something clinked against a
stone, and she was free. (*I forgot to take my clothes
off,* she realized.) There was the hole in the wall, as
large as she was now; she leapt through it and down
the narrow side-yard behind the wall, following the rat.

As she might have suspected, the world was full of
smells, rich and provocative: fish, mud, rot, salt, stale
straw somewhere; lentils cooked with onions, some
human's dinner; and twisting through them all, a clue
thick as a rope, the musty stink of the rat.

At first she thought her sight had also improved.
What had been deep night to her human eyes was cool
twilight now, enough to find her way between the
houses and over the rough ground. But she had lost
something in clarity; all the edges were fuzzy, and the
red light of the setting sun had gone gray.

She could hear every mouse's squeak, every cricket's
chirp, and the distant rumbling of the people's voices
within the houses, the scuttling of the rat's claws as
she came up close behind it—

It had taken her that long to realize what she was
not hearing. Her own paws were silent, that should
have clicked against stone and scraped against wood.
She looked down. Her forepaws were blunt and
rounded, the claws nowhere to be seen. She raised a
paw and flexed it; needle-sharp claws sprang out of

the toes. Her long tail lashed against her flanks; her back was long and supple. *Xanthe was right; I needed practice.* She'd *thought* she'd been thinking of a terrier, but somewhere along the line her mind had wandered and she was no dog now, but a cat.

I could easily have done worse. (The rat was standing on its hind legs, its body stretched up against a wall, its forepaws feeling along the edge of a shutter, seeking a weak spot. Finding none, it fell to all fours again and ran along the wall's edge. There was a door ahead that stood just a nose's-width ajar.) Cats, after all, had earned not only their keep but a place in Egypt's pantheon by keeping down the mice in the granaries. A rat was just a larger mouse. . . . Except that this was a disturbingly large rat, and the cat she had become was smaller than the dog she'd hoped to be. It would be no easy few minutes' work, to leap in, shake the beast till its neck broke and trot away again. She could still kill it, she thought, but it was going to be much more like even odds.

Belatedly she recognized the place, not from its appearance so much as from its smell: mussel broth, and bread and onions, and the heavy smell of sickness, and the sulfur candle burning on the hearth: it was Daphne's house. Inside she could hear the sick husband's voice, bewildered and irritable with fever, and Daphne's voice as she called on all the gods by turns and tried to soothe him. The rat had got its nose inside the door; where its head could go its body could follow. She leaped toward it, and got her claws into its backside long enough to drag it out.

The rat rolled over twice, fetched up against the opposite wall, and landed on its feet. Its eyes were big and black, and they sized up the cat in a glance: bigger than the rat, but softer. It snarled. Cynthia silently called on Bast, who had been a war-goddess as well as a cat in the days when men still believed in her, and crouched to spring.

It was a good leap, for a beginner, but the rat slipped aside and she hit the ground nose first. Before she could get her feet under her, its teeth closed on the scruff of her neck.

As a girl she had dreaded rat bites; they festered and took long to heal—and to go to her father for a poultice was to invite a dressing-down for having been on the docks in the first place. Now her thick fur made the bite no more than a painful pinch. She hunched her shoulders and tossed like a Cretan bull, and the rat flew over her back and lost its grip. She scrambled round to face it as it attacked again, hit it broadside with claws extended, and knocked it sprawling.

Again it charged, and again she knocked it base-over-apex. The rat regained its feet a stone's cast from her and sat glaring while it caught its breath.

She had seen a cat playing with a mouse often enough: bat, bat, bat till the mouse was exhausted or until someone intervened and brained the wretched thing with a rock. Otherwise, not infrequently, the cat would tire of the game and let the mouse crawl away to die or recover at its own convenience. It served well enough in the long run: what one cat spared, another killed, and among them they kept the mice down. But it wouldn't do here. The rat must die here and now, or go free to spread the plague, and there was not another cat in Syracuse.

(Except the one on the ship—but she daren't take time to go off and recruit it, even assuming she could get the message across.)

So she sprang again, teeth and claws bared. The rat dodged, but not quickly enough. She pinned it to the ground and her teeth sought its neck. The rat squirmed and kicked and broke free again, but she tasted pungent blood: she had marked it at least. The rat darted away between the houses, and Cynthia bounded after it. She opened her mouth to shout "Hellas and Alexandria!" but nothing came out but a caterwaul. With that scent in her nostrils, she could follow it from here to Lilybaion—

She turned a corner and stopped hastily. A householder's midden lay against the wall, reeking with unnameable smells—and a dozen rats roamed over it, foraging. The blood smell led here; her prey was one of the dozen, but how was she to tell it from the others? If she could get in among them she could pick it out by scent, but the rats weren't about to let her. They had drawn closer together, shoulder to narrow shoulder across the midden, teeth bared, eyes glistening.

One of the rats turned to its neighbor and sniffed; sniffed again, and licked. Another rat nudged its way in from behind, and licked, and snapped: teeth flashed, and a rat squealed. Its fellows all turned toward it like a school of fish toward a bit of dropped bait, and squealing the wounded rat burst out of their midst, torn ear bleeding afresh, before they could eat it alive. *Fine lot of friends you've got*, Cynthia thought as she ran after it. *Just when you need their help, they turn on you. I've known people like that.*

They had left the wharfside alleys, and were running southwest through a better class of streets. Cynthia had the edge on speed, but the rat was running for its life, and she gained on it only gradually. Neither animal was built for long-distance running, and both were tiring. *When I was in Persepolis,* the old joke ran, *it was so hot that I saw a jackal chasing a hare, and they were both walking.* It might come to that soon.

It was fitting, perhaps, that the rat turned at bay at the rim of Arethousa's fountain. Cynthia approached cautiously; it wouldn't do to pollute the spring by throwing the rat into it. She raised her paw to knock it sideways, but the rat leaped up and sank its teeth into the pad. Pain shot through her foreleg, and she jerked backward, but the rat did not let go. She could not shake it loose. The pain made it hard to think, but—

It was like working out a problem in logic, at dream-slowness, underwater at the bottom of a sack. If she couldn't put the rat away, she could bring it closer. She pulled it in—slowly, taking time to aim—and sank her teeth into its neck.

After a dozen cat-heartbeats the rat squeaked and let go. Cynthia hung on. The rat thrashed about, and scrabbled with its little claws against the ground, but to no effect. Cynthia hung on. She hadn't a dog's muscle, to shake the rat till its neck broke, but between pain, rage, and desperation she felt she could hold on forever. If she held on till morning, some man might come along and kill the rat with a stick.

It didn't take that long. The rat made one last desperate leap, and when Cynthia brought it down to the ground again, its body twisting, there was an audible snap. The rat shuddered and lay still.

Then its flesh began to move, slowly, like bubbles rising in yeast. Cynthia dropped the rat and sprang back in uncatly alarm. The hairs were falling out of its skin; the tail shriveling, the hind legs stretched out. She had heard tales, from time to time, of shapechangers who regained their proper form after death, and Xanthe had said something about it, but none had warned her it would be so slow.

The body was the size of a newborn babe now, and swelling visibly. If she started now, she might be able to drag the corpse to the shore and drop it into the sea before it became too heavy to shift. On the other hand, if the Punic sorcerer had had confederates in Syracuse, it would give them pause to find his body lying bloated and naked with the teethmarks of a huge cat in his neck—

And besides, she didn't want to touch the thing again. Her paw stung. She sat down and licked it for a few minutes, then rose and began to limp away. She would return to the privacy of the dark alleys and change back—

She stopped in her tracks, paw in midair. How was she to change back if she couldn't speak? The word of unbinding was a simple one, only four syllables, but a cat's mouth could not shape them. She tried, nonetheless, yowling in the dark air till "A-ma-wa-wa" echoed back from the nearby houses and a human somewhere flung open a window and hurled a broken pot in her general direction.

"Over here," someone said in a drink-thickened voice. A small group of men was approaching, five or six of them with three torches among them. Looking for her? No, no, they were returning from a party; she could smell the expensive perfumed wine from where she sat. "Here it is," the man in the lead said, and squatted to hold his torch near her. "I told you it was a cat." He rubbed under her chin with his free hand, and Cynthia found herself purring.

"My mother had a cat once," the drunken man went on. "She called him 'Thoth-Autolykos, Prince of Thieves,' and I called him 'Stinky.' This one looks just like him. Ho, Stinky, you want to go to a party? I don't suppose you drink wine, but you could have a fish. Squid in lobster sauce? Sparrows broiled in anchovy paste? Nothing too good for my friend Stinky—"

The man lost his balance and fell over on his rump. He flailed his arms, holding his torch higher, and that was when he saw what lay beyond Cynthia. The words he shouted were garbled, and his companions laughed, till they saw what he was pointing at. Then they screamed, and hauled him upright, and ran away in a clatter of feet. Cynthia could hardly blame them. She licked her paw again, and took a wide path round the twitching corpse, down the pathway to the base of the spring.

She dipped her paw into the water, and watched as one glistening drop fell back into the pool. *O Arethousa, help me,* she said in her heart. But there was no answer.

No more than she had expected, really; the gods had been going out of the world for a long time. A threat to her adopted city had been enough, once, to rouse Arethousa and bring her close enough to speak across the boundary between the worlds. No longer.

But she had left Cynthia the ring, which had seemed to keep at least some of its power. Maybe the ring would break the spell and let her change back—if she could find it. She climbed slowly up to the street level and hobbled back to the waterfront.

She heard Daphne's voice as she passed her door, giving thanks to Apollo All-Healer and to his sister Artemis and to Arethousa. Her husband was mending then; as Cynthia had hoped, the plague-spell had not survived its maker. And let the silent gods have the credit that should have gone to Cynthia—or to Xanthe. Neither had any need of glory now.

She would go and make a search for the ring, though it had been lying in the alley for hours for every passing thief to find, and she had no real hope of finding it again. She would go and make a search, and then she would come back and make her living as a cat.

It wasn't so hard a life, if one took it like a philosopher. She could get used to the taste of raw mouse, and if she didn't it was no matter. She'd known plenty of cats that lived on a diet of human food, better fed than many men; as a child she'd had a cat that ate fruit, cheese, and garlic bread (and anything else, so long as you were eating it and it wasn't supposed to have any). And people would scratch her ears and rub her under the chin and stroke her from head to tail. Nobody ever did that while she was human.

She would go and live with Daphne, maybe, who was a kindly soul; or make the venturesome journey up the Epipolai to Xenokleia's house, keep the mice down in the granary. There were no other cats about, of course. If ever she wished to have kittens, she would go back to Alexandria—or (remembering the prickly business end of a tomcat, and his tooth-and-claw style of lovemaking) maybe she wouldn't.

But she found the ring; she found it by the musky human scent of the clothes that had fallen upon it. She could smell fatigue, and fear, and the mutton stew that she had eaten for dinner many hours before.

And a trace of something else. To cat-Cynthia it was clear that human-Cynthia had been without a mate too long, and a grain of cat-sense would have sent her in search of a lover, even the little Demetrios for want of anything better. Yet she hadn't done so. Humans: their ways were strange and unreasonable, their lives complicated beyond all cat-logic. Maybe she'd do better to stay a cat: take ship to Alexandria where the granaries were plump with mice, the streets lively with toms, and kittens could be loved for a few months and weaned by the simple expedient of walking away when it was time. . . .

But all the time she was thinking this, she went on nosing through the pile of clothing till she found the ring, cold to the touch and smelling sharply of human, iron, and ice. She put her paw to it, but the toes were too wide to fit through. So she lifted it with her tongue and took it into her mouth.

Again the feeling of flux, the rippling and changing along her flesh, like the unchancy metamorphosis of the Punic sorcerer but notably faster. (He must be nearly man-sized by now, and a nasty surprise for the Punic spies and the rest of humanity when they found him in the morning.)

Day was breaking. The fresh breeze of dawn was beginning to rise, clammy cold over her bare skin; she transferred the ring from her mouth to her finger and dressed as quickly as she could. She left the sorcerer's clothing where it lay, for thieves to make a shallow profit on or mice to nest in; the sigil of Tanit she lifted gingerly by its neck-cord and carried at arm's length toward the waterfront. She'd drop it into the sea, so that none could put it to an ill use.

A single ring of ripples, smudged out by the waves. She turned her back on the night's work and walked back to the Egyptian ship.

The men were still filing up and down the gangplank, going away empty-handed now and returning with jars of oil and crates of salted fish. The ship would be ready to sail on the next tide. The cat still sat in the prow, licking its forepaw. Cynthia looked at the palm of her own hand; it was unmarked. "Now, I wonder," Cynthia said to it. "How did you come by that paw? Was I some other cat, or was I you?" The cat stopped licking for a moment, and stared at her out of great topaz eyes. Then it yawned, and began licking again. As one of the poets has said, no cat ever gave anyone a straight answer. Cynthia saluted it, and rubbed its ears, and turned away to climb the cliff-road to the Epipolai. The sun's red arc had just broken the gray line of the horizon.

WOLF HUNT
by Bobbi Miller

If there are themes to these volumes, one would have to be wolves; every year I find myself buying several stories with lupine themes. This year we have three "wolf" stories; this one, Mary Choo's "Wolfrunner," and Gemma Tarlach's "Black Wolf." I have for a long time loved these much-maligned animals, perhaps because the most beautiful member of our household is Signy; a beautiful part wolf, part German Shepherd and part Malemute dog. She is more loving and loyal than any usual dog, and far more timid; rather than fierceness, these fine animals are remarkable for their timidity. Anyone who is still brainwashed by tales of, "the big bad wolf" should read Farley Mowat's splendid true story *NEVER CRY WOLF*—to which the movie, though good enough in its way, did not begin to do justice—or his even better *A WOLF IN THE HOUSE*. Signy has only one major fault; when Lisa and I are both away at once; she refuses to eat, and simply lies in the garden and howls; so when we travel at the same time, we have to "send her home to Grandma" to her breeder, who is also a writer for this anthology; Dana Kramer-Rolls. Signy loves to "go home to Mommy" for a few days.

I don't know how much experience Bobbi Miller has with real wolves; but this might serve as notice that—almost alone among fantasy fans—I am a dog person, not a cat person. I am fond enough of cats; but I love dogs this side of idolatry.

Isabeau narrowed her eyes against the drizzle and squatted, hunter-fashion. She measured the depth of the spoor with her index finger and inhaled sharply. Leaning against her staff, she straightened slowly, shrugging the quiver into a more comfortable position against her back. Her weathered gray tunic and breeches blended into the greenland. Despite layers of wool underneath and a heavy overtunic roped to a snug fit, she still felt the cold. Her boots were of deerhide, fur side out, and sank into the wet muck of the forest floor.

Her lean frame moved with the intense energy of a fighter. Even as she examined the woodland, every move was calculated, determined, effortless. She stroked the rowan staff, searching the wood. The drizzle had drenched everything, the night's cold cast an icy mantle. The vegetation was losing its lifeblood again, tingeing gray with the passing of autumn. Hidden in the brittle branches and thicket were more of the woodland secrets—a twig showed white, snapped in swift flight, and black hairs were snagged on the thicket.

She braced herself against the wind, following the spoor's lead. Her hunter's eye plucked another fixed in the mud two strides in front of her.

"Demonshit," she muttered, taken aback with the size of the depression. Her lips thinned bitterly. Maybe this would be the end of it. She sighed, tired. Destiny had clawed at her features: her high cheeks gaunt, her brows pushed forward in a perpetual frown. Even the light in her blue-green eyes glowed with a hard glint.

She had moved quickly enough, across the stone ridge outlining the horizon, then down into the high grassland, circumventing the marshy lake. Despite losing her journeypack to the bog, and blunting her short blade hacking through the bramble, she reached the forest without incident just after sunrise.

She looked over her shoulders, catching the blur cresting the hill in the distance.

So, she smiled slyly, he had kept up with her through the distance after all.

Carefully she lined her step exact with her prior footfall, backtracking a few strides. Then she lunged for a hollow in the underbrush, so light the leafy carpeting didn't expose their moist dark undersides. Then she shucked the bow and quiver.

She waited, the staff aglow.

Eventually the man came along. He stopped, hunched over, his lungs stinging for the want of air.

"Blasted bitch," he muttered, wiping the sweat from his brow, not realizing she crouched three lengths away. "Demons guide your feet." He searched the ground, finding the wolf spoor near her footfall. He inhaled sharply, forced his breath to even, and focused again on the woman's track. He took another step and the trail seemed to disappear.

Too late he realized what she had done.

She erupted through the brush, thrusting the staff's end out hard. The man jumped aside. The staff caught his thigh sharply.

He recovered quickly, the hunter noted dryly, as the man regained his footing. Even beneath the heavy cloak of furs, she discerned him to be a burly man.

"Isabeau," his thick lips turned back in a derisive smile, one hand spread-fingered, ready to grab as the other weaved a hunter's blade in the air in front of him.

The man lunged. Isabeau sidestepped the attack easily, noticing the other's reach. His advantage lay only with his sheer mass, his movements were random and clumpsy.

She allowed him to close, but just enough. She dodged, pivoting to face him directly. The man pressed the attack, his rage emitted with a growl as, again, Isabeau evaded the attack. Her staff, alive with the witchfire, slapped his ear. He yelped in pain and surprise. Before he gathered his senses, she shoved the staff out again, striking his arm. The witchflame seared it useless, his blade dropped earthbound. She gave the rowan another thrust, the staff bit at his knees. As the man folded, she clipped his chin, and the man sprawled onto his back.

The stench of seared flesh and smoldering fur filled their noses. The man struggled to his knees, slapping at the cinders in his cloak. Raising his head, he met her glare.

"You hunt the wolf?" she asked dispassionately.

The man shook his head, swallowed convulsively.

"That's good." She kicked his blade beyond his reach.

"I sought Isabeau instead," he grimaced, his chin thrust up in defiance. He cradled his blade arm. "It seemed the easier of two demons and the bounty is the same."

She remained taut, allowing him to rise.

"Take those furs off," she demanded, stepping back. When the man hesitated, she struck his cheek with the staff. He screeched.

"The furs," she repeated through gritted teeth. He fumbled, then threw the cloak aside, his eyes darting between Isabeau and the staff.

"Now the boots."

She smiled inwardly, watching the man skitter out of sight, thinking of the stories he'd tell at his fire tonight—if he survived the cold. It would keep others away, if only for a few days, and give her time to finish her task. Retrieving quiver and bow from the brush, she turned and trotted into the forest, the rowan staff cool in her grasp.

The great oaks towered upright, full of themselves, the trunks with a circumference of five men with arms outstretched. Silver birch and ash vied for the light and rain that managed to penetrate the twisting oak canopy. Toadstools thrived at their roots and along the rutted ground she walked. The air smelled of mildew, mold, and decay.

She recognized this as the most ancient part of the forest, suddenly heedful of the tales of travelers, hunters, and wanderers entering these woods and becoming lost forever. She looked up, trying to see the sky. It was midday, the sun should be at its height. But it was dark where she walked, in the shadows of the oaks.

Soon enough she came upon an oak with a gnarled trunk, its roots heaved up and twisted around rock. Fresh water welled up and spilled over the granite, rambling farther down an incline to form a pond below.

She slowed to a near standstill, tense, her eyes darting around her, seeing everything. A skull, brown-stained in antiquity, was embedded high in the trunk, eyeless sockets staring out at her.

She gave a wide berth to the area, swallowing, looking over her shoulder to the skull. She was well enough versed in ancient knowledge to recognize that this oak had been marked by someone with great power. It claimed this part of the forest as its own. The fanatic may have long departed this place, but it made her nervous all the same.

. Long after midday, she came upon the hut. Just as the clouds pulled apart to allow the sun to penetrate the tangled canopy, the timber opened into a small glen. The low structure nestled serenely in its remoteness. Age had already taken its toll on the moss-ridden stone walls. Above the door and window hung thick, drooping eaves of thatch, with sparrows flickering from beneath. Smoke drifted in a thin, winding wisp from the stone chimney.

She approached cautiously, staying in the shadows, circling the structure in search of its resident.

She found him near the front, chopping wood. The druid turned to face her as she stepped into view. A rope belting the tattered cloak revealed the lean, wide-shouldered, figure beneath. She expected an old man, and was surprised, mildly so, as he turned back his cowl. Not too many years her senior, a brooding sternness had chiseled his features. Heavy brown hair waved back from a high forehead and brushed his collar. His eyes, an amber intense enough to burn through her, met her gaze.

"A traveler?" he asked in a voice more like a whisper. He was not tall, not even a head above her own. He spied her bow. "Or a hunter?"

"Both, of sorts," she saw the flash of disbelief as he realized her gender. "You say many come this way?"

"Very few travelers," he came closer, his arms now buried in the robe's wide sleeves and folded across his chest, "Too many hunters. But never a witch." He regarded her staff with a nod, recognizing the white rowan wood.

"I'm no witch," she relented with discretion, remembering the skull in the twisted oak. "It was a gift. It comes in handy at times."

" 'Tis a strange time we live in," the man chuckled. For a moment his features softened, almost pleasantly. "A non-witch carries witch wood. And a non-druid lives in a druid sanctuary. Laurent, I am."

Both looked up as gray clouds suffocated the sunlight once more, and thunder rumbled in the distance. Crows dipped and dove in, swarmed in the oak grove edging the clearing, their harsh caws irritating her.

"They seek something," she watched them momentarily, the staff burning in her palm.

"The rain comes," Laurent's expression darkened. "I've a fire and stew. You're welcome to share them until the rain subsides."

She remembered this quiet from once before, in an inn on the edge of another forest. The air was so still, so heavy it was hard to breath. The light within had been just as cool and shadowless, even though fire burned in the hearth. Her spine tingled. This was more than a druid's safehouse. Like that long-ago night when she entered the inn, she became aware her life was not her own, that she was being manipulated to play out a role.

Inside, a worktable flanked the wall, scrolls were unrolled and scattered at one end with a mortar and pestle harboring the other end. Bunches of dried herbs and onions suspended from the ceiling beam. Nearby shelves were stuffed with crockery jars, some spilling out onto the floor. Greens soaked in a basin of water. There was no other furniture, save the bed furs heaped in the corner.

Her eyes came to rest on a harp, the taut strings flickering in the light from the fire.

"Your things are safe," he said as he directed her to an empty corner nearest the door.

She looked at him with curious appraisal, as he bent over the hearth. The staff burned in alarm as she leaned it against the wall.

Easing cross-legged near the fire, Isabeau accepted the bowl and breadloaf he proffered. She held the bowl's rim to her lips, savoring the warmth more than the taste.

He shook his head, eyeing her bow and the staff. "I'd imagine quite a story behind that rowan."

"None quite as interesting as a druid who claims not to be." She cocked her head toward the medicaments and the harp.

Again he smiled.

"None quite. I came late into the studies. Here, at least, is sanctuary."

She didn't understand the force that drew men and women to lives of chastity and prayer. But she knew the need for sanctuary.

"Aye, 'tis the wolf you seek," He drank heartily, finishing his broth, then tore another chunk from the loaf. "It kills just to kill. It'll kill you as it has done to all who come this way."

His even, matter-of-fact tone was caution, she decided, not coldness.

"I'm sure it'll try." She sensed it again—the magic.

"Aye, this creature is everything you think it is, but never quite." He turned his gaze into the fire. "It's never heard nor seen until it's on top of its victim. It springs traps without getting caught . . ."

"Sorcery," Isabeau interjected.

"You know more than the rest," he arched his brow, facing her.

"Why hasn't it killed you, then, for its want of blood?" she held his stare.

"It can't kill me." Then his head fell back with the realization. "The merchant Keth hired you."

"You know Keth?"

"Too well, too long."

"He says this wolf causes a decline in his trade. And he thinks I can stop it."

"A bargain struck with the demon himself. What price does he give that's worth your death?" He gave her a cynical look.

She was silent a long time, tearing at her bread. Then she straightened. "My freedom."

"There is a truth about Keth that goes beyond knowledge. Trusting him may not be so wise."

She knew the wolf was bound in magic even as the merchant cajoled her into the bargain. So sure he had been that she would take his wager because of his connections that would lift the bounty from her head. But it had been the staff that brought her here in search of the witch who forged it. She would've come to this place with or without Keth's bidding.

"You're welcome to stay," Laurent went on, giving the woman a nod of quiet understanding. No more questions. It wasn't necessary for her to say what drove her, only that certain things had to be done in this life. "The rain will drive hard through the night. I'd welcome the conversation and the opportunity to play the harp for an audience." His lips curved slightly into a rueful smile, in contrast to the words.

"I'd welcome the harp. I'm footsore and tired. And the morrow will bring on the hunt."

Grateful he was, it seemed to her, when Laurent gathered his harp. His fingers melded with the strings, his voice became a part of the harmony. He sang a ballad of two brothers. The elder was boisterous and proud—the harp twanged loud and discordant. The younger was introspective and contemplative—the harmony softened.

The elder mirrored his father, a wealthy regent who loved his power—the chords struck a potent resonance. Together they hunted—the melody floated like a bird in flight; they drank—the music quickened; they sparred—a chord was stuck like the clash of steel.

Isabeau leaned back, swept into the tale of a father's quest for power and the fate of two brothers caught in its wake.

The music sparked: the elder held a great banquet to honor the father. There was drink and song and food, more drink, more food. But the company pressed for more—a match! The father wished the younger to prove his devotion by sparring with the elder. The company shouted, banged their fists on the banquet table.

Laurent's tone flared, his fingers danced across the harp. Isabeau was in the banquet room, hearing the cheers, watching the younger move into the center.

The elder attacked; the younger stood still. For all their differences, they were still brothers. The elder had forgotten. The younger realized it all the more. The two harmonies, bold and quiet, blended into a sad euphony.

The elder, goaded by his father, his mind reeling with wine, lunged forward. A great sweep—he thought his brother would sidestep easily—sliced the other's heart.

The harp quieted. His timing was impeccable, Isabeau commended.

Then he struck a fearsome chord. The father, stricken with grief, cursed the brother left standing, and banished him into the demon's world.

Isabeau knew Laurent sang his own song.

"Aye," she said when he finished, " 'tis a strange time we live in."

As she fell asleep she dreamt of a huge creature, black and powerful in the night. She felt its power reaching out to her from the abyss of her dreams. But it was not its hate that touched her soul. It was a sorrow so potent, so deep that her soul keened with its grief.

She woke in a start to the anguished screams ripping the night's silence. She bolted from the hearthside to the corner where her weapons stood. In a glance she realized Laurent was gone. Again, the screams resounded, reaching a fervored peak and abruptly, silenced.

She halted mid-stride as the quiet was replaced with a mournful wail. The very air vibrated with the howling.

She stepped outside, as dawnlight began to feather across the sky. The silence pressed in around her—not a crow called out, not a swallow moved from the thatch. No insect hummed, or toad quickened with the dawnrise, or wild cat yowled before it settled into sleep.

She felt the staff's fire, so bright it lay open a path into the forest. She crouched low, moving quickly and silently on the balls of her feet along the forest floor, her narrowed eyes seeing everything.

The howling rose again, all around her, fierce and hungry.

She went cold inside, slowing her assault. The rising sun cast an eerie red-orange glow against the green-land. Cautiously, every muscle tensed, every nerve open to her surroundings, she edged her way on, her sight darting from tree to tree, to brush, to branch. She smelled it then, the sweet tinge of blood. She came to the gnarled oak, the skull's grin chilled her, welcoming her back.

A body lay twisted about the gnarled root, parts of it strewn about as if ripped apart by hell-demons. She retched. There was not enough left whole of the body to distinguish whether it was the druid or not. Blood soaked the ground and colored the spring. She leaned heavily on the tree, sinking to the ground. Her fingers grazed something sharp. Looking down, she saw a hunter's knife, the blade broken close to the hilt. She recognized it as the blade of the bounty hunter she had disrobed the day before.

So, he had not returned to his camp, but chose instead to save face and seek her out again.

The staff whined in her grasp, forcing her back to her senses. The creature was out there, still.

She swerved to the sounds of snapping wood beneath a heavy step. Then a groan. She followed the sound, and coiled. Just then, the druid fell from behind the brush, his face ashen, his robe tattered and blood soaked.

He woke in a start, bolting upright to a sitting position. He screeched in his pain, falling back into the furs.

"Hold yourself," Isabeau whispered, wiping the sweat rolling down his cheek, across his neck.

"My leg?" his breath came in frightened blasts.

"I'm no healer." She shook her head, eyeing her crude sutures. The laceration was deepest above his knee, with the bone exposed, following a jagged line up his thigh. "It festers. I've used the herbs, but I can't be sure."

"It'll kill you," he moaned. "It'll seek you out." He wrenched, his eyes squeezed shut from the pain. "I cannot die. I wish I could." He lapsed into a restless sleep.

Isabeau relaxed, putting aside the rags and herbs, allowing the man to sleep while he could. She leaned back, her shoulders sagged. Her gaze ventured out the window. The clouds thinned, momentarily at least, and the forest lightened with the sun's haze. Wrens bickered beneath the thatch. She watched as crows swooped low against the glade's edge.

Her thoughts strayed to the wolf. She sensed its power, its rage. And more, now she'd heard its cry. She felt the aloneness, a sorrow so deep the forest keened.

Her gaze drifted hearthside, to the rowan. It glowed in the firelight. The light intensified, strands of interconnecting silver-white light danced across the wood. It reached out toward her. . . .

"Persippany," she whispered, eyes half-closed as if in dream-sleep.

In the witchfire, the strands bound together to form a face. Etheral features writhed in the waves of heat and flame.

"Isabeau . . ." the voice sang like wind through summer leaves. "The witch . . . touches . . . here . . ."

"I know." Isabeau arched her brow, wondering why

the Other felt the need to say the obvious. She inhaled slowly, deeply, and looked to the druid. He still slept.

"Soon . . . Isabeau . . ." Persippany's voice continued. "We find this witch . . . that traps us . . ."

"If I had not answered your plea, I would not be here." Isabeau's face darkened. The grim memory of that night swelled up to haunt her. She watched her mind's image enter the inn and search for the one who called for help. She found instead children, their mutilated bodies strewn the length and width of the great room. She should have run then. She should have turned and fled without looking back. But instead, she persisted after that voice. The voice of Persippany, leaning against the hearthside.

The image lifted her face, her laugh like a tinker's bell. "But ye hear me . . . I teach ye well . . . the ways to fight . . . to hunt . . . to see . . . I lead you true . . . to the witch . . . that murderer of children . . . the one who leads the prince to . . . kill your family . . . to punish ye . . . the prince who lay . . . the bounty on ye head . . . this witch . . . that traps me here. . . ."

She had learned long ago not to ask how the murders happened, and how it was the essence was trapped in the rowan. Or who the essence was. Persippany always refused to answer, resorting to heated means to let Isabeau know she disapproved. So Isabeau sought the one who did know—the witch whose name she didn't know, who seemed always one step ahead.

The sun was already past its zenith when Laurent moaned, stirring awake.

"Are you hungry?" she asked as she eased a bowl of broth to his lips.

"Leave here." He waved aside the bowl, struggling to raise himself.

"So you keep warning me. Why?"

"Because you listened to my harp without complaint." He smiled, weak. "Why do you stay?"

"Because you shared your meal with me." She pushed him gently back into the furs. He didn't flinch as she probed the skin around the wound.

"It seems better." She straightened. "The sleep did you well."

"Sleep?" the monk's voice quaked, his face flushed. "The sun—does it set?"

Isabeau gave a nod. She seized his forearm to steady him, his agitation increasing.

"Isabeau, forgive me . . ." he shivered uncontrollably.

Suddenly the man let out a screech, wrenching free from her grasp. He clawed at his chest, untethered by his wounds.

Isabeau moved back, mouth agape.

Laurent reeled off the furs, no longer quite a man. On all fours, he changed. He was no longer the druid, but a wolf, its sleek, black body corded with muscle.

Incredulous, Isabeau huddled as if to hide herself. Then rage swept through her—rage for not realizing the truth, even as the staff had warned her. A rage for losing control of the hunt, for being trapped in the hut.

She lunged for the staff, its touch fiery.

The wolf-demon stood, its jaws gaping, its hindquarters taut.

She kept her watch fixed on the amber glow of its eyes, holding out the staff in a horizontal position. She called upon the witchfire, Persippany. It was not a tame thing, with Isabeau as master and the fire at her bidding. It lived. It had its own purpose. It needed only a vessel to release its flame. She hoped that now, their purposes were the same.

Then she felt it, coursing through her as if it were her own lifeblood, a joining of will and strength. She felt the heat explode within the staff, the light of blue flames blinding the creature.

The wolf-demon yowled, whipped its head back and forth. It sighted the window, looking back to Isabeau. Its mouth curled back in hate.

Then it sprang, clearing the window, its doleful wail trailing behind it.

She stood, thanking Persippany. She inhaled deeply, bracing herself. Then, she pulled the heavy tunic over her head. She thought of her bow, but the force she hunted could not be stopped by arrows. She seized the staff, and followed the wolf into the night.

There was no sound; it was as if the forest held its breath.

Indefatigable, she moved fluidly through the greenland, the staff's blue light penetrating the darkness. There was no fear now, no rage, memory, or hate. There was only the hunt.

She stopped mid-stride, the sound of the wolf's cry luring her deeper into its territory. Pulsating, Persippany urged her on. Isabeau understood. Their magic was founded in similarity—the witch—and it drew them together.

Then she came to a standstill, the twisted oak loomed before her.

Abruptly the staff's fire exploded, a tree off to one side burst in flames. Isabeau stumbled back from the force, fighting to bring the magic to bear. She swerved hard, eyes catching the blur of the wolf as it darted behind her, in the underbrush.

Again the staff threw its fire, holding the demon at bay.

It howled from out of the darkness. She stood fast, holding the staff up as a shield. Then the demon was before her, circling her, its fangs lashing out at her. She pivoted with it, feeling the fire surge again.

But the wolf had witnessed the staff's power, and it remembered. It slowed its circling, eyeing the staff. It stood for a long moment.

Isabeau crouched, taut, ready. She blinked hard, thinking she saw the creature twist its features into a smile.

Silent and swift, the wolf lunged. Quicker than thought, Isabeau held out the staff and called upon the flame. Beneath the demon's hide, a man's heart still beat: Persippany launched an arrow of bluish fire, embedding itself true to the mark.

The wolf shrilled, twisting grotesquely in midair. Down it went with a hard thud. Still it was, like the forest around it.

But not dead, Isabeau knew. Only the man's heart died, his soul released. The demon still lived.

In the next instant it was on its feet.

The magic flared up in a blinding explosion. It caught the monster a glancing blow. The wolf swerved sharply, veering away from the fire.

Isabeau followed it, pivoting on her toes.

Again, the witchfire surged. Her hands and wrists burned in its power. But Persippany fought its own battle.

The demon rushed again, its rumbling snarl vibrating the air. It rushed past, knocking her violently back.

Still grasping the staff, Isabeau struggled to her feet, fighting the pain.

The blue fire rose again, strong. So strong that Isabeau had to choke down her scream, the pain stabbing her arms and searing her chest.

The flame struck the demon's face, boring through its lifeless eyes. It wrenched desperately, trying to break the flame's hold. Isabeau surrendered herself wholly to the flame, setting the magic free.

The fire intensified, pummeling the creature. The wolf writhed in its pain and fury. The fury swept through it. And when the flame died, long breaths after, only charred remains were left.

She coughed. Her lungs strained for air, her arms burned; the pain brought her to her knees.

Then, it was like a whisper invading her thoughts. Still clinging to the staff, she staggered to her feet. Her eyes narrowed on the shimmering before her.

"Keth," she hissed through gritted teeth. "We've waited for you."

"I've hired well," the man said, his arms folded across his chest. "You've earned your fate."

The staff burned with Persippany's flame. This time, Isabeau listened.

"You are not safe, witch. This forest is no longer your domain! It would take more than one of your demons to stop me from finding you!" She screamed out.

The image shifted. In its stead rose another figure, neither human, nor man or woman. Its face contorted with hate, its flat nose pushed up between small, yellow eyes, its teeth filed into fangs that clipped protruding thick lips. Its cloaked body was bent from age. Around it danced fire without light or heat. It skitted across the twisted oak, resting on the ancient skull.

Isabeau lunged. But not quickly enough. There came a crushing pressure on her mind.

I have you! It was a laugh, graveled and ancient. *I've always had you! Since the night at the inn, Isabeau. Isabeau!*

It crawled inside her, moving down through her, pushing the witchflame farther away. Her heart pounded, ready to explode inside her. The force sent her sprawling, the rowan sailed through the air, driven into the ground an arm length's away.

The witch's magic beat at her savagely, unyielding.

She turned her head, her mind seeking a hold with Persippany, her arm reaching out. She could see the familiar face dancing around the rowan, entreating her. But the flame needed a vessel to bring it out. And she could not reach it.

Isabeau dies! The hideous laugh echoed.

Just then, the witchfire exploded from the staff, blue flames engulfed the skull. The witch's laugh shrilled in surprise and shock.

How, Persippany? The wail heightened as the flames engulfed the oak. The translucence faded.

It was the first time Isabeau realized the essence in the rowan loved as well as hated. And that love had given it a life of its own.

She lay still for a long time, gasping for breath. The night closed in around her. The rowan cooled, asleep.

How it happened that the witch came upon Keth as he cursed his son was a question only the highest order could answer, Isabeau decided.

She shrugged her quiver and bow into a more comfortable position. She swung the staff in stride. The end of it grazed a stone, and she winced. Her hands, while packed liberally with medicinals from Laurent's storehouse, were still sensitive.

They not be true burns, she felt Persippany's presence reassuring her. *They heal fast.*

Laurent . . . her mind wandered to the forest, now a full day behind her. She smiled slightly, thinking of the druid. At least he was free. And Keth. And the witch no longer controlled the forest.

The sun broke through the cloud cover. Winter would wait another day, she thought, glad for it. She was still outlaw. And she wasn't sure if the staff had destroyed the witch, or only its hold on the forest.

But at that moment she didn't care.

PEARL
by Carl Thelen

Carl Thelen turned up in one of the short story work-shops which I run every two or three years from my garage; this, the shortest story in the anthology, proves that sometimes—not always—writing, which can't be taught, can be learned.

Carl earns his living programming computers, but is interested in such things as blacksmithing and carpentry. He says he wants to, "bail out of that racket and become a full time writer." Less than five percent of writers can support themselves doing it, so good luck; you've made a good start.

"Rape her?" the short, stocky man asked incredulously, his sword point wavering around the old woman's throat.

"Yeah, Bert," the short, skinny one replied. "Aren't you always supposed to rape a woman when you rob her?"

"Louie, this isn't a woman. It's an old hag! Raping a crone like this is . . . is like . . . it's . . . Oh, just empty her saddlebags!"

The woman had long white hair and wrinkled skin, but she stood straighter and taller than either of the thieves. "I prefer Carissa to 'old hag,' if you don't mind," she told them evenly.

Louie ignored her as he pulled the saddlebags off the brown and white mare and unceremoniously dumped their contents onto the road. There was bread and cheese, a few assorted coins, and a smooth white stone about the size of a man's head that glowed softly from within. Bert was so amazed he almost dropped his sword. "Louie, do you know what that is? That's pearl! That must be the biggest pearl in the world!"

"A pearl? I've never seen one before," Louie replied with awe, picking it up and stroking it gently.

"Be careful with it, Louie! Pearls are fragile. Put it back in the saddlebag and let's go."

"I wouldn't take that if I were you, gentlemen," Carissa cautioned them gently.

Bert laughed. "You can't pull that trick on me, old bitch."

"What trick, Bert?" Louie asked.

"When you're robbing people, they say 'Don't take that! It's cursed!' or something like that so you won't steal it. They do it all the time."

They both clambered aboard the horse, who whinnied unhappily and looked longingly at her former owner. "Be careful with Amber, too," Carissa said. "She bites when she's mad." But Bert and Louie again ignored her as they rode off into the dusk, chuckling over their success. When they were out of sight behind a bend, she gave a quiet sigh, then went into the woods where she made a couch of branches and magic, and waited.

Under the soft light of the full moon Bert and Louie made their camp, eating the stolen bread and cheese, and washing it down with equally stolen ale. Amber was tied to a tree close by, with her saddle and bags on the ground beside her. "How much do you think the pearl is worth, Bert?" Louie asked.

"A lot."

"A lot?"

"Yep. A whole lot."

"A whole lot," Louie repeated in wonder. "That's a lot."

"We could buy our own castle, with servants and slaves—and women."

"Our own women . . . Wow . . ."

"Get some sleep now, Louie," Bert commanded, curling up under his blanket. "Nobody'll bother us this far off the road, and we've got a long ride ahead of us tomorrow."

Louie gazed in wonder at the glowing pearl in the saddlebag. "Hey, Bert, does that pearl look like it's bigger than it used to be?"

"Of course not, idiot! Pearls don't grow. Now shut up and go to sleep." Among Louie's other mistakes, he believed everything his boss told him. Reassured, he was soon sleeping as soundly and snoring as loudly as Bert

The pearl, however, had other ideas. It twitched, and wobbled, then rolled out of the saddlebag, growing quickly larger, as its inner fire turned from white to yellow to green. In a few minutes it had turned into a small dragon, about four meters long, who looked around curiously. Amber gave a quiet neigh of greeting and moved toward her as far as the tether would allow. The dragon approached and nuzzled her friend, cutting the rope with her sharp teeth. After killing Bert quietly by dropping venom in his ear, she devoured him eagerly. By the time she turned her attention to Louie, she was almost full and she wasn't sure she could finish all of him. But given the choice between leaving a half-eaten corpse lying around and probably going hungry before her next feeding, she figured she had better eat while she could.

At that moment Louie was having one of his wild-and-willing-barmaid dreams, looking deep into her eyes and her cleavage. But, as so often happened in Louie's dreams, she suddenly slapped him, knocking him off his chair and waking him up. He went from looking into a pair of tantalizing blue female eyes to a pair of slitted yellow dragon eyes; his scream could be heard for miles. The dragon hadn't realized humans could move so fast.

*　　*　　*

A short time later, Amber and the dragon walked into Carissa's camp, and she hugged and kissed them both. "Ah, Pearl, I love you dearly," she said to the dragon, "But the things I have to do to feed you!"

NAME OF THE DEMONESS
by Jessie D. Eaker

Everybody makes mistakes. My late father used to
say, "There was only one perfect man ever created,
and you can read in the Bible what they did to Him."
Lisa puts it more simply: "If I were infallible, I'd be
Pope." And my second grade teacher used to say, "If
nobody ever made mistakes, they wouldn't bother to
put erasers on pencils."

With that good precedent, I can easily confess that I
am no more infallible than anybody else, and a lot
more fallible than some. In a previous volume, no bio
having arrived by the time I mailed off the manuscript,
and misled by never having seen the name on a
by-line, I introduced Josepha Sherman as an ama-
teur; well, she is in the sense of making her living at
something else—very few people can make a living
writing short fiction—but I apologize for not mention-
ing her sales. It seems she has a novel out from Avon
books. And since Jessie Eaker's letter didn't arrive
when I was writing introductions, I wrote that "her
characteristics are best left to the imagination, but for
all I know, she has three heads." Well, the bio arrived
when I had finished these introductions, but I am left
here with metaphorical egg on my face, for Jessie
Eaker is a man, a computer programmer, and has
sold, on and off, to the small presses, but this is his
first professional sale. He has three sons, and says
that the inspiration for this story came from the birth of

his youngest child. He and his wife purchased a home in "the far west" and currently own no cats or dogs, but have a large turtle who likes to visit. That's a new one.

"Push once more!" said the midwife.

Exhausted and sweaty from her labor, Freya firmly gripped the arms of the friends kneeling beside her and heaved up from the pallet. Taking a deep breath and groaning with effort, she pushed with the remainder of her strength. Expectantly, the other women held their breath; all eyes focused on the laboring woman. The room grew quiet except for the sounds of her exertion. The world seemed to pause, waiting for the result. . . .

Freya fell back and the midwife held up the infant. It began to cry.

The midwife briefly inspected the baby and laid it on Freya's stomach, where it squirmed and wiggled. The women began to excitedly whisper among themselves. It was a girl-child.

Freya leaned up to watch her infant. *So this is the little creature that changed my life,* she thought. She couldn't help but smile.

Despite her exhaustion, Freya anxiously waited for her turn to hold the child. But first came the blessing: thanks to the Goddess Mother for a successful birth—and a female. The midwife cut the cord and handed the babe to the waiting Priestess Lyris. But the priestess frowned. She took the child over to the window and threw open its shutter, allowing in the last of the day's sun. A light breeze ruffled the priestess's robes as she studied the infant's face. The room suddenly became silent.

"What is it?" Freya demanded. "What is wrong?"

Lyris shook her head. "I'm sorry, my child." She gave the baby back to the mother and pointed to a black mark on the child's forehead. "It is the mark of the Demoness Gilou. Before tomorrow's sunrise, she will come to collect what she has claimed."

The other women had left. Only the priestess remained to counsel the new mother—and console her to her fate.

"I am a warrior!" Freya shouted. "I will *not* give up my babe without a fight!"

"You can't fight the demoness," stated Lyris. "You risk your own life if you try to stop her."

"I *swear* by the Goddess Mother I will not give up my baby without a fight! Be they human or demon, my sword will just as easily cleave their heads from their bodies."

"You don't understand!" said the exasperated priestess. "Your steel is useless against the demoness. And if you anger her by your feeble efforts, she will take you, too!" The priestess shook her head. "It is best you set the child aside, don't even suckle her, and let the demoness take her."

"Curse you! If you won't help me, I'll prepare to meet her as best I can! Alone!"

The priestess shook her head in resignation. "You are a stubborn woman, warrior. I will do what I can, but it is very little I offer." She paused a moment in thought. "I will put you in the highest tower of the temple, which will slow the demoness, but not stop her. This will force her to wait until just before dawn, when the life force is at its lowest ebb. At best it will buy you a few hours."

Given the help she needed, Freya's anger subsided. Doubt replaced it. If the sword she had depended on for so long was useless, what was she to do? How could she defeat a demoness whose very name made mothers weep and babies cry. No doubt the priestess was right—to interfere was death. But this child had been hard won, and for her, there would be no more. She had no choice but to fight. "Is there no weapon I can use against the demoness? Some way I can kill her?"

The priestess laughed. "Can you kill a mountain?

Can you destroy the sea? No, my child. You cannot kill a demoness."

Freya shook her head. "Surely there is *something*. All things have their limits. Even demons must get their power from somewhere!"

"True," acknowledged the priestess. "A demon gets its power from its names: the more names it has, the more powerful it is. Demoness Gilou has three: Gilou her familiar name and Abyzu her second. But she has a third—a secret name, her name of power. If it were known, you could write it on a stone or amulet and place it on the child. Then, if the demoness touched the child, she would be destroyed. But only Gilou herself and her mistress know that secret name. And I doubt Gilou will volunteer the information." The priestess stood to begin the preparations. "I wish there were more I could do. I'll pray that the Goddess Mother is with you. But what you can accomplish, other than increase your misery, I do not know."

Freya awaited death's approach.

She lay upon a low couch in the uppermost tower of the temple, resting, saving her strength for the battle to come. The chamber she occupied was round and bare except for the couch and a small lamp. She had positioned the couch across from the room's only entry—a door on the room's north wall, bolted shut from the inside. Tall windows, with wide window ledges no higher than her knee, occupied the west and east walls. The priestesses used them for prayer at sunrise and sunset.

A chill pre-morning breeze blew through the open windows. Freya shivered and pulled her cloak tighter about her and the baby. She had spent half the night standing at the east window, looking out over the sleeping city, watching the stars dancing to their unhurried rhythm, and praying the sunrise would hurry.

Absentmindedly she fingered the amulet around her neck. The priestess had placed it there before leaving her in the tower. She had whispered it was an amulet of the Goddess Mother and would help protect her from the demoness. Then the priestess had kissed her good-bye.

In the time since then, she had developed a plan. It was her only hope. She touched the dagger concealed at her waist. Dipped in her own blood, she had used it for a stylus. If her ruse failed, she would use it on herself.

The baby slept in the crook of her arm. She had suckled a little. Although she took the breast eagerly, she was too young to really drink well. Freya had been pleased when the child grasped her finger and blinked up at her with unseeing eyes. These were good signs that the child would be strong.

The warrior occupied her mind with choosing a name for the babe. If they survived, the child could be named at the next dawn, as was custom. But Freya could wait for three more days if she wanted. Just as long as the naming was done at dawn.

She leaned her head back and sighed. Her whole body ached from her labors, and she was tired. Her body cried out for rest, but she could allow it none. The time was near.

A scraping noise from the door made her sit up. Despite having been barred, it now stood open, swinging gently in the breeze. Before it a figure stood, outside the circle of light the small lamp projected. Freya tensed. Waiting.

"I have come for that which is mine," announced a rasping voice.

"Who are you and what do you want?" Freya responded, trying to keep her voice from shaking.

Stepping forward into the light was the demoness: nude, with a woman's breasts and hips, she had the head of a dog, the feet of a hawk, and arms like snakes—the digits of her fingers waving of their own accord. The dog head grinned.

"Gilou," the word escaped Freya's lips. The warrior stood, clutching the baby to her chest. She darted her eyes to the east—the horizon was beginning to lighten.

"Fear me, mortal. I am the bringer of death. Give

me the child. The reward my mistress has promised
awaits my return."

"I have lambs to offer you instead. Or calves if you
prefer. I will make a great sacrifice to you."

The demoness laughed. "You pitiful mortal. I must
have the babe. It has been foretold that the child will
one day destroy me as well as my mistress. My mistress I care nothing for, but as for myself, I have some
care. I give no quarter. I take no chances." The demoness reached for the infant. "Give her to me!"

"No! Wait! She's protected. Look at the names
written on her forehead."

The demoness took a fearful step back. Freya held
her breath hoping the ruse worked.

The demoness cocked her head from side to side as
she studied the child. She suddenly laughed and Freya's
blood ran cold. "Foolish mortal. Yes, there are three
names there, but only two of them are mine. The third
is gibberish. *Now stop delaying and give me the child!*
The sun is rising. I have no time for games."

Freya drew the knife concealed at her waist. "You'll
have to take her, monster. A Guards-woman does not
surrender!"

The demoness hissed. "Fool! Your steel is nothing
to me." Faster than lightning, the demoness reached
out and seized the knife by its blade. She jerked it
from Freya's grasp and flung it out the window. "Pay
for your insolence, woman!" One of the demon's snake
arms reached for the warrior's throat. But the amulet
Freya wore flashed brilliant white. The demoness jerked
back as if stung.

"What!" she roared. "More delays. Woman, killing
you will bring me great pleasure." The demoness raised
her arms and chanted. "I am the demoness Gilou, also
called Abyzu. I destroy this treachery by the power of
my own secret name—*Neola!*"

At the mention of the name, the amulet flared and
blackened. It fell from around Freya's throat and shattered on the stone floor.

The demoness grinned. Again lightning fast, she
reached for the warrior and wrapped one of her snake

arms around Freya's throat, cutting off her air. With the other, the demoness ripped the child from her grasp and clutched the infant to its chest.

In one smooth motion, the demoness threw Freya against the wall. The warrior hit hard, landing on her face and knocking the wind out of her. Blood oozed from her nose and lips. She fell to the floor.

As the demoness approached, Freya unsteadily regained her feet and using the wall for support, slid away from the demoness. Freya's mind raced. She knew the demoness' name, but she no longer had the child or her stylus. What could she do?

The demoness lunged and Freya dodged. But not fast enough. Catching her by the arm, the demoness threw her through the air to land on the window sill—half in, half out the window. Freya teetered on the brink of falling. She barely managed to catch herself.

The demoness came up behind her and placed a clawed foot in her back, preventing her from rising. "I wish I had more time to enjoy your death, but the sun is about to rise."

Freya raised her head. Maybe there was a way.

The demoness continued, "Fortunately for you, yours will be a quick death. Now *die!*"

The demoness started to push her out the window. Freya raised her head and yelled at the sun just peeking over the horizon. "In the name of the Goddess Mother I give my child the name of the demoness— *Neola!*"

Instantly from behind her came a blood curdling scream and the pressure on her back released. Freya turned to see her child glowing where she was clutched to the demoness' side. With her other snake arm, the demoness tried to pull the babe away from her, but the limb stuck fast to the child. It screamed again, shaking the tower in its agony. Gradually the glow from the child spread to cover the demoness and she began to shrink away. Smaller and smaller she became, until nothing was left but a fine black powder on the floor of the tower—and her child.

The babe had slept through the whole ordeal, only to be awakened by the scream. Freya picked up the child and tried to comfort her.

Just then Priestess Lyris burst into the room, followed by two guards. "What happened? We heard the scream." The priestess drew up short. "You still have the baby!" she cried in astonishment.

Freya smiled. "And a fine daughter she'll be, too. Barely a day old and she's already killed a demoness."

HANDS
by Lois Tilton

When I first read this story, I almost dismissed it and rejected it as a horror story. It starts horrifyingly enough—but all I have to say about it is that it's not nearly as horrific as the first couple of pages would indicate. Lois Tilton is a part-time instructor in Philosophy and has had a good deal of poetry placed in various anthologies. Since neither philosophy or poetry is a good way to make a living these days, and she says that, "apart from this I do nothing which is at all interesting," we wonder what she's leaving out.

Tianne fought and kicked as the executioners dragged her to the block. The crowd gathered below the platform cheered her on, not out of sympathy, but that the spectacle enlivened their marketday entertainment.

Her struggles were futile. A muscular hand brought her down to her knees, others forced her forearm onto the block's stained, hacked surface.

"Better hold it still now, girl," the executioner warned. He raised his ax, brought it down again—a single, swift movement.

Tianne, looking away, felt something hard strike her wrist. Onto the gore-splattered straw at her knees fell a perfect human hand, brown and slim-fingered.

Distantly, she could sense pain beginning to gather, growing. But before it could burst fully into life, her arm was seized, the spurting stump thrust into a pot of bubbling pitch. That pain met the other, she screamed, then fell into darkness.

Slaps on her face brought her back again to the scene on the platform. It was not finished. She began to tremble uncontrollably. Her hair and shirt were soaked with the cold water the executioners had used to revive her. She was lifted back to her knees, her other arm laid on the block.

Tianne moaned, no longer capable of struggling. In the city of Khazad, loss of a hand was the normal penalty for a first theft conviction. A single hand only. The guild should have kept this from happening to her. There had been—she was certain—a betrayal.

The crowd watched now with only an audible intake of breath as the ax was raised again. At its apex, Tianne caught sight of a hooded figure standing just below the platform, and in the shadow of its face a darkness, a black vortex drawing her . . .

For an instant time seemed to stop, the axe suspended. Then the blade thudded through bone into the wood of the block, and this time, mercifully, Tianne slid unconscious onto the bloody straw.

She was released from the prison hospital after six days. Time for the pain in her wrists to abate, for the pain of betrayal to fester. *Both of her hands.*

Outside, the sunshine in the marketplace made her eyes water. It took a long time to cross the market square. She was still weak from bloodloss and wound-fever, and every footstep jarred her wrists, but she persevered, thinking only of her destination. There was going to be a reckoning. The guild had failed her. At last she passed into the shadows of an unpaved alley, leaned back against a wall to rest for a moment. She was home.

They recognized Tianne when she came into the Gamecock tavern and sank onto a bench. The walk from the prison had made her dizzy. A child came running with a cup of water, held it so she could drink. But after a single gulp she raised her head and demanded to see Hadro, Master of the guild of thieves. Soon an apprentice arrived to lead her up the tavern's narrow back stairs.

Hadro shifted his bulk in his chair and exhaled. The sour reek of ale and onions on his breath made Tianne's stomach heave, but her anger helped repress the reaction.

"What went wrong?" she demanded, holding the stumps of her wrists inches from Hadro's face.

"There was nothing more I could do!" he protested. "You should have known you were asking for trouble—breaking into a courtier's house. They must have bribed the judge. Or else you have a real enemy, girl. He refused to be reasonable."

"Oh? How much did you give him—thirty coppers?"

"I gave him two orii. It was no use."

Stunned by the amount, Tianne fell back into her chair. Hadro sounded almost sincere. Two orii was twice the usual bribe in a case like hers. If he had really paid so much . . .

"You were warned, you know," the guildmaster added. "Ambitious young journeymen—you can't resist the jewels, the gold. If you'd stayed in the marketplace, I could have bought off the judge with ten silver bits and this need not have happened."

Tianne closed her eyes, the anger that had sustained her draining away. You don't become a master-thief by lifting coppers in the marketplace. But she had not been born to the guild, and there was resentment of ambitious outsiders. She was willing to bet that Hadro had never warned his own nephew away from the lure of gold and jewels. Or that he would have let him lose both hands for it, no matter what the cost. But two orii—no one could say the guildmaster had not fulfilled his obligation in Tianne's case.

Seeing her slumped in the chair, Hadro pressed his advantage. "Well, I suppose we have to see to your future now. Gemmeine, at the Scarlet Hyacinth, has offered you a place, for your mother's sake."

"No!" At the name of the whoremistress, Tianne shook her head violently. "My mother slaved ten years on her back to buy my place in this guild, so I would never have to end up as she did!"

And had died not long afterward, Tianne did not have to add. She would never reject that hard-bought legacy.

Hadro shrugged, assessing her body as a piece of merchandise. "Too bad. You're not so old. It's an easier life than you'd have with the beggars."

But Tianne knew the business of the prostitute's guild well enough to be aware of the kind of man who would pay to have her the way she was now—crippled, helpless. She shook her head again.

"All right," sighed Hadro, "then it's the beggars for you."

He stood, dismissing her. The reciprocal arrangements among the underground guilds that had obliged the thieves to accept Tianne as an apprentice twelve years ago also ensured her a place now that she was incapacitated for her own trade. The beggar's guild would receive her indenture bond in exchange. Tianne, swallowing hard, got to her feet. She had her right to refuse Gemmeine's offer, but now Hadro was obliged to do no more. From now on, her future was a ragged gray robe in the streets, where one-handed beggars were as commonplace as thieves.

Tianne was granted a pitch outside the Three Black Hounds tavern, a place frequented by soldiers from the nearby barracks. Though soldiers were not much given to pity, they were all aware that a cripple's fate might one day be their own. They would toss a coin or two her way.

The beggars had also assigned her an apprentice, but when the boy realized she was helpless to beat him, he ran away to spend his time at the heels of the soldiers. Alone, she could not care for herself or pick up any coins that missed the bowl at her feet. There were armless, handless beggars who could use their feet almost as well as hands, but Tianne had no such ability. All her skills had been in her fingertips.

So now she sat in gray rags, her hair tangled, in the filth beside the tavern door. All day long her bowl had gone empty, her stomach as well. She was near despair when finally someone tossed a single coin, which spun around the rim and jumped out into the dirt. Tianne stared at it lying there. Then she lowered her head and used her lips and teeth to pick the copper from the ground. There was a drunken cheer from inside the tavern as she spit the coin into her beggar's bowl, and another coin came sailing out of the open door, past her head, rolling a distance into the street. Now Tianne did not hesitate. On her knees, she crawled to the street and retrieved the coin from the gutter.

Face flushed with shame, she turned, still kneeling, to display the copper clenched between her teeth. This time the cheers were louder, and as soon as she returned to her place by the door a serving girl came out in her soiled apron to set a mug of cheap ale down beside her bowl.

Tianne bent down to the mug and washed away the taste of the gutter with the sour brew, at the same time hiding her burning face. She wore a gray robe now. She could not afford pride.

Yet that day she ate, and paid for her food with the coppers she had earned unaided. Soon the soldiers came to expect her at the Three Black Hounds, laying bets to see if she would retrieve a coin from the horse dung in the street or a puddle of vomit left from a customer of the night before. They were only coppers, but enough of them were thrown her way that Tianne could pay her fees to the beggar's guild. Even a gray robe, she well knew, had its cost.

The coin appeared before her eyes, thick, gleaming gold—a ten-orii piece. Ten orii had been the price of Tianne's indenture as a thief, that her mother had accumulated night by night, copper by copper. Tianne raised her eyes from the gold to a dark robe of cobalt blue and a face hidden in the shadows of its hood.

A sudden flash of memory made her shudder. For a moment, she strained to see within the hood. Then the thick, white fingers brought the coin closer to her face and a man's voice whispered, light as rice paper rustling, "Do you want it, girl?"

Her mouth was dry. She could not answer. It was unimaginable, what she might have to do to earn a coin of that value.

"Well, do you *want it?*" the voice repeated impatiently.

Still stricken mute, Tianne nodded.

"Then it is yours, when you can take it." As he held it up, Tianne made an instinctive movement to reach for the coin.

"Yes!" his voice rasped, "Like that! No, I do not mock you. It can be done—*if* you have the will. *Do* you have the will?"

Tianne could not tear her eyes from the gold. Ten orii—with that amount invested with a moneylender, her guild fees would be paid for the rest of her life. She got awkwardly to her feet, all the while knowing that this was almost certainly a trick, a hoax, some amusement to be had at her expense. But the chance, no matter how remote—she had to take it.

The hooded man led her across the square to an inn frequented by the caravan-masters who crossed the deserts to Khazad. The innkeeper started to protest the presence of Tianne in her gray beggar's rags, but a coin silenced her objections. Tianne followed the blue robe up a staircase into an ample apartment.

The mysterious figure locked the door behind them, then turned to face Tianne without lowering the hood of his robe. "My name is Arad," he said. "I have Sought for one with your qualities. I know who you are—Tianne the thief. Now Tianne the beggar. You lost both your hands on the block two fortnights past."

She nodded slowly. None of this was a secret. Yet . . . "You were there. I remember seeing . . . a hooded robe."

The dry rasp of his voice was harsher as he answered, "So you did see. Yes, I was in the marketplace that day, I saw you lose your hands. Tell me, beggar, how would you like to be a thief again? You have the will, I have already seen that."

"How?" she whispered in a voice that matched his.

"*How* is not your concern," he said sharply.

"And the gold?"

"As I said, the gold is yours, the moment you pick it up. But that is not important. If you obey me, *nothing* would be beyond your grasp."

He snapped his fingers, and a gold coin appeared out of nowhere, spinning in the air. As Tianne stared in awe, he snatched it up, then slapped it down onto the center of the polished table in the room. Brusquely, he pulled a chair out from beneath it and ordered her to sit.

Still staring at the gold, she obeyed.

"Put your hands on the table—yes, I mean what I said. Your hands. You can feel them sometimes, can't you? There is pain, as if they were still there. Sometimes you forget they are gone, don't you?"

Tianne nodded.

"Yes, the nerves are still alive. Your *hands* are still alive—in your mind."

Daring to believe, she asked, "You mean I could become as you? A wizard?"

"No!" he said sharply, "The Art is not for you. But I can bring your hands to life once again. Here—"

Tianne's eyes widened as he threw back the hood of his robe. The wizard Arad was pale-skinned. With his soft, plump cheeks and shapeless nose, his face looked like a lump of unbaked dough. His hairless skull gleamed like ivory. But his eyes—one was a pale, water-colored blue. And the other . . .

The memory was clear now, the axe-blade frozen in time above her head, and the darkness, the deep vortex of black within the empty socket that she now saw exposed. She shuddered again.

Arad pulled the hood back up to conceal his face. "Now you have seen. And I tell you, my thief, the Sight I achieve with that eye far transcends mere vision. As can your grasp."

The wizard turned away to an embossed metal chest

in one corner of the room and made an intricate gesture before he lifted open its lid. He returned to the table with a green stone vial no larger than the middle finger of his pale, fleshy hand.

Tianne held her breath as he carefully removed the stopper and allowed a single drop of glistening oil to fall onto each of her wrists. For a moment, there was a sensation of intense warmth. It faded. She felt nothing else. Was this all?

The wizard had gone to replace the vial in his chest. Now he returned and tapped the gold coin on the table. "Reach for it," he ordered. "Pick it up. With your *hands*."

Tianne tried, but nothing happened. Tears of frustration burned beneath her eyelids. She could not. She *had* no hands!

But Arad simply said, "Don't look at your wrists. Look at the gold. Don't *think* about your hands. The effort must come from the instinctive part of your mind. Your hands are *there*—believe in them. *Use* them!"

Tianne tried again, her eyes focused on the gleaming coin, reaching out to close her fingers around it . . .

Fingers she no longer had.

"Again," Arad ordered her, and again and again. The effort was intense. They worked until Tianne's arms were shaking with fatigue and sweat made her dark, tangled hair cling to the back of her neck. At last Arad allowed her to rest.

"It takes time," he told her, raising a hand to the empty eye socket in the shadow of his hood. "This I do know. Time and, most of all, the *will*. But the reward is worth the pain. I would not have chosen you for this task if you were the type to give up."

Tianne did not ask what task she had been chosen to perform. That it involved a theft was obvious. And, perhaps, danger. Yet if the wizard could restore her hands to her, it would be worth the risk.

The training continued all that day and then the next, until Tianne could no longer keep her eyes focused. She had been allowed to eat and sleep, but little else. Arad was showing signs of impatience, but try as she might, Tianne could not grasp the golden coin with fingers she no longer possessed.

Or any other object. For hours now there had been a mug of cold ale standing on the table, forbidden to her. Mouth dry, she stared at the moist condensation on the glazed pottery, while Arad taunted her, "Go on, take it! Quench your thirst! Just reach out and pick it up! Drink!"

Sweating with the effort, Tianne strained for it, in vain, then dropped her face down onto her arms on the table.

Pain flared across her back. She spun around. Arad was standing above her with a stick raised to hit her again. "Worthless bitch-dog," he hissed as he brought it down on her shoulder.

Tianne had not endured such a beating in years, not since her apprenticeship. Arad had no right!

Furious, she saw the stick lifted again, descending . . .

And snatched it from him with . . .

She stared. *With her right hand.*

"So that is what it takes!" Arad whispered in satisfaction.

Numbly, Tianne reached out for the mug, felt her fingers close around the clay handle, felt the texture, the weight as she brought it to her mouth. The cool ale flowed down her throat. She drained the mug and set it blindly back down on the table, shaking all over. Only her unseen hands were steady.

His face rippling in a grin, Arad held out the tenorii gold coin. Tianne reached for it, closed her fist around it. But there was no fist! She almost let it fall, then looked away again and managed to drop the coin into one of the inside pockets of her beggar's robe.

"Excellent!" Arad whispered triumphantly. "Now we are ready to begin! Or would you stop now?"

"No!" Tianne breathed. Invisible, her hands tightened.

For a week she and Arad remained in his rooms while she learned control over her phantom hands. Soon she had regained her former dexterity. And more.

Her grasp now extended beyond the limits of mere flesh.

"*Reach* for it! Take it from me!" he urged her, holding a comb up above his head. He was at least a foot taller than she, but angrily Tianne snatched it from him.

"Very good!" he exulted as she began to draw the comb through her matted tangles. There was no need for her to look like a beggar any more. Suddenly she plucked in distaste at the tattered gray robe.

"I want different clothes," she said. "I can change the gold at a moneylender's."

"No," Arad said quickly. "We must not lose the time." He pinched the cloth of her gray robe between two doughy fingers and made a gesture with his other hand. For an instant the robe was dark, shapeless fog, and then it had become what seemed to be the same loose pants and shirt she had been wearing on the executioner's platform.

Speechless, she ran her hands over the clothes. Then, suddenly, she reached for the hidden pocket that should be inside the shirt. It was there, and the ten-orii gold piece inside it. She exhaled with relief.

"Will that do?" Arad asked her testily.

"I'd like to be able to do that," she said.

He turned on her. "I warn you, little thief, do not try to meddle with things you could never understand. One must be born to the Art, and even then it takes years of training to properly develop the talent. Do not mistake *that*—" he waved his hand dismissingly at the comb she had picked up again "—for a wizard's power."

Stung, Tianne turned her back to him and finished combing the last of the beggar's tangles from her black hair. The wizard's suspicion was a growing source of irritation. Why, for one thing, did he so jealously guard his mysterious metal chest, if only one born and trained to his Art could make use of whatever was hidden inside?

It was nothing to her, of course. She had her gold already, and the miraculous new grasp of her phantom hands. When this was all finished, when she had done whatever task Arad had in mind, then indeed she would be a master thief! Yet—

She caught Arad's single blue eye glaring at her and reluctantly tore her gaze away from the chest. The wizard shot one more suspicious look in her direction from the shadow of his hood. Then, reluctantly, he once again told her to practice alone while he disappeared into the adjoining bedroom. There, she knew, he Sought . . . whatever he sought. Let him find it soon, she hoped. Let this task be done.

Tianne spent some minutes reaching out through the room's windows to knock the hats from passersby in the street below. The sport soon palled. Once again her eyes were drawn back to the metal chest. What wonders did it contain? Impatient and restless, she drew closer and knelt before it. The chest was of beaten brass, embossed with cryptic signs and figures. Tianne brushed the lid with a phantom finger, aware that Arad always secured it with a locking spell.

Curiosity and a thief's impulses urged at her. She glanced back behind her nervously, but the wizard's door was still closed. His Sight, wherever it was focused, was not on her. With invisible hands, she grasped the lid.

It lifted easily.

Surprised, Tianne almost let it fall. But then she opened it all the way and stared at the wonders within. There were gems—unset, in rings, on chains, most of them carved with symbols like those on the outside of the chest. As well, there were rods of wood, metal and stone, tiny boxes, bottles.

She recognized among the jumble of objects the small green stone vial of oil Arad had applied to her wrists. She frowned and bit down in thought on her lower lip. The wizard was secretive. What if the power, her newly-gained phantom grasp, were to fade once she had done Arad's will? To return to the life of a beggar once again—no!

And was she not a thief, after all? Tianne clutched

the vial tightly in one insubstantial fist, then thrust it into her pocket with the gold coin. Quickly, fearing discovery, she shut the lid.

A few moments later, the door of the bedroom opened and Arad burst out. The pasty-pale flesh of his face was flushed with excitement.

"Now!" he whispered. "Now, while he is gone!"

Abruptly, he seized Tianne by the shoulders. "Are you ready?" He let go just as suddenly, without giving her time to answer. "Of course you are. This time I shall have it!"

"Isn't it about time you tell me what all this is about?" she asked.

"When we arrive," he said curtly. He hurried to the chest in its corner and began the gestures of the unlocking spell. Then he hesitated, turning a suspicious look in Tianne's direction. Her heart faltered for a moment, but her thief's training kept her reaction from showing on her face, and Arad completed his spell.

"Come here," he told her, standing with an intricately carved ivory rod in his hand. Holding it over his head, he shut his blue eye and began an incantation.

Tianne inhaled sharply. They were no longer in the room. Around her was a swirling, a blurred rush of wind, and she staggered with sudden vertigo.

Then there was the blinding impact of the sun on her eyelids, and she lifted them to find herself standing outside on the floor of the desert. She spun around. The city was nowhere in sight, only a crumbling ruin less than a league distant, a few ragged date palms brushing its roof.

Arad, beside her, was observing the sight with intense satisfaction. He whispered, "There it is, the house of Alkairiad. Inside is the thing you must take. Listen well—it is a smooth crystal, about the size of a swallow's egg, clear blue in color. I caution you, do not look closely at it! Place the crystal into this pouch and return to me immediately. You will find it inside a wooden box with a design of thorns carved on the top.

Here," he said, handing her a tightly-rolled scroll, "is a map to guide you to the room where it lies."

Tianne glanced up from the scroll. "You have been to this place? You have seen this crystal where you say it is?"

"I have seen." The wizard paused. "I warn you— the place is warded. But you need not fear." He placed a chain around Tiane's neck. She saw hanging from it a medallion of silver, incised with a symbol that made her think of flames. "As long as you wear this," he said, "you will be protected."

Protected against what? Tianne wondered. "If all this is so," she asked him, "why don't you simply take this crystal yourself? What do you need me for?"

Arad answered reluctantly, "He has ways of knowing . . . . And the box holding the crystal—there is a spell on it that I cannot break. If any hand—any material hand—should touch the lid . . ."

Tianne, recalling the ease with which she had opened the brass chest, understood. "I see," she said quickly and turned her eyes back to the scroll. "Now, is this where I enter?"

"Yes, through the wooden door," said Arad. He stood impatiently while she studied the map. "Enough," he said at last. "I must have the crystal and be gone from here before he returns."

He. Alkairiad. Whoever he was, Arad feared him.

"Remember," he whispered as she pulled open the cracked wooden door, "you must take the crystal from the box and put it into the pouch at once!"

Tianne did not bother to answer. It took a few moments for her eyes to readjust to the darkness inside the walls. Within, the house was no ruin. The floor's tiles were gleaming white, and there was no sign of sand blown in through the cracks in the door. Polished brass lamps hung unlit on the walls. Tianne shivered with nervousness, despite Arad's assurance that the owner was not present. She damned the wizard's secretiveness.

But there was no help for it. She was inside now, and there was a job to be done. Tianne glanced once more at her map and went down the left-hand corridor. She paused as she came to the door marked on the scroll. Arad had placed a symbol beside it. Did that mean some danger? What were these wards he had spoken of?

With one phantom hand clutching the silver medallion, Tianne eased open the latch. At once, flames leaped out to engulf her. She screamed out loud and leaped backward. Gasping, heart pounding, she collapsed against the wall, realizing slowly that she was unhurt. In the doorway, the flames burned on without consuming the wood.

Tianne exhaled a shaken breath. Either it was illusion or the medallion had protected her. She examined the silver disk again. Yes, the symbol was the same as the one on the map. Flame—she had been right! Cautiously she returned to the door and passed through the fire, untouched.

This was the room marked on her map. A table stood against the back wall. Tianne advanced slowly, lest there be more spells warding the place. There on the table was the wooden box, carved with a thorn design as Arad had described it. She reached out an immaterial hand to the lid. It lifted easily.

The crystal within was egg-shaped, a deep, clear blue and cool to the touch. As she stared into it, Tianne felt a sudden dizziness and recalled Arad's warning. She quickly looked away, but there was something compelling in the blue depths. Next to the crystal, the jewels in the box seemed lusterless and uninteresting.

Reluctantly she dropped the blue oval into the pouch and hung it from the silver chain around her neck. She started to the door, then cried out in shock.

The flames filling the doorway reached out to her, shimmering hotly, like a living, translucent being with the form of a man.

"Wizard-thief!" The voice was a high-pitched, dry crackling. "Wizard-thief, free me!"

Tianne approached the doorway, step by trembling step. "What are you? What do you want?"

"Free me, wizard-thief!" it repeated. "You have stolen the crystal. Be merciful! Save me from Alkairiad's wrath!"

"But what *are* you?" Tianne asked again. "A demon?"

"No! Only an elemental, bound here to guard the door of the wizard's workroom. When he returns, when he finds the crystal gone—"

Tianne touched the silver medallion, and the fire-being writhed, crying out, "No! Please! Mercy!"

She took her hand from the silver. "I'm sorry. But how can I help? I know nothing of this," she said, refraining from touching the medallion. "I am no wizard, only a thief."

"Wizard!" insisted the elemental. "Wizard-thief! You bear the crystal and perceive my true form! Your hands reached through Alkairiad's spell! You can free me!"

"How?"

"In the box," the being hissed. "The jewels. One of the rubies is carved with a symbol—I will try to show you."

"No," said Tianne, "I think I know what it looks like."

She searched quickly through the jewels in the thorn-carved box until she found the ruby carved with the same symbol as on the medallion. "Now what do I do?"

"Give it to me! That will break the bond."

The elemental reached out for the stone. "Wait!" said Tianne, pulling her hand away out of its reach. "First, tell me—why do you call me a wizard?"

The elemental shimmered, reaching toward the ruby. "Your hands! None have that power save those of wizard's blood!"

My hands! As Tianne stared numbly at her wrists, the being suddenly cried out, "Quickly, the stone! One comes!"

Alkairiad! Tianne tossed the ruby at the doorway just as a blue-robed figure appeared in the hallway beyond. There was a burst of flame and the being was gone.

With a surge of relief, she recognized the figure as Arad. "What are you doing?" he rasped, out of breath. "Do you have the crystal? Give it to me!"

Before Tianne could react, he snatched the pouch from around her neck and glanced inside.

"Wait!" she cried out. "My hands! How did you know—"

"No time," he whispered harshly. "I should not have come inside. We must be gone from here!"

Tianne followed as the wizard hurried back outside the ruined walls. She stopped in the doorway. He was holding the rod with which he had transported them to this place and beginning the incantation.

"Curse you, wizard!" Tianne burst out, but it was too late. The swirling rush of vertigo overwhelmed her.

There was light again, and trackless sand. Tianne whirled around, but the ruined habitation of the wizard Alkairiad had vanished. Arad was gone.

Then she gasped in shock and dismay. Once again she was wearing her tattered gray beggar's robe. In a panic she reached inside for the hidden pocket, for the ten-orii gold piece.

It had disappeared. Only the tiny stone vial remained."

And the merciless sun.

And the endless leagues of sand.

The heat shimmered at the horizon. Tianne shaded her eyes with the sleeve of her robe and strained to make out the solid form of the city walls. "Khazad?"

The nearest camel drover spit in imitation of his beast. "Khazad, that's right. Almost there!"

The caravan had come on her lying in the shade of a dune, blistered, dehydrated, and close to death. It had been six days since Arad had abandoned her to heatstroke and thirst in the middle of the desert. She had been meant to die, there was no doubt of that, but Tianne had stubbornly refused. With her phantom hands, she had dug tiny burrowing creatures from beneath the sand and sucked the raw moisture from their flesh.

The merchants and drovers were in awe that she had survived, a crippled beggar, and they did not press her to speak of her ordeal. This was as well, since Tianne had little to reveal.

But much to remember. *Arad.* His pallid flesh. His hideous dry voice whispering lies and deceit. The dark, hollow socket of the eye that had Sought her out—for her wizard's blood. No mystery how a whore's daughter had come by that, whose fathering had been at the price of a quarter-bit piece of silver.

Wizard-thief! the elemental had named her. And Arad had *known.* Had known as he stood watching, gloating below the executioner's block, as the ax-blade rose and fell, rose and fell again. As her hands fell severed into the bloody straw. A thief with wizard's blood—how long had he Sought for such as she? How much had he bribed the judge to ensure that the ax took both her hands, to render her apt for his purpose?

Now she knew why he had so jealously guarded the secrets of his chest. But not quite jealously enough. Tianne smiled as her immaterial fingers tightened around the vial within her robe, and one of the drovers shuddered to see the expression on that sun-ravaged face.

Arad. Tianne cherished her hate, which had kept her alive those six days under the sun. For all that he had taken from her—her hands, her livelihood, almost her life. *Arad.* She would find him. As she had wrung the life from the burrowing creatures in the desert, so her hands would close around the pale, yielding flesh of his throat.

Toward this goal the caravan brought her, to the city gates of Khazad. Tianne went directly to the beggars' inn, to her own wretched room. She locked the door, making no effort to rid herself of the beggar's rags or wash away the dust of the desert.

Arad might be here in Khazad or he might not. It

did not matter. Wherever he had gone, she would find him.

The vial of oil rested on the table before her. Tianne set her teeth. She raised one phantom hand to her right eye. There would be pain, but she would endure it. And then she would begin to Seek.

WOLFRUNNER
by Mary E. Choo

Another wolf story; this one by a writer who has appeared widely in various anthologies, and won many awards; far too many to mention here. She has also had a story accepted for a new Andre Norton anthology. She has written much poetry and placed twice as quarter-finalist in the "Writers of the Future" contest. Once again, for all I know about her personally, she might be a vampire, or have three heads.

The northern twilight spread like fire across the sky, riding the tips of the distant peaks. M'Lawn stared out toward the horizon and the snow-bound pass beneath as though she could will life from the icy desolation.

"They must come," she murmured.

She reached down, caressing the shaggy black head of the great wolf beside her. The horn of summons pulled at its chain about her neck, and she grasped the instrument with one hand, raising it to her lips.

"One more time, Asha," she said to the wolf.

She blew hard; seven sharp blasts that soared along the pass towards the mountains. As the echoes died away, she lowered the horn and listened. Sparks snapped and rose from the small fire she had lit nearby.

"Nothing," she conceded at last.

She could just make out the faint glitter of the Temple lights at the far end of the pass, and a hard, dark anger stirred inside her.

"They have no honor, Asha. I should have made the journey to the Temple, instead of calling, waiting like a trusting fool!"

There was a rush of wind at the edge of the forest to her right. Asha stirred and whined, cocking her head to one side as she stared out over the landscape.

"What?" M'Lawn demanded. "Show me!"

She crouched down, placing her hand on the top of Asha's head and concentrating. After a moment, she experienced the familiar, dizzying second vision that came with this intense touching, linking her to the wolf. She saw the drifts through Asha's eyes, with their pallid, luminous aura, perceived the distant, mounted figure moving with dreamlike clarity across the snow, accompanied by the muffled drum of hoofbeats.

She rose to her feet as the rider drew nearer. She could see well enough on her own now. The fading light gathered in a wash of scarlet behind the stranger, accentuating his billowing cloak and long, streaming hair. He pulled up before M'Lawn in a spray of snow.

"So," M'Lawn said. "You've come at last."

She strained, looking beyond him into the near dark and listening. After a moment, she turned her attention to him. She could not see his face clearly, but the light from the flames played over the lush, dark green of his Temple cloak and the sleek leather of his one visible boot. She held out her arm, displaying the attached leather badge with its golden wolf's head that designated her position.

"The Brotherhood agreed to send hunter-warriors in time of trouble. Where are they?" she asked.

"I haven't come to honor any agreement, Wolfrunner," he replied. The voice was soft and young. "I only heard your horn a short time ago. I was traveling in the forests on the northern slope."

He dismounted with the lean, easy grace that marked all the Blackglass priesthood, dropping the reins and starting toward her. She could just make out the three short, curved horns on the shaggy, tossing head of his horse.

He stopped several paces from her, the firelight flickering over his face. It was a beautiful countenance, chiseled and keenly intelligent. His eyes seemed to draw all the remaining light into their core, glittering like emeralds in his olive-brown skin. One gloved hand fingered a silver hammer that hung on a chain about his neck.

He has Seer's eyes, M'Lawn thought; *fathomless and cold.* It was rare to see one of the priesthood's gifted elite abroad.

"They must have heard my summons at the Temple," she said. "The air's been clear and still to the far end of the pass for the last two days—"

"The hunters are occupied elsewhere," he interrupted. The words were accompanied by a wry twist of the mouth. "I regret to say, I'm all the help you're likely to get for a while."

He was young, certainly, and not much taller than she, and he looked drawn and thin. M'Lawn hesitated, then shrugged aside her customary deference to the priesthood.

"I need hunter-warriors, not a lone prophet," she countered. "Unless you have some skill with the sword unusual to your kind. In what I'm about to face, you might be more a danger than a help."

"A greater danger than whatever caused you to summon Temple warriors?"

M'Lawn sucked in her breath, considering him.

"Look, there's been trouble in the mines—I mean, ''e priesthood's mines," she corrected herself. "I—"

"You're paid well enough to look out for the mines on your own. You have enough able-bodied villagers to assist you."

M'Lawn bridled at his words. "I thought, late today, that the Temple might choose to ignore my summons." Her voice hardened in accusation. "I looked after their sacred property, and my people, long enough and well enough, until the other night. All the capable men and women are either badly injured or dead!"

"Then I insist on helping you."

M'Lawn took only a moment to decide.

"I suppose you'll have to do." She jerked her head in the direction of the woods. "Come. We must go. I'll explain as I can, on the way."

She turned and started down the path toward the woods. Asha, who had been strangely silent throughout the exchange, rose and padded alongside her. In a moment, the young priest caught up, without effort it seemed, and M'Lawn could hear the muffled plod of his horse as it followed them.

The trees closed in above them, but M'Lawn could see well enough in the half-light emanating from the banks of snow on either side. To her surprise, Asha began to nuzzle at the young priest's hand. As he walked, he played with the wolf, catching at her ears, and she seemed to delight in his presence.

After a time, though, Asha lost interest. She began to whine, and there was an immediate burst of wolfsong from the lower forest.

"Asha's kin tell me that the moon has risen on the lowlands," M'Lawn said, turning to the priest. "We'll have to hurry."

The snow was well-packed, and she eased into the steady lope that she adopted whenever she and Asha ran together, patrolling the wilderness borders of the village. The horn of summons swung rhythmically against her thick cloak. She glanced back, half-expecting that the priest had fallen behind, but he maintained an even pace, his horse still following.

They descended a slight incline and emerged into a large, snow-packed clearing. M'Lawn halted, motioning the priest to her side. The ground sloped away in front, then dropped off sharply, diverging into a series of ridges that ended in the distant lowlands below. The newly risen moon hung leering over the landscape, with its ravaged face and great swollen bruise of an eye, its pale radiance falling all around them.

To their left and partway down the slope, the lights

of a small village glittered and danced against the mountainside, and there were faint sounds of activity. Off to their right and in a little, the jutting, peaked entrance to the mineshafts rose up into the night.

"Two nights ago," M'Lawn began, nodding toward the mines, "the miners were at work on a particularly good find. The gems were good, with almost no superficial encrustations. The miners grew preoccupied, careless . . ." She faltered. "According to one of the survivors, there was a noise, and the head miner turned, but it was too late . . ."

He made a low, sympathetic noise.

"It was a bloody fight," M'Lawn continued. "From their language and their stocky builds, the attackers were thought to be lowlanders, from the plains below the village—yet they hid their faces behind hideous masks . . ."

"Moon-masks," he interrupted, thoughtful. "The lowlanders are lately infected with an ancient form of moon worship, in direct conflict with our beliefs. They've grown quite fanatic, and seek to wrest authority from the priesthood. Your people happened to be their unfortunate target."

"My wolves and I have always been so watchful, so careful to steer strangers away from here—"

"And you? What was your part in all this?"

"I returned from patrol in the middle of the struggle. I was delayed to the west, and the enemy must have slipped past the village watch. I took out a fair number of them, but the rest managed to get away with a sizable sack of gems." She paused, fingering the thick, silver-threaded hair that belied her youthful appearance. "I failed my office," she finished.

"It seems you were overwhelmed," he said.

"Your superiors would not be so kind. I was careless, inept."

"Perhaps." He looked at her closely. "As for my superiors, they can be more cruel than you could imagine."

His horse strayed behind them, wandering off toward the woods. M'Lawn stared down the slope towards the village. As she had ordered earlier, the lights were being extinguished one by one. Already the exodus of remaining villagers and the wounded to the shelter of the forest caves would have begun.

"The attackers took some of the best gems. I heard them say they'd be back with more men. I calculated it would take them two days to return to their settlement and make their way back here. I hope I'm wrong, and that they come later, or not at all—"

Asha whimpered, and the keening of the rest of the pack was quick to follow. Note after note drifted up from the lowland ridges. The young priest grasped M'Lawn's arm, and she would not have thought he possessed such strength.

"They are coming now," he said. His voice dropped to a terrible, icy whisper, and she knew he saw, somehow. He was counting the enemy, the nameless fanatics as they worked their way up the mountainside.

"They are many—a hundred at least," he continued. He turned to her, his eyes bright and remote in their focus. M'Lawn felt the cold weight of desperation settle in her stomach.

"We must prepare," she said, pulling free of him. "I'll show you what I'd planned to do." She started across the crest in the direction of the mines, moving swiftly, with Asha at her side. His step was quick behind her, and he soon caught up with her.

"Wait!" he cried. He took hold of her and turned her on his arm, and Asha uttered no protest. "You must take me into the mines."

"That would be madness—a waste of time!"

"Please." He released her. "It's important. I must see the gems the miners dug up two nights ago. Whatever you're planning, it could make the difference—"

M'Lawn hesitated. Then; "You can't," she said. "The intruders took all we'd mined that day."

"All?" he demanded, his voice soft. His eyes grew penetrating, cold, as though they were focusing inside her, on the very core, the essence of her being.

"No," she said. "No!" Her resentment of the priesthood flared. "As you would have it, not all, young priest. If you want to see, then I suppose you must—you shall!"

She knelt down and fumbled in the thick, gathered folds of her boot, retrieving something from the generous side pocket.

"There!" She straightened and thrust a piece of stone into his hand. "They dropped one gem—just this one—as they fled."

He stared at her. "You kept it—hid it?"

"Yes," she said, without apology. "I thought, if the priesthood didn't see how good these stones were, if they didn't check in the mines for others when they came, they might view my carelessness a little more kindly."

"Somewhat of a gamble, don't you think?" he murmured.

He crouched beside her in a swift, lithe movement, finding a stray rock in the snow and beginning to chip at the stone in his hand.

"Yes," he said. "Yes." There was a note of intensity, almost triumph in the words. Fragments began to fall away, and he stopped, holding the stone M'Lawn had given him up to the moonlight. Even with the remaining encrustation, she could see the eerie, midnight-sun glitter of the rough gem's core. Generally, the jewels were heavily encased with deposits of coarser stone, a thing which concealed their value from the unaware.

"The ones the strangers took—were they all of this quality?" the young priest asked.

"Yes."

"Then they'll destroy your village and your remaining people for certain. The encrustations are so thin that the lowlanders can't mistake the fact that these are the priesthood's sacred stones."

"But why would that compel them to kill us?"

"They believe the stones to be evil, and a source of our power. It follows that they would attack your village and all the priesthood's other mining settlements, once they found out about them."

For a moment, his face wore an almost covert expression, and M'Lawn suspected there was much about the jewels he was not revealing.

The edge of his protruding sleeve had slipped back, exposing his forearm. In the moonlight, M'Lawn noticed several welts on his arm, and a livid scar showed just above his wrist, as though he had just been branded. She bent and snatched his hand, holding it in a firm grip, staring at the design of the crescent moon with the angular slash of a lance passing through it.

"You!" she said, sudden anger pulsing at her temples. "You're a heretic, a runaway! No wonder you came alone!" She released his hand. "And just what did you think you could do to help me?"

He rose to his feet and faced her, his eyes searching hers, finding some response inside her in spite of herself. The wailing of the wolves drifted toward them across the snow.

"I had to come," he said simply. "I'm the reason why the priesthood's hunter-warriors didn't respond to your horn of summons. They were on the other side of the mountains, tracking me. I'd doubled back along the pass and through the forests when I heard your call—"

"Enough!" M'Lawn interrupted. "Quickly, now! You must have run away many times, for them to have beaten and branded you. Yet they take you back, and from the cut of your clothing and your appearance, they seem to keep you fairly well. Why do you keep running from them?"

"Because they force me to abuse my gift."

The cries of the wolves grew more urgent. There was no time to ask him more, or what this gift was that the priesthood prized so much. Yet she sensed there was something about him that she had missed, some terrible, dark power that went beyond what she had seen of him until now.

"Come," she said, turning. "We'll probably die together, my young lord priest, but at least you can help me prepare for it!"

The howling of the wolves reached a crescendo as they hurried back towards the incline, with Asha following. Suddenly, M'Lawn paused, motioning the priest to a halt. There was a sound from somewhere below, on their right. It grew, rumbled, became a roar that shook the ground beneath their feet.

After some moments, the noise died away. M'Lawn beckoned to the priest, and with Asha they moved swiftly to the incline, pausing on the flat, sloped space above the crest once more.

She cursed softly. The way before them was much altered. What had been a twisted mass of rock and ice was now heaped with snow, forming a white trough that snaked down the mountainside, tapering off toward the lowlands. Just at its edge, a ragged line of torches bobbed against the glow and shadow of the lower ridges. Above this, and to their left, the entire village was in blackness.

"There." M'Lawn swung her head to indicate an overhanging mass of snow just below the mineshafts. Its edge was ragged, and powdered snow drifted on the air around it where the rest had just fallen away.

"That," she said, "was part of my plan." She took up the horn, which still hung from its chain around her neck. "When you blow a certain note on this, and conditions are right, the snow will shift, fall . . ."

They both stared down the slope. The lowlanders were near enough that she could make out the shapes of their hideous moon-masks.

"Fate mocks me," she said bitterly. "If the snow had held off until they were nearer, fallen when I commanded it to, it would have buried them . . ."

The lowland raiders struggled upward over the heaped snow towards the mines, some of them breaking off and heading for the village. Nothing slowed them. All at once, M'Lawn felt the weight of her years of service to the priesthood. She turned to him.

"I'd planned, as a secondary measure, to set the pack on them, then lure the survivors into the forest and pick off as many as I could." She reached inside her cloak and removed the sleek, coiled whip attached to her belt, then took the horn of summons from her neck and cast it to one side. "I have my whip. And you? Do you have a weapon?"

"I do," he said. He crouched in the snow, delving with one hand until he found a large rock. He still held the rough gem in his other hand, and he began to chip away at it with the stone.

"What are you doing?" M'Lawn demanded. "That's sacrilege!"

"Will it matter, if we die, and the lowlanders hunt down and butcher your fellow villagers?"

He stood up and held the gem to the scarred face of the moon. M'Lawn caught her breath as the light shot through the stone's core with a wonderful clarity, revealing its dark green color and the pale gold star at the center. Then the shouts of the raiders below drew her attention.

"Well," she laughed bitterly. "It seems we'll die with the wealth of the priesthood on our hands. Do you have a name, young heretic?"

"Dhane," he said. "And you, Wolfrunner?"

"M'Lawn," she said, summoning her pride. "And though I'm past my prime, I'll give them a fight to remember!"

"We both will," he answered. "M'Lawn, will you trust me?"

"Isn't it a little late to ask me that?" M'Lawn demanded, distracted as a raider set a torch to a village roof.

"You must have guessed that my gift exceeds that of the usual Seer. Didn't it occur to you that I might use my talents against the lowlanders?"

"Yes—but I'm not certain I want to be part of it."

He ignored this. His silver hammer had slipped inside his cloak, and he freed it. He raised it to the level of the gem and tapped the surface lightly. A low, sweet note resonated across the clearing. Asha began to prance about him, her topaz eyes glowing.

"This is hardly the time for games!" M'Lawn snapped. "Asha, here!" she called, but the wolf would not obey.

"Not games—no. But it is time for music," he replied. "My music."

The last was said with an eerie reverence. He turned to M'Lawn. His eyes seemed to have taken on a life of their own, so bright were they, so clear and green.

"I can stop them, M'Lawn. It's my duty, my penance for depriving you and your people of the priesthood's help. But you must stand by me. I need your strength, your courage."

"I hardly have a choice, do I?" M'Lawn snapped, frightened now.

He shrugged, then faced the ravine and began to tap the stone in different places; gently at first. The notes were varied and clear, and carried on the night air, growing vibrant in their intensity, like some ethereal, mesmeric command.

M'Lawn watched spellbound as the activity of the raiders below ceased, their torches growing still. After a moment, the men began to stir again, changing direction and starting up the incline toward the young priest, moving inexorably through the deep snow. Dhane stepped forward, so they could not mistake him in the moonlight, playing ever louder. Asha stuck close to his side, her tail beating against him, oblivious to M'Lawn's efforts to check her.

The raiders drew nearer, their masks with their painted scars and bruises plainly visible now, bobbing in the night. They were strangely silent, some tumbling and sprawling as they worked their way upward.

All at once Dhane stopped, dropping the hammer on the length of its chain. M'Lawn moved forward to stand shoulder to shoulder with him. The raiders crunched toward them. In the absence of music, the men began to mutter amongst themselves, shaking their heads as though they had just awakened from a dream, some of them cursing and gesturing with their weapons toward Dhane.

Asha crouched, snarling, making brief leaps toward the steep drop of the incline and retreating again. M'Lawn flexed her whip.

"Asha, my heart, stand fast!" she called. The raiders

stopped, growing silent once more, and she sensed their intense, disbelieving scrutiny.

"All right, lord priest—what now?" she asked, breathing hard.

"I'm going to tell you a story," he said. He reached out and touched her shoulder.

"You're mad," she whispered. Yet she felt bound by him, by something she had seen in his eyes, his face, and she could not move.

He held the gem to the light of the moon, and the stone's heart burned with a sudden and terrible light. At the sight of it, the enemy erupted in a howl of rage.

"We are prepared," Dhane laughed, and there was madness in his voice.

He pressed his shoulder hard against hers, rotating the gem. It flickered and blazed, and as M'Lawn stared at it she experienced a shock, a sudden bonding, as though the light had frozen her to his body. She could feel the pulse of his blood in his veins, the beat of his heart, just as she could feel Asha's when the link was forged between them. He began to talk, his voice carrying above the sounds of the lowlanders' advance.

"Look at the moon, M'Lawn," he said. He thrust the gem, almost blinding in its brilliance now, directly at the moon's ravaged face.

"Do you know, it was once very different—"

"I've heard a lot of stories about that, priest!"

M'Lawn lashed her whip, her muscles tensing from long habit. She was held by his words and her strange new bond with him, yet every seasoned instinct cried out for her to fight. Asha began to lunge and retreat again, perilously close to the steeper drop of the incline, the black shadows of the rest of the pack streaming over the lower ridges as they coursed toward her.

"But this story is true," he continued. "Once, before the coming of the great ice and the wars men fought in their silver sky-ships, the lady moon's face was whole and pearl and luminous, and she laughed at the night and the earth and the stars."

M'Lawn blinked, her eyes stinging from the light of the gem. A constriction seized her chest, grew like cold fire. Her shoulder felt completely fused to his, as if the garments that separated their flesh had melted away, and the light were drawing all the strength from her body into his.

"Look at her face, M'Lawn. See it in all its ancient glory!"

The moon paled, grew luminous as a pearl, the features melting, changing into a countenance so beautiful that it took M'Lawn's breath away. A warm rush of air caught at her hair, seemed to drag at her body and Dhane's, uproot them, though they were standing still. Towering, unfamiliar trees suddenly framed the clearing on either side, and the ravine before them shifted, filled, grew shallow and devoid of snow.

Asha still crouched a short distance in front of them, fierce, bewildered. Her confusion called to M'Lawn, and the Wolfrunner knew without touching her that they both saw as Dhane did, as he wanted them to. She had a blurred, complex vision of the lowlanders struggling, and heard their cries as the ground rolled and changed, though their voices seemed to come from a distance. There was an absence of wolfsong now, as though the darkness beyond were some endless space that had swallowed the rest of the pack. Some of the raiders' moon-masks fell crumpled to the ground, and a number of them struggled waist-deep in rattling, falling stones. Any hatred M'Lawn had harbored against them drained away as she watched their suffering and heard the strident terror of their curses as they slipped back into the darkness.

"Any moment now," Dhane said. Though his voice still carried, M'Lawn thought he sounded shaken.

"They're calling us devils—witches!"

"Never mind that! Call Asha back!"

M'Lawn whistled, called so loudly that her throat hurt, trying to reassert her hold on the wolf, but Asha had begun to panic. She lunged and snapped, starting after the terrified lowlanders.

"No, Asha!" M'Lawn plunged forward, but Dhane caught at her. M'Lawn struggled, surprised once more at his strength.

"M'Lawn, don't. I can't hold us here! The moon—look!"

M'Lawn stared up at the face of the opalescent moon. A great bruise began to swell under one eye, and streaks appeared on the face. The air grew bitterly cold once more, and the trees began to fade.

"I'll not leave Asha!"

M'Lawn broke free and started after the wolf. She had almost reached her when she heard Dhane cry out, and felt his arms about her waist, pulling her back. The ravine below began to blur. There was a stabbing pain in her foot, and she fell back, the sky spinning around her as the moon filled the limits of her vision. Her struggling knocked the ice-hearted gem from Dhane's hand, and it shot into the night like a dying star, then bounced down the ravine and into the growing darkness beyond. The returning cold seemed to penetrate her heart, to crush it. As her head slid sideways, the last thing she remembered was the sight of the moon behind the hooded mine entrance to her right, and the sound of the wolves howling.

M'Lawn was weary of the pain and the dreams. She tossed and turned on the bed, her skin slick with sweat, vaguely aware of the walls of her modest hut around her and the flickering fire to her right. Her mind was filled with wolfsight, and a vision of Asha vanishing, and her ears rang with the voices of the pack.

"Gone," she murmured. "Gone."

Several of her people were tending her, their touch and voices gentle, almost conspiratorial. A darker form moved in the background like a shadow, and she knew it to be the young priest.

At last she forced herself to concentrate, to call him, and he came forward and knelt beside her, his beautiful face coming into focus.

"I'm home," she said, her voice coarse, as if from fever.

"Yes, but I've cost you dearly, Wolfrunner," he replied.

"The lowlanders—?"

"I left them in the days of legend, M'Lawn, in the land of the opalescent moon."

"So that's where we all went," she said, remembering. *That was his gift, then,* she thought—*rediscovering the past—no—making it real, existing in it, with the help of the sacred stones.* There were those who would kill, and worse, to possess such power. Her mind wandered, and she felt a pang of grief.

"Asha," she muttered brokenly. "We left her there?" He took her hand, and for the first time she noticed the distant, keening wail of the pack outside.

"I'm sorry," he said. "I didn't mean to take her with us. Taking anyone else 'back' is new to me. I've always gone alone, before."

M'Lawn waited for a moment, unable to speak. She eased herself up on one elbow, looking down toward her foot, feeling the pain only now.

"It got caught—between 'then' and 'now,' " Dhane said. "It's a nasty injury, but it will heal with time, and if you're careful, you should walk without a limp."

"You know so much, for a heretic," M'Lawn said, her voice catching. She reached out to finger the edge of the coverlet, where Asha normally lay. Tears pricked at the corners of her eyes, but she would not show her grief. Not to this wayward priest who had used her in a way she would never fully understand.

"I'm that, and worse," he said. His face came alive with emotion; chagrin, anguish, remorse. "I've drawn you into my heresy, compromised you, risked your life—"

"I'd have done anything, to save the rest of my people," M'Lawn interrupted. She struggled with her feelings, unable to go on.

As they stared at one another, a drum of hoofbeats grew outside, followed by a shouting and general confusion so loud that it could not be denied. Dhane looked toward the door, then back to her, as though there were more he wanted to say, but could not find the words.

"Your village has been kind enough to keep my

horse for me. I have to go. Good-bye, M'Lawn," he said.

He rose and snatched up his cloak, making for the door. As he reached it, there was a loud pounding, and it burst open. Several figures loomed against the sudden flood of sunlight, pulling him outside.

"Wait!" M'Lawn cried. She gestured to one of the villagers who had nursed her. "Quickly! Help me!"

The old woman eased her to her feet, and at M'Lawn's insistence provided a stout staff from the wood by the hearth. M'Lawn slipped into her boots, taking some time to hobble across the floor and make her way outside.

The surviving villagers were gathered in the narrow road that passed by her hut, and milling among them in all their dark power and arrogance were the mounted hunter-warriors of the Blackglass priesthood. They were several dozen in number, the winter sunlight spilling across their dark hair and the coarse, jet manes of their mythical horses. Two of them were binding Dhane's wrists with fine leather thongs, and at their insistence he mounted his horse.

M'Lawn's anger was so sudden and so strong that she hardly felt the cold through her sleeping garment. One of the hunters eased his mount toward her, and she saw from the crest on his cloak that he was the leader.

"You come readily enough, when the worst is done," M'Lawn said coldly. "I take it that hunting runaways is more important than protecting your miners!" *Now it would come,* she thought. *The arrogance, the recriminations.*

"We'd have been here in time, if it hadn't been for our young friend," the hunter replied. He towered above her on his horse, and M'Lawn saw no mercy in the stern, handsome face.

"Without Dhane, I doubt if any of the village or the mines would remain—"

"We're pleased to have caught up with him," the other cut in. "He's just confessed to certain unorthodox methods in defeating the lowlanders. We understand that you couldn't help, because of the injury you sustained in the earlier battle. For the moment," his gaze traveled to her silver-streaked hair, "we'll pass on your earlier negligence. Provided your foot heals, as Dhane says it will, you'll remain here, Wolfrunner. We'll rebuild the population of your village from others in the highland settlements."

He turned his horse away. Dhane's mount was being led down the road and through the villagers, and he turned and gave her one last look. M'Lawn knew what he risked with his lie, for he alone would bear responsibility for the lowlanders' fate. She struggled after the leader, clutching at his bridle with her free hand.

"The priesthood is cruel, to brand its own!" she cried. "Have mercy on one so young!"

The hunter's expression as he looked down at her was cold and unyielding.

"He only seems young, Wolfrunner. In many ways, he's older than you or I could possibly imagine."

He freed the bridle from her grasp and gestured to his comrades. They turned and galloped away in a swirl of dark cloaks and flying hooves, the villagers scattering before them. M'Lawn stared after them as they moved up the slope toward the forest, her eyes half-blinded by the sun. An elderly villager nudged her arm.

"They'll flay him alive," M'Lawn murmured.

"Perhaps, Wolfrunner," the villager replied. Then, "Look."

He thrust a bundle at M'Lawn. She settled her staff under one arm and gathered the squirming mass in the other. A small black head poked out from among the ragged skins.

"A wolf pup!" M'Lawn gasped. "But where—?"

"The young priest went into the woods, while you slept off your sickness." The villager's voice was tinged with awe. "He said he found it near the pass."

More likely he dug up a stone in the mines and went "back" for the pup, M'Lawn thought. There were no litters at this time of the season.

She stared after the retreating horsemen, filled with

a mixture of gratitude and anguish. Dhane had understood only too well. The wind would carry the cries of
the grieving pack across the snow, and the moon would
rise with her scarred face as though nothing had
happened.

And now, M'Lawn had a new life to consider. She
buried her face in the pup's warm fur, the thought of
Asha, the final, terrible realization that she was gone
pulling like a physical pain inside of her.

"Niamat," she murmured, using the wild, sacred
name for wolf. The tears started from her eyes.

At once, there was a dizzying shock of both wolfsight
and something else; the now-familiar, chilling sense of
bonding she had experienced with Dhane, though it
quickly began to fade. She saw the forest as it rose
before the young priest's eyes, and she knew he was
unafraid, that he inwardly mocked the authority of
those around him as they bore him back to the Temple
at the end of the pass.

"Good-bye, Wolfrunner." His voice sounded somewhere inside her head, became a trailing echo before
it died.

She swayed, regained her balance, favoring her leg.
A new determination kindled within her.

She was still strong, and young enough yet, she
thought. When the time came and her grief had passed,
she would run again, and fulfill her duties to the
priesthood.

And she would remember.

She blinked, looking past the black blur of the pup's
head towards the forest, and through her tears, she
managed a smile.

UNTIL WE MEET AGAIN
by J. A. Brebner

Somewhere on my desk, there is (I have faith) a piece of paper telling me something about Jeffrey Brebner; but it appears to have been kidnapped by the Black Hole I keep there for losing important documents, and my memory tells me only that Jeffrey Brebner is married with a daughter, and that his household includes two "generic dogs" . . . a phrase fraught with promise against all those cat people out there in fantasy. Up with the canines!

The constant drone of insects was loud in the summer air. After two days in the village of Preavey, where a plague of locusts was quickly decimating the local fields, Valerea thought she was ready to go mad. She didn't know how the people living there stood it. She entered a building with TAVERN painted above the door and sighed with relief as the monotonous buzzing dropped in volume.

While waiting for the little man behind the bar to draw her a tankard of ale, Valerea turned and looked around the room. Some tables were occupied, many were not. Running a hand absently through her short red hair, she ambled over to a table where the only other woman present was sitting with three men. They

249

all looked up as she pulled a chair from a nearby table and sat down, then resumed their conversation.

"Of course I can do it," the woman said. "Removing locusts is no problem. I assure you that I can save your fields this very day, but I really must have payment first."

"What's the problem, Tess?" Valerea asked. She glanced at the short woman with the long dark hair, then let her blue eyes turn cold as they settled on each of the three men. They looked back at her uncomfortably, their eyes shifting from hers to the handle of the sword protruding over her shoulder to the table top.

"They don't want to pay before I've done anything," the dark-haired woman answered. She took out a small clay pipe and filled it from a leather bag around her neck. Lighting it with a touch of her finger, she sat back and looked at the three.

"You do not trust Tessia L'Argent?" Valerea asked the men. "Do you think the Silver Sorceress would take your money and then sneak out of town? Why, her honesty is exceeded *only* by her magical skills, and I don't like it when people cast doubt upon my friend's honesty."

Although the men were impressed at learning the identity of the sorceress, and nervous about the thinly veiled threat of the redhead, they were still reluctant to pay in advance. After some more talk, however, and several more less-thinly veiled threats by Valerea, they agreed to pay half in advance and half when the crops had been saved.

After the men had gone, Valerea picked up the money they'd left and placed it into a pouch at her waist. "Dogs," she muttered. "With your reputation, it's not bad enough that you must cast spells on grasshoppers in bean fields for paltry sums. These village idiots must also question your honesty as well."

"Maybe so," the sorceress replied, "but we cannot eat my reputation, and this paltry sum, as you call it, will buy enough supplies for us and our horses to last until we get to the High Mountain Games in two weeks. With what you should win there, plus what I'll make selling charms and amulets, we'll be able to take a sizable amount with us back to the Sisters at the Crystal Tower."

Valerea suppressed a groan. In the several years that she and Tessia had been together, she had never known the sorceress to be so obsessed with anything. Of course, if the Sisters had done for her what they'd done for Tess, she knew that she'd probably be just as anxious to help them out as her friend was.

The Sisterhood of The Golden Light was a group of women that taught those who were gifted with magical abilities how to use their skills. Tessia L'Argent had been a *very* gifted child, and her powers had become known to those who would have used her for their own evil ends. A plan was formed to kidnap the child.

But the gift of Tessia was also know to the Sisters, who watched over the child. So, when the kidnappers broke into the L'Argent home, young Tessia was not there to be taken.

From the safety of the Sisters' keep, known as the Crystal Tower, the dark-haired child watched in a silver bowl filled with a dark liquid as several men broke into her house. She saw them go from room to room looking for her, and she saw them kill her parents and younger brother.

The Sisters had cared for Tessia after that, slowly helping her through her shock and grief. Then they began to teach her how to use her power. Having an affinity with the metal that shared her name, she became known as the Silver Sorceress. As her power and skill grew, so did her fame, and she traveled all over the land, helping others with her magic.

Years passed, and Tessia finally settled down in a beautiful little valley to live in solitude. A few more years went by, and the Silver Sorceress began to fade from the public's memory. Until one day, when a young redheaded swordswoman entered the valley, investigating the tale of a hidden cave filled with bandits' treasure.

Valerea talked the sorceress into joining her, and though they never found the treasure cave, they'd been together ever since. Then, a few days ago, they heard about the trouble that the Sisters at the Crystal Tower were having, and helping them out had been the only thing on Tessia's mind since.

Lord Aldemus, the king's governor over the lands of which the Crystal Tower was a part, had recently increased taxes. The governor had always been a very public figure, and was well liked by nearly everyone. Yet now he had withdrawn into his castle and refused to see anyone other than the members of his own household, and no explanation was given for the tax increase. It was whispered that Lord Aldemus had been placed under a spell, and that General Tobray, leader of the king's troops under Aldemus, was responsible.

The new tax was heavy, and many people, having little or no money, were forced to pay by stored goods and/or livestock. Failure to pay the tax meant going to prison, from which few, if any, returned.

The Sisters of The Golden Light were a self-sufficient body, and had less money than most. But since their meager gardens provided barely enough food for them and their students, money was the only way they could pay the tax. General Tobray himself had come to the Crystal Tower and said they had until the end of summer to raise their tax money, or he would destroy their keep. There was no doubt that he would do exactly as he threatened.

When Tessia learned of the Sisters' plight, she saw it as her chance to repay them for all that they had done for her. She and Valerea had always done very well for themselves at the upcoming High Mountain Games, and though she didn't know how much the Sisters needed, she was sure that between the two of them, they could cover the amount.

The trouble was, Tessia had never *asked* Valerea to give up her share to help the Sisters; she'd just assumed that the redhead would do so. And Valerea was a little annoyed that her friend expected her to part with her hard-won money just like that. So, although she said nothing when Tess spoke about taking their money to the Sisters, her annoyance was visible on her face. The sorceress looked at her in surprise.

"What's the matter, Valerea?" she asked.

Valerea hesitated, wanting to choose her words carefully. But she could think of no easy way to say what she was thinking, and finally just blurted it out: "Tess, I never said I would give my money to the Sisters. I feel sorry for them, of course, and I'll be glad to give them *some* of my winnings. But I want to keep some as well. After all, I work hard for that money, and I want something to show for my effort."

Tessia said nothing, but Valerea could see that she was angry. The sorceress' eyes had narrowed and her jaw had tightened, the way it always did when she was upset. The redhead sighed and placed a hand on her friend's arm, but before she could say any more, Tessia jerked her arm away and stood up.

"Fine," she said, her voice cold. "If that's the way you want it, fine. I thought you would want to help the only family I have, but I guess I was mistaken. Good luck to you at the Games." She started to turn away.

"Tess, please don't be like that," Valerea said. "I said that I would be glad to give them *some* money, just not *all* of it. As you pointed out, we have to eat, too."

The sorceress turned back to her. "I said it's fine. You can keep your *hard-earned* money to buy all the food you want. I'm sure the Sisters will manage without your help somehow." She started away again, then turned back, holding out a hand, palm up. "Speaking of money, you have mine. I'll just keep it myself, please."

Without a word, Valerea handed her the money that the three men had left earlier. Without a word, Tessia took it and walked away. The buzzing of the locusts became louder momentarily as the sorceress opened the door and left the tavern. Valera watched her go, then shook her head and called for another tankard of ale.

Shortly afterward, someone came into the tavern and announced that the sorceress was going to the fields. Within moments, those in the tavern joined the rest of the villagers as they went out to watch the Silver Sorceress at work. Valerea went along, hoping that her friend had cooled off a little.

When Valerea reached the field where Tess had chosen to cast her spell, the sorceress had already begun. She was standing out in the field alone, arms spread and head thrown back. Her lips were moving, but the noise of the insects made it impossible to hear what she was saying. Not that it made any difference; Valerea knew that Tessia could've screamed into dead silence at the top of her lungs and the words still wouldn't have made any sense to anyone not skilled in magic.

The sorceress then performed a short ritualistic dance, which ended with her kneeling on the ground. After a few moments, she stood, reached into a pouch at her waist, and removed a small silver vial. As she opened the vial, a wind came up. From out of the vial, a small cloud of greenish-blue smoke emerged which quickly grew until it obscured the sorceress and covered the field. Then someone pointed at another field, where a similar cloud was appearing, then another, until all of the village fields were enveloped in clouds.

Valerea had moved up to the front of the crowd, at the edge of the field. A man near her reached a hand toward the cloud. The redhead quickly pulled the long knife from its sheath at her waist and slapped the reaching hand with the flat of the blade. The man pulled his hand back and looked at her in surprise.

"That cloud is deadly poison!" Valerea yelled, then looked around in surprise along with everyone else. The buzzing of the locusts had stopped, and the clouds were already starting to dissipate.

The villagers began to cheer as Tessia stepped out of the field, and Valerea went to help her friend, as she usually did after the sorceress finished casting a spell. But to her surprise and dismay, Tess brushed past her as if she were a total stranger. Valerea stood and watched as the sorceress was swallowed by the crowd of grateful villagers, which then began to head back toward the village. Within moments, the redhead was alone by the silent field.

By the time Valerea got back to the tavern, the place was packed. She could tell where Tessia was, even though she couldn't see her, because everyone in the tavern was trying to get close to the largest table in the room. After trying in vain to get the barkeep's attention, the redhead finally leaped over the counter and drew herself a tankard of ale. No one paid the slightest attention.

Holding the tankard up to avoid spilling it among the jostling crowd, Valerea made her way to the stairs at the rear of the tavern and up them to the room that she and Tess had rented. But when she got there, all of Tess' things were gone.

"Well, I guess there's no reason for me to stick around here," Valerea muttered. Fighting down a sudden lump in her throat, she quickly packed her few possessions. When she was finished, she went back down the stairs, deposited her empty mug on the bar-top, and left the tavern. She didn't even look toward the large table, and so did not see Tessia watching her leave, or the tears in the sorceress' eyes.

By the third day of the High Mountain Games, Valerea had won all of her preliminary events easily. In two events, she'd disabled her opponents. If the weapons used hadn't been dull and blunted, she would have killed them. People began to talk about the woman with the short red hair who fought so fiercely, and she quickly became a favorite to win in the finals.

While walking alone among the booths that had been set up to sell almost anything one could want, Valerea spotted Tess. The sorceress was working a small stand by herself, selling charms and amulets that she'd made. The redhead was about to turn and go in another direction when her attention was captured by two men who had stopped at the little booth. They did not look like the type who believed in good luck charms, so Valerea edged closer, curious.

"I hear you're trying to help those bitches at the

Crystal Tower," the taller, bearded man said. He picked up a silver necklace from the table in front of him. Tessia looked at him, but said nothing. The second man giggled, a high-pitched sound, and picked up a bracelet.

"Please do not handle these items if you are not going to buy them," the sorceress said at last. "It weakens the magic." She calmly reached out and gently placed a hand on each man's wrist. When she did so, their hands snapped open, releasing the items they held.

As soon as she let him go, the taller man reached for the knife at his belt, his face contorting in anger. But before he could draw the weapon, Valerea's sword was against his chest, the edge facing his throat.

"She asked you nicely," the redhead stated, her voice low. "You don't want to cause trouble to someone so polite, do you?"

The bearded man looked at Tessia for a moment, then at Valerea. "Not here or now," he said, "but we will meet again, I assure you." He stepped back, away from the sword at his chest, then the two of them turned and walked away, the smaller man's high-pitched giggle coming back to them over the noise of the crowd.

Valerea turned to Tessia after watching the men leave, hoping that her action had redeemed her to the sorceress. But the smaller woman regarded the redhead with a cool stare.

"Thank you, but your help was unnecessary," Tessia said. "I am not afraid of General Tobray, and I certainly am not afraid of any of his men."

"Was that who those two were, Tobray's men?" Valerea asked. "I've seen the one with the beard in competition. He's very sneaky and very mean, Tess. Maybe you should stay with me at night while the games are on, for your own safety."

"I told you, I'm not afraid," the sorceress replied. "Now, if you aren't going to buy anything, please make room for those who will."

Valerea didn't move. "Tess, what can I do to gain

your friendship again? You want money for your sisters? Here." Reaching into her pouch, Valerea took out her winnings and laid them on the table.

But the smaller woman ignored the pile of coins and moved to one side, where a man and woman were looking at amulets. After a moment, Valerea turned and walked away, leaving the coins on the table.

Later that day, as Valerea was going over her weapons and gear, a boy came up to her and said the lady with the silver wanted to see her. He gave her a necklace that the redhead recognized as the one that Tessia wore. Placing the necklace in her pouch, Valerea started to walk briskly to where the sorceress' booth was.

But when she got there, the stand was empty and Tess was nowhere to be seen. Valerea looked around, puzzled, and then heard a high-pitched giggle behind her. Feeling a chill down her spine, the redhead turned to face the smaller of the two men that had been there earlier.

He was standing well out of sword range, so Valerea kept her hands at her sides. She took a step forward, but the little man took two steps back, so she remained still.

"If anything happens to me, your friend dies," the little man giggled. "If you want to see her alive again, be at the practice area in one hour." He turned to go.

"Wait," Valerea called. He turned back toward her. "What makes you think I care what happens to her?" she asked.

He shrugged. "You're here, aren't you?" With that, he turned and ran off, his annoying giggle drifting back to her on the afternoon breeze. Valerea cursed under her breath.

When she walked into the practice area, Valerea wasn't surprised to see a number of men standing around, waiting for her. She'd figured there were more than just two of Tobray's men at the games, and that they would probably join the bearded man when he faced her. As she walked toward them, Valerea did a quick count. Fourteen standing, and two sitting on chairs that had been brought from somewhere.

Valerea looked at the two sitting down. One was old and thin, and carried no weapons that she could see. His hair was long and gray, and even from a distance the redhead could see that his face was lined with wrinkles.

The other man sitting down was big, but not fat. His bald head reflected the setting sun when he looked down, as he was when Valerea entered the practice area. He was smoking a small clay pipe, which she recognized as Tessia's, and fingering a dagger at his waist. When he looked up at the redhead, his small, close-set eyes looked dead, like a reptile's eyes.

"Where is she?" Valerea asked, stopping about thirty feet from the two men sitting. She directed her question to the bald man.

"She is alive and well, so far," he answered. "But to see her, you must first defeat Borz, if you can." He lifted his hand from the dagger, and the bearded man that had been at Tessia's booth stepped forward, grinning.

"I told you that we would meet again," he said, drawing his sword. "And now you'll pay for humiliating me today, just as your friend shall pay, once I've finished with you."

Valerea drew her sword as the men spread out to watch the fight. She could hear the high-pitched giggle of Borz's companion, as well as calls and insults from the other men. She ignored them all, concentrating on her opponent. As the two circled warily, looking for openings, the redhead let her gaze stray from Borz, trying to determine where Tessia might be hidden.

Finally, she thought she knew. The only place near the practice area large enough to conceal a body, even one as small as Tessia's, was behind or under the two chairs where the bald man and his elderly companion sat. She was thinking about how to get them to move, when Borz began his attack.

Valerea parried the bearded man's thrust with ease, but he evaded her counterthrust similarly. Grinning, he came at her again, and again they clashed and separated without drawing blood.

"You're not bad, for a woman," Borz said. It was the same ruse men always tried to get her angry with, hoping to break her concentration. Valerea had long since learned to let such taunts go in one ear and out the other, but she pretended that it was working this time.

Putting a scowl on her face, the redhead delivered a wild swing that she knew Borz would avoid easily. The force with which she swung seemed to spin her around, putting her back to the bearded man. Borz rushed forward, raising his sword to cut her down.

But Valerea proved that she was adept at trickery as any man. In the same motion that had spun her around, and as Borz advanced with blade held high, she brought her left foot up in a back-kick. Her heel drove into Borz's midsection with enough force to double him over. Valerea then brought her sword down across the back of his neck, and Borz collapsed to the ground, dead.

Valerea faced the bald man. "Now, where's the sorceress? Or do you intend to go back on your word, general?"

Tobray looked at the redhead with mild amusement. "Do we know one another?" he asked as he and the old man stood.

"No," Valerea said, "but I've heard the rumors of how you had Lord Aldemus placed under a spell. It figures that you would keep your spell-caster with you, and that old man is a wizard if ever I saw one."

Tobray laughed out loud then, and he and the wizard exchanged a look. They moved away from their chairs, and Tobray had four of his men lift them up to reveal Tessia, bound and gagged, lying on the ground beneath them. As the sorceress was lifted by her arms and held upright by two of Tobray's men, Valerea thought of a plan and put it into action immediately.

Moving slowly closer to the little group around the sorceress, the redhead casually reached into the pouch at her side and took out Tessia's necklace. Then, seeming to rest her hand on the hilt of the knife at her waist, she began to wrap the necklace around the handle. When she was about fifteen feet from them, she stopped.

"Perhaps I was mistaken about that old man," Valerea said, a sneer curling her lip. "If he were a real wizard, there would have been no need to tie such a small woman up."

"You think my magic is not strong enough to hold her?" the wizard asked. His voice was surprisingly deep and powerful for his apparent great age. "Untie the woman. I will make her as a statue." He turned to face Tessia, already beginning his spell.

The moment he started to turn, Valerea pulled the knife from its sheath and threw it at him. But as quick as she was, Tobray was faster. He pushed the wizard, knocking him to the ground. The spinning blade sank into the chest of one of the men holding Tessia.

"Kill her!" Tobray yelled, pointing at Valerea. His men began to run toward the redhead, drawing their weapons.

Valerea saw Tess break free of the remaining man that held her, reach up to pull the gag from her mouth, and fall to the ground before she was forced to run from her attackers. In the large open practice area, there was nothing for the redhead to place her back against for protection.

Valerea heard the pounding of her nearest opponent's feet on the hard-packed ground close behind her. She waited until she could hear his breathing as well, then she suddenly stopped and fell to the ground. The man tripped over her, and Valerea drove her sword into him, then leaped to her feet.

As the rest of the men surrounded her, Valerea jumped forward, screaming. The ferocity of her attack caused two of the men to step back several paces, and the redhead quickly broke through the circle and began to run again. As she passed the fallen Borz, she leaned forward and snatched up his sword.

She was running back toward Tobray and the wizard, who had gotten to his feet again by that time. The old man was looking at the redhead as she approached, and she could see his lips moving. Valerea knew he was casting a spell at her, and that she would never reach him before it hit her. Behind her, she could hear Tobray's men coming fast. Screaming in anger and frustration, Valerea put on a burst of speed, raising the two swords she held in the hope of throwing them at Tobray and the wizard before the spell hit her.

Suddenly, the wizard stumbled forward and fell to his knees. Tobray looked down at him in surprise, then looked over his shoulder. Tessia was standing there, holding the necklace that Valerea had put around the handle of her knife before throwing it.

As the wizard shook his head and climbed to his feet, he waved a hand at Tessia, and the sorceress staggered and fell backward. Valerea threw the two swords then, but lost her balance and fell facefirst to the ground. She began to roll, expecting to feel the swords of Tobray's men cutting into her at any moment.

But when nothing happened to her, the redhead looked back to see them all standing still, staring past her in awe. She looked the other way and saw that both of the swords she'd thrown had amazingly found their marks. But that wasn't what had captured the attention of the eleven men chasing her.

General Tobray was on the ground, writhing in agony as he tried to pull the sword from his thigh. The other sword had struck the wizard in the side, just below the rib cage. Yet he still remained on his feet, looking as if the blade protruding from his body was merely an annoyance.

Casually pulling the sword from his side, the wizard stepped over to stand above Tobray. Looking down at the bald man with contempt, the wizard raised the sword he held and drove it down through Tobray's belly, pinning him to the ground. The man screamed once, and his body convulsed several times before finally becoming still.

"Now *I* am in command," the wizard said as he turned to face the redhead and Tobray's men. They all stared at him as he pulled the sword from Tobray's body and walked slowly forward, his eyes on Valerea, who still lay on the ground. "Don't bother to stand, woman. You've shown great courage, and out of respect, I'll make your death quick."

Behind him, Valerea saw a slight movement. One of Tobray's men saw it, too, however, and started to say something.

"Silence!" the wizard roared. "I know the one behind me still lives. I can feel her attempting to use her magic against me, but she is too weak to succeed. Once I have . . ." He stopped suddenly, and his audience noticed that his gaze was fixed on a point behind them all.

Valerea and the soldiers glanced back to see what the wizard was watching, and they saw some dust-devils forming about twenty feet away. When the dust settled, there were five women standing there, all clad in long robes, and all with long blonde hair. It was hard to see them clearly, for there was an aura about the women that made it difficult to look directly at them.

Although she'd never seen any Sisters of The Golden Light, Valerea knew that that was who the five newcomers were. She glanced back at the wizard and saw fear on his face. He seemed to have forgotten about her, Tessia, and the soldiers. The redhead cursed softly over the fact that she had no weapons, for he was an easy target, standing still about ten feet away. She tensed her muscles, preparing to launch herself at him barehanded, when she saw Tess slowly rise to her feet, Valerea's dagger in one hand.

The sorceress had put her silver necklace back on, and it seemed to give off an aura of its own, pulsating slowly as Tess walked toward the wizard as if in a trance. When she was within arm's reach of him, she stopped and just stood there. Valerea could see sweat on Tess' forehead and cheeks, beading up until it ran in rivulets down the sides of her neck. The sorceress raised her chin slightly.

Looking back at the five blonde women, Valerea saw them begin to raise their arms. Hearing a hoarse cry from the wizard, she snapped her head around and saw him quickly throw his hands out in front of himself, fingers splayed. She felt the power of his magic as it passed over her, and sighed with relief that she was flat on the ground.

The soldiers were not so fortunate, however, and several were destroyed by the force of the wizard's magic. Valerea started to look behind her, to see if the Sisters had survived his attack, when Tessia suddenly raised the dagger she held and plunged it into the wizard's back.

He stumbled forward and fell to his knees. Leaping to her feet, Valerea kicked him as hard as she could in the side of the head. The wizard flopped over onto his side, and Tessia stood above him with one hand pressed to the necklace at her throat and the other stretched out over him. Her eyes were closed and her lips moved, but no sound emerged from them.

Smoke began to appear from the wizard's prone body. He screamed and began waving his arms and legs. The smoke grew thicker, and Valerea backed away, coughing. When the smoke cleared, where the wizard had been, there was just a burned-looking spot on the ground. There was a strong smell, like that of burnt hair, which made both women wrinkle their noses in disgust.

Then Valerea remembered the remaining soldiers. She dove for the sword that the wizard had dropped, rolled, and came to her feet with it up and ready. But they had had enough, and with Tobray and the wizard both dead, there was no one to stop them from leaving, which they did. As Valerea watched them go, she noticed that the Sisters had also gone. She remarked on the fact to Tessia, who laughed softly.

"But they were never here," the sorceress said. "The wizard said he could feel me trying to use my magic against him. He was partly right. I knew he was stronger than I, so I caused an illusion of five Sisters. I hoped to make him expel a great deal of force against them, which would leave him momentarily weak enough for me to attack him by surprise from behind. Fortunately, it worked."

"Good thing, too," Valerea said. "Or else we'd probably both be dead right now."

"Yes, well, we're not," Tess replied. "And not only are we alive, but with Tobray and his wizard both dead, the spell over Lord Aldemus should be broken."

They both fell silent as they began walking out of the practice area, the setting sun throwing their shadows far ahead of them. When Tess spoke again, her voice was softer and lower than usual. "I'd like to thank you for coming to save me, especially after the way I've treated you. Why did you do it, when you knew you were outnumbered?"

"Because you're my friend," Valerea replied simply. "Now let me ask you a question: How'd they manage to capture you in the first place?"

The sorceress glanced at the redhead, then looked away before answering. "A boy came up to me as I was packing my things to go eat and said that a red-headed woman had been injured in one of the games. He said a man told him to get a magician right away or she'd die. Naturally, I thought it was you and rushed after the child. We came to a large tent and the boy said the woman was inside. Then he ran off. I entered the tent and was immediately grabbed by several of Tobray's men. They took all of my silver away and had me tied up before I knew what was happening. I think you know the rest."

Valerea nodded. "Probably the same boy that brought me your necklace said that you wanted to see me," she said. Then she filled Tess in on what had transpired up until Tobray and the wizard had stood up from their chairs at the practice area. When she finished, Valerea looked up ahead and then nudged her friend with an elbow. "You can stop the illusion, Tess. We're not in any danger now."

Tessia also looked up ahead. Coming toward them were two women in long robes. Both had long blonde hair, and though they didn't exactly *glow,* they did seem to catch and hold the light of the setting sun.

"That's no illusion," the sorceress told her friend. "It really is two of the Sisters."

When the four women came face to face, Tessia hugged the two Sisters, then introduced Valerea to Karina and Milis. After greeting the redhead politely, Karina turned to face Tessia.

"We at the Crystal Tower were aware of magic being used in great profusion," she said, "but we weren't going to intercede, until Milis felt the drain of her image being used in an illusion. When several others felt it as well, we decided to investigate."

Valerea started to explain, but was stopped by the blonde's gentle smile and raised palm.

"We already know all about it," Karina said. "Even now, three Sisters are at the estate of Lord Aldemus, explaining to him what has happened, and convincing him to remove the tax and return what has been stolen from the people.

"And we've come here to thank you both for stopping General Tobray and his wizard, and to invite you to join us at the Crystal Tower." Karina finished speaking and looked at them expectantly.

Tessia and Valerea looked at each other in surprise. Then the redhead looked at the blonde sorceress again. "For what?" she asked.

Karina stared at her. "Why, as Sisters of The Golden Light, of course."

"But I'm no sorceress," Valerea said. "The only thing I know about magic is that I know nothing about it."

"Well, since this all happened, we've decided that we need more than just magic for protection," Karina explained. "And we feel that you are the perfect choice to lead the Sisters of The Golden Sword."

Tessia grabbed Valerea excitedly, her joy obvious in her expression. But when she looked at the redhead's face, she calmed down and grew concerned. "What's wrong, Valerea?"

The swordswoman gently pulled free. "I am honored that you've asked me," she said to Karina, "and it's probably foolish of me to turn you down, but I'm not ready to settle down yet. I think you should go, though," she added, looking at Tess.

"How can I go without you? After all we've been through, I can't just say good-bye and leave you," the soceress told her friend.

"Then say 'until we meet again,' " Valerea told her. "The Sisters are your family, Tess, and you belong with them. I'll stop and see you sometime, though. Here," she removed her sword and scabbard and placed it over Tess' shoulder. "Hold this until I come for it."

Blinking back tears, Tess removed the silver chain from around her neck and placed it around Valerea's. "And you hold this for me," she said. The two women held each other tightly for several moments, until Karina and Milis gently took Tessia's hands. Valerea stepped back and smiled at her friend as the three Sisters began to fade.

"Until we meet again," Tessia said, and then they were gone.

"Good-bye, Sister Tess," Valerea said softly, touching the silver necklace. Then, wiping her eyes, the redhead walked off into the darkness, alone once more.

BLACK WOLF
by Gemma Tarlach

Here is another "first story." Gemma Tarlach describes herself as, "a nineteen-year-old southpaw who likes to wear black;" all of the kids here went through a stage where they wouldn't be seen in anything else; I am convinced it's a stage all young people go through.

My daughter is convinced it's allied with a regular stage in adolescent depression; I am not so sure, but hope it will soon pass if it is.

Gemma Tarlach says this is the first story she has ever submitted for publication, though it is only one of many stories she has written. When people are willing to write for the pleasure of it, it often is the sign of a budding professional; at least it is in this case. I have seldom seen a first story told with such a sure hand. I'll be looking forward to seeing the rest of those stories.

Now mind you, I'm not the kind of man that exaggerates anything. But when she walked into the market, I swore it was the demon goddess herself. But like my dad always says, begin at the beginning.

It was an average day at the Cliosk—almost. The sun was bearing down on sea and sand and men with the usual ferocity of midsummer, and the Cliosk was brimming with all it had to offer. But there was a cool edge to the briny air, an odd chill that seemed to grow as the day waned. I was going about my business, haggling with rich men over silver and poor men over copper, and keeping my stall free of the undesirable sort. It was past the hottest hours of the day when most stalls close and everyone in the City finds some-place shaded. Business at the Cliosk was picking up as the merchants returned and the crowd grew. I was just about to reach for my afternoon piece of tauto cheese when I saw her.

Some women walk demurely, their heads lowered and taking mincing little steps. Others move with thoughts of ambition imprinted in their stride or wad-dle with detached complacency. But she—she stalked like the hungry diijuni that serve as the warking's pets. Every movement beneath her ebony robes was grace-ful, confident, and very dangerous. I studied her as she moved past the busy stalls, her black attire poorly camouflaged in a sea of white deeldi.

As she drew closer, I noted the way her cloak was tied, thrown from her shoulders warrior style. She was clothed entirely in the color of night, from the deep hood that allowed no light to enter to her low, steel-toed boots. Then I saw the sword. The sword. No woman carried a weapon other than her tongue in the City. It went against every tradition we had. And no man I knew had a sword like hers. Unlike the curved monsee blades thrust naked through the belts of my people, her sword was straight, sheathed in black leather and bobbing slightly from its shoulder sling. The hilt flashed silver—and my jeweler's eye told me it was worth half my stall.

I had no more time to appreciate the weapon, how-ever, for the stranger arrived at my stall and stopped. I felt something colder than steel pierce me from within the hood.

"You are jeweler, no?" The voice was low and musical—and definitely female. It was thick with an accent strange to even my well-traveled ears. I nodded.

"Canuh is the name, stranger," I said in my most pleasant tone.

"How much for this?" she demanded, placing a small black pouch before me. I opened it slowly and removed the brooch, keeping a blank face as my eyes danced over the treasure.

It was a braided silver circle set with emeralds and sapphires, a green and blue swirl of exquisite beauty. The delicate style was totally foreign to me, but then sword-bearing women in black were not an everyday occurrence either. I sighed and set it down.

"Ah . . . I'm feeling generous today . . . one hundred." For a moment, I thought she might lop off my head at the obscenely low offer. But there was only an uncomfortable silence.

"No," she said finally, "Four hundred." I went through the motions of throwing my hands up in the air and closing up my stall in disgust when I felt an icy grip on my left wrist. Her thin hand, starkly pale against the black sleeve, was exerting surprising strength.

"Three hundred," she whispered. The brooch was worth double that and we both knew it. But the edge of desperation in her voice intrigued me. I agreed, relieved to feel the release of her cold hand. She waited expectantly.

"Not here. Such an expensive transaction cannot be carried out in the middle of the Cliosk. We go to my pau-ton." I stepped back to put room between us. There was something about this one that smelled of sorcery.

'I have little time," she hissed, sending a shiver through me.

"We'll go now." I began to lock up my stall. The more valuable pieces of my inventory, as well as my money, were kept somewhere in the one-room adobe hut attached to the back of my stall. I gestured for her to wait at the pau-ton's front door proper and then went through the room to open it.

The dark insides of the pau-ton seemed to agree with her, for I felt the aura of tension about her lessen. Foreigners take poorly to the heat of Ditantia's

north coast, especially the pale ones like her from
colder lands. She stood in front of me, taller by a good
half-hand. Thinner, too, I thought. Good—if it came
down to a fight, every inch of me was muscle whereas
she was oddly slight. Then I remembered the intensity
of the handhold and shuddered.

"Wine?" I offered the lone bottle of my store. Jeweler or not, I was no rich man. She shook her head,
the fabric of her hood rustling slightly.

"Business," came the curt reply.

"I don't deal with faceless people," I stated flatly.
Normally I would lean forward and sneer a bit to
intimidate the customer, but something told me it
would have no effect on the creature before me.

"There are other jewelers." She turned.

"Wait." I said it too quickly, but the mistake was
made. She faced me again and I sensed amusement.
"Sit down, I will get the money."

Actually, the money had been in my inner pocket
since I locked up the stall, but I made a show of
bustling about my confines. The stranger watched me
indifferently, sitting cross-legged on my rug. I turned
to face her at last and dropped the money bag on my
foot.

She had removed her hood and face covering and
calmly looked at me, smiling almost at the look of
shock upon my face. White, pure skin stretched flaw-
lessly over fine features, her cheekbones pronounced
and chin pointed. Her lips were orange-red with the
telltale signs of desert chap, but their curves were
gentle nonetheless. Burgundy-colored hair—a shade
I've never seen before—fell halfway down her back in
a loose braid and wisped about her face. But it was
her eyes that struck me—the eyes that had been watching my reaction with quiet laughter. They were a bril-
liantly cold green, softened by long, dark lashes. And
the shape of them! They were perfect almonds, slant-
ing upward at the outer corners. Her heritage hit me
like an angry sailor.

"You are of Ryng." I whispered. Just the name of
the distant northeast continent made the room seem

darker, less familiar. The legends of the Wolves, the strange warrior people of Ryng, were known to few in the City. I was among them, thanks to a father who wove the best stories north of the desert. The girl (she was indeed a girl, with at least four years less than my own twenty-three) replied with a dark smile of pride.

"Does that surprise you?" she asked, her smile suddenly bitter. I nodded. What one of her kind was doing half a year from home selling jewelry was unfathomable. She shrugged and stared directly at the money pouch. I picked it up as I sat. We eyed each other as all those in my business do.

"What brought you to the hotlands?" I asked curiously. She frowned and I imagined that the room turned cold.

"My business, jeweler," her voice slashed the air like a blade. "Our business my jewel, your money."

Like I said, I'm not the sort of man to exaggerate, but by the sea goddess it turned freezing in the room. For a wild moment I thought she was a Black Robe, one of the sorcerers who thrive in the power of evil. But no . . . I've dealt with those before and could always sense the decay of their souls. The shadows of the room clung to her, I'll admit, but the darkness was drawn to her rather than oozing from within.

The coins spilled out onto the rug between us, and I watched as she counted them with thin, dextrous fingers. The payment was judged correct. She scooped it up and placed it in an inner pocket of her longskirt. Then she rose and began to leave. She stopped at my door and turned.

"Where I find lodging for night, Canuh?" she asked, her accent twisting my plain name into something beautiful.

"The best place is The Gold Tent." I offered directions to the place as well. She departed immediately, leaving me standing at the door in a private moment of indecision.

"Ah, by the gods, I'll follow her." I muttered to myself. There was something in her oddness, her desperate, mysterious circumstance, and aye, her beauty that dragged me out into the streets after her.

The Gold Tent is not far from my pau-ton. It's one of the smaller inns, frequented by merchants like myself and I expected to find it empty at this early hour. But as I rounded the final corner, a clash of steel and guttural shouts welcomed me.

She was being attacked by three men—two of them in the unmistakable crimson of the palace guards. Two more lay motionless, victims of her Northern sword.

Fighting agreed with her. Her footwork was lithe, her sword flashing in a stunning show of precision. And those eyes—even from here I could see how they gleamed like ice. In the heat of the afternoon, it had suddenly gone cold.

They had her cornered against the front outside wall and the side of another building that jutted farther into the street. I pushed my way through the gathering crowd, pulling my saradl across my face. Working toward her left side, I watched in fascination as she parried each attack to her advantage. One guard rushed her with his short blade and with a thrust and sweep he was disarmed and falling backward, his fingerless hand cradled in the other.

There was a shout to bring more guards, and I knew it was up to me to get her away before a pack of crimson guards descended upon the scene. As I mentioned before, I'm a solidly built man to say the least, and I know how to use my body to its fullest advantage.

I came up on her left as one of the guards happened to step away and leave the path completely open. Barreling into her full-power, I shoved her against the wall and into unconsciousness. Even as she slumped in my arms, her grip on the sword remained fast. I slung her over my shoulder and started to run, heedless of the long sword slapping roughly against my thigh. I ran through the Cliosk and its environs in a patternless manner, going past my own pau-ton more than once until I was convinced that no one was following.

Once inside, I put her down on my sleeping mat.

Then, leaning over her, I grasped the pommel of her weapon with hopes of prying her hand from it.

Ice. A wrenching pain of a thousand needles coursed through my hand and I released the cursed metal with a cry. Rubbing my throbbing hand, I waited for the pain to subside. I wrapped my hands in the heavy fabric of her cloak and clumsily freed the blade. With a grimace I tossed the ungodly thing into my closet where it fell with an offended clang.

She awoke with a start. For a moment she held her breath and squinted around the room. Then her surroundings became clear and she sat up. Too quickly, I guessed, for she winced in pain and lay back down.

"How dare you . . ." she hissed at me.

"You're welcome." I snapped. The run had cost me my breath, and the rescue could cost my life. Silently I brought a bowl of cool water and a cloth to her. Her face softened.

"I am sorry," she reconsidered, "I know you did what you thought right. I . . . I thank you." She took the wet cloth and wiped her neck.

"Are you hurt?" I wondered aloud. She nodded and gestured to her ribs. I helped her remove her cloak and longshirt, surprised at the thickness of all her clothing. What sort of land could it be where one had to live burdened with such a heavy second skin?

She sat up, frowning, wearing only her pants and an odd leather halter. The women of my land are by tradition clothed in flimsy silks with little underneath, garments designed to make them as desirable as possible. But the Wolves, judging by the one who sat on my floor, sought to hide their bodies from both the sun and the eyes of others. She sensed my stare and looked up abruptly. I turned away reluctantly and busied myself.

When I gave my attention to her once more, I saw the ugly mottled bruise on her rib cage. At first I thought one of the men had beaten her, but then it dawned on me. I had done the damage when I pummeled her. Other than that injury, she was fine save for some scrapes and smaller bruises. I noticed but said nothing about an older, jagged scar near her collarbone. Aware of my eyes upon her again, she pulled her longshirt back on and grimaced.

"I'm sorry." I said quickly. "How did you get yourself into that mess?" Her eyes darkened.

"The men always the same in such places. I only defend myself." Then she stared at me with a look that clearly informed me she would do so again if I tried anything.

"I see." I rose and brought some tauto cheese for us. "And how exactly did you get here? You're a good five moons from home."

She did not answer immediately, her face filled with shadows. "I . . . I had to run from very bad union . . ." she murmured.

"A marriage, eh? Here the woman may refuse the man chosen for her if she can find good reason. Is it not so in your lands?" The question withered in the air when I saw the disgust on her face. She sighed and looked away as if I could never hope to comprehend her world. I decided to try again. "I'm sorry. What's your name, anyway?"

"Elya mi Glaimrista, Sar Glaeden." The liquid sounds of her language danced off her tongue. "In your land I am known as Elya, Black Wolf."

"Why did you come here, of all places, from Ryng?" Her story was as interesting as she was, I wagered.

"I make my way south, to eeshi Waeshtral, in the Nil'ganut."

"The Wastrel?" I exclaimed, calling that cursed place by its common name. "That's on the other side of Ditantia! Besides, what would you want with that evil place—a pit of thieves, Black Robes, and mercenaries!"

Elya smiled bitterly up at me, her young face suddenly imprinted with the look of a wild diijuni—the lone hunter. I realized then that sword-sporting was no hobby of hers. The stories of my father came flooding back into my mind, tales of the Order of the Wolves, and of the highest rank being that of the Black. Elya, Black Wolf. I felt very stupid. So, I had rescued a creature from a fight that she could have easily won. Now I understood her initial anger. Composing myself as best I could, I smoothed the creases in my deeldi and tried to hide my embarrassment.

"I have been to the Wastrel before, Elya. It is not a place to be taken lightly." I gave her my most meaningful look. My next statement would be a plea for her to stay. She sensed it, perhaps, for she looked hard into my brown eyes, past them even. and into my soul.

"Then you give me directions to it." Her voice was so cold. Now, don't get me wrong. She wasn't emotionless or hollow like some. There was just something in her, an edge as sharp as her sword. I thought of the two men lying outside The Gold Tent, scarlet blood spilled onto the crimson of their uniforms.

"I will leave soon as possible. Someone see me here with you will be trouble for you." She stood slowly and went to my closet, retreiving the sword though I had said nothing of it to her. Holding it as a mother might cradle her child, she wiped the sword carefully, rubbing the dried blood off the blade. The sword itself was as beautiful as she.

It was finely polished steel, and its long blade was etched with runes that twisted and curled, forming an endless pattern. The hilt was decorated with a heavy silver braid much like that of the brooch.

"Do all Wolves carry such fine arms?" My question brought that smile of subtle pride to her lips.

"No. I win mine in final trial for rank of Black Wolf . . ." She continued with a touch of darkness in her tone. ". . . so, too, I win set of broke ribs and the scar." Her fingers ran over the unnaturally whitened flesh below her neck.

"It must have been painful . . ." I whispered, wondering what weapon had caused the injury.

"It was meant to behead me." she replied flatly, ignoring the shock on my face. "That how I live, Canuh. I accept it because I chose life of fighter. To be free, to be independent—that is what is good." The words did not surprise me as much as the tightness in her voice. I knew there was much she was not telling me.

Remaining silent, I poked at the tauto cheese and tried to understand her. She watched me, motionless. Together we let the sounds of the street take over our conversation—a boy selling levka, the clattering of a chariot, the sound of sandaled feet marching in careful precision—

Elya was on her feet, long sword ready in her grasp, when the guards broke open my door. I had time only to stand before I saw four charge and slam her against the wall, the sword falling to the ground with an eerie, almost-human shriek. Then a crimson-sleeved fist met my chin and all the world turned flashing white and then soothing black. . . .

The smell of fouled water greeted me as I awakened. The tiny cell had a layer of the stagnant liquid in which I happened to be sitting. Repulsed, I rose too quickly and the dim outlines of the wall before me wavered. I steadied myself as best I could and ignored the dank stench, examining my surroundings.

The cell was half my length across and twice as deep. There was a windowless door on one side and a low stone ceiling. Remnants of a straw floor floated about my ankles and I nearly vomited at the slime. The sound of footsteps, those same marching sandals, drew nearer.

Blinding white exploded in my face as the door was flung open and I cried out at the sudden light. A gauntlet reached in and pulled me out by the neck of my deeldi. Shoved ahead of the guard and his two companions, I was escorted out of the dungeon and into the palace above.

I've never been to the warking's home, and in spite of my situation, my jeweler's eye delighted in its artistry. High, arched ceilings painted in the softest blues and pinks, gilded columns with jewel-encrusted bases— Diinia the Mighty spared no luxury. I felt pitiful in my state of filth.

And by far the most fantastic was our destination, the throne room. An ivory bridge spanned the ring of tinted water skirting the domed room. The ceiling was a fresco of the heavens, the sun and stars made of pure gold. At the far side of the room, ringed by half a dozen of the ruler's special guards, sat Diinia the Mighty.

He was a man in his prime—tall for my people, and well-muscled. Wavy black hair was pulled back from his face in thick, oily braids. His heavy nose and prominent brow gave him a brutish appearance, but glinting black eyes belied a dangerous intelligence. The brown of his desert tan was scored with reminders of the wars he had fought while younger and he flaunted them by wearing a short, sleeveless deeldi of gold. But as we came closer, I saw not all the scars were old—there were several deep scratches newly clawed onto his cheek. Yet the wounds seemed insignificant upon the hulking man in gold—the warking looked every inch his title.

The guard in back of me pushed me forward, across the bridge and closer yet to the warking. I bowed as deeply as my sore body would allow. A sound from the door told me that they were bringing in Elya. I glanced at Diinia to see the slightest flicker of hatred on his face.

Then she was beside me. Her cloak was shredded and her hair spilled over it in defiant disarray. She was very pale, but I saw anger rather than fear flash in her eyes. Diinia rose and sneered at her before focusing his attention on me.

"Canuh Jewelman, how is it that this foreigner came to be at your home?" His voice shook me in its sheer strength. I opened my mouth and froze. I've always been the worst liar in Ditantia, yet telling the truth, that I aided one who killed his men, would be my death. Then I felt Elya's eyes on me and the words came to my tongue without thought.

"Almighty warking, I found this woman outside my door, begging for shelter. Normally I would not host a stranger, but this one offered me a great many things in return. May I ask, my lord, what I have done to be brought to your just presence?" The words made me nauseous, but I could not control them. It was as if I had become one of the cork puppets sold in the Cliosk that children move about with strings. From the corner of my eye I saw that Elya remained expressionless, her eyes lowered but dangerously bright.

But Diinia seemed satisfied with the lie, especially the allusion to Elya's virtue. He stepped down from the gilded throne and inspected her carefully.

"As I suspected. These foreign women," He half-spoke to the guards, "They come here and corrupt my city. And yet, my little wolf, why did you show your claws to me last night? Perhaps you like common, nothing men." He bared his teeth at her in a savage grin. Without a second thought, Elya spat into his face, smiling hatefully. Diinia grew mottled with rage.

"Death! You will die by my own hands!" He yelled, wiping his eye and cheek. As he fumed, a sudden chill seeped into the air like the dark smile slowly spreading across the Black Wolf's face. Diinia felt the unnatural cold and paused. To kill a magicker was to invite revenge from her spirit, and this woman stank of the dark arts. Another, less dangerous plan entered his mind. "Ah, no. I have a better contest. You will face my diijuni in the pit. And you will die.

Elya smiled wider, and perhaps Diinia reconsidered, for he added with a malicious grin, "Without any weapon other than your claws. I want it to be fair, of course."

They stared at each other for an eternity, and the tension in the room drew my muscles taut even as the cold coursed through me in a shiver.

"My lord," I barely whispered, "What is to be my fate?" Diinia replied by waving his hand, his thoughts on the warrior witch alone. My freedom granted, I bowed and was escorted out of the room, a thousand plots for Elya's rescue brewing in my mind.

As I reached the street, however, the blare of horns shattered my thoughts. The contest was to begin immediately! I turned back into the palace courtyard—already people were gathering. Pushing my way to the center, I came upon the pit.

It was circular, set into the ground by the length of

three men. There were four doors, one for each compass point, that led to the pens of the diijuni and other fighting animals. On the first day of the sea festival each year, Diinia held matches against his desert cats and guard dogs for the public. But now, in the heat of the high afternoon hour, there was no sport in the air. There was only the sandy death circle, a blistering sun, and a crowd of crimson guards wagering on a woman's death.

The crowd cheered with bloodlust as Elya appeared. She was surrounded by guards who pushed her through the crowd, ever nearer to the pit. As they passed by me, I saw that her cloak was gone. Her hair was pulled back severely and dangled in one tight braid.

Another fighter might have entered such a weighted contest with a trace of fear on his face or a false countenance of pride and the self-assurance of impending victory. But not Elya—her face was made of stone, and any emotion she might have had was not visible. Only her eyes were alive, with the eerie emerald glow I had seen before.

She entered the pit by a rope ladder that was quickly drawn up after her descent. I thought I saw the start of a frown as she tested the sandy ground. It was probably slippery to her Northern boots. There was no more time to think about what lay ahead, however, as Diinia appeared at the south overlook of the pit, a cruel smile creasing his face.

"It has been declared by the all-king Diinia," proclaimed his second, "that the foreigner will enter combat with two diijuni to the death." And then there was silence.

The door on the east side of the pit flipped open as the first of her opponents bounded out. The diijuni are not the largest of the desert cats, but Diinia bred and conditioned his well. This one, a male of prime age, was a tight coil of muscle. His large jaw yawned at Elya, revealing two rows of deadly teeth. He looked at her with golden eyes, sure of his prey.

Elya watched him motionlessly. When he began to circle toward her, she moved in the opposite direction,

keeping the distance of the pit's diameter between
them. For a moment I forgot the barbarity of the
contest and was lost in observing the graceful dance of
the two foes. Each stalked the other, sizing up their
opponent with careful scrutiny.

The diijun halted and turned. Elya began to walk
backward, always keeping that precious distance. He
quickened; she matched him. With a sudden show of
speed, the diijun jumped, his heavy back legs propel-
ling him directly at her. At the last moment, Elya
ducked and spun away. The crowd murmured at her
agility. Perhaps, I thought, she has a chance.

He came at her again, angrier this time. The tawny
hairs on his back bristled as his prey eluded him again,
this time by tumbling beneath him as he was airborne.
I'm no fighter, but I could grasp that Elya was testing
her opponent before taking offensive action. Diinia
was impressed, I could see. He frowned from his view-
ing place, hands balled tightly into fists.

The diijun below suddenly moved in close to Elya
too swiftly for her to escape. He swiped at her leg but
missed as she leapt forward and over the beast, her
hand on his back for balance. There was scattered
applause from the crowd for such a dramatic move,
but I doubt Elya heard. Her face was colorless and
beaded with sweat, the merciless heat as dangerous as
the beast stalking her. Both warrior and cat weaved
slightly in the glaring sunlight as they began to circle
once more. The diijun hissed and growled, his eyes
almost red with fury. He rushed her and she scrambled away. For a moment, he chased her around the
small pit and the outcome seemed inevitable. The
crowd cheered.

Then she turned swiftly as he made the deathleap.
Elya dropped down hard and rolled as the beast hit
the ground inches from her. She rolled back over and
onto his back. Pinning him with her own body weight,
she struggled to get a firm hold on the diijun. Beyond
fear, Elya snaked her sword arm around his neck, her
sleeve rubbing against the eager jaw. As she pulled
her arm tighter around his neck, the diijun sensed his

precarious position and pushed up on his back legs. Elya lost her balance momentarily, her feet slipping in the sand, but she kept her stranglehold. The diijun sat again, his breath a wheezing hiss in the pit. Elya pushed more of her weight onto the exposed neck, causing one of the legs that straddled the cat to straighten and slide beneath his powerful back legs. I winced as his claws raked her thigh, making ribbons of her pant leg and tearing into her flesh.

Elya growled in pain and increased the intensity of her grip. With a final burst of energy, she reared up, pulling the diijun's head one way and pushing his neck the other. There was a crack and then both lay very still.

After a moment of tense silence, Elya rolled off the body. She pulled herself up to a sitting position and shook her head. The world must have been spinning, for I saw her squint purposely as people sometimes will when they cannot see clearly.

"Bring the next diijun!" Diinia thundered. Elya did not look up but allowed herself a grim smile. She tried to rise and fell back down. There was no question who would win this time.

Then she looked around the pit's rim at the swarm yelling for blood. Her eyes froze just to my left and I saw her face darken and twist with hate. I looked over to see what caused this reaction and shuddered. A Black Robe stood at the rail, a good measure of space around him. Nobody I knew liked to stand near one of the dark wizards . . . but there was something unusually malevolent about this one. The way he stood, motionless and calm, hands hidden in the folds of his velvet robes and his deep hood revealing just the fringe of a white beard, made my blood ice.

"Ator'pol, glaerung," shouted Elya to the Black Robe. She pushed herself up and stood defiantly tall. "Ator'pol dll simoovata."

There was no reply from the wizard. The east door opened and Elya turned to meet the next diijun. This one was a female, no doubt the mate of the male, for she ran to his body and sniffed. Wheeling around to

face Elya, the female unleashed a roar of pure hatred.
Elya smiled. Her arms crossed in front of her, she
shifted her weight onto her good leg. Slowly, never
breaking eye contact with the cat, she straightened her
arms and stretched them out to the sides. Her wrists
were loose, her fingers dangled. With grace that drew
a hush over the crowd, she lifted the knee of the
wounded leg and balanced on her right.

The diijun sprang without warning, but Elya was
ready for her. Pushing off with one leg, she kicked the
other right into the cat's jugular. Both went down with
a brutal thud, but Elya was up first, gasping in pain.
She threw herself onto the diijun, again hoping to
break the neck. Only this time there was no precision
or grace to it. Elya wanted to be done and fought with
a mad ferocity that the diijun, stunned from the blow,
could not match. Twisting her neck with her stronger
arm, Elya rubbed sand into her eyes and nose.

Her legs stretched out for grounding, but she made
no sound as they came under attack from the back legs
once more. The cat clubbed her head with the back of
her paw, but even that did not deter the Black Wolf.
Again there was the sound of bone breaking and the
diijun collapsed. Elya pushed away from the dead
creature and then dropped.

After a time, a guard jumped into the pit and kicked
at her. There was no response. he bent down and
examined her for a sign of life.

"She's dead, m'lord." he said, straightening. I looked
away, my eyes happening to fall on the place where
the Black Robe had been. He was gone.

"Does anyone claim the body?" boomed Diinia.
There was no answer. I thought of what the rest of the
diijuni would have for dinner.

"I do, my lord." I heard myself saying. Heads turned,
there were low mutterings everywhere. I pushed my
way to where the guards had carted up her body. I
took off my cloak and covered her face with it. Then I
picked her up and walked out of the courtyard, oblivious to the noise behind me.

Again I carried her through the streets to my pau-ton. There were tears in my eyes for the life she would never have. She should have stayed in her cold, distant land and married whatever man had been selected for her. At least she would be alive.

I laid her down on the sleeping mat, removing my cloak, and went outside to be sick. I came back in and sat down next to her, wondering where I could find a priest willing to perform the proper burial rites. Brushing a piece of hair from her finally peaceful features, I marveled at how the coldness of her body pervaded the room.

Then her chest rose and she drew in a ragged breath. I gasped. She gave a long, low moan and coughed.

"You live . . ." I whispered in the unnatural cold. She looked at me and nodded weakly. "But you were dead."

"No . . ." She licked her lips and swallowed shakily. "I went to other place for while . . . I have water?"

I got her a drink quickly, spilling half a cask as I shook with excitement. She was weak; all her energy was concentrated on breathing. I had to hold her head as she drank, her eyes a dark, unfocused green.

"How . . ." I began, but she shook her head.

"Not now . . . sleep . . ." She closed her eyes and slipped away. While she rested, I tended to her wounds. The backs of both legs were red and maroon with drying blood, but I was relieved to find that the injuries were not deep. There would be scars, but no permanent damage. The rib bruised in the tavern fight, as well as a few more, were broken and all her limbs were purpled with bruises and scrapes. Still, even in such a bad state, her loveliness stirred passion within me. I traced the curve of her neck with my fingers, smiling until I felt the jagged ridge of scar tissue against her collarbone. Black Wolf. I pulled my heaviest deeldi over her and began to brew some tea.

It was late afternoon of the next day when she awakened. Inhaling deeply, she murmured a chant in her odd language. I listened, deciding after a while that she was praying. When she stopped, I moved closer and sat down beside her.

"How do you feel?" I asked. Her eyes were alert now, though she was still grayish white. She nodded and managed a small smile. "What happened to you before?"

"I went to place . . . restful place I been to before." Her voice was a soft, sibilant breeze in the room.

"After your final trial for Black Wolf?" I guessed. She nodded again. "Do all your people have this ability?"

"No," her voice had an ethereal quality, "I was born seventh child under first Spring Moon. I have mark of Shitan . . . I have . . . special powers." Then she frowned.

"So I wasn't imagining the cold, the way you put words in my mouth . . . but what about the Black Robe at the pit?" Elya inhaled sharply.

"Do not speak of him . . . ever." And her eyes bore into me almost painfully. I moved away shocked as she turned and got up weakly, padding to the far wall. Her sword was still there, awaiting her caress. She buckled the harness around her shoulder and let the sheath hang against her back.

"You're leaving." I said in disbelief. "I won't allow it. You're too weak—" She silenced me with a look.

"I must go, Canuh. My past very close, following me. I have to go south, find new life. Please . . . understand." Again the green eyes met mine, shadows lurking behind their brilliance. I felt sorry for her then, more sorry than when I had thought her dead.

"The soldiers took your platnum. How do you plan to survive?" I was on my feet, wanting more than anything to tell her to stay with me.

"I will find way." The resolve in her voice told me that it was impossible to reason with her. Still, there was something I could do.

"I'll give you some gold." I put my hand up when she started to protest. "I insist. You'll have enough for a horse, food, whatever else you need."

"But I have nothing to give in return." She argued. I shrugged. I'm not a generous man by nature, but I felt compelled to help her as best as I could. She dressed quickly, leaving the deeldi on beneath her other clothing. I guessed that she was still cold from whatever limbo she had visited.

I went to my coffer, hidden in the sand beneath my bedmat. Calculating quickly, I found that there was enough for a decent horse and a few weeks' rations plus some to spare. I gave it to her as discreetly as I could, knowing that she was in pain as much from her wounded pride as her injuries.

It was the blackest part of night when I guided her to the southern edge of town. The desert of Kaedani stretched before us. It was a several-hour journey to the oasis of Bacaen, and I knew she would feel more comfortable traveling at night.

Elya quieted the anxious gelding as I sketched out a map, that, unless my memory failed me, would take her to the Wastrel. She had adopted both my deeldi and a black saradl to cover her face. She was still limping, but the bright look in her eye told me nothing would keep her in the City.

"Thank you for all, Canuh." She stood before me, speaking in that dark voice once more. Yet I knew she was sincere. Then she stepped closer and took my brown, weatherworn face into her hands. She brought her lips to my forehead, the kiss cool like the breeze that rustled my deeldi. I heard her murmur something in her native tongue.

"Know this, Canuh. You can travel to my lands and walk with my people. No harm come to you though you not Wolf. They will know you my friend. I am sorry, that is all I can give you."

I forgot myself and pulled her to me, wanting to express all the passion I had for her. Elya was shocked and squirmed in my arms.

"I . . ." I began breathlessly. She stopped the protest and smiled, putting her finger on my lips.

"Hush, Canuh . . . do not think of me. You will find pretty girl of your people, settle down, have many laughing, black-haired babies. Be content you can have such happiness."

"How do you know this?" I demanded as she escaped from my grasp.

"I know it . . . it is just something I can see ahead." She replied, mounting the ebony gelding.

"And you? What does your future hold?" I ran up to the horse and grabbed the reins, not wanting her to leave. She gave me that bitter smile for the last time.

"I will survive." Her whisper lingered in the desert breeze.

"Take this . . . as a symbol of our friendship." I pressed the silver brooch into her hand. She accepted it with a gentle smile.

"Shitan be with you, my friend," she said in farewell. Then horse and rider were off, galloping to the south. I watched them until the black of the night took them. Even then, I stood until sunrise, watching the southern horizon turn pink and then gold in the eastern light of a new day.

DAW

BESTSELLERS BY MARION ZIMMER BRADLEY

THE DARKOVER NOVELS

The Founding

☐ DARKOVER LANDFALL   UE2234—$3.95

The Ages of Chaos

☐ HAWKMISTRESS!   UE2239—$3.95
☐ STORMQUEEN!   UE2310—$4.50

The Hundred Kingdoms

☐ TWO TO CONQUER   UE2174—$3.50
☐ THE HEIRS OF HAMMERFELL (hardcover)   UE2395—$18.95

The Renunciates (Free Amazons)

☐ THE SHATTERED CHAIN   UE2308—$3.95
☐ THENDARA HOUSE   UE2240—$3.95
☐ CITY OF SORCERY   UE2332—$4.50

Against the Terrans: The First Age

☐ THE SPELL SWORD   UE2237—$3.95
☐ THE FORBIDDEN TOWER   UE2373—$4.95

Against the Terrans: The Second Age

☐ THE HERITAGE OF HASTUR   UE2413—$4.50
☐ SHARRA'S EXILE   UE2309—$3.95

THE DARKOVER ANTHOLOGIES

with The Friends of Darkover

☐ DOMAINS OF DARKOVER   UE2407—$3.95
☐ FOUR MOONS OF DARKOVER   UE2305—$3.95
☐ FREE AMAZONS OF DARKOVER   UE2430—$3.95
☐ THE KEEPER'S PRICE   UE2236—$3.95
☐ THE OTHER SIDE OF THE MIRROR   UE2185—$3.50
☐ RED SUN OF DARKOVER   UE2230—$3.95
☐ SWORD OF CHAOS   UE2172—$3.50

DAW

DAW PRESENTS MORE BESTSELLERS BY
MARION ZIMMER BRADLEY

NON-DARKOVER NOVELS

☐ **HUNTERS OF THE RED MOON**   (UE1968—$2.95)
☐ **WARRIOR WOMAN**   (UE2253—$3.50)

NON-DARKOVER ANTHOLOGIES

☐ **THE BEST OF MARION ZIMMER BRADLEY**
                                                    (UE2268—$3.95)
☐ **LYTHANDE**   (UE2291—$3.95)
☐ **SPELLS OF WONDER**   (UE2367—$3.95)
☐ **SWORD AND SORCERESS I**   (UE2359—$3.95)
☐ **SWORD AND SORCERESS II**   (UE2360—$3.95)
☐ **SWORD AND SORCERESS III**   (UE2302—$3.95)
☐ **SWORD AND SORCERESS IV**   (UE2412—$4.50)
☐ **SWORD AND SORCERESS V**   (UE2288—$3.95)
☐ **SWORD AND SORCERESS VI** (6/90)   (UE2423—$4.50)
☐ **SWORD AND SORCERESS VII** (12/90)   (UE2457—$4.50)